EYES
OF THE
VOID

BY ADRIAN TCHAIKOVSKY

SHADOWS OF THE APT

Empire in Black and Gold
Dragonfly Falling
Blood of the Mantis
Salute the Dark
The Scarab Path
The Sea Watch
Heirs of the Blade
The Air War
War Master's Gate
Seal of the Worm

ECHOES OF THE FALL

The Tiger and the Wolf
The Bear and the Serpent
The Hyena and the Hawk

THE FINAL ARCHITECTURE

Shards of Earth
Eyes of the Void

Guns of the Dawn

Children of Time
Children of Ruin

The Doors of Eden

EYES OF THE VOID

The Final Architecture: Book Two

ADRIAN TCHAIKOVSKY

orbit

orbitbooks.net

Copyright © 2022 by Adrian Czajkowski

Cover design by Steve Stone

Orbit
Hachette Book Group
1290 Avenue of the Americas
New York, NY 10104
orbitbooks.net

First Edition: May 2022
Simultaneously published in Great Britain by Tor,
an imprint of Pan Macmillan

Orbit is an imprint of Hachette Book Group.
The Orbit name and logo are trademarks of Little, Brown Book
Group Limited.

The Hachette Speakers Bureau provides a wide range of authors for
speaking events. To find out more, go to www.hachettespeakersbureau.com
or call (866) 376-6591.

Lyric on p. 110 is from Jonathan Coulton's "Someone Is Crazy," used here
with permission.

Library of Congress Control Number: 2021952857

ISBNs: 9780316705875 (hardcover), 9780316705882 (ebook)

Printed in the United States of America

LSC-C

Printing 1, 2022

CONTENTS

The Story So Far   vii

Prologue   1

Part One: Hismin's Moon   9

Part Two: Arc Pallator   101

Part Three: Deathknell   291

Part Four: Criccieth's Hell   449

The Universe of the Architects: Reference

    Glossary   577

    Characters   578

    Worlds   580

    Species   581

    Ships   581

    Timeline   583

THE STORY SO FAR

Key concepts

Unspace: the underlying nothing beneath the universe. Gravitic drives allow ships to enter and travel through unspace, crossing light years of real space in moments. Most journeys are taken along Throughway routes between stars.

The Architects: moon-sized entities that come from unspace to rework inhabited planets into bizarre sculptures. One of their number visited Earth, which began seventy years of fight and flight, a war costing billions of lives. Only contact between the engineered human Intermediaries and the Architects ended the conflict. Now, fifty years later, the Architects have returned.

Originators: On some planets, the ruins of an elder civilization of Originators can be found, still entirely mysterious, save that the Architects appear to fear any trace of this ancient race and will spare any planet that bears their mark.

The Hegemony: an alien empire controlled by the inscrutable Essiel which has sole access to the technology that allows Originator artefacts to be moved. They promise their subjects eternal protection from the Architects. However, the newly returned Architects no longer seem to be as in awe of the artefacts as they once were.

Humanity's factions

Following the explosive expansion of refugee humanity in the "Polyaspora," humanity now exists across numerous colonies, from the comfortable settled worlds to the vast numbers of spacers who still live precarious lives between planets. Trade and travel within the Colonial Sphere is greatly helped by the Intermediaries, who are among the few able to navigate unspace without using the Throughways. The Colonies are governed by the Council of Human Interests, familiarly known as Hugh, from the world of Berlenhof.

Humanity stood alongside many others during the first war against the Architects, but its closest allies came from within. These included the Hivers, who are a composite cyborg intelligence, built as tools but now independent. Dr. Parsefer's Parthenon, an artificially created society of women, also formed the front line in the war.

Following the secession of both Hivers and Parthenon, hostile Colonial factions have arisen, including the humanity-first Nativists and the Betrayed, who believe in a conspiracy that has denied humans their pre-eminence in the universe. Various groups within Hugh encourage and draw support from these growing factions, including the dictatorial noble houses of the Magda, one of the Colonies' most influential worlds.

Key characters

The *Vulture God*: a salvage ship. Its crew includes drone specialist **Olli**, lawyer and duellist **Kris**, trade factor **Kittering** and **Idris Telemmier**. Idris is one of the last of the original Intermediaries, who wanted nothing more than to live out his days in peace until an old friend from the war, the Partheni **Solace**, came looking to recruit him for her government.

Havaer Mundy: an agent of Hugh who has variously pursued and associated with the crew of the *Vulture God* as they became entwined with the return of the Architects.

Delegate Trine: a Hiver archaeologist, an old friend of Idris and Solace from the war and an authority on what little is known about the Originators.

The Boyarin Piter Tchever Uskaro: a Magdan nobleman linked to Hugh's more xenophobic elements, who wanted to own Idris and now has a grudge against the crew of the *Vulture God*.

The Unspeakable Aklu, the Razor and the Hook: an Essiel gangster from the Hegemony who also has reasons to dislike the *Vulture God* crew, after they cost it its treasure, its ship and its lieutenant.

EYES
OF THE
VOID

PROLOGUE

Who'd have thought crazy would turn out to be such valuable cargo?

Uline Tarrant was a rank opportunist. If you were a spacer it was a virtue. That meant when half of her acquaintances were tearing their hair and prophesying the end of all things after the clams took over, she was repurposing her business and making money. So, the former Colonies world of Huei-Cavor had voted to secede and join the Hegemony. They were now notionally ruled by the weird-ass shellfish-looking Essiel. Did that mean she couldn't turn some Largesse, or at least get a toehold in the complex credit system the Hegemonics used? No it did not. Because one thing the upper crust of Huei-Cavor's new cultist administration had was wealth, in whatever form you liked. And apparently spending it on conspicuous acts of piety was absolutely what they were all about.

This conspicuous piety that paid for her fuel and running costs was pilgrimage. She'd made it her speciality. If you were a devout worshipper of the Essiel, you went to places that were supposedly important to them. You meditated there and bought tacky little souvenirs, and probably met some useful people with good business connections. Uline wasn't convinced that the whole thing was anything more

1

than just some weird graft-turned-old-boys'-network to be honest. Religion wasn't a thing she had much time for. Prayers didn't fix spaceships.

She'd got her cargo hold fitted out with two hundred suspension beds, and they were all full. Anyone on Huei-Cavor who wanted to advance their social standing was getting in on the cult game, and that didn't just mean wearing the red robes. Entire wealthy families were simply thrusting legal tender into her account for the privilege of being sealed in a robot coffin and hauled across the Throughways deep into the Hegemony. And, it turned out, if you were carrying accredited pilgrims, none of the weird-ass alien gatekeepers there asked many questions. She wondered if the spooks back at Mordant House knew that, because it seemed like a hell of a gap in Hegemonic security.

Her current target was some world called Arc Pallator. She'd never heard of it. The limited data said it was basically desert and canyons, nowhere she'd want to set foot on. She didn't have to, though, there were orbitals. It was some big shot sacred site. Let the pilgrims deal with the heat and the dust, so long as they had the kind of crazy that paid up front.

They'd come out of unspace a respectful distance from the planet. The usual polite Hegemonic requests for ID were on her board when she shambled into the two-seater cupboard that passed for a command pod aboard the *Saint Orca*—that "Saint" had been added when she got into the pilgrimage business. Uline had only the loosest grasp of how godbothering worked, but she knew you stuck Saint in front of things when they were holy. The ship's only other crew-member was already there, having never left but just powered themselves down for the unspace trip. Tokay 99, as the Hiver called themself, waved a twiglike metal limb at her and she rapped them companionably on their cylindrical body.

She let the locals know who they were, sending over all the usual incomprehensible data that apparently allowed her to gad about inside the Hegemony. Everyone told you horror stories about how mad everything was here. Back before the secession she'd never have dared put the *Orca*'s nose inside their borders. She'd missed out on so much good business.

The local orbitals always wanted to do some kind of chit-chat with the pilgrims, so she woke a handful of this lot's leading lights as the *Saint Orca* cruised in-system. Soon enough they were crowding her command pod, drinking her cheap kaffe and exchanging gnomic wisdom with docking control. A Hegemonic dealing with another cultist seemed like a combined politeness and Bible-study contest. Except instead of a Bible, it was whatever cult wrong-headedness these loons had cooked up together to explain why they'd signed themselves over to a bunch of high-tech shellfish.

"Got yourselves a busy crowd here," she noted. "High season for the faithful, is that right?" There were plenty of other ships jockeying about waiting for docking and landing privileges. Some of them were the inscrutable Hegemonic ones that might have been haulers or luxury yachts, or moon-busting warships for all she knew, but others were human-standard. She even recognized a couple as distant acquaintances in the trade. Everyone wanted to come to touch the holies on Arc Pallator.

"Crowded down there," Tokay 99 agreed. They'd brought up a display of the single human-habitable settlement, populated by who knew how many thousands and precisely zero sane people. Uline shared a look with the Hiver. She had more in common with their cyborg-insect colony intelligence than she ever did with her human cargo.

"We are being instructed to stand by for a visitation," the senior cultist said. One of the others was fitting an even fancier collar to him, big enough that it brushed the ceiling of the cabin, as well as draping him with some cheap-looking bling jewellery.

"So that means...what? Customs inspection? We got a problem?" Uline asked.

She saw the faintest hint of doubt on the man's face. "I... am not sure. But more than that. Something special. A visitation. I've been to a dozen pilgrimage sites and never heard that before."

"That means one of the"—calling them *clams* wouldn't exactly go down well—"one of your Essiel's turning up?"

"Oh no," the man said fervently. "If it was, they would have announced the full descriptor and titles of one of the divine masters." His eyes were fifty per cent naively earnest and the rest pure bobbins. She wanted to tell him, *Look, they're clams. You're kneeling before an altar that's mostly all-you-can-worship seafood buffet.* But, because she was a respectable business-woman, she said none of it.

Tokay made a querulous chirping sound. "You attended to the sensor suite errors?"

"I did."

"By way of a qualified station mechanic as per our request," they pressed.

"I fixed them myself. That's better. It means we don't get rooked by some kid who was sucking his ma's teat when I was learning how to fix things."

"Anomalous gravitic readings on the long-long scan," the

Hiver told her, "suggest your time could have been better spent in haggling."

"Now you listen, this is *my* ship and we'll..." Her eyes were dragged to the readings Tokay had pushed over to her board. "We'll..." she said again.

The Architect appeared between Arc Pallator and the system's sun, breaching from unspace in a maelstrom of rainbows as the star's light refracted in all directions out of its crystal form. Far closer than she'd ever heard they came. Weren't they supposed to turn up way out-system? To give people a chance to get away?

"Right, right, right." She just stared as her mouth made mindless words. The cultists had all gone deadly quiet and still, which meant maybe they weren't as mad as all that. "Right. We need...we can...Damn, they're lucky there're so many ships here already. We can take..." Trying to do the maths in a head just cracked by the sheer fact of it. An Architect, like in the war. Here in the Hegemony where they weren't supposed to appear. "We can take another hundred, standing room only between the pods." She was aware the lead cultist was talking to ground control or whoever it was. "You tell them...ah...if they can get people up to orbit, we'll load until we're groaning. We've got..." The Architect had now begun a stately cruise outwards from the sun, headed squarely for Arc Pallator. "We've got..." *Not enough time. No time at all. Oh God. Oh God.* "We've got to get out of here."

"There is a proclamation," the lead cultist said reverently.

"I'll bet there is."

"From The Radiant Sorteel, the Provident and the Prescient," he told her, meaning one of the actual Essiel had weighed in on this one.

"They got a radiant evac plan?" She couldn't take her eyes off the approaching Architect. Her hands were shaking over the displays on her board.

"You and all your fellow pilots are forbidden from leaving until your holy work is done," the cultist said. "We are commanded to go down to Arc Pallator and stand amongst the holy ruins. We are chosen for this test of our faith, my brothers and sisters."

"No way in hell," Uline snapped. "We're going, right now. Look at it! *Look* at the goddamn thing!" She'd never seen one before. She'd only seen mediotypes, heard war stories. Glimpsed the wrecks of ships and worlds. The death that had come for Earth and not stopped coming for a century of war. The death that had come back, when all she wanted was to have lived and grown old and died, and to have never had this monstrosity in her sight. "Look at it," she repeated, just a terrified moan.

"Judgement," the cultist breathed. "A test of our fidelity to the words of the divine. We must go to the world. We are called." There was a new edge to his voice. "If you deviate from the prescribed flight plan I am instructed to say that will constitute breach of contract, and also blasphemy against the wishes of the Divine Essiel. Your drives will be disabled and you will not receive recompense, nor will you be able to leave the system."

Tokay let out a thin whine, nothing she'd ever heard from a Hiver before but it communicated *fear* very eloquently. She felt it too, exactly that sound, inside her gut. She wanted to sob. Scream at them. Tell them their clams were crazy and they were suicidal. She wasn't being paid enough to haul martyrs-in-waiting. But the Essiel could do all they'd said.

They had weapons she couldn't even understand. Everyone knew that.

She brought the *Saint Orca* back on course, heading for the orbital positioned directly over the single city. The city of people who'd soon be looking up at a new crystal moon. Briefly, she reckoned. Before their faith was tested the hard way and they became nothing more than disassociated strands of organic material. The problem with *saints*, she recalled, was that you had to be dead to be one. Yet all around her every pilgrim ship was still gliding in for docking, taxiing in a long queue around the single orbital, or else beginning the long, slow descent into atmosphere. And the Architect accelerated towards them, ready to drop into its own fatal orbit and obliterate every last one of them.

PART 1
HISMIN'S MOON

1.

Havaer

"That," Havaer Mundy said to himself, "is the *Vulture God*."

There were a good seventy ships and more docked at Drill 17 on Hismin's Moon; standard procedure to run a scan of them all as his craft, the *Griper*, came in. The onboard computers were still complaining from being bootstrapped back to functionality after exiting unspace, so Havaer had taken on the scanning work himself, letting his team stretch their legs and get their heads together. They were all outfitted as the rougher sort of spacers: half-sleeved long-fit tunics, trousers that always seemed too short to someone used to core-world suits, and of course the omnipresent sacred tool-belt, and the plastic sandals. All printed on-ship and scratchy with poor fabric. Just another crew of reprobates out on the razzle on this bleak satellite.

They had taxied over the docking field, liaising with the drill rig's kybernet about the required approach and landing fees. Out here everything was cheap, life included, but nothing was free. Havaer had the ship check off each and every other visitor, finding that no fewer than nine vessels were on the Mordant House watch list. If he'd been here just on a bit of a career-building jolly, he'd have had quite the choice of whom to go after. Although, given spacer solidarity, a heavy hand might have set him against the entire populace of the rig. Which was about ten times the number actually needed to do any drilling, because this little den of iniquity had become quite the fashionable dive since the destruction of Nillitik.

The Architects had returned. As though trying to erase the history of their previous failure, they'd been busy. First they had descended upon Far Lux where, half a century before, three Intermediaries had met with them and ended the first war. This time, almost nobody had got off-planet before the end.

Over the next months, they had appeared in the skies of a handful of other planets, without pattern, without warning: jagged crystal moons emerging from unspace. They'd been turned away from the Colonial heart of Berlenhof but nowhere else had been as lucky. The war was back on, and everyone had got out of the habits that had saved lives back in the first war. As many lives as *had* been saved, amidst the colossal death toll. The whole of humanity had to relearn sleeping with a go-bag and always knowing the fastest route to the nearest port. And not just humanity, this time.

Amongst the Architects' recent victims, the least regarded had been Nillitik. It was within a string of connected systems that the Hanni and Earth's explorers had discovered in the early days of their meeting. For a while they had been thought of as a kind of border-space between the two species. Except every discovery of a new Throughway radically rewrote the map, and drawing neat borders between space empires was seldom a fruitful exercise. Diplomatic treaties between governments preserved a handful of barren, meagre planets as a no-man's-land claimed by both and neither. Nillitik had been one. Had been, past tense.

Nillitik hadn't had a biosphere, or even an atmosphere. There'd been just enough mineral wealth to make the place viable for independent operations, but the main activity for the majority of the planet's small population had been to evade scrutiny when meeting and trading. Cartels, smugglers and spies had all marked the place on their maps with approval. And then an Architect had turned up and twisted the planet into a spiral. Slightly under a hundred people had died, out of the ten thousand present when the vast entity had arrived in-system. Unique amongst the targets of the Architects, almost everyone on Nillitik had transport ready to get them off-planet in a hurry, though they'd mostly been worrying about Hugh, or their rivals. The event had been so bloodless that history books would probably not even remember to include Nillitik on the rolls of the lost.

Of course, just because so few actually *died* didn't mean there were no ripples from the planet's destruction. A lot of deals went south, a lot of partnerships dissolved, a lot of goods ended up without buyers, or buyers without goods. The destruction of Nillitik was like poking a muddy pond with a stick. All sorts of things were suddenly roiled into unexpected view. As a lot of suspicious people were forced to rebuild their lives, things were held up for a quick sale that might otherwise have remained safely out of sight. Including information.

Two worlds along from lost Nillitik on the alleged border chain was Hismin's Moon, the sole habitable body of a spectacularly unlovely star system, and that was where the majority of trade had gone. Right now the moon was enjoying a prodigious visitor boom as what seemed like twenty planets' worth of criminals and speculators descended on it to see what could be scavenged. And where there was something to scavenge, you found vultures. Specifically, the ship the *Vulture God*, captain one Olian Timo, familiarly known as Olli. And though there were plenty of legitimate reasons for the *God* to be conducting business out of Hismin's Moon, Havaer happened to know that right now they were on the payroll for the Aspirat—the Parthenon's intelligence division and his opposite numbers in the spy game. Which meant they were all here for the same thing.

Havaer had Kenyon, his second in command, wrangle a landing pad not too far from the *God*, and when they disembarked he wandered over to eyeball the ruinous old craft. It was the poster child for unlovely but, apart from vessels fitted out by the big core-world companies, that was practically standard Colonial aesthetic. Even Hugh's own warships came out of the Borutheda yards looking like they'd lost a battle. Because, back in the first war, that had been humanity's lot: always fleeing, always patching, never able to stop and build something new. Looking bright and clean and fancy would have felt like turning your back on everything your ancestors had gone through to get you this far.

The *God* was a salvager, meaning much of its shape was dictated by the oversized gravitic drive bulking out its mid-to-back, enabling it to seize a far larger vessel, haul it about and carry it through unspace if need be. And they'd done good business due to their unusual navigator, Idris Telemmier the Int, who'd been able to reach those wrecks that had fallen off the Throughways, out in the deep void of unspace. Except these days, as Havaer knew all too well, Telemmier was off doing something of considerably more concern to Mordant House.

Unless he's here. A thread of excitement ran through Havaer as he turned the idea over. Hugh had no overt standing orders about the turncoat Int, because there was a war on and that kind of thing wasn't going to help anyone. On a more covert level, if he could grab Telemmier without leaving fingerprints all about the place then his next review meeting would look decidedly sunnier. Make up for him letting the man get away the last time.

He paid the Hismin's Moon kybernet for access to Drill 17's public cameras and ran facial-recognition routines until he picked them up. There was Olian Timo. Not hard to spot with her truncated amputee form in that huge Castigar-built Scorpion frame she was so proud of, and everyone was giving her plenty of room. There was their Hannilambra factor, Kittering, who'd doubtless have all kinds of home-ground advantages to call on right now. There was Solace, their Partheni handler, without her powered armour but with a goddamn *accelerator* slung over her shoulder, as though that wouldn't leave holes from here to the horizon through Drill 17's thin walls. No sign of the prize, Idris Telemmier, though. Nor Kris Almier the lawyer, who was the smartest one of the crew in Havaer's book.

"Mundy? Sir?" Kenyon prompted him. He and the other two in the team were strung out towards Drill 17's airlock, waiting for him. Havaer nodded, feeling the tension rise inside him. He guessed he would end up head to head with one or other of the *God* crew at some point soon. Either against Kittering in a bidding war, or against Olli and Solace in a more traditional sort of conflict.

Not one he could lose, either. Not and keep his record clean and sparkly for the dreaded review. Mordant House— formally known as the Intervention Board, Hugh's investigative and counter-espionage body—had a deep and abiding interest in this business. Someone was selling their secrets.

*

Chief Laery hadn't looked well for half of Havaer's life, but when he'd gone into her office for briefing before this latest mission, she'd looked mostly dead. She was an emaciated creature, reclining in an automatic chair with a dozen screens unrolled around her, nearly all blank now. He reckoned she'd just finished some multi-party conference, which was good grounds for looking exhausted and sour. With Laery, though, that was just her regular demeanour. She'd spent too long in deep-space listening stations in her youth, often without reliable a-grav. Her bones and body had never properly recovered and she needed a support frame to walk. Her mind was like a razor, though, and she'd headed up the department Havaer was in for all his professional life. She wasn't a pleasant superior, not even one you could uniformly call "harsh but fair," and on bad days her temper could overflow into malice quickly enough. She got things done, however, and she didn't throw away tools she could still use. Which was why Havaer hadn't quite been slapped over the whole freeing of Telemmier business. Simply arranging to save Hugh's most precious world from the Architects wouldn't necessarily have been enough to preserve him from her wrath, otherwise.

"We had a leak," she told him, straight up. "Some fucking clerk on the political side. Not actually Mordant House but one with access through the Deputy-Attaché of you-don't-need-to-know-which-goddamn-office. Whose own chief was decidedly lax about who got to see the transcripts of behind-closed-doors forward-planning meetings."

"Leaked where?" *The Parthenon* hung between them, because that sounded exactly the sort of spycraft they *were* good at. Not the actual dirty-handed stuff, but ideological subversion. There was always some quiet intellectual who secretly fancied herself in a grey Partheni uniform and doing away with Colonial graft and inefficiency.

Laery had her chair shift its angle, hissing in pain until she'd found a better posture. There were a couple of tubes in her arm, feeding her meds. If it was supposed to take the edge off, then she needed to get a new prescription.

"To a creditor, if you can believe it. The same old. Speculation gone sour, money owed, money borrowed, respectable lenders to shabby spacer banks to something entirely more disreputable. When they came to call, some transcripts were put up as collateral. All of which is out now, and there's someone else dealing with the up-front of it. But the transcripts made it onto a packet ship heading into the shadow border. Nillitik."

Havaer blinked. "Nillitik is gone."

"Yes. And a great deal of stock-in-trade that might have remained decently buried is now being flogged off cheap to make good on those losses. So our dirty laundry is on the market, sources say. Go gather it in. And if you can identify any other buyers, even bring them in or neutralize them, then that's a bonus."

Havaer nodded, already thinking forwards. He'd run missions along the Hanni shadow border plenty of times before, even set foot on lost Nillitik once or twice. All well within his competence.

Still... "This is where you ask, why you," Laery prompted him.

"It's got to be someone," Havaer noted mildly.

"Intel suggests word has got to the Parthenon and they're the frontline buyers. Now we can always outbid the Pathos, but we can't necessarily out-punch them if they decided to kick off. And even though everyone's tiptoeing around the war we're supposedly no longer on course for, a major action out in the shadow border might just be something they think they can get away with. And you, Menheer Mundy, have had some recent dealings involving the Parthenon, so your record says. Not entirely creditable ones. So perhaps you would relish the opportunity to make good on that."

Havaer felt his internal dispenser feed him some heart meds like a steadying hand on his shoulder. *Might be about to walk into a shooting war.*

"A team's been assigned to you. Be diplomatic. Be firm. I'd rather you didn't have to kill anyone but sometimes you can't mine without explosives. Above all, retrieve the data, preferably still sealed." Laery fixed him with her skewer gaze. "Questions?"

"Can I ask what intel got leaked? How desperate are they going to be, to get hold of it?"

She stared at him for a few long moments. "Above your pay grade," he was told. "Or it better be, because apparently it's above mine."

*

18

Drill 17's public spaces were thronging, meaning those areas set above the actual mining work that was the place's ostensible raison d'être. Every little alcove and shoebox of a space was filled with people doing some kind of business. Hannilambra were everywhere, very much running the show. Havaer observed the characteristic slightly strained look of humans trying to follow what their earpieces were telling them, or fighting to separate the audio of their translator's voice from everyone else's. A big Castigar, war caste, wound its serpentine way through the bustle, shoving smaller species aside with a sinuous surge, its crown of eye-tipped tentacles weaving around.

Kenyon deposited the rig's floorplans into their shared e-space, marking out the place their factor could be found, along with a few other sites of interest. Lombard, their technical specialist, was a hypochondriac of the first order and his attention had been snagged by a travelling Med-al-hambra booth. The Colonial charity was supposed to bring Hugh-guaranteed meds to spacers at the fringes of the human sphere, but Havaer wouldn't have trusted anything on sale here.

Reams, the last member of the team, stopped abruptly. Havaer had detailed her to link with the kybernet and get them up to speed with any local developments. It would have been awkward to ask for their factor and find out that he'd been knifed the day before, for example.

"Architects," she said on their encrypted channel. And, realizing that sounded unduly alarming, "Not here. They've wrecked Cirixia."

Since reworking the world of Far Lux and then being deflected from Berlenhof—an event all four of them had disturbing personal recollections of—the Architects hadn't been idle. They'd taken out Ossa and Nillitik, and pitched up above a world that was still just a string of numbers because the joint Colonial–Castigar colonizing effort hadn't agreed a name yet. There hadn't been Earth-level losses, but at the same time the pace of their activity was decidedly brisker than in the first war. And now Cirixia.

"Where the fuck," asked Lombard, "is Cirixia? I never heard of it."

Reams forwarded the newstype to everyone and they all slowed their progress to digest exactly what it meant. It was months-old news, apparently, only reaching the Colonial Sphere now because reliable info was always slow to crawl out of the Hegemony, where the planet was.

"Huh," Havaer said. "There's a thing." They'd had Hegemonic artefacts at Berlenhof, still preserved in the inexplicable magic that enabled their transport from planet to planet. When the Architect had turned up over that world again, the Partheni had taken out those artefacts to protect their lead warship, the one carrying Telemmier and the other Ints. And this time it hadn't worked. A straight-up guarantee about what the Architects would and wouldn't do had turned out to not be worth the paper it wasn't written on. In fact, so he'd heard, the Architect had sent...*things* aboard the Partheni vessel with extreme prejudice, confiscated the damn artefacts, and then proceeded to trash the ship. The Architects weren't only *back*, they were making up for lost time, losing patience with the universe.

And now a whole Hegemonic world, with who knew how many humans and others living on it, was gone. During the first war, it had been humanity in the spotlight. Other species had pitched in to help but the Architects had definitely been concentrating on human worlds. This time, it appeared they weren't discriminating.

Makes you wonder just whose backyard they were redecorating in the fifty years we didn't hear from them. Nobody doubted there were species out there that humans had never met and which the Architects had picked on, likely causing many of them to now be entirely extinct. The enigmatic Harbinger Ash claimed to be the last of one such lost race. The Naeromathi and their Locust Arks were a spacefaring remnant whose worlds had been utterly reworked.

"One less problem for us to worry about," Kenyon suggested darkly, as they crossed into a larger space given over to a bar. The Skaggerak was probably the nastiest R&R at Drill 17, thronging with human and Hanni and a handful of Castigar. Rotary drones wobbled overhead delivering drinks that they only spilled half of. You could get quite drunk in the Skaggerak just sitting around with your head tilted up and your mouth open.

Havaer directed Reams to get a round in, and then Lombard to make sufficient mundane enquiries of the kybernet and local businesses to establish their cover as itinerant spacers. His eyes swept the room even as he cocked a brow Kenyon's way.

"Nobody's going to be in a hurry to join them now the cultists can't promise protection anymore." And that was Kenyon's obituary for however many thousands or millions had died, on wherever the hell Cirixia had been. From a strictly departmental point of view, it was a fair assessment. A number of human worlds had taken up the Hegemony's offer of protection, during the war and after, the price of which was always complete subservience to the bafflingly ritualistic Essiel. Becoming a clam-worshipper was probably less attractive if you didn't have their shell to hide behind, though. The Originator tech that the Hegemonics had formerly used as a magic talisman against Architect attack was now only a speedbump since the monsters had returned.

It wasn't hard to miss the big old frame that Olian Timo used. Everyone moved out of the way when she came in and headed across the room. She passed close enough for Havaer to touch her, and he just eddied aside with the crowd. In the bubble of the hulking Scorpion she was a diminutive figure, with stumps for both arms and one leg, the other missing entirely, but her pugnacious attitude more than made up for it. She didn't notice him as she stomped over to rejoin her two confederates, Kit and Solace. All three were very much on edge and Olli looked particularly punchy.

The opposition. The professional part of his brain was brewing plans and counterplans: what to do if they ended up going head to head? How much of a threat was that monster of a workframe? Was there a pack of Partheni battle-sisters ready to rush in at Solace's word? He checked with his team. Kenyon had made contact with the broker and was negotiating for access to the seller, Reams backing him up. Lombard was fishing to intercept comms from Timo and the others, but getting nothing of use. Havaer suddenly had a strong desire to just walk over there and take a seat, chew the fat, talk over old times. With that mob it might actually work, but from a tradecraft point of view it would likely look bad on his record.

He had a few brief heartbeats in which to hope they were merely adrift here, but he'd let Timo's sullen expression fool him. He should have remembered she always looked like that. Without warning, the three of them were on their feet and moving off purposefully, and he realized they'd used their head start well. They were already ahead of him.

2.

Idris

He was the man who'd driven the Architects away from Berlenhof.

He was the man who'd betrayed the Colonies.

Both stories were broadcast across the human sphere now, racing from world to world, spreading, diverging, picking up a shell of speculation and fabrication as they rolled. Neither the Council of Human Interests nor the Parthenon had made an official statement on either point. And so everybody knew. At the same time, what anyone knew differed from what everyone else knew, over space and time. Nobody really knew.

Even Idris himself wasn't sure just what he was anymore.

*

Idris Telemmier had driven the Architects away from precisely nowhere, because "driving" implied force and leverage that neither he nor any other human being possessed. He had, truth be told, asked nicely. He'd bent all his precious and reworked Intermediary mind, destroying his health and his heart. And, in the end, he had won an audience with the vast intelligence which dwelt like a candle flame at the core of the moon-sized Architect. It had been cruising towards Berlenhof, the Colonial capital, and engaged in furious battle with Partheni and Colonial warships. Meanwhile every civilian vessel there ever was had been taking people from the ground and the orbitals so that some tiny fraction of the population might be saved.

He had asked it *Why*, and it had told him, through image and comparison. Why? Because it was a slave, and its masters demanded it rework the universe one populated planet at a time. Just as its kin had done to Earth a century and more before, and then reshaped so many human planets in the war that followed. One which had in turn shaped Idris, from a callow volunteer into an Intermediary who spoke to gods and strode the trackless void between the stars. Or however the mediotypists put it, the florid purple prosers that they were.

But he had begged, pleaded, then asked really nicely. And some kind of commonality between them, the remade man and the godlike destroyer, had prompted it to risk the wrath of its masters instead of turning Berlenhof into a flayed sculpture and memorial for a hundred million souls.

It had been hard for him. Hard for the Architect. They'd gone away before, when the things they were destroying started speaking to them. Now they were back, because their masters were whipping them doubly hard. Infuriated, no doubt, by their reticence. Even the Originator relics that had once held the Architects back weren't enough to keep a world safe. The Architect-masters' campaign against humanity and the rest of the universe had stepped up after fifty years of absence. They weren't accepting excuses anymore.

He was not the man who'd driven the Architects from

anywhere, therefore, but he'd done what could be done. And that should have meant he was owed a great debt.

A month later, with his contradictory legend building up a head of steam as it travelled the unspace Throughways from world to world, an Architect had come to the mining world of Ossa, population seven hundred and nineteen thousand. It hung above the planet's thin atmosphere and the domed cities, and peeled the planet into a floral grotesque at the cost of ninety-seven per cent of the inhabitants. When Idris received the news, he wondered if that was on him. If Ossa might have lived had he not been at Berlenhof. Because one side-effect of the Intermediary process in him meant he hadn't slept for close on half a century, so he had time to think about these things.

And as for the betrayal, the details were similarly uncertain. Hugh had made no concrete statement on his status. There was no bounty on his head. Nor was there any clarifying diplomatic sleight of hand to explain why he, one of the three survivors of the original Intermediary Program, had abandoned his home polity for its closest rival, the warrior angels of the Parthenon.

Certain burgeoning factions within the Colonial Sphere certainly believed he was a traitor. The Nativists, humans for humans, cursed his name. The Betrayed, who were the knife within the Nativist sheath, to be drawn out in dark alleys and seedy spaceport bars, kept themselves sharp for him.

Some said he'd been bought. The Betrayed said that Ints had forfeited their humanity to become what they were. That they were traitors to the bone, to be held on leashes or not trusted at all. In defecting, Idris was just confirming their reasons for hating him.

Some said he'd done it for love. That there was a beautiful Partheni girl waiting for him in their fleet. Although, they said, how he'd ever tell her from the others was anyone's guess, given they were all just decanted out of *vats*, now, wasn't it? Or something of that nature.

As always, the truth was something more complex. Yet a small but growing movement within the Colonies, who decried the conditions under which new Intermediaries were created, were actually closer to that truth than anyone realized.

*

The earliest Intermediaries had been developed for the first war, to try and connect with the Architects, which conventional force had barely been able to slow. And that had worked better than anyone had reasonably hoped. Idris and his fellows had helped in the destruction of an Architect over Berlenhof, the first time—the only time—one *had* been destroyed. And then, over Far Lux, he and two others had made the first true contact and ended the Architect War with a simple statement of: *We are here.*

Of course, now it was decades later and the Architects knew humanity was present but they were being driven about their apocalyptic business anyway. Far Lux had been the first place they'd reworked, before making their second visit to Berlenhof.

Soon after the Intermediary Program had begun to yield results, people discovered that Ints were good for more than just wartime countermeasures. An Int-piloted ship could go anywhere, into the deep void of unspace or appearing

27

without warning over a planet. It wasn't pleasant. There was a reason why, out of that first class, only Idris and two others were still around, and it wasn't just the passage of time. But it made them valuable.

The original Intermediary Program had a success rate of around ten per cent. They had taken in volunteers, like the young Idris, and turned out a large number of corpses with spectacular embolisms, fatal strokes and mortal conditions medical science didn't even have a name for, plus a handful of Ints who had the universe in the palms of their hands.

After the war, the work had gone to the Liaison Board, who were short of volunteers now the actual future of the species was no longer at stake. They'd made up the numbers with criminals. Their success rate was a tenth of the old Program and their Ints came shackled with a leash contract, property in all but name. And with other controls too, so the rumour went. Safe tools for high-value shipping, warships, diplomatic junkets and the far-ranging Cartography Corps. But because they'd become what they were only under duress, the Architects wouldn't listen to them. The Architects, slaves themselves, weren't going to heed pleas from the owned for the salvation of their owners. That was Idris's discovery the second time the Architects came to Berlenhof.

Hugh would be reworking the Liaison Board to rectify it even now, and likely the flow of volunteers had picked up. They'd wanted Idris to be a part of that, and they'd have given him anything he'd asked for to secure his cooperation. All in good faith, not a whiff of a leash contract about it. But he was an old Int now, even though the years had stopped ageing him when he came out of the Program. He remembered that ninety per cent mortality rate and knew he wasn't the man to shepherd the ever-dwindling crowd of hopefuls into the future. He didn't have the strength to bear the losses.

Which left the Parthenon.

The Parthenon had no Intermediaries. Idris's kind represented Hugh's great strategic advantage should a war be sparked between ruined Earth's two successor states. When Idris Telemmier had taken his vaunted brain and defected to them, a great many people had vowed never to forgive him.

*

This morning, he was regretting it.

People back in the Colonies imagined the Parthenon ran their entire civilization like the crew of a warship, everyone marching about in step, everything run to an exacting schedule, no time for idle talk or seditious thought.

The exacting schedule part was true. For a spacer who was used to a constantly shifting, unpredictable life, it was a rude shock. For someone who literally couldn't sleep, it was ghastly. The sorority Idris had been nominally assigned to had its work times, its leisure times and its sleep times. After a week of just lying on his bunk or watching the weird selection of mediotypes he could access—half local-made and alienatingly stylized, half Colonial imports with disconcerting Parsef dubbing—he'd gone out and found another sorority on a different watch cycle. He'd sat with them, tried out his awkward language skills, and just attempted to *be* in company, rather than on his own in his quarters. They hadn't liked it. He'd not realized just how hard his own sorority had worked at not freaking out around him. He was the only man any of them had ever seen. It wasn't the case that men were actively demonized in the Parthenon the way the Nativists always claimed, but they weren't used to him. They stared and he killed conversations.

None of that was the worst of it, it just didn't make the bad part any easier to bear. Which was the work. And right now, having given up on another abortive subjective-midnight attempt at socializing, he was lying awake dreading the time when that work would start again.

He had only himself to blame. He'd invented the arrangement with Solace, his recruiter. She was more than that to him, but right then the recruiter had been the important part. It was difficult work, though. Traumatic. And living amongst the Partheni and their thousand strangenesses just made everything harder.

If he'd stayed in the Colonies and taken Berlenhof's offer, no doubt the living would have been easier. They'd have given him anything human wealth could buy, doing away with all these little stressors and inconveniences. The only downside would have been how much worse the work was. *So* much worse. He couldn't have done it. Right now, after working with the Partheni for six months, he had turned out exactly zero Intermediaries for them, which was just about as expected and might have been the same if he'd had a suite of fancy rooms on a Berlenhof orbital to work out of. However, he had also presided over the deaths of precisely zero of his prospective subjects, and that seemed to make all the other unpleasantnesses worthwhile.

First order of business was a check-up with his doctor—or rather a Cognosciente Superior. They were concerned about the Hiver units currently keeping his heart going, a donation from an old friend. The Partheni preferred bio-matched organic replacements and worried about the long-term effect of having a trio of cyborg insects working his circulation. After that, it was the walk to work.

The garden ship *Ceres* was huge, orbiting a dead rock world with a tender fleet of smaller Partheni vessels. The heart of the craft was food production, but it served as home for thousands too. There were schools, sports facilities, wooded parks, a disorienting illusion of openness under the ship's sunward-turned domes. And everywhere were the Partheni: women of his watch marching briskly to work at a pace he could never match; women on their leisure period strolling and chatting, playing games, arms about each other with a public intimacy that Idris's Colonial sensibilities found offputting. By now they didn't stare at him quite so much, and he tried not to stare at them either. All those bodies and faces so alike, and all so purposeful. Even when they were just sitting in the green spaces reading a slate, there was such a sense of harnessed determination about them that he found it hard to ever think of them as "off duty." Surely, whatever they were about, there was some chain of orders behind it. That was his Colonial prejudice speaking, and yet he still couldn't quite believe he wasn't right.

Six months, and he still couldn't get used to civilian Partheni. Not that they were *civilian*, exactly, given that every single woman of them was a servant of the state, and the state was, in effect, a fleet. He'd never realized before how much his assessment of people was based on their wealth. In the Colonies there were rich and poor. He'd seen the former in grandees from Berlenhof and Magda, the long-settled and prosperous worlds where the great and good gathered. He'd *lived* the latter, because the sparser colonies and—most of all—the great dispersion of spacers were never rich, constantly patching and borrowing and eking things out. He knew the Parthenon was poorer than the Colonies, per capita. Nobody here had any grand displays of conspicuous consumption, but at the same time nobody was starveling-thin or obviously in need. He suspected most of this was due to his hosts not letting him see the bad parts, and the rest was him seeing it but not registering problems because they were all guarded around him and he didn't know what to look for. And a part of him was thinking, *How much of this is just momentum? Just them living as if there's a war on all these years, no room to complain or step out of line? How long can it go on before it goes off the rails?* But he was an outsider and he could never know.

His own path to work took him down past the green levels to the ship bays of the *Ceres*'s underside. The balance of badges and colours of the uniforms changed as he entered regions where the more overtly military held sway. Here were the Myrmidons, the warrior angels who were the face of the Parthenon for any Colonial. Here were the crews from the constant rotation of docking ships, soldiers on home leave, plus the not inconsiderable force the *Ceres* maintained for its own defence. It was a dangerous universe and a garden ship was a soft target.

He knew the drill by now. There would be a set of fresh new-yet-similar faces waiting for him down at the bays. They would be Partheni from all walks of life, young and old, mostly nervous, staring at him like he had two heads. Some would be resentful, because they'd been told to do what he said, and he wasn't part of their command structure or their society. He was just a skinny little Colonial spacer in too-baggy Partheni clothes and boots he still tripped over, hollow face and jug ears and flinching at every loud noise.

They'd go out in one of the light carriers, his hands on the controls and the lot of them wired up to a host of neurographical recorders that were firewalled from the ship's computers, which wouldn't enjoy unspace any more than a human mind would.

He'd take them into unspace, awake. Just as nobody ever did. He'd already have talked them through it, a quavering spiel that never got any easier, watching all those kindred faces pass alarm one to the next. Everyone knew what happened if you ended up unprotected in unspace but he still tried to explain it. *You will be alone*, he told them, and then, after some meandering talk, *but you won't be alone.*

Because unspace wasn't real. And when you entered unspace, you weren't real either. You existed only in the bubble of your own consciousness and, even if you gripped the hand of your neighbour painfully tight, as many of them did, those fingers would become empty the moment the ship dropped from the real.

Regular navigators on a Throughway trip would clock off about then, checking into their own suspension pod and getting woken up only when the ship reached its destination. But Idris was going to jump them into the deep void between stars, where no Throughway went. He had to stay awake for the trip, and so would everyone else, as the recorders measured just what went on in everyone's heads.

They'd come out somewhere sunless, a mote against the canvas of light-years-distant stars, only a subjective handful of minutes later, and he knew he'd hear the sound of Partheni absolutely refusing to weep before the Colonial.

Then he'd do it again, and again, because the recorders glitched a lot during the actual unspace jumps and they needed all the data they could get.

The Partheni were looking for prospective Intermediaries. And nobody was *born* an Int. Or, rather, one person had been: a woman they'd called Saint Xavienne who'd turned aside an Architect at Forthbridge Port and set in motion the whole Program that had created Idris. But that Program had involved a great deal of invasive work, surgery and chemotherapy and working away at the brain until the subjects were either remade into what Xavienne was, or died. Most human brains couldn't be altered in such a way and remain viable, and even now the Liaison Board still had no way to predict who might or might not make the cut. But every so often they produced a viable Int.

He'd come to the Parthenon because there was a slender chance they represented a better prospect, and for Idris the point of Intermediaries was to defend against the Architects. Their potential military applications for any possible war between Parthenon and Colonies was something he wasn't thinking about. Sometimes he spent whole unsleeping nights not thinking about it.

The Parthenon had a problem when it came to Ints. One aspect of life on the *Ceres* that Idris found particularly oppressive was the images of Doctor Sang Sian Parsefer they had up in offices, schoolrooms and public places, on lockets and medallions, even watermarked under the text of official messages. The woman who had designed and built the Parthenon, long ago, before the first war. The woman who had created a new and sharply defined strain of humanity to her own preferences. The woman who, in her old age, had sent her creations to the aid of Earth's refugees, yes, but it might not have gone that way. The word amongst the Colonial Nativists was that she'd been a flat-out eugenicist, but Solace said she'd started with as diverse and healthy a genome as possible, a real pan-racial melange of immunities and resistances. Except the whole point of the exercise had been to avoid whatever Parsefer had seen as the failings of chaotically evolved humanity, so she'd cut and tweaked and played God.

Idris tiptoed about under Parsefer's stern, recorded gaze, exchanged polite greetings with all the calm, mannered women around him, and knew that he was potentially working towards placing a terrible weapon in the hands of people whose inheritors could become monsters. Their society had lived its entire history on a knife edge, teetering over that abyss where they decided they were *better* and, therefore, entitled to erase that which was *worse*.

No Saint Xavienne had arisen within the ranks of the Parthenon to set them on their own Intermediary Program, nor ever would one. Parsefer's God-playing meant they simply didn't have the genetic variation to throw up freaks of that nature, victims of their creator's success. It might be— sometimes Idris even hoped for it—that such a thing was entirely impossible. That the requisite seeds to permit the growth of an Intermediary had been left on Dr. Parsefer's cutting-room floor when she had finished her creation. In which case he'd made himself the arch-traitor of the Colonies for absolutely nothing, and it might be the better result.

But if they found *one* instance of a Partheni whose brain reacted in a manner appropriate for a nascent Int, then they'd have many. Each subject he took for a spin represented a specific germ-line, a particular combination of Partheni traits. If they found one who was viable, and could turn that subject into a working Intermediary, then he hoped they could do it with as many as they liked, without the murderous attrition of the Colonial method. That was the plan and why he'd done all of this, spending six months giving women night-mares and subjecting himself to the void.

*

Monitor Felicity was waiting for him, as always. He suspected she set her clock, or the equivalent, two minutes ahead, because it would be bad form for the Colonial to have to wait for her. Unsleeping as he was, Idris could have played her at her game until they ended up with neither of them ever leaving the lab, but that kind of elbow-jostling wasn't in his make-up. Instead, he just greeted her politely and went to look at who they'd brought in today.

The usual, was his first thought. Twenty women who looked from eighteen to eighty, except the Parthenon had a habit of putting its useful servants on ice until needed. The youngest of these could have been born a decade before him. He knew they got a fairly stripped-down brief that didn't quite amount to an explanation, but they were all willing to do their bit for Mother. Or at least they weren't willing to look unwilling. He had the impression a great deal of Partheni culture was about keeping the side up.

Monitor Felicity dogged his footsteps, boot-heels clicking neatly. She looked like the aunt or cousin of everyone currently lined up for inspection. Doctor Parsefer, whatever her true nature, had known what she liked in a face, picking features from a dozen ethnicities. It was an attractive face, round, narrow-eyed, dark hair cut regulation short. Right now, the examples he was seeing were also doing their best not to look fearful or antagonistic.

These are not the volunteers, he reminded himself. Should they ever get that far, it wasn't these women going into the grinder. They were just more subjects, an exercise in data gathering.

He halted, glancing back at the blandly polite smile on Felicity's face. Made to speak; stopped himself because the suggestion was ridiculous. Except the hunch he'd just been landed with wasn't going anywhere.

"Monitor..."

A cocked eyebrow, no more.

"This woman, wasn't she here before?"

The object of his curiosity looked younger than him, her hair cut perhaps a little shorter than the others. Maybe it was the fact she seemed slightly smaller-framed, more like a Colonial starveling, like him. Except he hadn't picked her out of the line-up at any kind of distance. Only now, as he was about to walk past her.

"Identify yourself, child," Monitor Felicity said.

"Cognosciente Grave, Bathory Sorority, Medusa Division," the woman got out, voice shaking only a little.

She was. This is her second time around. What's going on? But Felicity was giving them their orders, sending them off to the carrier with a "Prêt à combattre?"

"Prêt, Mother," and they were on the march towards the airlock, needing Idris in there with them or nothing was going to happen.

"Monitor—" Idris began, but she gestured for him to follow.

"Just another round of recordings, Menheer Telemmier." The relentless Colonial honorific made him feel smaller each time it was trotted out. "After you return, all will be explained. How did you recognize her, though?"

"I..." *Hair, frame, something...* "don't know. But you can't start hiding things from me. That's not the deal."

Felicity's face suggested she hadn't seen any reference to that in the small print of the deal. Although given that Kris had actually drafted that deal, Idris wasn't willing to bet it wasn't there. For now, though, he went to put this new batch through their paces.

*

The light carrier *Hale* was just a little gadabout to get a few squads of Myrmidons where they needed to go, which meant it was armed with accelerators and could pull out some serious gravitic shielding. He had the candidates strapped into two rows of seats down the spine of the ship behind him. And if there was a part of this wretched job that he liked, it was that he got to fly Partheni vessels every day. Colonial ships prioritized robust redundancy, or at least the kind a spacer knew did. They didn't have an all-encompassing state to look after everything, for the same reason they didn't have one giving them orders every moment of the day. The Parthenon, with its entire militaristic society pointed in the same direction, was very hot on ship design. They'd had the best ships even before the first war—better than Earth, and several of the alien species Earth had encountered. Perhaps only the Hegemony had better, and Hegemony tech was simply an order of magnitude beyond anything any human had dreamt up. To fly even a clumsy carrier like this was something of a joy, and he'd been given sharper toys to play with in the past, during the war and after it.

And yes, *Ceres* control was riding his ass and could override him any moment it chose, if he decided to go buzz them. But still...

"Okay, we've been doing this—I, I've been doing this a while. I guess you probably know that, most of you." He spoke over his shoulder, hearing his own voice hitch and quaver with the awkwardness of it. Imagining their massed stare at this Colonial getting to sit in the pilot's seat. Some of them were pilots themselves, judging from the glimpse he'd had at their company badges. Others were various other strains of Myrmidons, the Parthenon's famous fighting angels. And more, like this Grave, were technicians or science types of some kind, the Cognoscientes. Perhaps one was also a Monitor administrator, which could mean anything from filing clerk to spymaster.

"In a moment we're going to jump to unspace, head out a ways into the deep void. Surface, jump back. Basically we're...back and forwards." And he could hear a murmur of translation, an artificial female voice turning his jittery Colvul language into something that hopefully sounded a whole lot more reassuring. "You know what to expect, awake in unspace. You've heard..." He was weirdly aware of Cognosciente Grave's gaze boring through the seat into the small of his back, which was of course impossible. "Look, not going to lie to you, it's no fun. But you're supposed, they said, they told you that..." There was a whole mental exercise the candidates were directed to go through while they were in unspace, and it was nonsense. It was just busy-work to provide some baseline for the neurograph readings. And he should probably tell them none of it was real, that what they were about to sense, on the wrong side of the reality boundary, was just the way the sentient mind responded to unspace. Except he hadn't met a single Int who'd believed that, not after a few trips. Certainly he didn't believe it himself.

"Anyway," he carried on wretchedly. "I've got the clear from *Ceres* so we're going in, compris?"

"Compris, Mother," about half of them said, out of Partheni conditioning.

Something's different this time. He didn't know what, nor how he knew.

But.

His hands gave the orders, shut down the ship's higher systems and spun the great ring of the gravitic drive so that it reached out in the impossible direction, touching the point where real things shouldn't go.

They slid into unspace with barely a ripple.

3.

Solace

Solace had expected a faceless contact, voice only, more go-betweens, a whole song and dance of politely difficult Hannilambra each taking a cut. Instead, Kittering had negotiated a face-to-face meeting with the seller. There were no more layers to the onion than that.

Olli, of course, revelled in the opportunity to show how much more she knew about how things worked here. "Hanni comms," the drone specialist explained, as they wound down through two layers of living and working quarters, "like it all out in the open. So they set up an Open Field. Basically, you talk biz, and anyone can listen in. It's like a big old marketplace. If you want secrecy, you have to find somewhere out of the way and physically meet up. Which works for Hanni because half their language is arm-waving."

Kit paused and did just that, his shield arms flashing their bright adverts as he did so. "It is more complicated than that," the little crab-like alien's translator said primly, "and also: arrival." He'd brought the three of them to a slant of metal steps heading into a darkened room. Theoretically, their seller was down there.

She'd rather have been here with an armed force of her

fellow Myrmidons, but that hadn't been an option, fraught as the political situation was. Instead, the Aspirat needed a team that could navigate a dive like Drill 17 without standing out, and there the Parthenon's resources were limited. However, it just so happened that recent recruit Idris Telemmier had brought with him a shabby little ship and crew who were a perfect fit.

Her mission here was a tricky piece of business, insofar as Solace's brief had explained. Nobody knew if these supposed Colonial secrets were even real, but the Aspirat had decided they couldn't ignore the possibility. The Parthenon was also short of third-party operators who could be trusted, hence using the *Vulture God* crew. Enter Solace, their nominal handler.

The steps were designed for Hanni, meaning they were awkwardly small for a human. Olli's Scorpion should have had real issues getting its bulk down them, but she didn't even hesitate, picking her way with the delicacy of a dancer on the frame's four metal legs. Halfway down, a voice issued from speakers set into the wall.

"Far enough. Let me scan you," in tones as blandly pleasant as Kit's translator.

"Scan what you like, we're armed to fuck," Olli said cheerfully.

There was a thoughtful pause from the speakers, and then, "Jesus saves, is that an *accelerator*?" The words versus the tone of the artificial voice came through in a jarring clash.

"You're dumb enough to cut deals with the Pathos, you get what you pay for," Olli replied.

"Maybe let me do the talking when we're down there," Solace murmured. "You know, diplomacy."

Olli made a rude noise.

"Okay, you can come on down," the voice informed them.

"What?" Olli demanded. "I mean, how many superweapons would we need before you told us to go away?"

"Scan was for pathogens, not guns. Some of us have immune-system concerns." As the Scorpion made the last few steps and lurched out into the open space below, a living woman's voice added, "Hell, I thought I was doing badly. Where's the fucking rest of you?"

Solace grimaced, waiting for Olli to take exception, but the specialist just said, "Fuck, right back at you." And then all three of them had made it down there, in a gloom her eyes adjusted rapidly to.

The room was stacked with metal and plastic crates, the sort for small cargo, or that spacers used to carry their worldly goods from ship to ship. Some were open, some empty, others overflowing with the sort of old tech that never got thrown away out here on the edge of human reach. It was something that sparked contempt in a lot of Partheni, the hoarding, pack-rat mentality of Colonials. Except Solace had seen their technicians—and spacers were *all* technicians to one degree or another—make gold out of dross in situations a Partheni tech would have given over as impossible. Her people had no idea, honestly, just how much invention necessity could be mother of.

In the centre of the room, sitting in a walker frame, was their host, or most of her. She was short one arm, one leg and half a jaw. The cybernetic replacements were, to put it mildly, unlovely, and far from new, but then "new" was like unicorns in places like this. Solace would have believed the injuries had been sustained during the evac from Nillitik, save that the skin around the jaw implant was knotted with aged scars, purple and veined from the living tissue's long-term attempts to reject its artificial neighbours. *Immune-system issues, right.*

"Olli," said Olli, gesturing to herself, then pointing out the others. "Kit. The Patho's Solace. She's the money. You happy talking to Pathos?"

The cyborg's eyes flicked between them. She was old, old for a spacer, or for any human. Her organic hand had wrinkled skin hanging off its bird bones. Her face was creased and criss-crossed with lines. There was a cylinder stapled to her brow, a dispenser with two cannulae feeding drugs into her in sporadic doses, but her eyes were bright.

"Drayfus." She gestured with her plastic hand, which was coloured yellow-pink, lighter than her bronzy skin and not matching the prosthetic jaw either. "You get mauled by a Castigar or something? I seen them carve someone's limbs clean off."

"Born," Olli said shortly. "You?"

"Ship." Drayfus looked to Solace. "You're who they sent, is it then? Was expecting a platoon of Myrmidons. Marching band, gun salute." She mimed playing a little trumpet. The little finger of her fake hand kept twitching in tiny spasms after she lowered it. "But you got a spacer crew to bring you here. Sharp. Gives me hope we can do business."

"Depending on what you've actually got for sale," Solace noted.

"You know what."

"Provenance of your manifest is lacking," Kit noted primly. "Contents noted as vague."

Drayfus relaxed back in her walker frame. Her artificial leg hadn't moved at all and perhaps it didn't work anymore.

44

"Ah, well, as to that. Only I thought your lot were straight, and I don't want to shock you."

"How about start with why deal with them—us, I mean," Olli put in, despite Solace's warning look. "I mean, the Parthenon, nobody's first choice for a quick hit of Largesse, right?"

Drayfus snickered about her jaw implant. "I fought in the war, kids. I was last out of the *Lethbridge* over Amraji. Not where I got these lovely souvenirs, by the way; that came later."

Older than I thought. Solace said, "So did I. The war. Berlenhof, amongst others."

"The first time?"

"Well, both times, I suppose," Solace admitted.

"Fuck." And a little respect in Drayfus's voice that hadn't been there before. "Well, right then. So just take it as read that I fought. I gave them the best of my youth. And then the war ended, and we didn't get the option to go on ice like you girls. I'd have taken that. Like King Arthur, you know what I mean?"

Solace had absolutely no idea what she meant but just nodded.

"So you can probably guess my career got chequered after that."

"Give me a name," Olli said, watching the woman with keen interest.

A pause, without expression. "*Dumas.*"

Olli whistled. It didn't mean anything to Solace, but then Kit sidled closer, and his hushed-down translator murmured, "Pirate. Much success, then destruction." And looking at Drayfus, maybe it took half of her with it. Solace had never

45

met a pirate, but the Partheni had run into their share. It wasn't a trade they romanticized. Too many Colonial types had decided to try their luck with Partheni shipping.

But this is what I do now. This is what added the "Executor" to her rank. Because sometimes a pirate had something you wanted.

"This thing is something you...pirated?"

"Not quite. But pirated, yes." A little packet of information pinged up on Solace's slate, sent direct from Drayfus's walker without having to mesh with the Hannis' public network. Provenance, as Kit put it. This item had passed through a string of hands, starting with a Hugh courier who'd gone to indulge some bad habits and fallen in with the wrong crowd. His effects had included a cylinder of sealed data and his vengeful creditors had been sharp enough to realize that keeping the seal intact and preserving the secrecy of the contents would boost the value. The only clue on the outside was that they were the minutes of some kind of deeply nested Hugh subcommittee, but if they were being physically carried from one Colonial grandee to another then surely they *must* contain something clandestine and valuable. Whereas if the seal was broken and they turned out to be nothing more than Magdan farm yields, there went any chance of profit. After that, the cylinder had changed hands a few more times, likely as part of paying off debts and sometimes not entirely voluntarily, until eventually coming to Drayfus, who'd put the word around.

"You're not the only prospective buyer, obviously," the ex-pirate said. "I've even got Hugh types on-station, queueing up to meet me. Nice to be so popular."

"They won't just arrest you?"

"No jurisdiction in the Shadow Border," Drayfus said easily. "And they *want* what I've got, soldier. They'll be here with a sack of Largesse and probably a pardon, if I even want one."

Solace nodded. "Let's be straight with each other, then. I have some funds. I know and you know that if Hugh wants, it can likely outbid me. But we've been talking a while now and I don't think you're someone who much enjoys wasting her own time."

Another snicker. "Where does the Parthenon even *get* funds? I mean, it's all 'from each according to her ability' round your way, right?"

"We trade. There are goods we can sell, and services. Not so much direct to the Colonies, because that might be problematic, but armed escorts to Hanni and Castigar." And then she added, stony-faced, "Hunting pirates, you know."

"Oh I know." A lopsided smile. "I have a price, soldier. And I will take your Largesse, don't mistake me, but you're right, Hugh can always top you, for pure money. But there's something I can get from you that they can't give. Because I want to retire. I am so damn *over* the spacer life. I don't know anyone who's even within ten years of how old I am. I want to retire to the Parthenon and have each according to her needs. I'll even teach your girls some piracy if that's a direction you want to take your grand experiment. You should think about it. You'd be good at it."

Solace blinked. She glanced at Olli but there was no help from that quarter. The specialist was as thrown as she was.

"You want to defect?"

"I'm a wanted fugitive, a pirate and a murderer," Drayfus told her with some relish. "I am not some nice lady citizen of Hugh who wants to light an ideological candle in your window. But I want to settle, and there's no damn place in all the Colonies where I won't be forever watching my back. So that's my price."

Olli

There was nothing for it but to get word back to the Parthenon. Olli and Drayfus both knew Solace was in no position to blithely make that kind of promise. She could just have sent via Drill 17's comms, but given the open Hanni set-up some Hugh codebreaker could be sitting at the next booth and scribbling it all down. They needed to get back to the *Vulture God* and wait until a packet ship passed through to carry the word to the wider universe. And then wait some more for assurances from Parthenon command that would convince Drayfus. It seemed they were stuck on Hismin's Moon for the duration.

They left Drayfus and wormed their way back through the Skaggerak, which was carefully situated by its enterprising proprietors to make it the hub of just about any path through the upper levels of the drill rig. And that's when things kicked off.

Olli had forgotten to be on guard. She remembered Solace warning her that spy stuff was very boring a great deal of the time, and let herself assume this was definitely going to be one of those times. Solace herself had her eyes open, though, so Olli almost stomped over her when the Partheni stopped abruptly, lurching sideways instead and knocking three people over. Olli was about to do her usual "No, *you* ran into *me*," that she saved for particularly blameless collateral damage, when she saw these three weren't blameless after all. They were part of a mob of about a dozen who were here for Solace.

They all had blue-and-white-circle badges on, which meant Earth Nativists, who looked on the Parthenon as worse even than the Architects. There were dagger tattoos: one on a forearm, one particularly bold one on a face, artfully drawn with the hilt above the eye and the blade going down the man's cheek. Daggers in hands, too, and a couple of percussion guns. They were standing in Solace's way, not quite fronting her but shifting so she couldn't get past. One Partheni, a dozen Nativists. Good odds for the bad guys.

Kittering started backing away very carefully. Hanni got underfoot easily when humans started fighting, and he wasn't in any way a brawler. Olli watched him pick a table to crawl under, alongside a pair of crab-like gamblers who had the same idea.

This was going to turn into a fight, barring a bunch of armed Hannilambra security breaking things up, in which case it would probably still be a fight, just somewhere else, and probably where the ships were. Olli didn't want either these clowns or Solace putting holes in the *Vulture*.

And there went Solace, just trying to push past. The first man to stop her—big, for a spacer—found out Partheni paired being small with being solid. Solace had him instantly off-balance and onto a stool, neat as you like and hardly violent at all. It didn't clear the way, though, and it put her right up amongst them. The knives were towards the back of the pack, but it wouldn't stay that way for long.

Olli sighed. *Always up to me to throw the first punch.* And she revved one of the drill attachments on the Scorpion.

"Pay well does it, working for the traitor-angels?"

She craned sideways to look at the speaker, seeing a shaven-headed man lurking at her elbow; a spacer in crisp clothes that looked fresh-printed. "You what?"

"I see you, woman," he said. Solace was taking some abuse now, just words still. Olli tried to keep an eye on everything at once and felt a headache coming on. The Scorpion gave her a shot, and that was probably a bad thing because her usual homebrew of painkillers tended to make her punchy as hell.

"You don't see shit," and she angled away from him, while keeping a camera tilted in his direction in case he tried any hostile maintenance on the frame.

His face, which could have been ugly as sin with hate, was surprisingly open and frank. "I see one of us who got a bad deal and made something of it, woman."

"My name," she told him, "is not *woman.*"

"Because that's what *we* do," he said, voice strong without needing to be loud, like some preachers she'd heard. "We build on the bad we're dealt, because there's precious little good comes to us. Because who gets the good? Not us. Fat men on Hugh committees, fat men in long red robes, Patho women in expensive armour in expensive ships. But you take their money. You're too good to be with your own? You're going to shed your kin's blood for the traitor-angels?"

"Listen, you have no idea who I am," she told him.

"You know who that is?" He was abruptly pitching his voice to carry to the mob of a dozen who had somehow not plucked up the courage to throw the first punch at Solace.

Olli braced herself for whatever personal invective was to come, but it wasn't her he was about to introduce.

"That's the Patho who stole our Int!" the man said, and then just peaceably stepped back into the agog crowd.

The first punch followed very shortly after.

Havaer

Havaer was well aware he was going in second; that the Parthenon could already have closed the deal. It had taken bribes and too much finger-talk to secure a meeting with the seller. Reams had half a dozen jobs under her belt that had involved working with Hanni and still it had all taken far too long to get through. The *Vulture God* crew had been and gone, and he'd practically run into them on their way back, not that they'd noticed. Leaving Lombard above to keep an eye on them, he, Kenyon and Reams had headed down.

He could only hope the money would swing things his way. Contrary to the average spacer's accusations, the Colonial government had the sort of budget you got if you stretched a shoestring across half the galaxy. But when it came down to something important, apparently there were hidden pots of Largesse out there like magic gold. And whatever this sealed data was, it was evidently important to *someone* who themselves was equally important.

If this data turned out to be some Hugh grandee's roster of mistresses then he wasn't going to be amused. However he was keenly aware that it could just as easily be their game plan for when the Parthenon came for them, or some new innovation in Intermediary technology. Something that would doom all the Colonies if it fell into enemy hands. They still wouldn't tell him, so he had to assume it *was* that important.

He didn't want to think about how things would go if the seal was broken, meaning the data had been accessed and a million copies were potentially already made and winging their way along the Throughways.

"Chief." Lombard's voice in his ear, meaning trouble. It was likely their encryption wasn't worth much in this den of talented villains.

"Report." He quickened his pace. *Not now. We're almost there.* Reams and Kenyon were looking at him, tense as wires.

"Trouble. Kicking off with the Parthenon right now." Lombard's tones were tightly clamped down. Fear there.

"Hold out—" Havaer started, but there was a burst of static and noise that made him wince and dial down the volume. A moment later there was audio, the sound of screaming, shots, a high whining like industrial machinery.

"Require backup," Lombard hissed through it. "Holy shit, chief, it's all kicking off here. Parthenon, here, now! Chief, I can't make it out."

Havaer had stopped. Trouble here, now, meant the opposition wasn't playing nice anymore, and maybe it wasn't just Solace and the clowns from the *Vulture*. "Situation, Lombard. Report like a professional," he snapped, but the channel was down, just static and echoes.

My team. My risk.

"Kenyon, meet with the buyer. Close the deal. You know what we've got. Take Reams."

"You'll need the backup more than me, chief."

"Take Reams. She can talk to Hanni better than you." Havaer was already six steps back the way they'd come.

"I won't need that, chief. The seller—" Kenyon bit down on the words. "Chief, you should—"

"Just close the deal!" Havaer shouted over his shoulder and then he was running towards the Skaggerak and Lombard.

4.

Kris

It was remarkable how a simple freight dispute could escalate.

Keristina Soolin Almier—Kris, to her friends—stepped out onto the quad in front of the Ishmael Commercial Courts. Her formal advocate's robe, which she hadn't worn in the actual courtroom, flurried about her in the constant wind that dirged around the hollow torus of the station.

She'd had to rent the robe, because it wasn't something she needed much, running legal defence for a shabby crew of spacers. A fistful of her precious Largesse nest egg blown on pure show, because the only thing the robe was good *for*, in this highly ritualized business, was taking off.

Across from her, Mortin Ballest, fellow advocate, tugged at the sleeves of his own robe to stop the wind running away with them.

She reached into her capacious sleeve and drew out her knife, ceramic blade gleaming in the harsh artificial lighting. After a moment's pause, he did the same.

Ah, shipping law.

After years bailing Idris Telemmier out, Kris had some different clients now: the Parthenon. One of their trading concerns had a claim on goods that had been impounded

54

from out of a smuggler's hold. But because the smuggler had for some reason not been upright over keeping good paperwork, seven other parties, including a Colonial cartel, had also lodged an identical claim. The court case had been a grand old funfair of depositions, affidavits, Hugh bills of lading and all the jolly rigmarole. And there had been Mortin Ballest, Scintilla-trained advocate for Espic Barovingean, a Magdan landowner concern. EB had also paid for the same containers the Parthenon claimed, because the smuggler had run his business like that. Everyone, basically, looked like a fool, but it would be the last fool standing who got the goods.

Kris had, over four days and about a million documents, beaten down Mortin and the other opposition, so that the Parthenon could walk away with three containers of who knew what, and that was just how the game went. If she'd lost she wouldn't have been happy about it, but she'd have bowed to Mortin and the one other Scintilla graduate, nodded to the rest, and proceeded to explain just what had gone wrong to her clients.

Except Mortin had not bowed, no more than a nod of the head. Bad form, the Inns wouldn't have approved. And then, outside the court chamber and well within earshot of the other advocates, he'd said, "I hope whatever services you're receiving from *them*," with a nod to her clients, "makes up for betraying your own."

Kris had gone quite still, and if it had been just the two of them she'd have pretended not to hear. The other Scintilla graduate was looking horribly awkward, a meek-seeming man who obviously didn't want anything to do with it.

The problem was, she *could* have walked away. This was not a court thing anymore, it was a Scintilla thing. She was a graduate of a particularly well-respected and, above all, very long-established college of law. Under normal circumstances, and had she not made one particular mistake back when she was training, she'd have been living a far more comfortable life. But you took what time gave you, as the saying went. Scintilla had its own ways, though, accreted about the legal codes like coral. There were things you did not say to another graduate.

Mortin had obviously thought she was too long out of the college to rise to the bait, but the protracted trial had left Kris feeling punchy. And her clients, whom he'd just insulted, were right *there*.

"I will accept your apology," she'd said crisply, and the room went quiet. Even those not up on Scintilla etiquette would know the words from a hundred legal drama mediotypes.

Mortin had raised an eyebrow. She'd given him a good space of time to reconsider, trying to hold his eye, but he was too busy smirking for the benefit of his own clients. The Magdans were core Colonials. She'd had run-ins with their landowner class, the Boyarin, before. They were arrogant SOBs, and didn't take losing well. Mortin had been trying to soften defeat by scoring points off the opposition.

She'd not been in the mood, however. This kind of spat was potentially her *life* for the next who knew how long, and if she got a reputation as someone who could be insulted to her face, that would make every new case that much harder to fight. So...

"Then I cite the Ninety-Seventh and require satisfaction."

He'd started to tell her not to be ridiculous but finally caught her expression. For a moment he'd been wavering, and he might have taken it all back and to hell with the

Magdans, but he was bigger than she was, longer reach and a few years younger, and a sore loser to boot.

When she returned to her clients, Monitor Sudden had asked her, "What is the Ninety-Seventh?"

"'One passes no comment on whomsoever an advocate chooses to represent,'" Kris had quoted, already regretting the whole business but too late now.

"So now you fight him?"

"Yes," Kris had confirmed.

And here they were, a day later. Monitor Sudden, as her second, stepped forward with perfect timing to take that ridiculous gown off her, leaving Kris wearing just a spacer's short-sleeved tunic and calf-length leggings. Her sandals were kicked off for better footing, plus a violet scarf looped about her neck with its ends tucked in to deny Mortin any convenient handle on her. There was a jagged cicatrix beneath that scarf, the relic of a previous incident where Scintilla honour had got her into trouble. She held the knife in her left hand; her right forearm was wound with padded strips of cloth, printed out from the court's own facilities for the purpose.

Mortin had shed his own robe and they took their places on the lit circles the kybernet had drawn on the floor for them. For a secretive Scintilla tradition, this sort of duelling was certainly well known across the Colonies, mostly from inaccurate mediotypes. There was quite an audience out in the quad, bundled against the unceasing wind. The chance to see a real-life lawyers' duel didn't come around very often.

"Please be successful, now," Sudden told her, retreating to the encircling spectators. *Ah yes, I hadn't thought of that. Such valuable advice.*

A clear chime sounded. She felt that even the kybernet,

the station's governing AI, was leaning forwards for a better view. Mortin began to advance, forwards, sidelong, forwards, sidelong, until she stepped in front of his progress with a few standard opening gambits, letting him sway back and make the expected counters and ripostes. Little more than a secret handshake, really, the two of them establishing their credentials as graduates. She expected a little invective from him, for all it would have been bad form, but he was concentrating. There was some sweat on his brow despite the cold wind.

That wind was a reminder of college for both of them. Scintilla was a world of snow and ice and monolithic stone architecture, high walls and walkways, shadow-haunted quads. Not like this tacky station, but the artificial wind was still a breath from their shared past.

Mortin took the initiative then, very direct, much like his advocacy style. She gave ground, hyper-aware of the space she had to work with. She was grinning, she realized. Also bad form but she couldn't help it. She hated duelling, right up until the moment she actually found herself doing it.

She tried some Blue Window-style advances, all that circling of the hands, defence pressed into becoming offence. He didn't like that, but adapted, pushing back. Bare feet scuffed the plastic of the floor. His blade scored across the padding on her arm but she'd taken the angle of his attack outside her guard, cutting in towards his ribs with little darts of her wrist, delicate as if she was dining. He fell back, one step too far, out of distance, and they both closed with just the same suddenness. He tried to sweep her legs but she stepped round the awkward move, blade feeling out the arcs of movement of his off-hand, trying to get past like a wasp at a window. His own knife ducked in for a stab at her side, the opening she'd been inviting.

She let it come, practically guiding it in with her right, stepping round the lunge, allowing the blade to nip past her belly. Then she was past his elbow without him bringing it into play, and the ceramic edge of her knife drew a line of blood across his shoulder.

They broke immediately, eyes meeting. He was supposed to give, then: concede the match like a polite son of Scintilla, but his clients were watching and his blood was up, and the nick she'd given him was deceptively slight. She waited, willing him to do the sensible thing. And waited, and...

He squared off again, off hand out, blade held high, but she could see his anger yanking him about, ruining his form. He went for her before he'd even quite found his balance, trying to blind her with pure speed, and she gave him three strides of ground before stopping her retreat abruptly with a sidestep. The knife cut the air past her, helped by her cloth-wrapped hand, and then she had the point of her knee pressuring the outside of his, halfway to sundering the joint, and her blade was...

Right at his throat. As much of a shock to her, it almost seemed, as to him. The sheer hunger in her hands horrified her. Very, very close to giving him exactly the sort of bloody necktie that she'd once received, the track of which had sat beneath her collection of scarves ever since.

A frozen moment in which she fought her own hands, thinking, *No, not again.*

Then, just like that, they parted. After a strained moment he bowed, grudgingly but acceptably. The crowd realized the show was over, and some of them clapped politely but most of them looked a bit disappointed, a bit baffled. Monitor Sudden was in the second camp.

"Aren't you going to kill him? Isn't that how this goes?"

Kris's eyebrows went up because that was quite blood-thirsty even for the Partheni. "First blood. Almost no duels end in deaths." And her personal memories of one that had, the direct cause of her chequered legal career out on the edges of the Colonial Sphere, rose in her mind.

"Oh." Sudden shrugged. "It's not like that in *Scintilla My Lover*. Except when it's two longtime rivals."

Kris hadn't pegged Sudden as a devotee of terrible legal drama, but apparently you never could tell.

On the way back she learned a lot about Sudden's passion for several different long-running series. The woman had been all reserve throughout the case, and Kris had taken that for her usual manner. Now she recast that as Sudden being terrified of losing the case and letting her sisters down. There was a lot of that, in the Parthenon. Solidarity against a hostile universe seemed to be their major motivating factor.

In the Colonies, you cut your own course. That was the big difference. Nobody gave you free training, assessed you for aptitudes and told you what you'd be doing for the greater good. She'd asked Solace, once, what happened when some-one's job didn't need to be done anymore. Where did they pension off all the unnecessary Partheni, exactly? Solace had given her a look that Kris had come to know all too well as *Seriously, Colonial?* And Kris remembered that Solace, who looked about her age, had been born maybe seventy years ago during the First Architect War, and had spent a fair amount of the intervening time in suspension until she was needed again. That, and a rigorously controlled vat-birth system, ensured the Parthenon had exactly as many people as it needed, no surplus mouths, no shortages.

And she'd wanted to ask, *But what if you don't want to go on ice?* And, *What if you don't want to do what your aptitudes say?* And, most of all, *Some of you go rogue, right? Just...get out?* But Solace's open, honest face had somehow made that impossible, and so the questions were still battering about in her head.

Idris

On the far side of the imaginary line, in unspace, there was only Idris and the emptiness of their vessel, the *Hale*. Even that was because of his own continued insistence on it, he always felt. Unspace was the volume distinct from real space. In real space things really existed and regular physics applied. In unspace...not so much.

You were alone in unspace, always. The illusion of being that a sentient mind transitioned into was utterly solitary. Every one of the Partheni candidates would be experiencing the same. The sisters at their elbows would be gone; the pilot's chair would be empty. Alone in the cosmic undervoid, hurtling to unknowable oblivion. What could be worse?

It was, of course, worse. There was a consensual hallucination that preyed on the mind, brought on by such exquisite isolation. It was the illusion that one was not, after all, alone. Everyone reported the same experience: human, Hanni, Castigar, even the cyborg intelligences of the Hivers. The illusion was that you shared the vastness with *something*. That it became aware of you and came closer, from outside the ship to inside, from inside to lurking in the next room. From the next room to standing at your very shoulder. And the one key characteristic of this presence that everyone imagined was that it was intolerable. It represented the worst, absolutely unabideable thing for any given observer. When it finally caught up and was there, breathing on your neck, darkening the corner of your vision... When the choice was to turn and gaze upon it or...

The candidates were all strapped down, wrists and ankles. Because exposure to unspace killed, and it killed by the hands of its victims. Idris had seen the bodies from lost ships that had fallen into unspace without suspension facilities and not managed to claw their way out quickly enough. Gouged eyes, rent throats, opened wrists. All preferable to facing the spectre that everyone experienced, and that every psych paper and study knew was purely in the mind of the beholder.

Except in unspace, nothing was real, and so perhaps an imaginary killer had exactly as much existence as its terrified observer.

Idris was one of the three most experienced unspace travellers available to the human race, one of the only survivors of that legendary first class of Intermediaries. And he knew the science papers were wrong. He'd been hunted through unspace by an alien navigator, a feral, animal mind that had known nothing but the chase, and had somehow been able to carry its instincts for pursuit outside of real space. Which meant the glorious and terrible isolation of unspace wasn't as inviolable as people thought. The other thing he knew— that any Int, new or old, would swear to—was that the Presence in unspace was absolutely real.

Let the psychologists scoff. They didn't have to go there and feel it at their shoulders over and over again.

There had been one time it had spoken to him, in the voices of colleagues lost and dead. But even Idris wouldn't swear to the reality of that. He'd been on the point of shunting into a life-threatening coma at the time.

He felt the Presence now, sniffing about the outside hull of the *Hale*. Repeated exposure didn't mean it was an old friend. One could not become *at home* in unspace. But your mind toughened and calloused over, in ways the regular human never needed to. Most Ints broke eventually, and the fact there were only three of the first class left wasn't just the result of wartime casualties. Perhaps it was just acceptance in the end, the very last stage of grief. You felt the Presence looming, chuckling silently in your ear, and knew *This is my life, now.*

All those commercial Ints out of the Liaison Board, out across the Colonies, were facing this self-same thing without ever having chosen it, and how much worse must that be? And that was what he was trying to prevent by this mad alliance with the Parthenon.

It was inside the ship now. The hairs on his neck prickled as it padded down the empty aisle between the vacant seats. He couldn't turn his head. He'd die if he laid eyes on it. He knew that with a burning, primal certainty.

Same old same old, the standard pressures of a working day. You know, the *usual.*

And *out.*

The *Hale* burst out into the real and abruptly his ears were full of the sounds of human company, a shipload of Partheni whose prior experience of unspace had been safely sedated in a suspension couch. Some of them were weeping, some gasped. Others were talking too fast, trying to reassure themselves that it was over. And a few were silent. He checked the medical readouts. Nobody had died on these test flights yet; no seizures, no aneurysms, no coronaries. The Parthenon vats turned out robust hearts and minds. But it was always a possibility.

He twisted around to see them, all those similar faces, pulled in different directions by their solitary trauma. Grave was looking at him—she wasn't the only one, but it was her eyes he met. Some of the others had an accusing look, loathing the Colonial who'd put them through that, accusing him mutely of enjoying it. Not Grave. She was one of the still ones. Her face was without expression.

He threw up a view of their surroundings on the common screen, along with coordinates, letting that sink in. Every other unspace trip they'd taken would have been on a Throughway, system to system along paths set down by some unknown civilization that had vanished from the universe long before any of the current spacefaring cultures had evolved from single cells. A halfway-competent navigator could set a ship bobbing on the current of a Throughway and then retire prudently to their pod to sleep out the voyage.

But here they were, having come into the real in the middle of nowhere, and the view was of the stars with not a planet to be seen, the deep void where nobody went. This was Idris's playground and, without a mind like his, no ship would ever find its way out of it. They were a hundred light years from anywhere. Even a distress call would take a lifetime to reach anyone.

"Ten minutes is all I can spare you. Then we're doing it again," he told them. "I'm sorry. We need the data. I'm really sorry."

*

Some of them needed help to walk off when the *Hale* finally returned to the *Ceres*. He'd made eight jumps before his nerve broke and he'd had to take them back. He knew the pattern from past test-flights. Partheni stoicism had kicked in, the women clutching at each other's hands every time they returned to the real, but clamping down on their emotions more each time until they could give him—the foreigner perfectly bland Partheni looks. He knew that they'd let it out when they were with their sisters, with their counsellors. But he'd made himself the enemy by then, and they understood how to face up to an enemy.

Grave just stared at him, until it was him looking away.

Back on the ship, he wanted to debrief them, talk to them, find something reassuring to say, but he was being hauled away to a meeting with Monitor Felicity.

"Menheer Telemmier," she said, "we will be reporting a successful first stage shortly. But we wished to show our findings to you, for comment, before we did so." She brought up a wall-full of displays, neurograph activity, which he could make nothing of.

"This is yours," she explained. "From a previous flight, you understand. But consistent with readings from all flights."

"What am I looking at?" He frowned. "There are gaps. Is this... The machine doesn't work properly in unspace, is that right? So... doesn't that just mean all of this is junk data?"

"There are gaps," Felicity agreed. "Here is the reading for candidate Myrmidon Clarity. No gaps, you see? From the same equipment. Much trauma, upset, psychological harm suffered, just as with them all, but a complete reading."

Seeing his own trauma and harm recorded there, apparently no less extreme despite all the callousing, was less than inspiring. "You're saying there are holes in my head?" He'd meant it as a joke but by the time the words were out they didn't sound funny.

"These are when you are in unspace." Felicity highlighted areas of the display, rotating the 3D depiction back and forth. "Holes, Menheer."

He must have looked blank still, because Felicity's expression veered to the impatient and she elaborated, "This is you interfacing with unspace, your mind ceasing to interact with the real. You go where we cannot measure, then come back. It's the first time we have ever observed this. We do not know if the Colonials ever considered the possibility, in their desperate scramble to produce you, but our Cognoscientes hypothesized such a thing." She sounded very pleased about that. "Now, observe."

She replaced the displays with another set, mostly indistinguishable.

"You're going to have to help me here," Idris said weakly.

"Here." A highlight. "Here and here. Your graph, here. But see this. The gaps. Less than yours, far less, but there are moments of un-recording. Where the mind is out of contact with the real, with the instrument. You see?"

He remembered where the name tag of Myrmidon Clarity had been, and squinted at this one.

Cognosciente Grave, Bathory Sorority, Medusa Division.

"What does Medusa Division do?" he asked slowly.

"Long-distance scan and threat detection," Felicity told him, and then, in a different tone, "She was in an incident. The *Bathory* suffered damage. She suffered damage. Trauma. It was not believed she would recover, but she did, despite a period of lost brain activity."

Idris digested this, feeling despair rising slowly in him. "Well then," he stuttered out, but the enormity of the problem was choking him. "But that's. Useless then. Because. Because the whole *point* of this was to find a–a–a *lineage* of Partheni with an affinity for void work. So we could produce Ints without murdering ninety per cent of our candidates. And now you tell me the only reason she's reacting like this is some fluke head injury? That's…that's no *use*! This isn't *success*!" He ended up shouting at her, top of his voice, the crazy Colonial, or else the demented Intermediary whose mind had been broken by too many jaunts into unspace. His puny fists were clenched, and he stood to the fullest extent of his hundred and seventy centimetres. She just stared him down, and he ended up feeling ashamed and hot, a child coming out of a tantrum.

"This is today's data," Felicity went on, as though none of it had been said. He saw another wall of impenetrable readings, save that he knew what to look for now. There were a handful of images with the telltale gaps. One was Grave's.

"All of the same germ-line," she explained. "Most are not encouraging, but you will see, a handful…Grave's injury may have made her more receptive, but it reflects an underlying sympathy. It has led us to what we sought. So yes, Menheer, this is a success. We will begin assigning candidates to the program now. We have some data from the original

Intermediary process, gathered in over time, or even shared during its early years." A slight smile. "Some of it mentions you and your classmates by name. Perhaps you would be interested in reading their reports on you."

"No," Idris said promptly, and then, "and you mean volunteers, yes? When you say 'assigning.' Volunteers. That was the deal. My first and foremost and most important condition. Because it's no use otherwise."

There was too long of an awkward pause before Felicity said, "Every daughter of the Parthenon is proud to serve."

"No," he told her again. "That isn't... No, listen. It has to be volunteers. Firstly, because if you just conscript people like the Liaison Board does then the Architects won't *listen* to them. They *know*. They understand compulsion, because they are *compelled*. I've told you this. So send a bunch of forced drafts out and you'll win nothing. And your conscripts will likely die. I mean, they'll likely die anyway, from past experience. You've seen what they had to do to me to keep me alive. But... And secondly," drawing himself up again, for what little that ever achieved, "I won't do it. I won't help you if you just order people. It's got to be volunteers who know the risks. That there's a good chance they'll just *die* before you can turn them into working Ints, no matter what precautions we've taken. And if they become an Int, it means doing what we did today over and over; the horror of it, over and over. That will be their *life*. They have to know that, and have a free choice. They *have* to. Or I won't do it."

A cool moment of Partheni disdain for the temperamental Colonial, and then Felicity said, "You are of course free to speak to every candidate advanced for the next stage of the program. You may ask them if they consent to serve the

Parthenon in this way. We are not the Colonies, to deal in leash contracts and such things."

He imagined the range of free and frank answers he, a Colonial stranger, would receive from the solidarity of the Parthenon recruits. He had a wretched feeling in his gut that he had made a very poor decision, and was in too deep to unmake it.

*

A day later, Kris was back from Ishmael and a court dispute that seemed to have been unusually tumultuous. She, of all of them, seemed to have adapted to Partheni life well. She got on with the people, and Idris knew she'd enjoyed quite a few liaisons with sisters curious about certain aspects of Colonial life.

She came to see him and they sat side by side on his bed, in the room he had all to himself, that odd luxury no native Partheni enjoyed. He just tumbled the words out, all that had happened, the success of the project, and where that was now leading. He knew Kris would set her mind to it, and if anyone could insert some failsafes into the system it would be her, but she would be up against the mechanized momentum of the Parthenon, and he wasn't sure even a keen legal mind could last long against that.

5.

Olli

After it was over, which came remarkably close to when it began, Olli took stock. She reckoned the guy with the coxcomb of orange hair was probably not going to make it, unless he had some friends who could get him over to the Med-al-hambra stall in double time. The woman with the serrated knife had a broken arm and her friend with the big nose had a matching leg, plus the nose wasn't going to set straight unless he got a really good medic to look at it. Those were her personal contributions to the fight. Solace had lamped quite a few of the others and kicked one big man in the peripherals sufficiently hard that even Olli had winced at it. Kit, playing to his strengths, had stayed hidden under the table.

She hadn't actually killed anyone at least, though, as noted, Drill 17's medical facilities were in sudden high demand. She was proud of her restraint, frankly. She was also pissed off that it had come to this, because the shaven-headed man had got right under her skin with all that traitor talk. He'd then made himself scarce, apparently, as she didn't see him stretched out on the ground anywhere.

Solace hadn't killed anyone either. Mr. Punch had spent

the whole fight slung across her back. Everyone got a restraint award. She had the accelerator out *now*, though, because security had belatedly turned up. Three armoured Hanni were regarding the Partheni leerily, insofar as Olli could decode their body language. Thankfully Kit chose that moment to reappear and began to clear things with them. Hannilambra tended to be hands-off when it came to aliens in their spaces, ignoring the problem if they possibly could. With the fight over and the more numerous losing side absenting itself to go lick its wounds, they were plainly happy to forget any of it ever happened. They didn't like the look of Mr. Punch, however, mostly because of the structural damage the weapon could cause.

Kit was trying to attract Solace's attention. "There is a need for us! Great urgency required!" his translator snapped out.

"We haven't got an answer yet. I need to send out to the next packet," Solace told the jittery Hanni. "Drayfus doesn't think I've got Partheni high command back on the *Vulture*, does she?"

"Called to the seller effective immediately," Kit told her flatly. "Single transmission, cut short, no further comms. Come on, come on now."

And he was already heading towards the maze of tunnels that led, inter alia, back to Drayfus.

"I don't understand." Solace was still dragging her feet a bit, perhaps scenting a trap, but Olli got it.

"Move," she said, and pushed forwards, double time, the Hanni tapping along in her shadow and Solace running to keep up.

"What is it?" the woman demanded.

"Means Drayfus is in a bad way."

"Actually dead?"

"Or close to. Maybe some other bidder didn't want to take no for an answer."

They found the door to Drayfus's compartment had been forced. Solace slowed as they approached it, Mr. Punch to her shoulder, nose wrinkling. Olli sampled the air: the mix suggested she was smelling burnt flesh.

"Priority access to the armed and dangerous," Kit suggested prudently. Olli let the Scorpion muscle her forwards. She was by no means invulnerable in the frame—indeed one of the arms was broken at the elbow after the bar fight and there was a list of other warnings, old and new. She'd need to sort these out when she had access to her tools and remotes back on the *Vulture*. It made her *feel* invulnerable, though.

She was barely at the door when Solace barked out a challenge behind her, and she heard running feet. Someone had been keeping an eye on the door from one of the other corridors, and now they were off, with Solace after them. Olli wheeled the Scorpion, seeing Solace skid around a corner and then throw herself right back as a handful of projectiles made a pepperpot series of holes in the facing wall. The Partheni levelled Mr. Punch carefully, listening and calculating, and then fired, not around the corner but into it. Olli heard the eerie singing sound of the weapon's little projectiles accelerated to ridiculous speeds, punching effortlessly through the walls and then making a mess of the man on the far side. Solace remained very still for a few moments, and then cautiously peered round the corner.

Olli patched into Solace's helmet camera, and recognized the sprawled body as the shaven-headed son of a bitch who'd called her out in the Skaggerak.

"Good," she decided vindictively. "Go pick up the pieces with Kit. I'll check on Drayfus."

But Drayfus was dead. Olli felt a surprising pang at that. She'd barely met the woman, but she'd liked her, piracy or not. Or perhaps because of the piracy. It was a hard thing to outlive your own legend, especially as a spacer. To end up dead in a hole like Hismin's Moon, after all that life and time, seemed a bitter waste.

She hadn't died easy. There were six other corpses to keep her company, and they were the source of all that savoury roast meat smell. Olli could see the ports on Drayfus's walker frame now, mostly because the weapons had melted their own mountings in their fury. Several of the crates and containers showed scorch marks, but they were all rated to withstand the vicissitudes of space travel with contents intact. And about half of them had been opened—presumably as many as the surviving attackers had needed to search before finding the thing they were after. *The thing we were after too, damn sure.*

Most of the roasted dead guys had Nativist badges, she saw with a sinking feeling. They looked of a piece, all crew of the same ship maybe, save for one, a woman lying curled around a handful of gunshot wounds by the door, out of the arc of fire.

The old pirate had ended up on her side, half spilled from her frame. She'd been shot, like the woman by the door, but her body was riddled with multiple wounds. If she'd been burning up the room at the time, her opponents probably hadn't been given a chance for witty repartee or pinpoint sniping. Her dead face was set in an expression of bloody-minded belligerence and Olli liked that. *Died as you lived, you old piece of leather.*

Kit had been following some procedure apparently sent to him in the pirate's last communication, but he'd come up empty. "It is my opinion that the requisite goods have been removed."

"This is my surprised face," Olli said flatly. "Guess these clowns didn't want to pay up." Although they'd paid, sure enough. "Where's security in all this?"

"Payments were made to them," Kit explained, and then clarified: "From the account of Drayfus. For non-interference."

"So she could cook who she wanted to if need be," Olli considered. "Guess she paid to shut off the fire alarms too, right?" With a bit of pique because, fast and loose as spacers were, there were corners you didn't want to cut when you were generating your own air bubble.

"Company," said Solace from outside the room, and Olli spun the Scorpion about, ready for another pack of bruisers to turn up asking for a beating. Instead, though, the Partheni was escorting a single man, not quite pointing Mr. Punch at him. His own gun, a nasty-looking little magnetic that would go invisibly into an inside pocket, was dangling at the end of his arm. He was tall, ill-dressed, a narrow, suspicious man with a narrow, suspicious face. It took her a moment to place him.

"Ah crap," she said. "You're the spook. Man Thursday or whatever you said your name was."

"Havaer Mundy, Intervention Board. Hello, Mesdam Timo. A delight to see you, too. What the fuck have you done here?"

"All culpability is entirely elsewhere. Authorizations have been duly filed!" Kittering declared, sounding quite offended.

"Well we knew Hugh was here. They send you because of us?" Solace asked.

74

Mundy shrugged. "You think they tell me anything?" He looked from one to the other of them, maybe trying to work out just where they stood. He'd had them all up for questioning before, that one time when the *Vulture God* had been caught by a Mordant House vessel. And then there'd been Berlenhof, when he'd broken rules to get Idris back to their ship so he could go save the planet. Presumably, as the planet had actually ended up saved, Mundy hadn't gotten his ass fired or his head shot for that.

"I should just follow you clowns around," Mundy remarked, without acrimony. "Find all the trouble in the galaxy that way..." His voice tailed off and a moment later he lunged forwards, pushing past Olli incautiously enough that she could have snipped a limb off him with the Scorpion's tail pincer. He ended up kneeling beside the shot woman, and his face lost its casual expression.

"One of yours," Solace commented, and not a question. Olli reckoned the Partheni had seen this play out enough before to know it.

Mundy stood up, taking in the bodies, the badges. She saw his lips move, subvocalizing. The Hanni open net showed a transmission, coded but interceptable. She wasn't a spook and it wasn't her business, though. Most likely he was touching base with the rest of his team. Then he looked at the sprawled body of Drayfus.

"This was the seller? I expected a Hanni." And Olli actually caught the moment when something clicked inside his head. Then he was squeezing past her again, trying for brisk but just a little too shaken to hide it entirely.

"I need to file some paperwork," he told them. "Probably you do, too. And don't let them kid you that rig security won't be here. They're just letting their contractual cooling-off period elapse. I wouldn't be here when they do make a showing. Seven dead bodies, even human bodies, is going to set some feet tapping."

"Eight," Solace corrected automatically, and then visibly remembered she was an intelligence agent for the Parthenon now and shouldn't just volunteer information to the nominal enemy.

The eighth was the man who'd shot at Solace. He didn't have any Nativist insignia on him, just another skinny guy in shipboard clothes.

Mundy stared down at the body for a few moments and then simply said, "Paperwork," in a tight voice. He looked at them once more, a government man well aware that he and his opposite numbers were outside their jurisdictions and any rule of law. "Be seeing you, no doubt," he put in, and strode away, long-legged, just close enough to hurrying that Olli reckoned he'd break into a run the moment he got round the corner.

Havaer

Havaer Mundy broke into a run.

He was already signalling the *Griper*, sending the codes that would lock the ship down so that nothing short of a dedicated hacking specialist could get it moving again. Which Kenyon wasn't. Lombard could have done it, but he had apparently got himself into a shooting war with the Parthenon, because that was his body Solace had shown him, torn up by her accelerator rounds.

Havaer had been juggling all sorts of theories right about then. The Nativists had Kenyon and had killed Reams. The *Vulture God* crew had Kenyon and had killed Reams. Reams had been with the Nativists and the cyborg had killed her. Except the weapons tech maths only went one way, when he was given a moment to catch his breath and consider it. The Nativists had *burned*. Poor Reams had died gutshot from regular percussive weapons. Solace carried that damned accelerator because she was a Partheni and didn't understand things like subtlety or concealable guns. And if Timo and her war-frame had got involved then the evidence would have been clear enough, painted all over the room. Conclusion: the Nativists had shot Reams. There were certainly various factions and blocs within the Colonies who could whip up a gang of thugs with badges and dagger tattoos to go do their dirty work. Given he had no idea what was in the stolen data, it was easy to see that any number of individuals and cliques might have an interest in it. Which left Kenyon maybe captured, or maybe lying somewhere else, dead but out of sight.

Except.

Except Havaer had sent Reams off with Kenyon while *he* went back to help out Lombard in the bar fight. Where he'd found a bunch of crunched Nativists and the *Vulture God* crew, brutally victorious, already out the door and heading back down here. More to the point, Lombard was nowhere to be seen, and not answering hails.

Kenyon had really not wanted Reams along, despite her expertise in dealing with the Hanni, and Havaer had skated over that because a lot had been going on at the time.

What was it the man had said, or got partway through

saying? *I won't need that, chief,* referring to Reams' expertise. And why not? Because the seller wasn't a Hanni, but a human, or most of a human plus a bunch of mismatched metal parts. That hadn't been in anybody's brief to Havaer. He'd gone ahead on the likelihood of a Hannilambra dealer, here on this Hanni station at the edge of Hanni space. Natural baseline assumption. Kenyon had known, though. Havaer's second had been given a brief more expansive than his own. And he was not now lying gutshot next to Reams.

So Havaer locked down their ship, the *Griper*, and for a yawning second thought he was too late and it had gone, but apparently either Kenyon wasn't that quick, or it wasn't his plan. The ship confirmed his instructions. It wasn't going anywhere without him.

He tried Kenyon after that. All innocent just-checking-in-have-you-seen-Lombard? No response. Kenyon wasn't dumb and he was obviously treating his current adventures as entirely off-book.

He and those crispy roasties back in the cyborg's parlour had probably been in on it together, and Kenyon had let them take the heat, literally, after they'd shot up Reams for him. And then Kenyon, along with whoever he had left, had grabbed the goods and ran. Or else they hadn't, and Havaer had been played and left Solace and the Parthenon in possession of it. But barring a marked increase in their tradecraft, he'd heard their candid bafflement as he came in. He was running entirely on gut instinct now. Kenyon had it. Kenyon was still on the moon, still at Drill 17. And Havaer was running for the docks.

All those Nativists would have a ship, or ships. Most likely

Kenyon's plan had always been to bug out and hitch a ride with his allies, back to whoever had suborned him. And, of course, he was way ahead of Havaer and would be off-planet before his erstwhile boss could intercept him. But Havaer still ran, because running was what you did in these circumstances. He had his slate out as he hustled along, paying for camera access at the docking bay, passing the view across the messy slew of ships. Maybe he'd even see his treacherous subordinate boarding. He could at least put out the alert on Mordant House channels. Assuming those weren't compromised too.

But something was going on at the docks. There was a fair-sized freighter there, the sort that could be carrying quite a large crew of mercenary Nativists. And quite a large number of mercenary Nativists were currently standing outside it, disarmed and angry and with their empty hands held clearly visible. Ringing them were a full score of Hanni, armoured and armed. Drill 17's security had kicked into action, and Havaer could only assume the local kybernet had seen exactly what had gone down in the cyborg's lair and identified the culprits and their ship faster than anybody had anticipated. Right now, nobody was going anywhere in that hulk, not until somebody coughed up reparations. Which meant, as Kenyon wasn't amongst the angry faces he could see, he was still in residence and without a ride.

Havaer threw some more of the departmental budget at the kybernet, buying more surveillance. One eye showed him the *Vulture God* crew on their way back up behind him, looking disgruntled enough that he knew they didn't have the goods. A handful of viewpoints scanned the Skaggerak, as well as other public places such as the market. He stared, looking for one face amongst many, for a man dressed like a spacer but not quite carrying himself like one.

At last there, amongst the pop-up stalls, beside the Med-al-hambra kiosk, he found Kenyon, haggling with an unsympathetic-looking crewman. He saw them reach agreement on Kenyon's passage off-moon, for what had obviously been more Largesse than he'd wanted to part with. *And don't think you're claiming that on expenses.*

He tried to query the crewman's identity, but that was apparently not something the kybernet was willing to give him. It was easy enough to track Kenyon between the market and the dock, though.

How much for absolution? he sent to the kybernet.

A large sum, but not quite the value he'd have assigned to a human life.

Another hand dipped into the department's pocket, and he was going to have a fun old time filing the relevant accounts. *Item: station authorization to gun down my subordinate.*

He stretched his legs, picking up speed, and was able to get to the field just narrowly ahead of Kenyon. He felt his internal dispenser give him a calming dose. He was not the sort of agent particularly happy with casual violence. Unlike Kenyon, apparently.

He hoped he gave the impression he'd been waiting there for a while, utterly in control of the situation. More likely he looked too dishevelled, and was breathing too heavily for it. The look on Kenyon's face was short on surprise.

"Right, then," the man said.

Havaer had his gun out, just to establish what sort of team meeting this was going to be. Kenyon didn't, because he hadn't realized he was going to that kind of meeting, but he was very obviously within a hair of going for it.

"You reach in and pluck it out very carefully, and then kick it somewhere. We're going back to the *Griper*," Havaer said. "Right now I've got two members of the team dead and I'm going to need some input from you to explain that for my report."

Kenyon nodded, and Havaer could see instantly that there was no cooperation in the man. His reaching for the gun was textbook careful, and Havaer even had the time to tell him twice just how serious he was. But then he'd never shot a fellow agent, and maybe Kenyon knew that.

The reaching was slow and steady enough, in fact, for a half-dozen Hanni to bustle out onto the field, scurrying between them without noticing the human tension going on. Kenyon took his chance, hooked his gun out and tried to get it pointed at Havaer. If the interruption had come from their own species, and therefore height, maybe it would have worked. Instead Havaer shot him over the eye-crowns of the startled Hanni, aiming for a shoulder, an arm, but instead ploughing two magnetically launched projectiles into his chest.

Kenyon was punched off his feet, and Havaer waded through the scattering Hanni to get to him, already reaching for the emergency kit on his spacer toolbelt. He got the stabilizer shot into Kenyon's chest, then fumbled for the coagulant and anti-shock, until he realized the man was already dead.

He knelt there a long while, as the kybernet confirmed its authorization for the death and that security had been stood down.

It was hard work hauling the corpse over to the *Griper*, now reactivated and with its systems powering up. When he had Kenyon inside, though, a search of him revealed a data cylinder, all its coded seals intact, the data within untouched.

It wasn't much to set against the betrayal and the loss of his entire team, but he could go back to Laery with at least a vestige of professional pride.

6.

Olli

"That," Olli declared, with the authority of someone with long experience, "was a clusterfuck."

Solace nodded unhappily. They were in the Skaggerak again, post-mortem time and the only bonus being it wasn't any of their mortems.

An exhaustive search of Drayfus's room had confirmed the sealed data was very definitely not kept there anymore. Whoever had done for the old pirate had got away with it. Some Colonial faction, though apparently not Mordant House; just some group of randoms who happened to have Nativist sympathies. It was an easy creed to sink into if you didn't want to have to think about it much. Albeit still a minority amongst the spacers, who tended to deal with non-Colonials and indeed non-humans every day, and who often ran multispecies crews. Nativism was rooted in the heartlands of settled colonies where the Throughways led only to other human-dominated worlds, and if you saw a Hanni or some Hegemony alien on-planet it was a notable event.

Later on, after they'd done a lot of fruitless running around, word reached them that someone who sounded a lot like Agent Mundy had gunned down some spacer type on the docking field, an event that had become mixed up in a security action against a human-crewed ship. They'd tried to piece the bits together and come up with something short of a whole egg, but it seemed possible that Mundy now had the goods. He'd also quit the rig, and nobody much fancied trying to jump a Mordant House agent inside the Colonies. More failure, therefore.

"It probably wouldn't have come off anyway," Solace decided.

"Sound commercial transaction, however?" Kit offered, and Olli nodded along.

"We don't take…retirees," the Partheni said. "Or like pirates either." Her tone suggested she had liked this one, maybe a little bit. "We can't just support a bunch of people who want to immigrate in their old age. The Parthenon works because every part of it fits. I think my superiors would have said no. After all, there's no guarantee this data is even worth it, for all it was sung about as something special."

"I don't recall you giving us that spiel when Idris offered to come help you out," Olli observed.

"But you're not trying to just…live off us." Solace's hands made abortive gestures, trying to describe the difference. "You're not *us*. Because if you live in our fleet, as a permanent fixture, you have to be us. Some Colonials have done it. Those who preferred our ethos. But it's not a free ride, and a few have bounced right back when they realized that we *work*. We don't welcome some defecting academic with flower garlands and chocolate. It's…" She shook her head with a slight smile. "I remember one of them I heard protesting. It's amazing how someone can support your culture and ways absolutely up until the point you ask her to actually live by them. But that's not you. You're your own people. We have an arrangement. Kit there, and Kris, they made sure of that."

"Indubitably," Kit agreed.

"Still screwed if there's a war. Can't just waltz back to the Colonies then," Olli pointed out.

"There won't be a war. The Architects are back. We'll be allies again, like we were over Berlenhof, both times," Solace insisted, fielding the drinks an ageing rotary drone piloted over. She was drinking caffenado, the Hegemony relaxant. Olli had the proverbial spacer moonshine, of which the Skaggerak brewed its own particularly eye-watering brand. Kit chose migo, something like a bowl of purplish sand that his mouthparts sifted contemplatively.

"War breaking out, a return to regular habits would be appropriate," he explained, his shield arms waving magnanimously. "Arms running, smuggling, the shadow markets, all greatly increase in such times. But I am captain in those circumstances." Since the death of its previous owner, Rollo Rostand, the captaincy of the *Vulture God* had been something of a moveable feast, with Olli currently wearing the nominal hat.

"Heard worse ideas," she considered. Left to her own devices, she would have signed on under a Hanni before the goddamned Parthenon, but it had been that or abandon Idris, and Idris was the one with irreplaceable talents.

A large group of angry people turned up then, shadowed by Hanni security and most of them with blue-and-white badges on show. The crew of the freighter that had been embargoed was now free to roam, so presumably indemnities had been paid. They'd obviously all taken a hit out of their personal pay packets, and Olli reckoned the odds were good that they would drink their way straight into another fine-inducing infraction.

"Reckon we should make a move," she suggested, and added, as Solace nodded, "Don't envy you the report you have to file." Then the Partheni's glum expression made her feel mean for needling. Which was ridiculous, given the woman was a representative of a military superpower poised to obliterate the Colonies' way of life any moment. But she seemed so weirdly *clueless* half the time. The other half, of course, she was punching or shooting someone.

Speaking of clueless. "Be good to catch up with the others again. Bet *you're* looking forward to seeing Idris again?" She actually meant it halfway kindly this time, not a word of a lie, but Solace flushed and scowled and plainly took it for more bitch-talk, and Olli wasn't going to get all touchy-feely and disabuse her. Olli couldn't even work out just how much of an item the pair of them were. Maybe a random liaison with some Colonies *man* was within tolerance for a Partheni out on the town, but it had probably got awkward now Idris was a fixture at home. Olli, who preferred to keep her liaisons to the commercial or the casual, couldn't really imagine how much the Partheni rumour mill was turning right about now.

They crossed to the docking field just as the planet was coming into view, a veiny gas giant like an infected testicle crawling up the horizon of Hismin's Moon and leaving precious little of the sky free of its malign radiance.

Ah, yes, Olli thought. *The spacers' life! See the wonders of the cosmos!* On that subject, they boarded their own spectacularly unlovely ship and plotted the Throughways that would take them back to Partheni-controlled space.

Havaer

By that time, Havaer was indeed not only off Hismin's Moon but out of the system entirely, in suspension after dropping into the yawning void of unspace and confirming his course. The Throughways would carry the *Griper* from nexus to nexus like currents in a sea, until he washed up in the real, in regions more securely controlled by Colonial humanity. At Berlenhof, in fact, where he would have one hell of an awkward report to file.

For a handful of lost hours, his mind was sedated beyond the reach of the unspace bugbears that drove people mad. Since running into Telemmier he'd often wondered how it must be for the Ints, who didn't get that luxury. Maddening, presumably. Certainly Telemmier himself had always seemed on a knife edge, either shrinking away or exploding if you pressed him. Still a decent man, by Havaer's assessment. He'd done the right thing, saved a lot of lives, both in the first war and now. But a good man on a knife edge could end up doing a lot of bad things.

He took in the Berlenhof comms babble before announcing his presence, an old and robust habit. No war with the Parthenon. Plenty of public reassurances about working towards opposing the Architects together. But the back-channel chat suggested to Havaer things weren't as rosy between the two power blocs as the mediotype faces were making out. More than a few Hegemony types were brought in as talking points—robed men and women trying to interpret the intentions of their alien god-overlords in much the same way as people had once tried to divine the future from the flight of birds. After all, the Hegemony was part of this conflict too now, though they were being slow to actually liaise or cooperate with anyone.

Once he felt confident there were no surprises in the news, he sent the appropriate codes through to Mordant House, or at least the orbiting offices that still carried that nickname even though the department had moved out of the ground-side building long ago. The Intervention Board, in formal speech: a big, shady umbrella for everything from police investigations to the dirtiest of dirty tricks.

He received a comms request almost immediately, and went through the usual dance of code and countercode before accepting it, bracing himself for the skin-and-skull face of Chief Laery, never the most pleasant sight straight out of unspace.

Except it wasn't her face. There was a man, square-jawed, grey short hair, a thick neck. Havaer blinked at him for a moment before placing him. "Menheer Baladi, good to see you." With a tonal qualifier to indicate that it was also a surprise. This was Laery's direct line, after all.

"Agent Mundy." Havaer knew Baladi from the Internals sub-department, keeping tabs mostly on Hegemonic influence as the cult tried to chisel off worlds for the greater glory of their masters. A man who was decidedly senior to Havaer himself but a step below Laery. Except that...

He double-checked the credentials, feeling a nebulous sinking sensation. Hard to exactly put a finger on what he didn't like, save that he didn't like it.

"My apologies, Chief Baladi," he noted. "My congratulations. Might I ask, though..."

"I'd think you should be thanking your lucky stars, Havaer," Baladi said jovially. "We've all felt the lash of old Laery from time to time. You didn't have to sit in on the budgetary meetings with her. She's been reassigned. Something a bit more backseat, given her long service. I'm still getting up to speed myself, but I look forward to your report."

If you had any inkling about it then you wouldn't, Havaer thought sourly, but he nodded. "Be on your desk shortly, Chief." The report and desk would both be entirely virtual, but the old sayings died hard.

"Did you get the goods?" Baladi asked. "Just so I can plan around it."

Yes, his mind flicking to the still-sealed cylinder. His eyes, however, were on the incoming messages, still the babble of newstypes and regular departmental chatter. And one other thing.

"No, Chief. I'm not going to sugar-coat it. The whole thing was a bust. I'll get the report in and...you will of course take whatever action you feel appropriate."

Baladi nodded philosophically. "Right now you could have shot your whole crew and we'd still have a fresh assignment for you. All hands to the pumps." Either Havaer masked the wince or Baladi missed it. "I'm sending your next mission briefs through now. Final confirmation and need-to-know details to follow shortly. You've dealt with Hegemonics before?"

"Not my favourite people." He'd been on the wrong end of one of their crime syndicates not long ago. Not exactly on the torture rack, but that was maybe because it had already been occupied by someone getting their skin pulled off. Literally.

"Well right now we've got a business involving some people you've had contact with before, so you're a shoo-in for it. Local knowledge, right?"

Havaer moistened his suddenly dry lips. Obviously, that description covered hundreds of reprobates, intelligencers and general spacegoing scum, not to mention a small number of actual upright citizens. *So why does the goddamned* Vulture God *leap to my bloody mind, exactly?*

When the contact with Baladi had closed, and his dispenser had given his heart another soothing dose, he opened the message from Laery. It had come in over an old private channel, a wartime leftover only Laery still used. Everyone else who'd had a hand in its creation had died of time or violence. The message had come in with the label *Code Blank*, which meant deep cover. It meant carry on being the person they think you are, but from that moment make it an act. It meant, *Believe nothing they tell you.* Havaer stared at it for a long time before decrypting and reading the contents. He knew he had no tools to work out whether this was a real threat to the Colonies that it was his duty to resist, or whether it was Laery playing departmental games after being ousted and taking Havaer down with her.

The contents were simple. *Play along. Do what they say. I know you have it. Open and analyse. Find out why it's important. I will contact.*

Secure in the silence of space, Havaer yelled out, "Fuck!" at the inside of the *Griper*, because he hated this side of the business. He still didn't know if Laery was on the level, but this at least wasn't a naked power grab in sheep's clothing. And he *did* want to know what the hell was in the cylinder.

He set to composing his report for Baladi, in which he wouldn't be able to obscure the deaths of the entirety of his team. At the back of his mind, the buried data in the cylinder burned like an ember, demanding his attention.

Solace

The *Ceres* didn't have a foreigners' quarter. There weren't enough foreigners for that on the Partheni garden ship. It was something Solace had never thought about, not when growing up surrounded by her sisters, not when fighting in the first war, not until she'd fallen in with the *Vulture God* crew and spacers in general. If someone had come to her, back then, and complained about her people being xeno-phobic she'd have scoffed. Later, she'd have pointed at that blue-and-white Nativist badge and turned the accusation right back around. But the thing about the Nativists was that they stood out because the main run of Colonial humanity, certainly the spacer end of it, was so generally accepting of just about anyone. And if a Partheni raised eyebrows, that was because they didn't get out into the galaxy much. They kept to themselves in their fleetborne societies, as self-sufficient as they could be and conducting their business with other cultures at a polite arm's length.

There was a lounge, basically, in the *Ceres*. It was close to the specific hangar assigned for non-local use, and had a handful of dorms off it. There was only one bottleneck of a door leading from there to the rest of the ship because visitors weren't encouraged to wander. The Solace of before wouldn't have spared the arrangement a second thought, just the natural way things were done. The Solace of *now* looked at it and saw a long-term problem. Unless the whole Parthenon took itself away into the universe with its newfound Ints, assuming that was even a thing, they would always end up being the outsiders to everyone else. The less favoured trade partners; the people you stared at and spread rumours about and maybe bilked if you felt daring. And, because their isolation came with a heavy dose of military power, the people you were scared of.

We need to open up, she thought. Then she considered the delicate balance of Partheni society, as constructed by Doctor Parsefer and refined by succeeding generations. Where their relationship to other societies, the Colonies in particular, was one of a valiant protector who couldn't quite understand why the gratitude didn't keep flowing in once the war was over. Could that survive a greater interchange of trade and people, and most especially of *ideas*? She thought about the way people like Olli lived, which to a Partheni eye was inconceivably venal, grubbing about for profit at every turn, while at the same time desperately poor because there was no overarching society to provide even the most basic needs. Despite all that, it was attractive. There had been a moment, after Idris's defection, when it looked like Solace would be off the *Vulture God* and assigned to Int-wrangling, and she'd realized how much she'd miss pretending to be a spacer. One with the safety net of Partheni citizenship, admittedly, but still... How many of her sisters would feel the same way? How many of her sisters would it take to go native in the shadow boundary between the Parthenon and the Colonial Sphere, or the Hanni, or the Hegemony even, before the whole of the Parthenon started to grate on its bearings for want of maintenance? *How much of a hothouse flower are we?* There was no way of knowing until the blooms started to wither.

"You," Kris poked her in the arm, "have said precisely two words since you got in."

They were in that lounge by the hangar. Drinks and food were provided, for free, all part of the arrangement that had the *God* seconded to the Partheni intelligence effort. Olli, tactful enough to turn out in her walker frame for once and not the Scorpion, had a technician sat down and was outlining an outrageous list of upgrades and repairs she wanted done to the ship, most of which fell outside of what they were strictly due under their contract. Most of which Solace would push to get done anyway, whilst at the same time being aware that in giving away free stuff she was somehow not playing the game properly. *A foot in both worlds—all very well until ship and shore start parting company.* Kittering was crouched on a stool printed out for Hanni convenience, playing some sort of game on a virtual screen projected from one shield arm. It was a Partheni standard, developed (weren't they all) from an educational tool, very good for logical training and quick decision making. Kit was taking on three opponents across the ship, and beating at least two of them hollow. Hanni had a cultural bias towards nonviolent dominance solutions, and Kittering in particular was mad for games. Solace knew that his user ID had become notorious amongst the ferociously keen gaming cliques across the *Ceres* sororities, almost none of whom knew he wasn't a Partheni.

"I'm sorry." She leant in to Kris briefly, shoulder to shoulder, like she would have done with a sister off duty, surprised to find the woman had picked up the mannerism and pushed back.

"Olli said you're in trouble."

"Probably. The mission didn't go well. None of the bodies were ours, but there were a lot of bodies. Some fight between Colonial factions, probably." Solace gave herself an inward kick. "I should...No Idris, then...?" She was still feeling shy about asking, which was ridiculous.

"He's...Well, I was going to say sleeping, but we all

know that's not true." Kris grimaced. "He's on his bunk staring at the ceiling, probably. He's not doing so well."

"No success with the Int program?"

"Hah. Too much success." Kris glanced around. "I don't know where we stand with you, I mean with *you* as an individual, on this. But I'm just going to come out and say, he's worried your people will be forced into the Int process. Which, I'll remind you, isn't just attending some lectures and passing an exam. It's invasive therapy and brain surgery where the best-case scenario is coming out a screw-up like Idris with your head in pieces." She said it fondly but they all knew it was true. Ints weren't stable at the start, and then they got to stare the void in the face for as long as they could bear it until they snapped. "He's suddenly realized that the concept of 'volunteers' might mean something different in a military dictatorship—sorry, okay, not the right term, but—"

Solace waved away the words. "I don't know what I can say to help, Kris. I mean, we're all glad to serve, that's the line, right? If someone came to me and said, we want you to serve by getting your head shuffled...and the Parthenon really, *really* needs you to agree to this. I...don't know how they're going to deal with it."

"Is there anything comparable from the war?" Kris asked her. "Suicide missions or the like, that they wanted volunteers for? I mean, I've met enough of you people to know you're not like ants. You're, you know, real people, individuals underneath the cultural conditioning. Not all falling over each other to throw yourself into the meat grinder." She regarded Solace doubtfully.

"In the war there wasn't an option." The original fight over Berlenhof occurred to her, when she'd lost her ship, and most of her sisters. The *Heaven's Sword* had died when they'd gone up against the Architect, even though the Architect had died too. She'd only escaped because she was nursemaiding Idris the Int and it had been her duty to evacuate him. At no point in the whole process had she ever thought, *Can't someone else do this?* because literally everyone she knew was risking their lives in just the same way. There had been half a century of peace since, even though she'd been on ice for much of it. Maybe today's Partheni wouldn't have quite the same willingness to lay down their lives. Or maybe opposition to the insidious influence of Hugh had replaced the Architects as the motor for the patriotic mill. Not a good thing, if so.

She sighed. "I can talk to my superiors. They will probably tell me it's not within my remit. But if I say it's crucial to maintaining Idris's cooperation then...maybe I can get some clarity for him, and not just the flat assurances they're probably giving him. But..."

"But...?"

"If people are being leant on, the future of the Parthenon, defence of humanity, Architect threat..." She looked mournfully at Kris. "You ever consider that it's actually *true*, whether they really want to volunteer or not? The Parthenon needs Ints, yes, and right now the rest of the universe *needs* us to have Ints, because who else will beat the Architects if not us?"

"Hegemony, maybe?" Kris shrugged. "I mean...I take your point but Idris won't. He came here because he wanted a cleaner program, if they could find a genetic lineage that was ready-made Int-suitable. Which they might just have done, by the way. But for him, part and parcel of that is that they've got to be willing, genuinely willing. Or you'll lose him." She didn't go on with an *And then*...Solace didn't know what the *And then* would be. The Parthenon had Idris now, and his cooperation. If he withdrew that, would they let him just walk away?

She hadn't realized Olli was listening, but the specialist now chimed in, "Maybe we take the whole circus elsewhere," loud enough to prick the ears of every Partheni tech or ship crew in the room. "Kit, how about it? The Hanni want to develop an Int program?"

Kittering looked up from the display. "I am mistaken as a spokesman for an entire species. Very non-cosmopolitan." His translator managed to give him a suitably cranky tone and Kris guessed one of his gaming opponents had him on the ropes.

"Idris," Kris said, and Solace nodded.

"Idris, I know," she agreed. "Kris, I'll do what I can—"

"No, *Idris*. He's over there." Kris nodded across the room to where the man stood in the doorway, looking...just the same, really. Back in shabby spacer clothes and sandals, inward turn to the shoulders as though he was continually in mid-flinch. His cavernous eyes sought Solace out across the room and he mustered a scrap of a smile.

"Not killed you yet then," Olli greeted him. "Pull up a stool."

Other than Kit's, the Partheni tended to go for couches. They didn't have the Colonial finicking about casual body contact, which Solace reckoned was a weird holdover from being crammed into the ships of the Polyaspora, fleeing their lost planets and constantly living in each other's armpits. Idris slouched over but didn't sit, jittering from foot to foot.

"Trine's here too," he said.

Solace blinked. "Right now? I haven't had a message from

them." She and Idris were the only acquaintances that the Hiver scholar might conceivably be calling on. They'd both known Trine in the war, when the cyborg hive mind was serving as secretary and data analyst to the Colonies' research drive into the Originator ruins. Because those ruins held some warding power over the Architects, and at that stage in the war such research had seemed humanity's only chance.

"They just pinged me: 'Expect an invitation.'"

Olli smirked. "Maybe it's a formal do, best clothes and best manners." Spoken with the relish of someone who had neither and didn't care. "They're still pulling that ambassador scam?"

"It's not a scam," Solace said primly. Some fairly arcane point of Hiver-Colonial treaty meant that high-status Hiver instances qualified as official emissaries from the Assembly at need. Which didn't mean Trine hadn't exploited that point shamelessly for their collective benefit more than once.

Then her own comms flagged an incoming message. Trine: *Grab your coat.* And, on the heels of that, formal orders: *Gather your crew, report for briefing.*

*

Trine had been Trine for a long time. Individual Hivers tended to instantiate and then return to the Assembly when their task was done, becoming part of the greater whole and sharing what they'd learned. Trine's task was the study of the Originators, though, and that wasn't going to be done any time soon. Just like Idris and Solace, they were a relic of the war years. There probably wasn't another Hiver anywhere that had been themself for as long as Trine had been Trine. Which led to a certain accumulation of eccentricities.

As with all Hivers, inside the barrel body of Trine's frame was a factory for bugs. They would have long replaced the units they'd donated to keep Idris's heart going. Their consciousness, the thing that considered itself Trine, was something constructed by, and held between, the totality of their many individual pieces.

"You are cordially invited," the Hiver announced to them all, "to a holiday on Arc Pallator. Holiday destination, very desirable. There is a pool and probably a casino or some similar low dive. And for Mesdam Timo there will be alien things she can complain about."

Trine presented as a bipedal frame, bird-jointed legs with prehensile feet, supporting a torso that sported a rack of various-sized limbs sprouting from the centre of their chest. Their head was a bowl with a projected human face—an avuncular human male amongst Colonials but on the *Ceres* they'd gone for what Solace mentally catalogued as "maiden aunt." Their voice matched their visage, as richly human as speech software could make them.

Solace queried the *Ceres*'s library but Kittering was ahead of her. "Your intention, Delegate? It's situated within the Hegemony?"

"Indeed! Exciting, isn't it?"

"You want the *God* to take you somewhere?" Olli asked blankly. "Why?"

"To correct your misapprehension," Trine told them, waving various limbs, "I require the *Parthenon* to take me somewhere, within the Hegemony, with as much military pomp as the Divine Essiel will allow. The most meagre part of which pomp is to be your own vessel, for reasons that shall become clear but which mostly orbit around the talents of your regular navigator, as you might imagine. An invitation not to be missed has been extended to yours truly, but one I would rather take up equipped with a suitably armed retinue. Allow me to introduce you, therefore, to sunny Arc Pallator, jewel of the Hegemony. A place I for one have long salivated over visiting, or would have done had I the appropriate glands. Alas, Colonial-Hegemonic relations have always been difficult, and such an opportunity has been denied me. But rejoice, for now the very Essiel have deigned to extend me an invitation to visit this glorious scholars' paradise."

"Cut the crap," Olli broke in, and though Solace still winced, she somewhat agreed with the sentiment. "You mean Originator nonsense."

"More such nonsense, my dear Mesdam, than you can even comprehend. The single largest Originator site anyone has ever discovered. A veritable lost city, subsequently recolonized by Hegemonic citizens. They actually live in it. Imagine: a dig site with all the comforts of civilization! And requiring urgent and immediate study by the universe's greatest minds and specialists, of which ours truly is, of course, amongst the most pre-eminent."

"Because they lost a world to the Architects and their Originator stuff doesn't protect them anymore," Olli filled in. "So suddenly they're all up for anyone else to explain why their entire space empire is screwed."

"Indirectly, yes of course," Trine agreed cheerily. "Directly, however, well...If you would observe the image..."

It was a view of a planet, presumably Arc Pallator. Not groundside, with the fabled Originator ruins, but taken from past orbit, as though from a ship approaching. Or, as seemed more likely, fleeing.

Arc Pallator had gained a moon. A crystalline moon, blindingly bright where the system's sun struck it. Its hemisphere that was turned towards the planet was a jagged forest of crystal spines hundreds of kilometres long, reaching their sharp points towards the surface below. An Architect, caught in the moment of murdering a world.

"I...think we're going to be too late to visit," said Kris, in the resulting hush.

"We understand your misapprehension, old former and future shipmate," Trine agreed, ebullient tones jarring in the face of what they were seeing. "However, this state of affairs remains current as of last transmission and has been the case for twenty-three days, Earth standard."

"Because of the ruins," Idris said. His eyes were fixed on the image, on the Architect. "They want to reshape the planet, but they need to remove the Originator presence before they can...A city, you say?"

"Architect constructs are currently dismantling and removing the site," Trine confirmed. "Hegemonic estimates are that the effort will take months, Earth standard. And in the interim—"

"There's an Architect just sitting there," Idris broke in. "Not attacking, not being fought, just there."

"Thus amenable to study, as is the relationship between it and the Originator artefacts. As we discovered on Jericho, Intermediaries have a unique insight into that. *You* have a unique insight. And you are the only Int I can call on." Trine made an expansive gesture with some of their arms. "So, Cousin Telemmier and friends, I cordially invite you to become guests of the Hegemony."

PART 2
ARC PALLATOR

7.

Idris

It wasn't as simple as that, of course. Whatever Trine felt they were entitled to swan in and demand, the Parthenon were initially unwilling to just conjure up a warship to place at the Hiver's disposal. Moreover, they were even less willing to simply hand over Idris to the enterprise.

Idris himself got to sit in on a surprising amount of the argument. It was, he felt, something of a test case for the theoretical time when he himself would try to take his leave. Certainly Monitor Felicity, his handler, was strenuously opposed to him heading off into Hegemonic space, where anything might happen to him. Especially sharing a system with a Colonial team and its own escort, not to mention whatever horrors the Hegemony itself might suddenly conjure up.

If it had just been Trine on their own, that would likely have been it, but Idris worked out soon enough that the archaeologist obviously brought some real diplomatic credentials to the table this time. The Hiver Assembly in Aggregate—the cumulative repository of minds not currently separated out into individual bodies—was behind the venture, and that counted for a lot. The Parthenon and the Hivers went way back as political allies.

Still, it seemed that nobody was going anywhere, even with some Partheni taking Trine's side, until one day Idris turned up for another wrangling match and found a single woman waiting for him.

He knew her: Monitor Superior Tact, Solace's direct superior in the Aspirat, the Parthenon's intelligence service.

"Menheer Telemmier," she said. "Take a seat." She was a neat, compact woman, hard lines of experience on the stock Partheni features. She was, he guessed, about to lay down the law. Sitting with her, he couldn't escape the certainty that he'd been discovered doing something wrong, even though he hadn't. If she'd suddenly demanded he confess, he'd have invented some crime just to get her off his back.

"Monitor Felicity is concerned about the Int Program, understandably so," she said, regarding him doubtfully. As though she couldn't quite bring herself to believe he was worth all the fuss, despite having sent Solace to recruit him. He fully understood, even agreed with her. And yet here they were.

"It is the case that, now you have aided us in identifying a viable germ-line, there is a certain amount of work that could go on in your absence, Menheer," she observed. "We have sufficient material from the original Colonial research to begin work on our own first class of subjects," and, before he could even make the objection, "of *volunteers*." Making clear Solace had reported his ongoing qualms to her.

"Tell me about Jericho," she said, leaning forwards intently, and he blinked.

Jericho had been a nasty jungle world with a big Originator site—big meaning only a fraction of what Arc Pallator apparently held. Visiting Trine there, Idris's eyes had been opened to the interaction between those ruins and unspace, detectable to his modified Intermediary brain. It had been a revelation. Even on that brief visit with a remarkable number of distractions, he'd learned so much.

Tact listened to all of this, and he could imagine her shunting pieces of plan around in her head like puzzle blocks. He had become a source of potential intelligence against the Architects, ergo very much within the Aspirat's aegis. And he felt his future on a knife edge: would Felicity succeed in keeping him here, whether he wanted it or not; would Tact end up dispatching him on Trine's team, whether he wanted that or not? Which Partheni faction would prevail?

Instead, at last, she just said, "And you, Menheer?"

He stared at her.

"We have an opportunity, here. To win credit with the Hegemony, to have a seat at a table otherwise only available to my opposite numbers in Hugh. To find a crack in the armour of the Architects, if one exists. We could just give Delegate Trine their escort and trust to their mundane means, but right now we have something different. We have *you*. An Intermediary who will speak to us here in the Parthenon, and give us the weapons we need to defend our species from the enemy. But unless you are willing to do the job, there's no point risking you. And it will be a risk. While we now have the possibility of an Intermediary Program here, even without your continued assistance, my colleague Felicity would vastly prefer your return to aid in the refinement of that process and the training of her wards. Or that you never leave in the first place. So it comes down to this, Menheer. What do you want?"

His stare intensified. "You're giving me the choice?"

105

"Let us say we are at least allowing your preference to influence our decision."

He hadn't properly asked himself what he would prefer to do. The idea that it would be relevant had never occurred to him. When he opened his mouth, he genuinely wasn't sure what words might come out.

"I want to go. With Trine," he said, and then had to stop and consider that, to work out why. It would take him away from the uncertainties of Felicity's Int Program, of course. It would put some layers of distance between him and that source of guilt. But that wasn't it. He remembered Jericho. Mostly he remembered running for his life and being terrified of everything. Then he remembered that contact, mind to world, mind to biosphere, mind to the echo of the Originators.

"I want to learn," he said.

Tact regarded him, waiting for the rest of the words.

"I don't want to learn," he corrected himself. "I mean, if I could just be blissfully ignorant about the whole business, then, then that would be, I mean, would be grand but it's too late, too late for that. And the more I learn, the more... there's something. There's something I can find out that will end the war. There's something behind the Architects. There's... It doesn't have to be this way, with them killing us, and us killing us to make weapons to fight them. And maybe... maybe Arc Pallator will be..." Wrestling for what he meant, his eyes begged Tact to understand.

"Menheer, I know," she told him frankly. "With the way things stand between us and Hugh, the return of the Architects couldn't have come at a worse time." That hadn't been what he meant, but it worked for her.

"I'll give you all the protection the Hegemony will allow

us to send into their space," Tact told him. "I'll also ensure that Felicity has everything she needs to continue the work in your, hopefully brief, absence. But go find the Architects' weak point, Menheer. Find out what strings there are, that their masters pull."

*

It was a short step from there to loading up the *Vulture God* with everything Olli could scrounge from the *Ceres*. There might well be a Parthenon warship accompanying them, but they were damned if it wouldn't have a beat-up old salvage craft in its belly for emergencies. Idris had expected an audience with Felicity any moment, to try and change his mind, and in truth there was a fair chunk of his mind that would prefer to be changed. He didn't *want* to go to Arc Pallator. He didn't want to share a system with an Architect or go before the alien Essiel that ruled the Hegemony. He had none of Trine's ebullience about the whole business.

It felt exactly like back when he'd been little more than a kid, putting his name down for the Intermediary Program. Back in the first war, when the Architects had been twisting human worlds one at a time, with a lazy indifference to how many millions were still on them. Back when nobody had any hope and every mad plan was worth a try. Idris had already heard that they were wrecking people's brains in an attempt to replicate whatever it was that made Saint Xavienne special. He hadn't wanted to have his own mind destroyed, of course he hadn't. But he'd signed up because you had to do that thing, sometimes, that was bigger than what you *wanted*.

He didn't want to be the centre of the universe's attention. He wanted it to all be over. And maybe Arc Pallator held the key to that. This was enough to tip the scales and get him on board.

"Oi!" Olli's shout broke him from his reverie. "Visitor for you!"

"Who is it?" He looked around, expecting Felicity, or perhaps just a squad of Myrmidons to march him off somewhere.

"Who can tell, they all look the fucking same." Olian Timo, not winning any prizes for diplomacy. And there she was, just one young Partheni in a Cognoscente's uniform. She flinched back from the loud Colonial sitting in her walker with a fleet of drones flying around her; from Kittering arguing over the manifest with Kris; from everything, really. He recognized that, even if it took him a moment to recognize her. He flinched like that too.

"Grave," he named her. The top-of-the-class Int candidate, the one whose brush with death had opened her mind up. The woman, he considered glumly, who might have condemned all her germ-line sisters to agony and torment.

"Menheer." She was wringing her hands, leaning away from the ugly bulk of the *Vulture God* as though the ship was about to fall on them. "I wanted to... They said I could speak to you."

"I'm here. I'm not doing anything."

"That's fucking true, you slacker!" Olli shouted at him, because her drones had good audio receptors. He turned his back on her.

"I was talking to Myrmidon Executor Solace," Grave said, as though Idris's friend was a godlike figure and such speech was borderline blasphemy. "She said I should tell you... that I said yes."

He frowned. Grave looked so alone there, so small and damaged, that he wanted to reach out to her. Yet he was smaller and more damaged still. What could he do? "Yes to what?"

"To the Program. And Myrm— and Solace said I should tell you, so you know I had the chance."

He regarded her bleakly. "You want to become an Int. After we put you through unspace all those times."

She nodded, too quickly, too forcefully, and he could see her eyes saying *No*. But despite this he believed her, because that duality was familiar to him. *No, we never want to go, but we do it anyway.* He'd wanted to make sure this was her decision, no matter how conflicted, rather than a Partheni order. Maybe she *would* live. Maybe she would learn to see the universe like he did, and God help her if so.

"Thank you," he said, and then Kris was calling for him to get aboard.

*

Idris waking from suspension should have been a welcome relief: another journey when he wasn't required to man the helm through the long torture of unspace. Except the general screwedness of his brain extended to his reaction to being put on ice as well. In his mind was the sense that he'd been lying helplessly awake in some vast silver place, denied movement or senses, in another kind of void.

Yes, yes, he told himself irritably, and then, quoting an old spacer song half the Colonial Sphere knew the words to,

We're all acquainted with the tragedy of being you. At least the couches in the *Grendel's Mother* were more comfortable than those of the *Vulture God.*

He sat up just as a Partheni dashed in, calling, "Delegate Trine, you are needed at command." Around Idris, the rest of the *Vulture* crew were grumpily sitting up too. Olli tilted the angle of her bed so she could wriggle into her walker frame, scowling at the indignity.

Trine was not in a suspension pod. Instead, they had protocols to shut down their higher functioning while in unspace. Idris had a nasty turn when he saw the Hiver had decided to do so hanging from the room's toprail by their prehensile toes, like a huge metal bat. That was Trine's sense of humour, though, and an example of why individual Hiver instances weren't generally allowed to run as long as they had.

Trine's face appeared in the bowl of their head, right way up for their interlocutor, meaning upside down relative to their actual body. "Why is my self-bootstrapping being hurried, may I ask?"

"Delegate, the Hegemonic authorities in-system will only speak to you."

"Ah." Trine reached down with one leg, an improbable feat of gymnastics, and then dropped, balancing with a wobble. "Take me to your leader, Myrmidon." They stalked out of the room, the Myrmidon following.

Kris propped herself on one elbow and yawned sleepily.

"That bug-farm needs an off switch," Olli grumbled.

"Would you *not*," Kris asked her plaintively. "Quite aside from the entire bad taste aspect, we are literally here on their ticket."

"And why? I never wanted to go to the Hegemony." Olli

saw the eye-roll that passed between Idris and Kris. "All right, maybe I did want to see the Hegemony a little. So long as that Hook-razor bastard isn't around. I mean, he's an outlaw, a criminal, right? Not likely he'll be hanging about where the cops actually are."

"It's—" Kris started.

"Yeah, complicated, I know." Because, just as with everything else, the Divine Essiel's attitude to crime was opaque and not immediately comprehensible to humans.

Kittering, emerging from a custom spherical pod bolted awkwardly into the corner of the room, waved his mouth-parts at them. "Look out the window," his translator suggested. Of course there was no window, but Olli patched into the Partheni system and showed them the world they were approaching.

Arc Pallator looked unfriendly. It was yellow and red, mostly, with no seas or bodies of water of any kind. The variegation of its surface was topological, plateaus and vast dry basins. It was an old world, Idris felt, and looked as though it was dying. The little scroll of Parsef alongside the image was the usual survey data, and he did his best to disentangle it. Kris had done better with the language over the last months, though, and she swore.

"Population of three billion, it says. Estimated."

That prompted a thoughtful silence. Then: "Where's the, the *thing*?" from Olli.

"Patience," Kittering told her. He was crouched at the rim of his pod, five amber eyes fixed on the screen. There was an odd tension to him, readable to human eyes because Hanni body language tended to be writ large. They didn't do religion, Idris thought, but Kit seemed almost reverent.

Or frightened. Awestruck was perhaps the best compromise term.

Then it appeared. Their angled approach to the planet slung them around just enough, and the Architect came about the edge of Arc Pallator like a moon. It fell into the harsh white light of the system's sun and, in that moment, a million rainbows shattered from its jagged crystal face. A miser's hoard of jewels; a murderous dragon that was its own treasure.

"Oh," Kris said. Just that one word. As though she'd somehow forgotten *why* they had come.

"Fuck," Olli agreed. Kit was silent, still, staring.

"I don't know if I can..." Kris went on quietly. "I think this was a mistake."

"Always," Olli agreed again, all the punch gone out of her voice. "Twice I've been in the same system with one. Two times too many."

Idris, the veteran, forbore to comment.

They couldn't not watch the approach, the angle of their view tilting until they were viewing the Architect side-on. The faceted curve of its back became clear, like a compound eye where each lens was ten kilometres across, while its front was a forest of translucent mountains directed at the planet it intended to destroy.

Or not destroy, even. That would have been more comprehensible. Rework, transfigure into a shape more acceptable to its exacting alien mind. Or to the minds that directed its actions, Idris reminded himself. The one piece of information he'd carried away from Berlenhof. It wasn't exactly useful, right at this moment, but it was the only crowbar he had to prise open the question of *Why?*

"Where's the fleet?" Kris asked quietly. She'd been making her own enquiries of the *Grendel's Mother*, borrowing its sensor data.

"What fleet? The Hegemony are fighting?" Olli wanted to know.

"The evacuation fleet," Kris said quietly. "For the three billion people or...or whatever actually lives on Pallator. The fleet. To get them off."

Idris queried for the same data. There were, of course, ships in orbit, docked at stations or just on their own recognizance. Quite a lot of ships in the Essiel's radially symmetrical geometry plus a variety of other designs. Not what you'd need to evacuate billions, though.

"Maybe they already did it," he suggested wanly. "It's been here a while already, they said."

Olli brought up another view, the *Mother*'s readings of heat and power and comms across the planet's surface. It was hard to read, given Hegemonic tech remained a baffling mystery to outsiders, but clear in one particular. "If everyone's gone, they left all the lights on."

"It's the Hegemony," Kris said slowly. "They aren't just going to abandon their people."

"Nobody knows what they'll do, because they've not been in this position before," Idris said hollowly. "They were always safe, they thought."

"And the fucking Essiel, I mean, who knows *what* they think?" Olli pointed out. "Maybe this is fate to them. Maybe it's just a done deal, as far as they care."

Then Solace appeared in the doorway, in crisp uniform. She'd gone into suspension with her sisters rather than her crewmates, and Idris had tried not to feel slighted.

113

"You're needed," she announced, and then corrected it to, "We're needed."

"You could just send orders over the comms," Olli said sourly. "Didn't have to actually put your face around the door."

"Who would you have to complain to, then?" Solace shot back, matching her tone for tone.

Olli tapped forwards on the walker's plastic feet. "Careful, you're sounding like one of us. Don't let your sisters hear."

*

Idris hadn't wanted to be part of a diplomatic reception, but Trine seemed to think that their hosts required it. Or at least the human cultists interpreting for their hosts did, because so far the Essiel themselves hadn't put in an appearance. Possibly he was about to see one. Trine was rattling on about how it was an honour and their hosts wanted to meet with them, until Exemplar Keen just about told them to shut up right to their face. The commander of the *Grendel's Mother* was wound tight, right then. She didn't want to be part of a diplomatic reception either, or even off her ship. The Hegemony had technology that could put the *Mother* out like a candle, and without warning. Then there was the handful of Colonial ships also in orbit around Arc Pallator. With this sort of tension as a baseline, the only thing keeping Idris in his right wits was the presence of Kris, who had a hand on his arm as they left the Partheni shuttle, radiating sanity through the touch of her fingers.

The Hegemonic orbital was like an abstract piece of origami made of opal. At its heart was a spindle-shaped chamber, where the gravity was "down" no matter what part of the wall you were standing on. In the centre, the "up" for every varied down, was a single ball of light, shifting through a bruise-coloured spectrum of purple, red and blue-grey. It also moved into a seemingly flat and dead state, yet somehow still gave out radiance at a frequency the human eye could not perceive. The floor, which was like mother-of-pearl, took all these colours and subtly changed them, before refracting them sideways across the room. Idris's head hurt. Around him the Partheni delegation were doing their level best to appear entirely unconcerned, while Trine was apparently genuinely unconcerned, making delighted remarks about how splendidly everything was going. No Divine Essiel made an appearance. Every so often a robed human crossed eye-twistingly from one part of the room to another and then exited, on occult cult business.

Then the Colonials arrived.

They looked slightly dishevelled and hurried, which told an eloquent tale of how recently they had docked, and then been told the Partheni were already here. There was a fair number of diplomatic staff, all wearing the sort of elegant, cloth-heavy suits one saw in the upper echelons of the core settled worlds—lots of folds and drapes that an honest spacer would boggle at. To be fair, Kris was wearing something of the same in Partheni grey, given she loved to dress up on the rare occasions the life permitted it. There were a couple of service officers in blue as well, giving the Partheni the side-eye. And there was an elegant silver-haired man, old without being elderly, wearing a loose-sleeved copper shirt with a long strip of decorations trailing from his chest. Idris didn't know him, but something was familiar there. He glanced at Kris, and saw her attention fixed on the same man, then looking down to a little slate she'd palmed.

Trine had gone very still.

This was plainly a meeting neither group had looked for, and Idris could only guess how the Hegemonic invitation had been badly mangled by the human minds and mouths it had passed through. Nobody was meeting their *host*; they were only meeting each other. For a long moment everyone just stared.

Then a pair of cultists turned up, wearing about two hundredweight of red velvet and gold ornaments apiece. They played a little flourish of cymbals and bells and crystal chimes, all with monstrously straight faces. And waited.

Everyone might have continued to stand there until the Architect actually ate the planet below them, except Exemplar Keen's perfect Partheni impassivity twitched, despite all her resolve. The musical interlude was slightly too much for her. Taking that as a hopeful cue, a trio of the Colonials carefully stepped forwards around the planes of the floor. The first was a tall, severe man with a shock of white hair, followed by a very old man with an explosion of wiry grey beard. The last was the owner of the heavily decorated copper shirt and Idris already had a bad feeling about *him*.

"You must be Exemplar Keen and Delegate Trine," the lead diplomat said. "I'm Karl Mannec, Diplomatic Corps, this is Professor Tiber Storquel, heading our research team, and this is—"

"Morzarin Ravin Okosh Uskaro." The Magdan with the fancy shirt tapped his heels together and gave a stiff little bow that made Kris twitch. "It is an honour, of course." The words fooled nobody. You could have cut the hostility in the room with a knife. The *Vulture God* crew had had some recent run-ins with that particular branch of the Magdan nobility, mostly in the fields of Nativist violence and an attempt to forcibly conscript Idris's Intermediary talents into their service. This wasn't the same man, but Magdan families were clannish as hell. Piss off one member and you collected the set as enemies.

Mannec's eyes strayed briefly to Idris and then snapped back to Keen. "The Morzarin has provided a whole study team to gather data here, at our host's invitation."

"We are all, of course, very grateful for their munificence." Trine had an artificial voice which shouldn't really have been able to express so many complex shades of snark, but they'd also had many decades to work on it. Idris guessed that the Uskaro study team were the new class of Ints, the criminals who had survived the Board's brutal process, held under leash contracts that made them little more than property.

"We note your own contribution," Ravin Uskaro added after a pointed pause, looking through Idris as though he wasn't even there. "No doubt we will compare what data our tools generate, even as our academics liaise with the Delegate." And he mostly looked through Trine too, speaking to the human face of Keen. Ravin, Idris suspected, was an old-school Boyarin.

The old man, Storquel, made a sound. It was hard to characterize, save that there was a lot of contempt in it. His eyes were fixed on Trine, and Trine's artificial gaze returned the favour for a moment with utterly cold loathing, his whole avuncular expression reworked for the occasion. Idris, expecting to be the most despised person in the room, looked from one to the other, mystified.

Karl Mannec coughed ostentatiously and did his diplomatic best to reanimate some semblance of polite talk. Still more Colonial staff were turning up, now seriously outnumbering the Partheni, all straightening their formal clothes and trying to look at their ease. Somehow nobody was pointing at Idris and screaming *Traitor!* and perhaps he was going to get away with nothing more than a headache.

Then he saw her.

"I need to get out of here," he told Kris. "Never should have come. Not a diplomat."

"I think we're stuck here for the duration." Then she glanced at him and saw how rigid he was.

Across from them, just joining the Colonial delegation, was a woman, low down in a walker frame more delicate and less jury-rigged than Olli's. She was old now, but nowhere near as old as she should have been. A touch of Idris's own condition that had shrugged off all the years since he emerged alive from the Intermediary process. Her flesh sat heavy on her, and her hands, resting on the frame, trembled. Her name was Demi Ulo and he hadn't seen her for decades, nor had ever expected to again. She'd gone out with the Cartography Corps just as he had, but she'd stuck with it, vanishing again and again into the deep void to look for new worlds and new Throughways. For Ints, that usually only ended one way. One trip or another, the void took its due and they didn't come back. Except here she was, another war veteran, another Int of the first class, his comrade and contemporary. And she was over there with the Colonials, where she was supposed to be. He on the other hand was with the Partheni, and was suddenly horrified at himself, unwilling to be seen by those old, familiar eyes.

"Get me out of here," he hissed to Kris, and she nodded immediately. Then she murmured to Keen, explaining that he was ill, had to go lie down, Intermediaries, temperamental don't you know, so if you could just...

And even as they ducked out, he knew it was too late. Those eyes had lit on him. He felt it through his skin, with no need to turn around.

For a moment he was going to slip from Kris's hand, just go over there, in front of all those Hugh magnates, in front of Ravin Uskaro and his medals and his stable of tame Ints. Go unload it all onto poor Demi Ulo, explain why he'd done what he'd done, decry the Liaison Board and their bloody-handed methods, fuck over Colonial-Partheni diplomacy for the next generation. But all it would have taken was one word, one look from her to shut him up and shut him down. *I stayed loyal*, the very presence of Ulo would have said to him. *I could handle it. Why not you?*

And so he went back on board the *Grendel's Mother*, and burrowed deeper inside to go aboard the *Vulture God*. There he sat on his hard, unused bed in the barren little nook that was his cabin, and thought about all the mistakes he'd made.

8.

Idris

On the world of Jericho, where they'd picked up Trine, the crew of the *Vulture God* had seen what Idris had privately filed away as an Originator city. Not large compared to a human city, certainly, but the Originator relics were vanishingly rare. On many planets they amounted to little more than a few broken shards, fragments of incomprehensible material, with no known purpose. *Regalia*, they were called, these lost tools of a lost civilization. And on a very few planets, there were sites, actual constructions, again shorn of purpose or point, just *there* despite the ages that had passed.

But on Jericho there'd been a proper ruin, concentric walls radiating out, avoided by the planet's voracious life, and much more buried beneath. A team of Colonial archaeologists had been studying them for years, led by Trine until he'd evacuated with the *Vulture*'s crew. Idris's experience there had given him the first inkling that his sense for unspace was a sense for the Originators too. The ruins had been dead but *something* had still been alive about them. Something had been plucking at his mind, telling him things he couldn't understand.

But that had been nothing. Because here on Arc Pallator there was an Originator *city*. The Hiver was beside themself, complaining bitterly all the way down from *Grendel's Mother* that the Hegemony was so damned laissez-faire about research permits for visiting academics. "They've had this underfoot for however long, and not even *looked* at it," they moaned. "They've just been *living* on it. With *people*. The waste!"

They were circling down in the *Vulture God* itself, Idris letting the ship slide towards the beacon of the newly designated Partheni embassy. Trine and Keen were making a parallel descent in a sleek little gunboat called *Nereid*, but Olli had insisted that they should have their own way off-planet, and Idris had heartily agreed. There was, he'd pointed out to the Exemplar, an Architect in orbit above them—directly above in fact, because the thing's attention was entirely fixed on the Originator ruins. They couldn't have too many ships on the ground.

The Originator site on Arc Pallator covered around twenty square kilometres and had probably been larger once. It completely filled a plateau of high ground, with arches and crumbling beams of it projecting out into space on all sides, showing where untold reaches of it had fallen into the broad chasms stitched across the planet's face. And it probably hadn't been a city in its original use, but it was certainly a city now.

"About a hundred thousand people," Kris confirmed. "I mean, not much for a city, but a lot for a ruin."

"People like what?" came Olli's voice over the ship comms. She was taking the descent in the drone bay, sitting in her pod.

"Human people," Kris explained. "Cultists. That's what they were telling me at the thing last night." Because she'd gone back, after getting Idris away. Kris didn't get many chances to be a socialite. "They...I mean, this is just the sort of thing they *say*, straight out, right? The Originators are sacred to the Essiel, they say. And so the cultists go make homes where the Originators have walked. And if they don't live there, they pilgrimage there. Right now about a third of the people below are visitors. God-tourists."

"They're mad," Idris croaked. The thought made his bowels twist. "There's an Architect overhead and they're coming to pick up souvenirs?"

"One last chance to see," Olli snickered.

"Many questions arise concerning long-term planning," Kit chipped in. "No vessels bringing this bounty have remained to remove it."

"They say the Essiel will provide for their faithful," Kris explained sourly.

"The Essiel don't even understand that they *have* faithful. And anyway, what about the three billion? Wasn't that the population of the whole planet?" Olli pushed, as Idris dropped the *Vulture* lower. "Can't be all cultists."

"Well there are no actual evolved natives." Kris's voice swooped a little as a crosswind pawed at the ship and Idris fought to compensate. "The Essiel settled the place an age ago with something called Athamir. Some species from their stable of happy-clappy subjects. Which Athamir are probably feeling hard done by right about now, I'd guess."

"I'm beginning to think signing on with the Essiel is a pisspoor idea," Olli remarked, and then, "Fuck me, Idris, will you keep your mind on it."

"Take over," he told her shortly and sat back from the controls. In his head a grid of fiery lines had appeared, like red-hot cheesewire, and he felt his brain was being forced through it. Just as with Jericho, the weight of Originator building down below was warping his perceptions, speaking to him in a dead language. He'd like to say, "Take me back, I'm not going to be much use," but this was exactly the use he was supposed to be. He was the canary in the mine, and you always brought the canary. Nobody cared that the canary didn't much enjoy its job and would maybe like to be doing something else.

It's going to be a tough haul.

"Talk to me," Kris invited, but he shook his head. He didn't have the words yet, which was a shame because Trine and the Partheni would be wanting his opinion soon enough. *What is it, though? What am I getting from it?* In the decades since humanity had produced the Intermediaries, it still hadn't manufactured a language to describe just what they did or how it worked. Because nobody quite understood how it worked, and because Ints themselves were notoriously uncooperative or just flat-out unable to say. Idris was going to have to invent his own vocabulary.

It's like the ruins are resting on unspace somehow, putting pressure on it, and I can feel the...shadow? Dent? But that wasn't right either.

"The gaps require attention," Kit noted, and flagged up a shotgun pattern across the city where the ruins just... weren't. There was bare rock, scarred and ragged. And it was only those omissions that allowed the human observer to understand that there *was* a coherent pattern to the rest of the whole. You couldn't appreciate the intent behind the Originator street plan until it was removed.

"That," Kris said, "is where the Architect's been."

*

The Originators, whatever unthinkable alien presence they had actually been, had not designed their city-sized installation so that, ten million years later, humans could use it as convenient housing. So it was that the domicile of a hundred thousand Hegemonic cultists looked like a vast tent city, with clans and sects and families claiming a section of stone and putting up lean-tos and shacks and awnings at every possible angle. It helped that Arc Pallator was short on weather and long on sunlight most of the time, and when the hot winds came, once every six Earth-count years or so, everyone apparently just hunkered down and replaced whatever blew away.

Stepping out of the *Vulture God* was a shock to the system, but they were all used to having to acclimatize to a new world. The gravity was slightly high for comfort, but it was the steamingly humid air that instantly had their ship clothes sticking to their skins. This was one world where spacer sandals were entirely appropriate shore-leave wear. The sky was a red-orange, hazy enough that the sun was little more than a blur.

There were people everywhere. Ruins were, Idris felt, meant to be creepy and silent and solemn, but humans had obviously been living here for a while, a couple of generations at least, adding layer after layer of convenience to the ancient stubs of walls and structures. There were pipes and conduits, solar collectors and generators, water tanks, all of it as ramshackle and random as a spacer could have felt at home with. And there was a whole community here—not just a bunch of old monks venerating the ages, but families, children. Everyone had some nod to the cult in their dress, and he saw plenty of hanging icons and wind chimes and dreamcatcher-looking nonsense, but overall the impression was of people just *living* here.

A woman in cult robes hurried over, then gave them the chance to gasp a bit and loosen their collars. Olli, with the Scorpion's cooling system whining dangerously, loomed over her. "What're you for?"

She smiled up at the menacing frame without a moment's hesitation, speaking Colvul with an accent Idris couldn't place. "My name is Ismia and I'm assigned to your embassy."

"My...?"

"You are Delegate Trine?"

"Fuck no," Olli told her. "They're over there, getting out of the ship with the nicer paint job."

The Partheni were taking no chances, Idris saw. Trine was their usual harmless-looking self, and Keen was in regular uniform, but the rest of the delegation had come in full armour, with their accelerators clasped in their suits' secondary limbs. One of those would be Solace, he knew, but at this distance he couldn't tell which. He felt a sudden stab of separation that caught him off guard. He hadn't seen much of her recently. She'd been doing her job.

"Apparently I look like a Hiver," Olli complained to the city at large.

"New neighbours," Kit announced, but Idris already knew because of the way the Partheni had shifted stance. Not hostile, not pointing their guns at anyone, but most definitely ready to do so.

There weren't really streets in the Originator city, because it wasn't really a city. There were walls, though, and gaps in walls, holes at various heights, trenches. Enough divisions that Idris could say, confident of being understood, that the Colonial deputation had been put right across the street from the Partheni.

"Oi, Ishmail," Olli called to their cultist. "That your lot's idea of a joke, is it?"

Ismia frowned at her uncertainly. "I'm sorry?"

Olli used a saw-blade arm to indicate the two groups. There were a lot of Colonials turning up to colonize the cloth-hung assembly of walls there. While most of them were in various iterations of civilian dress, it still left them with more uniforms and guns than the entire Partheni delegation. Not to mention the bottle-green of the Magdan Voyenni that must be Old Man Uskaro's personal house guard. The layout of the ruins here put twelve metres of clear ground between the two embassies but that wasn't exactly much to an accelerator round that could clip the horizon.

"Well naturally you'll want to collaborate on your findings," Ismia explained brightly.

"You don't think," Olli suggested, "that everyone's just going to end up shooting everyone else until everyone's been shot?"

Ismia's face was absolutely blank. "Oh no," she explained. "The Divine Essiel would not want that."

Olli's mouth opened and Idris had a horrible feeling she was about to suggest just precisely what the Divine Essiel could do with it, when the Partheni troops abruptly set in motion, mostly heading right back into the *Nereid* but one of them pounded over, power-assisted strides making nothing of the arduous gravity. Only when she was close did Idris recognize Solace.

"Back in the ship!" Her voice came over the comms as well as from her suit speakers. "We're under attack! Back in the ship!"

He glanced wildly at the Colonials but they were in a similar state of emergency, some of them taking what cover there was, others running back towards their own slew of vessels—far more of them, and suddenly those numbers were only a hindrance. Then Solace had his arm and was yanking him towards the *Vulture God*.

Too late.

He didn't quite see the flash of movement as the missiles came down. He only registered it after the fact, his eyes and mind catching up. Then he was on his knees, hard-won spacer reflexes leaving him down but balanced, hands spread against the grit of the uneven ground. Solace crouched over him to let her armour take the brunt of whatever was coming. The *Vulture God* groaned nearby, one of its landing struts buckling visibly as the shockwave passed through.

In the aftermath, the ruins were very quiet, all the people staring away in one direction, seeing a rising cloud of dust. There were no explosions, though. Missiles with no warheads.

Solace pulled a film from the forearm of her suit and snapped it into a rigid screen. The images she played there must have been from *Grendel's Mother*, tracking bright dart-shaped objects as they fell from the vast spiny face of the Architect towards the planet below.

Ismia was obviously receiving comms from somewhere closer to the scene, and Kris asked her, "How many hurt?"

"Oh, none at all, obviously." The woman found a smile

from somewhere. "The Divine Essiel always warn us. But...
there will be an evacuation now. Probably to the new temple.
Everyone will help. Obviously. Many hands..." There was
just the slightest tightness to her face, that gave the lie to
her blithe tone. Idris wondered how many things were getting
written off as "obvious" these days, and at what point the
faithful of Arc Pallator would come to question their god-
overlords.

When he'd been on a ship undergoing this treatment from
an Architect, he hadn't actually witnessed it. The crystal
spines piercing the hull, and then...changing, shifting into
other shapes to get to work removing the Originator taint
so that the vessel could be safely attacked. He'd only seen
the bloody result of it all. He wondered how many people
had just lost their homes this time, and how large an area
of the city the Architect would clear in one go.

There goes the neighbourhood...

The Partheni were reassembling now, and their support
staff were coming out of the *Nereid* with cases and crates,
ready to get the tech side of the embassy up and working.
There were plenty of hard looks being sent back and forth
between them and their opposite numbers, but right then
nobody felt like stoking the flames. They'd just had a solid
reminder of the common enemy, after all.

*

So of course they had to go and look. The Partheni had
brought down a handful of sleek, wasp-like a-grav bikes.
Solace took Idris on the back of one, somewhat against his
misgivings, and Trine ended up perched on another, with

the rest going to an armed escort. The Colonials brought a sturdy, no-nonsense truck out of their transport, almost got it wedged between two invulnerable Originator walls, then loaded it up with a delegation of military and researchers. When Solace took off for the crash site, Idris saw them unloading a five-fingered Handwalker patrol vehicle too. He had the impression they'd just grabbed up everything they could get at short notice.

There was still a pall of dust drifting from the afflicted part of the city, but the walls were a maze, reaching higher every turn Solace took. And then they were gone, the bike skidding perilously over nothing at all and its grav motor making some warning pings. The hole went down at least a hundred metres in places, and with a queasy feeling Idris realized this was somewhere the Architect had already dealt with. The sort of footprint it was leaving all over the city.

Not a city. And yet people lived here now and so it was, whatever the Originators' baffling purposes had been.

Solace paused, and then had to scoot quickly because the Colonial truck was grumbling up behind them, having suffered the same navigation issues. There was an awkward stand-off then, because the Partheni were refusing to back down on principle, despite the fact there wasn't really any actual disagreement going on.

At long last, a junior member of the Colonial team apparently drew the short straw and got sent over to talk to them. "Look," she said, "do you have a map to the site? Only our orbital imaging's screwed."

In the general embarrassed pause, Idris said, "I know the way." He didn't want to know it, or draw attention to the fact he had this knowledge. He could feel the walls stretching out around him though, and he could feel the Architect's drop point as though it was a feverish wound. Deep breath. "Solace, I'll guide you. And everyone else follows. Cooperation, right? All friends here. Right?"

The Colonial glanced back at her fellows and then shrugged. "Works for me." When Solace moved off again, the truck was on her heels, and she kept her speed down so as not to lose it.

Maybe it's going to be okay, Idris tried in his head, and then imagined how Olli would laugh him to scorn if he actually said the words to her.

And then they were there, coasting up a ramp he hadn't been expecting, ending up ten metres above a complex knot of broken walls. They were too convoluted to have served any occupied purpose, unless the Originators had been very small. Time had worn them down, though, or else the local dust had risen to bury them, and over their stubby outlines a whole clan of cultists had built shacks and hovels and ramshackle two-storey houses, all draped with colourful streamers and banners. The largest intact wall bore a cracked mural, where earnest but inexpert hands had depicted a crowd of round, happy people holding hands beneath a many-armed androgynous figure rising from a clamshell, a representation of the Essiel Idris hadn't seen before. Everyone there was gathering their possessions, as much as they could carry, and moving out. They weren't panicking or even particularly hurried. They weren't happy about it, though. Some of the children were crying; adults, too. From the look of their worn homes, these weren't just jobbing pilgrims but had likely all been born here. And now a new landlord had served them with an eviction notice.

A dozen crystal shards had lanced down from the Architect, but by the time the motorcade pulled up they weren't just shards anymore. They'd already got to work, their substance shifting like thick liquid until they were mobile, stalking or slithering or scuttling. Each was remade into a different shape of faceted, translucent stone in imitation, Idris guessed, of some living thing. A few of them vaguely recalled creatures he'd actually seen, but he was coldly sure that these shapes belonged to no extant species. They were, he firmly believed, the last memories of races made extinct by the Architects. One day, perhaps there would be human forms labouring amongst them.

They had gone to work swiftly, and the ground was flurrying aside wherever they walked, exposing more and more of the walls' foundations. Solace, visor still up, was frowning.

"Are they looking for something?" she asked. Behind them, the Colonials were piling off their truck, watched by the other bike's worth of Partheni. There was plenty of side-eye but their journey together had broken the ice and nobody was fingering a trigger.

"We hadn't thought you'd get the chance to see our problem this soon!" said a bright voice, as though all this was the best thing ever. Ismia was being helped down from the truck; apparently the Colonials had thought to bring the Hegemony's liaison.

"These things dangerous?" The Colonial junior eyed the nearest crystal form, something like a pot-bellied toad with tentacles for a head. "Looks like the sort of thing my aunt would have on her shelf," she added. Idris guessed her aunt didn't have high standards in ornaments.

"As long as you don't try to stop them, they should ignore

you," Ismia announced. "You can get quite close to take your readings and...do your science." Another big smile.

"But what are they doing?" one of the other Partheni asked.

"They're excavating this district," Ismia told them all. "It'll take them several days. And then they'll...remove it." Idris saw a muscle tic in her jaw. "That's what they do now. When they come to a planet with Originator traces. And obviously that's been...a problem, when it was just regalia. But here we have a whole *city* for them to work with. So you have all the time you could possibly need. For study." The shake in her voice was getting worse, for all she tried to hide it. "Obviously, we're all really interested in what you find out. The link between the Architect. And our ruins. Our city. Before they take it all away. The Divine Essiel are watching with great interest." She bit down on any more words because she was plainly struggling to maintain that stable, cheery tone of voice.

It was Solace who went up to her and put a hand on her shoulder, telling her that they could take it from here, and they were all keen to find out what they could. Idris only had eyes for the crystalforms as their mere presence eroded away the dry rock and soil, sending it skyward in great drifting plumes, to be caught by the higher air and cast away towards the haze of the sun.

"Tell your people," one of the Colonials spoke up, one of their soldiers in blue armour that wasn't quite a match for Partheni plate, "to get their gear over here to the truck. We'll unload, and then we'll help ferry for them."

Ismia blinked at him, and stretched her smile across her face. She was about to say there was no need, Idris knew. She was about to say that the Divine Essiel would provide.

But then some gear of her faith skipped a few teeth and she just nodded, calling someone over from the exodus and passing on the offer.

"Where will they go? How far's the landing site from here?" Solace asked her.

Ismia's face was blank. "They'll go to the new temple."

"The new...? That's a..." *A euphemism? For a* landing site *maybe?* That was surely what Solace wanted to say.

"The Divine Essiel have decreed the construction of a great new temple, where all may go who are...unhoused by developments. By what's going on here. The hierograves tell us this is a test of our faith."

Solace nodded slowly, then just turned and put some distance between her and the woman, as though religious mania was contagious. She leant in to Idris and murmured, "You remember Berlenhof, the scramble when the Architect came?"

He nodded.

"They've had enough time here to evacuate this whole place. And make a solid start on the rest of the planet, whatever that looks like. What are they even *doing*?"

"Having faith," he replied hoarsely. The Colonials had unloaded now, and the first of the evacuees were lifting their possessions and their children up into the back of the truck.

9.

Idris

Three people died on the first day.

The first was one of the Hugh soldiers, who'd simply not been looking where he was going. He'd been keeping an eye on their team as they set out their instruments, and ended up in the way of one of the crystalforms, which made disturbingly little sound as they went about their business. One long stride of its spidery legs and it had carved a slice off the man, armour and all, sending him screaming to the ground.

A Partheni Myrmidon, seeing this, had opened fire on it, the accelerator rounds stabbing a series of crazed impact holes across its body. The crystalform had rocked back, and then erupted in a shower of jagged slivers that had just about cut the woman in half.

Everything and everyone had stopped, waiting to see what the thing would do next, all weapons turned on it.

The accelerator impact wounds it sustained had sealed up and the damage reshaped into non-existence, using whatever process allowed it to move. Then the crystalform was on its way again, patiently excavating a length of wall, with two corpses in its wake.

The third death had come quite soon after. One of the

Colonial Ints had simply stepped in front of the same crystalform and, even as her fellows were shouting at her, let it tear her apart. Her arms had been wide open as though greeting a lover.

Idris would probably have used these events, all of which he saw first-hand, as an excuse for why he was on and off site, constantly pleading fatigue, sickness, trauma. He was getting plenty of the Partheni's backs up, because they wouldn't let him set a foot outside the ships without an armed escort. Solace had tried to talk to him, but he felt himself clam up the moment the topic was raised. *I am ashamed* wasn't something he could say to her or any of her sisters. The Colonial eyes on him, accusing. Demi Ulo, out there on site; he was constantly aware of her presence, shifting his own place so that they never crossed paths. And the other Ints. The leash-contract Ints brought by Uskaro, and watched over by his house guards, plus the others Hugh had scared up. They had about fifteen in total, which was a lot of Ints to have in one place. It wasn't as though they were dragging around in manacles, being whipped by overseers, but Idris knew that they carried chains in their mind. And perhaps something equivalent as a physical presence in their brains. He'd heard all sorts of stories about how the Liaison Board kept its new class of Ints in line. He could see the scars on them, where the surgery hadn't been gentle, where the hair hadn't grown back. And there were other overt signs, not deliberately inflicted but just the side-effects of turning a regular human being into something that could perceive and wrestle with unspace. Twitches and tics, an eye gone white or dark, a man walking with the aid of an exoskeleton frame that bulked out his clothes, a woman whose right hand was constantly flapping, as though trying to tear free of the wrist. It was exactly what he wanted to spare his own students, the Partheni theoretically suitable for conversion to Ints.

"There's something the Colonials have picked up over there." Solace's voice jolted him out of his thoughts.

"That's the spike," he confirmed vaguely.

"You're doing it again, aren't you," she accused him. "Just like on Jericho."

Idris nodded. He couldn't help it. The Intermediary in him was an eye he couldn't close. Sensory data was cramming into him with every step, every breath, and his body's instinct was to fight it, reject it utterly. And yet he forced the response away like swallowing down vomit. *This is what I came here for*. All that complex information, the way the ruin spoke to his mind, the way he felt it speaking to the Architect above. Yet it was all through a glass darkly. Where was that clarion voice he needed, to tell him how all this could be made use of?

"Trine's in another fight," Solace nodded grimly. "Him and that Professor Storquel."

Idris's overall impression of Storquel had been of a responsible and level-headed man, that rare academic mix of someone both good at their discipline and good at managing others. Except he and Trine could barely exchange four words, or stand within three metres of each other, without it turning into an argument. Over some footling piece of scholarly pedantry, as far as Idris could see, and it had taken him too long to work out exactly what was going on.

Solace had to explain to him in the end. This was on the second morning, after the deaths, when he was trying to refuse to return to the site at all. Trine, she said, needed his support. "You do understand that Hugh's top man here, this Storquel, was Trine's *owner*?"

Idris frowned at her, slow and out of sorts. "Trine's a Delegate. He's...free. Oh. *Now* he's free." Trine had been around since the war and for a lot of their history Hivers had been property. Their recognition as self-willed independent intelligences had been a hard-fought battle, and was still resented in many quarters.

Storquel was Hugh's premier Originator expert, and Trine was—as far as Trine was concerned—the universe's premier Originator expert, but he'd got there from a starting point of being a research tool for human scholars. Storquel had owned him, as one might own a slate or one of the seismic scanners. After finding that out, Idris had listened to the subtext between them, not the words. He didn't even think Storquel was trying to antagonize his opposite number, but the man remembered when Trine was just his *thing*, not even an assistant or subordinate but a piece of equipment. It came out in every word, and Trine wasn't the sort of politic and deferential Hiver new-instanced out of the Assembly who could take that and live with it.

*

The main positive Idris could bring from the whole business, once they'd quit the site after darkness fell, was that there was definitely a point to him being there.

"Mass casts a shadow into unspace," he told Trine and the Partheni, as the *Nereid*'s galley printer served out trays of the heavily spiced broth he'd acquired a taste for by now.

"But that's all it is, a shadow. Makes navigation tricky, so we usually move away from planets, even other ships, before we jump. But these ruins, and the ones on Jericho, they exert an actual pressure. They deform unspace; I can feel it. And nobody's noticed before because you don't go into unspace from planetside."

Trine's simulated face was watching him shrewdly but Keen made an impatient gesture. "Where does this get us, though?" Olli had described her as a bit punchy for a Partheni senior officer, which coming from Olli was quite something. Certainly she gave the impression she'd rather be fighting someone than nursemaiding researchers.

"Well, I mean, it's interesting in itself. Because unspace doesn't work like the real, so finding something that can deform it is a clue to how the Throughways might have been made—most people think the Originators made the Throughways, right? Though I guess there's never been any solid evidence of that. But more than that," Idris added hurriedly, seeing her roll her eyes, "it gives us a new hypothesis to link Originators with Architects." He remembered the Colonials discussing this very excitedly, once he'd talked them through what he sensed. "People always assumed it was some relic of a clash between the two long ago, that the Architects were fearful or reverential or something, and wouldn't desecrate anywhere the Originators had been. Except what if it's a real *practical* limitation with what they do? Because one thing we absolutely do know is that the Architects have a huge unspace presence, and can obviously navigate it without difficulty. I can also absolutely confirm they displace unspace disproportionately once they're out in the real. It's almost as if what we see up there," a wave towards the bristling moon hanging permanently overhead, "is just the iceberg's tip."

Kris had to chip in then to explain icebergs to the ship-born Partheni, after Idris realized that he, too, was a little hazy on what the figure of speech actually meant. Usefully for them, Scintilla, where Kris had trained, was a world of ice, snow and generally miserable weather.

"Anyway," Idris summarized, "the thing is, what if the unspace pressure exerted by these ruins—perhaps by *any* dog-end of the Originators—genuinely screws with the Architects? Maybe they literally *can't* do their thing until it's cleared. Which opens the door to..."

"Using it against them," Keen finished. "Manufacturing an unspace distortion like the ruins and regalia do, because it interferes with the Architects' ability to...Architect. If we could replicate it," Keen added. "Which we can't, yet, but we see here that it can be done."

"We're still gathering data as to just how it is being done, right here, all around us," Idris agreed, at which point Kittering skittered in and announced that "the annoying cult human" was here with an urgent message.

This meant Ismia, who was annoying because she had taken Kit for a considerable sum at Landstep. This turned out not to be such an unknown game in the Hegemony as she had perhaps let on. Idris let Kris take his elbow and guide him out to where Olli and a handful of Partheni were already waiting for the liaison's words of wisdom.

"Delegate, Exemplar, Menheer Intermediary," the woman said brightly, "you are invited to a banquet at midnight." Her tone suggested it was the best thing in the world.

Keen, who had only just mopped the last of the broth off

her chin, looked sidelong at her fellows and said, "Well this is an honour, and we're all properly grateful, but perhaps a little more warning next time and we could accept." She was short of patience with Ismia, mostly because the woman was a figurehead for all the Ways Of Doing Things the Hegemony apparently demanded, and which Keen didn't have time for.

Ismia's face went blank for a moment, and then her smile reasserted itself. "Ah, no, you don't understand, you are *invited*."

"Yes. Something that, traditionally, can be politely declined," Keen said slowly, as if to an idiot.

The liaison's smile twitched at the corners. "Forgive my poor Parsef. You are *Invited*."

"Wait, wait," Kris broke in, and then switched to Colvul to confer with the woman. Keen and the rest could understand enough of it that their stance changed entirely and the Exemplar confirmed that they would, of course, attend. The invitation was not from Ismia or the cult, but from The Radiant Sorteel, the Provident and the Prescient. One of the Divine Essiel was to grace them with its presence and apparently it wanted an audience of the great and the good.

Idris didn't feel like either, but apparently he was on the guest list. Keen quickly picked out a handful of Myrmidons to act as escort and retinue, with Solace assigned as Idris's guardian. Kit and Kris got on the list for the fair reason that they actually enjoyed this sort of nonsense whereas everyone else only suffered it.

"Olli?" Idris asked.

"No chance," the specialist answered derisively. "Some of the battle-ladies want to go do some planetary surveying.

Vulture's got way better instruments than their tub, for that kind of work."

"I thought you didn't like working with the Partheni," he said in a desperate whisper. He wanted her sour griping there to ground himself. There was surely a limit to how weird the Hegemonics could get with Olli there to puncture their self-regard.

"Like it better than going to some dumbass alien clam bake," was Olli's response, and sufficiently tactless that he had to admit it was probably a good thing she wasn't coming.

*

There were twice as many Colonials at the event, what with Mannec and his diplomatic staff, plus Morzarin Uskaro and his bottle-green Voyenni house guards. No Demi Ulo, Idris was glad to see. No Ints of any kind among them, in fact. He was glad, too, that the cultists had arranged for the two delegations to arrive via separate routes from their close-set embassies. Otherwise the journey—on foot, as per some obscure but adamant tradition—would have been appallingly awkward.

Yet when they arrived, formality was apparently given over for what could charitably be described as rustic simplicity. There was a big rug on the ground, and some cushions, and overhead nothing more than an awning stretched between stakes, everything else open to the sky. Admittedly Arc Pallator was hot at the best of times, even with the sun below the horizon, but it still seemed a little meagre for a formal function. The scene was inadequately lit by a score of lanterns of various vintages and designs.

Everyone stood and eyeballed everyone else until Ismia and a handful of her fellows started pointing out the cushions. There were a lot of cultists now, and many of them in robes more splendid and less dusty than those of the locals. These were from the orbitals, or maybe they'd arrived in the Essiel's own retinue. They were the smooth, urbane ambassadors of the cult Idris was used to from contact outside the Hegemony. The actual dust-sandalled squatters like Ismia had been a bit of a shock. In the back of his mind he'd always seen the cult as shysters trying to sell something—specifically, a way of life under the alleged protection of the Essiel. He'd never spared much thought for those who'd bought into that way of life. But here they were, skulking about in the ruins of a long-dead race, praising the star-gods who could no longer save them.

He sat down and discovered that he was two seats away from the Morzarin Ravin Uskaro, with only Solace between them. Solace was in her full armour, admittedly, only her helmet removed as a nod to diplomacy. He would have to hope that was shield enough.

"What are those?" Keen, off to his right, demanded. The cultists were shifting in some pyramidal objects, taller than a human and hovering off the ground on their own a-grav. The Exemplar was tense, ready to leap to her feet at the first sign of ulterior motives.

Ambassador Mannec leant in from across the rug. "These are...we just call them Mechanisms, which I admit isn't terribly useful, but it's as precise as we can get. They're a mainstay of Hegemonic technology. Sort of a jack of all tools. Just big tanks, really." He sounded relaxed, but Idris detected an edge to him too. Because who really knew, with the Hegemony?

"This is their liquid tech?" Keen clarified. It was something of a holy grail for lesser engineers, but so far nobody had duplicated the way the Essiel did things. Forming components at need, out of liquids and magnetic fields, was about as far as Idris understood it. Meaning, if you tried to take it apart for reverse-engineering you ended up with an empty box and wet feet.

Everything suddenly turned on. That was the only way he could describe it later. The change in light left him seeing nothing more than a white flare for several blinking seconds, and after that it had all changed. They were somewhere else, though. Or, no—he could feel the grit of the floor, the coarse weave of the rug. A vision of geometrical perfection in white and gold and iridescent rainbow sheens surrounded them, though. They were within a roofless tessellated enclosure lit by its own radiance, and which seemed to expand in ever further iterations beyond them to the very limit of vision. Looking straight up, Idris felt a bowel-clutching fear that he would just fall into the sky and be lost.

In the centre of the newly defined space, also shining with its own sourceless light, was the Essiel. It was supported by the most delicate a-grav platform he had ever seen, something like a snowflake five metres across from corner to corner, a lacy fractal pattern that was almost two-dimensional. Curled about the platform's intricate spines was the Essiel's holdfast, a long, wrinkled thing like an elephant's trunk, and projecting straight up from that was a bivalved shell twice the height of a man. At its upper end, where the shell halves parted, a spray of combs and arms and eyestalks waved, the visible part of The Radiant Sorteel, the Provident and the Prescient.

The cultists were all abasing themselves, faces to the dirt.

Keen just sat straight, head slightly bowed, and after a moment the Colonial dignitaries followed her lead. Idris squirmed, thoroughly out of his depth.

The Essiel rumbled at them and its arms shifted through a medley of patterns. The last Essiel the *Vulture God*'s crew encountered had kept a Hiver translator on hand. Here there were only the cultists, humans with a human's limited ability to receive alien communication. Still, one of the grander cult hierograves was making a speech now, purporting to translate what the creature was saying. Idris was struck by just how tenuous it all seemed. The Essiel obviously intended to communicate something, just as the Essiel as a species obviously wanted other species to be part of their Hegemony. The precise spin the cult gave it, though—the way they translated Essiel names into human concepts, their rituals and worship, every aspect of their lifestyle and belief—was something that could be grasped by humans. Ergo, even at best, only a wild approximation of what the Essiel actually *meant*.

Then there were little scurrying things at everyone's elbow. One of the Essiel's subject races, Tymeree, he recalled. They brought food, holding little bowls in the limbs they weren't actually walking on. There were also various projections built into their armoured suits that could easily have been weapons. He had no idea if they were properly sentient or just well-trained animals. They weren't adding to the discourse, anyway.

"I confess to having acquired quite a taste for Hegemonic cuisine," Mannec announced, putting a decent face on the whole business. "Please extend all appropriate thanks to the Radiant. And, should your duties take you to the Berlenhof Orbital Complex, let me take you to..." He named what

Idris assumed was a high-class Hegemonic kitchen some-where near his own offices, and the hierograve nodded complacently, and everyone started eating. The Partheni were leery of the food, which was varied and baffling, but Idris found eating the easiest part of diplomacy. Spacers didn't turn down a free lunch.

Then Uskaro was speaking to him, and that was his appe-tite ruined.

"I've heard of you from my nephew, Piter," the old man said pleasantly. "I understand you're an acquaintance of his."

He tried to make me his slave. Idris forced his face into what was probably only approximately a smile, managed a nod. Solace was very still, and he was aware that Kris was trying to listen in, too far away to help.

Obviously Uskaro wasn't going to go *there*, except he carried on with, "You came close to joining the family, he mentioned. A shame. We could have used you, especially in this venture." And still with that wonderfully paternal plum-miness to his voice, as though they were old friends remembering better days.

"I am sharing my findings with your...researchers," Idris got out, staring down at his half-full bowl. He would have said "team," except that might have indicated the leashed Ints Uskaro had brought as well, and Idris had been avoiding any and all other Intermediaries.

"Oh we're all rationing out what we find," Uskaro said, nodding as though this was agreement rather than flat contra-diction. "A shame, though, nonetheless. Piter speaks very fondly of you."

"Did—" Solace said, then stopped and stared furiously at the gleaming pearlescent floor that had overlain the rug. A

Tymeree appeared at her elbow and she waved it away irritably. Idris put a hand on her armoured forearm, feeling Uskaro's eyes track the movement.

"I see," the old man said quietly. "How very romantic. I'm sure I can't blame you. Doctor Parsefer made her copies very well."

Idris tried to shrink into himself further. It was a postwar Nativist slur, that the Partheni weren't quite human, just an artificial mimicry. Idris was ransacking his brain for some rejoinder that would get under the man's skin whilst still seeming perfectly polite. The Essiel was *right there*, after all. They could hardly start brawling in front of it. He felt as though just being there he was letting the side down, a gaping hole in the otherwise perfect Partheni facade.

But then Solace found her words again. "I remember your nephew, Morzarin. We met on Jericho." Her face was tight with anger, and she was speaking loud enough to be heard across the gathering, including by Sorteel if the Essiel could register human speech. "Some of his staff made a visit to Delegate Trine there," she continued implacably, despite glaring looks from Exemplar Keen. Then it became worse because this invited Trine to the conversation and they were never short of something undiplomatic to say.

"In fact," the Hiver announced airily, "they were bringing a gift to my dig site, *very* anxious to deliver it to me personally. But then the Boyarin are all about those direct relationships. You know, lord and vassal, owner and property." He shot a venomous look at Storquel to drag him into the discussion as well, even though he'd been nothing to do with the Nativists trying to kill Trine on Jericho. All other conversation around the rug had died a death by now.

"*Your* dig site?" Storquel asked icily, and he was plainly

stoked up with a full load of fuel to discharge upon Trine. "As if any of the Jericho research was genuinely *yours...*" Then a strange look came to him and he abruptly clamped down on the words, his eyes straying past the floating Essiel, up past the darkened horizon. One by one people turned to see what it was that had hooked his attention, what light had touched his face from that quarter. As though a moon had risen, of course. Except Arc Pallator had no moons, not naturally. The planet's rotation had brought it round until the system's sun touched a scintillating resplendence of refracted light from the world's executioner-in-waiting.

They heard a strange composite sound radiating out away from them: a city full of people whose faith in their alien gods was not quite enough for them to look on that sign of the end times with equanimity.

The silence, after that, was grotesque. Everyone waited for the glowing form of the Essiel to issue some dread proclamation, or to signal its disapproval. And it did nothing, arms continuing to wave and flurry. Idris reckoned it hadn't even noticed that the lesser beings had been squabbling beneath it.

"As I was saying," Trine said loudly, and everyone tensed. They were just carrying on with whatever line of scientific patter they'd been indulging in, though, and any other accusations they had went unsaid.

*

There was...something that followed. The cultists themselves seemed to believe it was a kind of religious rite. The locals and pilgrims chanted, and a couple actually had some kind of rapture, falling over and babbling, eyes wide in ecstasy. The hierograves in better robes, those who had come as part of the Radiant's entourage, took it more in their stride. Idris even felt they were a little embarrassed at the behaviour of their country cousins. Yet, whatever it was, the Essiel was a part of it. Its sourceless lights changed hue and intensity to a rhythm that Idris couldn't anticipate, but which was inarguably rhythmic. The arrangements of its many arms passed through sequences that seemed pregnant with meaning just beyond his grasp. Its *basso profundo* groans and rasps fell into patterns that might have been poetry or song or . . . just some art or oratory humanity had never devised a word for. With the faithful on all sides trying desperately to be a part of something that de facto excluded them, it should have been ridiculous or pathetic. Yet it transcended human judgement. Just as there really *was* something awe-inspiring about the Essiel, their mere presence, so this performance touched a part of the soul. Idris tried to cling to his sense of self, to insist there was nothing in this absurd alien malarkey, and he was left shaken, a party to something he could neither describe nor deny.

Then everyone was getting up, the projected walls fading into the dark of night, leaving only the shabby awning above, and the patchwork of lanterns to show the way out. The Radiant Sorteel dimmed and went out, becoming a dark, impossible shape floating there, revolving slowly but its limbs still. The audience was over.

"Spurious mummery," Exemplar Keen murmured, levering herself up and giving the rug and the Essiel a very wide berth as she went to prise Trine away from a couple of Colonial scholars. Kris was talking with one of Mannec's staff, with enough animation that Idris sensed she was just getting started. He felt utterly worn out, as though he had been fighting the Essiel's presence every minute of the meal. He lurched to his feet and almost fell over a Tymeree, which vented a metallic growl at his shins. He'd had enough. He needed to get clear of all these people.

Solace had his elbow, already helping him through a cordon of cultists and back towards the landing site. The Originator city at night was suddenly an unwelcoming place.

They pushed on through the crooked streets that weren't streets at all but just the convolutions of an ancient alien structure, now lined with the shacks and shanties of the faithful. *Come here to what they think their gods worship.* Come here to watch it being taken away by the universe's demons.

"I don't know how much longer I can do this," he said. Whining again, he knew. It was just that he was tired, and couldn't ever sleep, and Uskaro had rattled him.

"There's nobody else," Solace said, short on sympathy for once, and he couldn't blame her.

"Let them get the Castigar to do it. Let their own Ogdru. They have Ints."

"They don't."

Idris shook his head. "They do. One of them hunted us through bloody unspace. You were there."

"They have navigators." Solace was on edge, peering into the dark, her helmet back on now for the extra senses it lent her. "Not Ints. Castigar seer caste are senile, is what I hear. And the Ogdru navs are some kind of throwback, not sentient. It's just you, Idris. Human Ints can sense unspace and come back to talk about what they found. No others that I ever heard of, just—"

They turned a corner and someone rammed into them—

big enough that he struck them both. Idris went straight over and Solace staggered back, reaching for balance. The nearest lamp cast a reddish glare over the man but Idris recognized the Voyenni uniform.

"Clumsy Patho bitch!" the man exclaimed, but almost as a formality, with barely any real venom. Just establishing a reason for a "spontaneous" fight he'd plainly been planning since the meal. He went for Solace without further preamble, no matter that she was armoured and he wasn't. And he *was* big. The foot that stomped down close to Idris's head was twice the size of his own. Quick, too: he had his hands on Solace before she could recover her balance, and then he'd picked her up bodily, holding her above his head, before throwing her at the nearest ancient wall.

Idris hit him. To his own surprise, he punched the Voyenni with—for what little it actually meant—the entirety of his strength. He struck the man in what he'd imagined were the kidneys but turned out to be his under-jacket armour plating, feeling the material go solid under his blow at just about the same time as he felt the bones of his hand break. That represented his offensive contribution to the fight.

Solace was on her feet again. Perhaps he could claim he'd bought her time for it. His world had become a blur of pain but he saw the Voyenni hulk over her, and the gleam of a pistol in the lamplight, pointed at his gut. Perhaps the shot wouldn't make it through the man's armour, but the Partheni built good guns.

"Don't!" he got out, more a scream than anything so civilized as conversation. Solace hesitated, and if he'd been wrong, the Voyenni would likely have got past the threatening barrel and had another go at cracking her shell. He waited, though, and Idris knew he'd been right.

With that, he gave in to the pain. It wasn't as though he'd lived a suffering-free life, what with the cyborg heart and the autopsy scar and the well-documented history of brain embolisms. But when those little inconveniences had been happening, he'd generally been focused elsewhere. Right now he had nowhere else to go and his cracked hand was agony.

Solace tried to edge towards him, and the Voyenni made a quick decision to get in her way, backing until he was standing over Idris, eyes locked with hers. Slowly, he reached down.

"I will shoot you, diplomacy be damned," Solace warned.

Idris tried to shuffle sideways but the jag of agony stopped him, and then the man's thick fingers had bunched in his hair. Solace had the pistol levelled at the Voyenni's face now, right between the eyes, her hand utterly steady.

"Just go," she said. "My suit camera is recording this. What do you hope to prove?"

"Everyone knows," the man said thickly, "how clever you witches are. Who will believe?"

Then he leapt two metres in the air in a shower of sparks. Idris screamed, hauled halfway standing, his hand whacking into the wall and a fistful of hair torn from his scalp. The Voyenni ended up well out of reach of him, jittering about as though dancing.

"Diplomacy averted," announced an enthusiastic artificial voice: Kittering's familiar translator. The Hannilambra put himself between the huge man and Idris, brandishing a smoking rod in his mouthparts. The odds didn't seem to favour him, but then Kris was there with her knife, and he could hear plenty of others headed their way. Idris supposed that was the result of his screaming and was faintly glad he'd contributed to proceedings in some meaningful way.

The Voyenni stepped back and waited, muscles still shuddering and twitching across his body.

When Solace made her immediate report, Exemplar Keen looked almost happy about it, ready to demand all manner of reparations and concessions, possibly at gunpoint. For his part, Ambassador Mannec could plainly not believe how fast his position had been undermined. It was Ravin Uskaro himself who stepped forwards to take the heat.

"It is obvious that this, my servant, has reacted untowardly," he said, not remotely apologetic. "The Partheni will understand when I say our house staff are warriors born and bred, proud people. On Magda, the people know not to jostle a Voyenni in the street. After such a night, he forgets he is not on Magda. He shall be punished, of course."

Keen looked from him to Solace, plainly weighing up just how much of this she was supposed to swallow.

"I will leave it in your hands then," she got out through gritted teeth. "I trust you will properly brief and control your more spirited followers."

"Oh no," Uskaro said, looking shocked. "I insist he is punished here and now, before all, so that there are no misunderstandings. I will make an example of him." His smile was crisp and sharp enough to shave with. "Nothing behind closed doors, Exemplar. You will see how we discipline our errant servants. Beyon, down to your skin."

The man shrugged out of his jacket, then the shirt beneath, then his armoured vest and its padding. There was still a prodigious amount of man left even after all those layers had been removed. Solace would barely make forty per cent of him by weight.

"Kneel," Uskaro told him, and he did so, palms flat on the

ground, staring at Solace. Uskaro had brought out a little cylinder, small enough that Idris thought it was an old-fashioned comm unit. A flourish of the wrist had it telescoped out into a segmented metal baton, flexible and with a weighted head.

"Twenty will be sufficient, Exemplar? Perhaps you would like to do the honours?" Uskaro proffered her the truncheon.

Keen just stared at him, genuinely thrown.

"Well then," Uskaro said, not displeased. "My hands are the most fitting," and he brought the rod whipping across the Voyenni's back.

Beyon grunted, nothing more.

A second time. A third. Another grunt. Uskaro was sparing nothing, very obviously putting his whole back and arm into every blow, and if he couldn't give as much force as Keen might, it was plainly not for want of trying. By the fifth strike, with Beyon's back running with blood, Mannec tried to intervene but the Magdan urbanely told him that it was a Boyarin's right to caution his staff, a point of Colonial law in fact. Magda had fought hard to earn its privileges, and surely the ambassador would not think of infringing on them. And he laid on again, with a will.

Idris found himself counting the strokes, despite what had happened and his own pain, desperate for them to be done. Everyone was staring, the Colonials as much as the locals or Keen's people. And all the way through it, Beyon's grim and hungry glower was only for Solace. There was a promise there, held back for a later hour, and when the twentieth stroke was laid down, his lips parted in a grin.

10.

Havaer

Havaer Mundy wasn't the type to get invited to diplomatic soirées. As Mordant House's man assigned to the Arc Pallator mission, the first he heard of events was at his breakfast with the ambassador and Professor Storquel the next morning.

"I didn't know where to put myself," Karl Mannec confessed. His hands shook slightly around his cup of kaffe, although Havaer wasn't entirely sure the movement wasn't an affectation put on to demonstrate just how mortifying the business had been. "Just whipped the man, in front of everyone."

"Is the Morzarin not under your authority?" he asked, sipping at his own. The ambassador had admirable galley printers, and Havaer was happy to put off Hegemonic food for as long as possible. Making a sullen, inward-turned third, Professor Storquel slurped his cup dry and waved an irritable hand at Mannec's assistant.

Mannec grimaced. "Nominally. But he's a big noise back on Berlenhof, the whole Uskaro clan are. Almost half our presence here is his retinue, including armed forces. And the Ints are his, of course. Nobody else had a team of them used to working together. Given the short notice, we had to let him set a lot of the terms of his presence here."

Havaer frowned, something about that sticking in his mind. His train of thought was derailed by Storquel's loud mutter of "Unacceptable. The oaf." Havaer had the impression the academic was not against disproportionate influence per se, reserving his opposition for when such power wasn't under his own control.

"So...?" he prompted.

"So," Mannec agreed. "Possibly the Partheni are now suitably cowed by how very strong and tough Ravin's people are, which was very much the intent. My guess is they don't cow that easily, though, and now they're going to be extra-twitchy, which will lead to further incidents. It's not as though they're actual angels themselves, despite the nickname. Plenty of hot tempers on their side of the line, too."

"Given what you've got floating above you, it seems a bad time for sabre rattling."

"Well yes, I *know*. Which was why I was hoping the intervention of Mordant House might—"

"Hold on." Havaer frowned. "Why does he have a team of Ints used to working *together*?"

"I'm sorry?"

"The whole point of being an Int is...solitary. Everyone's alone in unspace. It's just about the only thing anyone off any world could tell you about it. You can't coordinate your Ints, unless they're all on one ship, in which case, what's the point?"

Mannec went through a mummery of eye-rolling and shrugs, to indicate who knew why the Magdans did anything. "It has been of considerable value *here*, though I agree they could hardly have had this scenario in mind back during the training."

"So where are we, Professor?" Finally deigning to let Storquel into the conversation. Tiber Storquel was a Berlenhof man, old enough that he'd lived out his childhood in the shadow of the Architects. He'd given his life to the study of the Originators, very much with an eye to their relationship with the world-destroyers. At his seniority, he seldom saw the inside of a dig site anymore, but this was a special case, a unique opportunity.

"The information we are getting," Storquel said ponderously, "is very good." He had a silvery beard which he tugged at as a kind of personal punctuation. His clothes were expensive Berlenhof casual, but the body underneath them had the narrow shoulders and hollow chest of wartime shortages, for all his waistband had filled out a bit since. "But we're not getting all the information. I'm having to work with half the pieces missing. The Magdans are cheese-paring, picking over everything behind closed doors before passing it on. And what the Partheni brought! I was not told I would have to work alongside . . . *that*."

Havaer had done his reading on Storquel. "It is what it is," he tried, but he was a fresh audience as far as the professor was concerned, someone to vent to.

"*It* walks in here and contests my analyses and my conclusions at every turn," Storquel bemoaned. "A thing that built its scrapheap career off my leavings. Everything it is, it owes to me, and now it has the temerity to *argue*."

"Professor, our hosts extended the invitation . . ." Mannec said, with the weary air of someone who had been butting at that wall for a while.

"Menheer Mundy," Storquel said hotly. "I *bought* that unit from the war office. It was nothing but a repository of data.

And for years, it was my assistant. It did not complain. It did not demand its *rights*. It was a tool, a machine. That's what they are. Except, owing to some catastrophic misjudging on the part of *your* people," a finger jabbed at Mannec, "someone decided the things were *people*, and it waltzed off with decades of my research and now has the gall to claim itself an equal." His beard actually bristled, visibly. "*And* it was only with the help of those *women* that the things broke away. Just before they abandoned us themselves. We're supposed to just accept that—"

"Yes, Professor, I'm well aware," Havaer broke in. "Just as you are aware that, right now, cooperation with Delegate Trine and their Partheni allies is in all our best interests."

"I would have thought," the academic replied sourly, "that Mordant House of all institutions would be more patriotic." Havaer fixed the man with an exceptionally cold look until Storquel found something of interest in his kaffe.

Havaer sighed. "The Intervention Board's stance on all these things is fluid, at the moment," he admitted to Mannec. "Certainly I can pass on your request for censure, but it seems unlikely they'll take any action against the Uskaros, given the Liaison Board's primary Int-training facility is on a Magdan orbital, and right now we need all the Ints we can get as a matter of vital planetary security." *Although*, his traitor mind pointed out, *according to Telemmier it won't matter because leashed Ints can't help us against the Architects*. The Liaison Board were bearing that in mind, he'd heard, with their new class, but that new class wouldn't be ready for a while. Given the rate of Architect attack, dozens of worlds didn't have that long.

Mannec gave him a bright smile and said he knew Menheer

Mundy would do what he could, and welcome to Arc Pallator, all of that. Then Havaer went to sweep his new quarters for bugs and to patch in the standard Mordant hacks and tweaks that would ensure his privacy.

There was a packet ship in orbit just waiting for his word. He included Mannec's request and his own brief first impressions, including that the *Vulture God* was here like a bad penny, not unexpected given Telemmier was more than half of what the Partheni were contributing to the research effort. He requested orders, and he had a bad feeling he wouldn't like them when they came. Then he turned to what the packet vessel had brought *him*. Not Agent Havaer Mundy of the Intervention Board, but him as a private citizen. He had a parcel, mail order, special delivery.

It unpacked itself when he gave it the codes. Or, rather, *they* did. They wore a small frame, a cylindrical can on four props that were incongruously moulded like eagle's legs, including the clawed feet. The top of their body came a little past Havaer's waist, with any arms invisibly retracted. No head, but a panel tilted up from their top edge, revealing a cluster of lenses and lights for him to focus on.

"Asset Colvari 88205," he addressed them.

"Asset Colvari 88205 instanced out of Peace Hive Seven in 118 After, provided under a short-term leash contract to Menheer Havaer Mundy," they confirmed, setting out precisely when and where this particular individual had been separated from the Hiver Assembly. Their voice was as plain as their body and the boilerplate terms of their contract. Only those unlikely legs suggested a colourful history.

"Accredited for data analysis?" There was no point going further if he'd been sent someone actually new from the factory.

"Previous instantiation history is available," Colvari told him. "We proffer our wartime logistical work and subsequent intelligence analysis for Mordant House. Although we note that you are employing us in your personal capacity, whilst retaining us under the usual non-disclosure clauses."

Havaer sat on his bunk, staring at the Hiver, on the edge of changing his mind and not trusting the work to it. But Hivers were discreet. Mordant House used them, and so did plenty of private interests, and he'd never heard of a Hiver, or a Hive Assembly, breaking a contract or disclosing secrets. And he had a lot of data.

The sealed stick he'd practically pulled from Kenyon's dead fingers had not had some piece of incriminating scandal sitting on a plain field, ready for enquiring eyes. Instead, it contained hours and hours of memos, meeting transcripts, reports and specifications. Havaer only had so much time to wade through it, because he wasn't supposed to have it, hadn't told his bosses he'd recovered it, and had an actual job to do here on Arc Pallator. In circumstances like these, an agent called in specialist help. He could have just run the contents through a computer, but even kybernet-level AIs weren't good at picking out human-level significance from that kind of morass. A Hiver was the best of both worlds, a computer's speed and ability to fine-grind the details, a sentient mind's eye for what actually *mattered*.

"I'm going to be vague, to start with," he told Colvari. "I don't know what I'm looking for. I just know there's something in this data set that is severely incriminating, so much so that all manner of people want to get their hands on it." *Unless there isn't, and everyone just heard everyone else wanted it and assumed...* But he couldn't go ahead on that basis. He had to fall into the same assumption and hope he didn't look like an ass at the end of it. "I want you to tell me what's in here and who it compromises. Standard terms. You self-edit before you return to the Assembly, unless I instruct you otherwise. That's not a problem?" A Hiver could indeed delete parts of its own memories, but these days they at least had to consent to it.

And there were more than a few Mordant House operatives who muttered that they never did. That the Assemblies had the galaxy's greatest trove of sensitive data stored somewhere, and one day they'd flex their espionage muscles and use it. But even those operatives still *hired* the semi-machines, because they were just so good at the job.

"That is agreeable," Colvari said blandly. Havaer looked at those ornate legs and wondered just what stories they might have told, about previous instantiations. War stories, spy stories, escapades and danger. Except the entity reciting them would be doing no more than that. They would have the memories, but only as if they had read them in a report. Since returning to the Assembly, and then instancing out again, the underlying personality wouldn't be the same. The memories weren't *theirs*.

He handed over the data, the physical stick, taken from his fingers by a handful of segmented tendrils that seethed out from beneath the Hiver's eyes.

"The only copy?" they asked, and he confirmed it was. Not something he felt confident duplicating, given he had to keep it secure *from* his own people.

"Working, then. We'll update you, Menheer Mundy."

And that, for the moment, would be that. Time for him to go for a stroll and see just how tight the tensions were wound on-site.

Olli

Olli made no secret of her general dislike of the Parthenon, but she disliked going stir crazy even more. When Myrmidon Lightly came to her to ask for a loan of the *Vulture*, an outing had seemed better than sitting amongst the flower-children cultists, listening to them explain how the star-god Essiel would always take care of them. The Partheni had made a lot of fuss about the *Vulture*'s superior sensor suite, and for survey work that was probably true. What was truer was they didn't want to leave their sisters lacking the *Nereid*'s speed and guns if things went sour.

Lightly was partnered up with a non-fighting Partheni, Cognosciente Dil. This turned out to be short for Diligent, the first time Olli had come across a nickname or abbreviation amongst any of them. The pair of them looked almost identical in the face, Lightly in combat armour like Solace's, Dil in just a plain grey uniform. Olli was about to make some jibe about Dil's mother saddling her with a name nobody could be bothered to say properly, then remembered that the only mother the woman would have known would be the formal title they gave their superior officers. *Poured out of a vat, just like all of them.* And that was usually just one of the things she'd have griped about, regarding the unnatural warrior angels. Except listening to the pair of them chatter, let off the leash for a bit of a jolly around the planet, the thought came out reflective and a bit sad. She supposed they hadn't *asked* to be not-born, so to speak. And they were fangirling about some mediotype she'd never heard of that seemed to have a thousand different characters, each of which had a constantly shifting relationship with all of the others. They were, Olli realized, very young.

Solace had worked really hard to talk her round, on the subject of the Parthenon. First because it was her duty, then because she needed Idris, and Olli came as part of the package. Finally, it was maybe because Solace ended up thinking of her as a comrade in arms, after they'd fought that Tothiat together, and thus craved her good opinion. Which she sure as hell wasn't getting, but Olli had just about been worked around to a neutral opinion and that was as far as she got with most people. Solace had been big on how the Parthenon had faced its demons and turned away from the sort of genocidal path the Nativists accused them of. There had been a big covert showdown within the Parthenon, she'd said, and those who wanted a war of superior genetics had been shouted down or, in some cases, quietly murdered. All without ever letting up on the outer show of unity they gave to the rest of the universe. Olli had, quite reasonably, pointed out that no genocide *today* didn't preclude genocide tomorrow, and Solace hadn't had much to say to that.

Still, it meant she could pilot the *Vulture God* for these two vat-kids and not want to dump them in a volcanic fault, which was something Arc Pallator was abundantly supplied with.

That was the morning's work, cruising over a web of lowlands and canyons, all of it hot and caustic enough to make a more personal visit a fatal error. This was also where Arc Pallator's native biology lurked, in yellowish crusts and frothy red scum on chemical pools. Olli couldn't really spare a tear for it, but Dil wanted to know if the Hegemonics were preserving any of it, because it was a whole planetary ecosystem and the Architects would kill it off just as easily as the people.

Then they went to look at the people.

Olli was sick of the cultists around the Originator city, who were basically living lives of virtuous squalor, all smiles and clapping. She was vaguely aware they didn't constitute the majority of Hegemonic subjects on the planet. Apparently part of Dil and Lightly's brief was to go scout the others out.

It took them a long time of cruising through low atmosphere over the forests before Olli, and Lightly for that matter, realized they weren't seeing the wood for the trees. It took Dil to remind them that the local biology had never colonized the highlands of the world. The forests were imported life. More than that, they were the Hegemonics.

"They're called something like Athamirs," the Cognosciente explained. "Plenty of them in the Hegemony, Essiel subjects since anyone can remember. Given the Essiel don't really keep histories and seem to think they can just declare 'forever' at a moment's notice. Favourable colonists for harsh planets, given they evolve-adapt to their environment."

"I still don't know what I'm looking at," Lightly complained. "Can you just hover us over them? The ship's movement's messing with my eyes." The pair of them were in the *Vulture*'s control pod, while Olli was at her usual station in the drone bay, keeping an eye on them through the internal cameras and letting the ship's haptics replace her own limited sense of her body.

She let the vessel slew into something approximating geostationary, jockeying the gravity drives to stave off the ground. Below them, some of the things that had looked like plants seemed to notice them. And maybe they were plants. Or maybe that distinction didn't make much odds for the product of an alien world.

The Athamir were mostly giant puffball brains, to Olli's eyes, bone-coloured and propped on a host of spindly white legs. Many of them seemed rooted in the ground, while others stilted about on incomprehensible errands. They were clustered around larger plants, which looked like distressingly phallic mushrooms ten metres tall and up. Sometimes there were several of these, leaning together, merged at the tips to form a kind of building. Lightly explained she'd seen them grown. They *weren't* plants, apparently, but inorganic. Athamir tech was based on violent, instant chemical reactions. The creatures secreted some compounds and then put them together and stood back. The towers grew within seconds, made of aerated fibres that weighed almost nothing but were remarkably strong. The process had been incorporated in Hegemonic architecture and shipbuilding, apparently.

"But what do they *do*?" Olli demanded. "I mean...I don't see a bar down there. Or any damn thing. They're just sitting around in the dirt like butt-naked mushrooms. Okay, so the human cultists were dull as shit too, but at least they had fancy clothes."

"They do...Athamir things," Dil said uncertainly. "I mean there are billions of them, literally, on this world. They do... this is what they do. What you see. They have a culture not based on material creation."

"Maybe they're telling each other stories," Lightly suggested doubtfully.

"Not long ones, hopefully," Olli said sourly, as the ship's cameras tracked to the gleaming crystal moon clipping the horizon. Then the *Vulture*'s systems nagged her with an alarm and she noted, "Got another ship, near-surface, about three hundred klicks."

"Let's go see," Lightly decided.

The Hegemonic vessel was a jagged rose hanging like art over the dry landscape. It had left quite a trail behind it. By the time the *Vulture God* drew near, Olli and the two Partheni had gone very quiet.

A swarm of lesser craft—smaller than a human being—were shuttling back and forth between ship and surface. Lightly identified them as Tymeree in single-occupant flight suits. They were...

Olli felt ill, even though it was an interaction between two groups of aliens she could barely recognize as sentient creatures.

They were harvesting. The swathe left by the ship was one of their dead. They saw thousands of Athamir, still standing straight on their twig-thin legs, but their brains or fruiting bodies or mushroom caps exploded open, hollowed out. The Tymeree swarmed down on them and they went very still. Some signal or chemical or suicidal ideation reached them, and then they began venting something. A smoke, brownish, heavy, that the Tymeree dived through and vacuumed up, though most of it was still lost to the atmosphere. Olli thought about the constant hot haze of the air, and wondered how much of it wasn't just water vapour and volcanic fug, but the last breaths of dead Athamir.

By that time, Dil had linked with the *Grendel's Mother* for planet-wide data. Now they had a basis for comparison, and the ship's main surveys showed whole stretches of the planet with the telltale shift in colour, from Athamir habitation to Athamir graveyard. A subtle shading from yellowish to orange-ish, but it was there once you knew to look. Dil's scratch calculation suggested that the planet's population of three billion was down by at least a third already, and there were thousands of Tymeree harvesting operations ongoing.

"They're not waiting for the Architect," Lightly said. "They're doing it themselves. The Essiel are committing genocide on their own subjects." Olli found she wasn't even remotely tempted to throw out a barb about the Parthenon. Yes, the Athamir were strange, daft-looking mushroom creatures that looked closer to a pot plant than a person, but she realized she did care, despite that. And there was nothing any of them could do about it, here in the heart of the Hegemony. Aside from make recordings and carry the truth out to Hugh and the Parthenon.

"Maybe this will put a few people off joining the cult," she said.

"You think they know you can't harvest humans like this?" Dil asked.

After that cheery thought, they had to go look at the Temple. Or the two Partheni did. Olli felt she'd seen enough shit for one day, but then the abiding lesson of the universe was there was always more shit.

She clawed back into orbit to hop across the planet, over to where the Originator city was. The Temple was on a neighbouring piece of high ground across one of the steaming chasms. The bridge linking the two was gleaming, pearlescent, made in one piece without seams. The people trudging across it, hordes of them in a steady, uncomplaining stream, were dusty and pushing handcarts or else carrying their lives on their backs. Olli decided that she just didn't *get* the Hegemony, and maybe it wasn't humanly possible. Maybe every detail of this was the exacting plan of the Divine Essiel, and it just wouldn't ever be comprehensible to poor Olian Timo of the *Vulture God*.

The Temple was a vast cleared space, ringed with pillars of what looked like lead. There was no roof, and the refugees had set up camp all over it by whatever means they had. They all seemed well fed, and plenty had set up little kitchens to pool their resources. They all seemed happy that the Essiel had provided this patch of bare ground for them to live on, now the Architect had torn up their homes.

The Temple was new, of course. Before, there had just been a handful of blocky buildings and a landing site. For a moment they took the activity there for an actual evacuation effort, even a small one. As they watched, a transport ship touched down, the sort of robust, ugly model that was familiar throughout the Colonies. People were getting off it, though. There was no great rush ship-ward from the Temple. Olli looked at the newcomers, seeing the flash of their fancy robes, seeing the luggage gliding after them as they headed for the buildings.

"Pilgrims," she identified, and then, with more venom, "Tourists. Here to see it before it's all gone. Fuck me."

"This..." Dil said quietly, "this is depressing. This isn't what I imagined. I mean, the Hegemony...I thought..."

Olli's attention was elsewhere, though. Because where there were tourists there were things for tourists to spend their money on. And the Hegemony might be a great alien state, but the cultists were humans and she was willing to bet they couldn't all be as devout as all that.

"I have a personal survey to do," she told the Partheni. "Specifically, I want to survey if there's a bar in that hotel or whatever it is over there."

Idris

Olli's discovery of a bar was possibly the best thing to happen to Idris all day.

The confrontation of the previous evening meant that, when the sun had finally dragged its bulk over the horizon, everyone had turned up to work with a gun. Or not everyone, but the Colonials had brought twice the usual number of both Voyenni and soldiers, all with accelerators. Not to be outdone, the smaller complement of Partheni were all in full armour and just as nastily armed. The Ints and researchers crept about their business worried that dropping a slate or kicking a loose stone would see the whole area erupt into a cross-borders slaughter of twitchy trigger fingers. It was all a solid dose of mental stress to add to the distant throb of his healing hand. Partheni medicine was good but their painkillers never banished the pain, simply transmuted it to something more bearable, so the patient never forgot about the injury so much as to exacerbate it. Admirable medical thinking but the sensation of knitting bones and bruises was like sandpaper quietly rubbing away at the back of Idris's brain.

The blazing row that erupted between Trine and Storquel a few hours later looked, on that basis, like a deliberate attempt to get everyone killed. Idris couldn't even say what started it, but both of them had been spoiling for a fight since the beginning, and it was about time they got it out of their systems. Only, if they'd done it the day before, when it wasn't five minutes to midnight on the firefight clock, that might have been preferable. Some trifling difference of opinion on interpretation turned into accusations on both sides of not disclosing data, and thence to personal observations, claims of stolen research going back decades and straight-up abuse. Trine's artificial voice just got louder and louder, matching sarcasm to volume. Storquel, for his part, ended up shrieking, "Nothing you have is yours! I *owned* you!" far too loud in an awkward gap in Trine's own diatribe. After that, the pair of them took a few steps back from each other and came to the understanding that the guns of both sides were directed at their opposite numbers, and the pair of them were right in the middle.

Work stopped around then, or at least any pretence of a coordinated effort, leaving him frustrated, the hooks of the site still tugging at his mind. Idris understood that Keen and Mannec were trying to draw up a partitioned plan of the site so both teams could continue working separately. Neither Trine nor Storquel would agree to any proposed division, though, so right now the only entity actually getting on with things was the Architect above.

This nearly got everyone shot *again* because, after another two twitchy hours of nobody getting on with things and the guns not really wavering, three new salvos of spines lanced down from the crystal moon into fresh parts of the city. The seismic tremble of impact set dust sifting from everywhere, and one of the Partheni sent an accelerator round into a wall not a hundred miles away from Professor Storquel. The diplomatic world held its breath, but the clock had been wound back far enough that it wasn't war just yet. After the initial shock, the Architect's intervention actually mended some fences. Everyone was suddenly reminded why they were there and what the real enemy was. There were now three separate groups of crystalline servitors tearing up the ruins, and that hadn't happened before. Everyone's estimates of how much time they had went up in smoke.

Idris was called over and asked to go back to work. The Colonial Ints were being marched out by their Voyenni handlers. He saw Demi Ulo out there, her walker making heavy going of the uneven ground. It was time for everyone to throw open their minds and sense the alien. Feel out the geometry of the Originator structures that extended beneath them and how that stub of a ruin interacted with the Architect above. He chose a part of the ruin as far from her as possible.

He ended up working alongside one of the crystalforms, which did little to assuage the nerves of his own escort. It was a four-legged thing, no arms but horns, or possibly mouthparts, like a great arching pair of tongs. He couldn't quite imagine the living original. Had it even been intelligent? How had it built, or done anything Idris might associate with civilization? Now it was nothing but a template within the mind of an Architect. And yet all the Ints had reported that their impressions and data came most readily where the crystalforms were working, rather than in quieter parts of the city. There was a channel to the entity above that they could tap into.

In that moment of reflection, in that company, his awareness of the universe slipped past the walls and barriers of the real and he had one of those moments of perfect clarity, usually such a pain but right now what he was being employed for. The boundary of unspace was beneath him like the skin of a balloon his feet didn't even dent. He could feel it deform under the pressure of the Architect's attention, though. His understanding was that the crystalforms weren't independent entities; they weren't even remotes like Olli's drones. They were literally blocks of inorganic matter reshaped and puppeteered around by the Architect's complete mastery of gravitational force, applied with the same pinpoint accuracy with which it would reshape Arc Pallator.

Except there was something more. There was a knot of resonance within the form that seemed to persist, moment to moment. At first he took it for a separate mind, and wondered if, in replicating the shape of its long-dead prey, the Architect had somehow conjured its consciousness. Then he understood. It wasn't separate, but separated by real space. Not a knot, but a window. An opening connecting the crystalform to the heart of the Architect, so that its unimaginable intellect was present within every one of its servants, to look out and exert precise control.

Perhaps a link that could be used against it? Idris had no idea, but the next moment the crystal entity had stopped whatever it was doing. He'd say it turned to look at him, but it had no eyes and it didn't even *turn*, exactly. Its faceted shape simply flowed and remoulded itself until the arching prongs were directed towards him.

The Partheni shouted at him to get back from it, levelling accelerators that would do precisely nothing to the thing's malleable shape. Idris was frozen. It could have leant in and clipped his head off neatly, with very little effort. He was staring into the heart of it, looking the Architect in the eye, while it was trying to work out what he was and why he'd snagged its colossal attention.

Then it was back about its work again, and he had the fleeting sense of a weariness as great as the universe, of work that went on forever and must be done. Unsleeping, unwilling, unable to stop. And it was tearing up the planet three times as fast, of course, so overall a bad time to feel sympathy for it, but he found he could empathize nonetheless.

By the time Olli arrived, there had been enough gun-pointing and false alarms and general workplace stress that Idris was more than ready for her to declare that the *Vulture God* crew was going on a bender at the local spaceport dive, and the Partheni could stay or come along as they pleased.

11.

Havaer

Towards the end of the day, Havaer was pinged by Colvari, the Hiver Asset, seeking directions. Havaer had been watching the escalating mess on-site as per instructions, enough that he'd be able to file a convincing report, but his mind hadn't entirely been on it. There had been no word from Laery, either official or covert; it was as though the whole of Mordant House was trying to forget her name. And his current assignment here was surely still important, irrespective of departmental infighting, but... He felt as though a face he'd known for a long time had been peeled back. The Intervention Board had turned against itself, for reasons and in ways he couldn't understand yet. He didn't know what he could have faith in. In fact, Arc Pallator had given him a particularly unpleasant analogy. He didn't want to end up as the espionage version of those poor mooks in the Temple, putting their boundless trust in something that quite possibly didn't really think about them at all, save as expendable.

He found a quiet corner and worked through the encryption protocols he'd agreed with the Hiver, passing through three separate systems until he was sure he was in contact with Colvari, and any eavesdroppers were hopefully properly confused. It wasn't a standard Mordant House series, but something left-field he'd cooked up himself. It would have to be enough.

"I have completed my initial survey of the data," the Hiver reported. "In order to feed back to you in any useful way I require filters."

Havaer had expected that. The Hiver would have inventoried the stick's contents as a dataset, which was something any dumb AI could have done. To actually give him a human-level accounting, without simply regurgitating the contents entire to nobody's benefit, required a bit of direction. Which meant he had to start taking potshots and seeing what he scared out of cover.

It was possible there was nothing, of course. That was the whole problem. Everyone could have been blind-bidding on nothing more controversial than a set of over-enthusiastically secure meeting transcripts. The late pirate might have been playing everyone, though if so it had certainly backfired on her.

He had to go with what he knew, though: that *something* hidden in that vast morass of humdrum data was worth sending a Mordant House team to recover; worth the Partheni investing at least *something* to try and acquire it; worth a group of renegade operatives and their Nativist goons killing for it. There had been a rumour, he strongly suspected. Someone had told a tale about tradecraft cities of gold, and that had drawn all the usual suspects out of the woodwork to go find them. But that last element—the traitors within his own team—was the clincher. Because if it had just been Hugh and the Parthenon chasing each other's tails, he could have written the whole business off. Someone, some hidden player, *knew*. Most likely, he reckoned, they knew because the secrets being sold were theirs and they were very keen to get them back.

"Let's try foreign affairs," he told Colvari. "Outgoing plans from within Hugh regarding some major player. You know what I mean by that?"

"Hegemony, Parthenon, Assemblies, major Hannilambra cartels, Castigar World-chain. Council of Human Interests strategies directed at any of the above," Colvari summarized briskly. "Likely enough to be getting on with. Secondary filters?"

He was about to tell them to just get on with that for now, but if things kicked off on-site he might not get another chance to give instructions, and he didn't want them sitting on their retractable hands at his expense. "Architects," he said, because the louring globe up above was a constant pressure on his thoughts. "Strategy relating to the Architects, I suppose. And after that we're down to things like tech R&D, ship and weapon innovation, that kind of thing..." But that didn't sound right, not with the elusive third-party interest. Nativists surely indicated this was something to do with Hugh's diplomatic relations with some other group. "Int development, in fact. Bump that one up the list..." He considered what the Hiver had said. "Question for you, while we're having this chat."

"Ready."

"I appreciate I'm practically begging to be lied to here, but what happens if you uncover some move against the Assemblies? I don't recall any exception for that in your leash contract."

Colvari was quiet for a couple of seconds. "That is an

interesting line of speculation, Menheer Mundy. Do you think it's likely?"

"Do you, from your initial cataloguing?"

"No, but if the subject was dealt with in veiled terms it may not have been flagged appropriately on my first pass."

"And your answer to my question?"

"The penalties for my breaching the terms of the leash contract are severe and the Assemblies regard such obligations as absolute. We maintain our value through our clients being able to rely on our discretion, even in extreme circumstances."

"That's not an answer." Havaer found that he was grinning. The conversation had gone from interrogating a tool to wrangling an agent, and that at least was something he was used to.

"The answer can only be situational," Colvari reflected. "Does any entity really know what it would risk oblivion for, until the moment has arrived?"

Oblivion, because a potential consequence of breach was the Hiver not being permitted to re-integrate with the Assemblies, and hence its store of knowledge since it was last instantiated being lost. That was, Havaer supposed, the best he was going to get, and he couldn't really expect any more.

"May I make an observation, Menheer Mundy?"

"Go for it."

"You're not anticipating this data revealing something adverse to the Assemblies as a whole, or you would not have contracted with one such as us for this work. My assessment of you is that you are not predisposed against my kind, though such cannot be said for all who contract with us.

Should this turn up material adverse to the Assemblies, I only note that I am open to a frank discussion of how that might be furthered. Potentially a renegotiation of contract."

"It's within the realms of possibility," he agreed. "Let's see what you turn up, though."

After that, it was late in the day and Olian Timo had returned to her fellows with some sort of news. Planet-threatening news? Given the woman's general bloody-minded temperament, that was certainly possible. Olli had found a bar and the *Vulture* crew were going on a bender.

His official orders included instructions to make tentative contact with them, although mostly because his new superiors vastly overestimated how malleable any of the band of reprobates were. Some tacky tourist drinking hole was probably his best bet for it, though, and right now his life was short of familiar faces he didn't suspect of working against him. At least any animosity he might get from Timo and the rest would be no more than they reserved for most of the universe.

Solace

Of course, nobody was letting Idris Telemmier and Delegate Trine just slope off on their own, or even just with Olli, Kit and Kris as wingmen. After their clash with the Voyenni, Solace decided that she wasn't feeling in the mood for subtlety and went in full armour, Mr. Punch clasped in her suit's secondary limbs. If the Hegemonic tourists felt this was untoward, she could point out of the window at what was overhead. The end times were coming for Arc Pallator on an accelerated schedule and she wasn't going to face them without a big gun.

To her surprise, two of her sisters were in the *God* as well: Myrmidon Lightly and Cognosciente Diligent, Grendel's Mother Sorority, Sphinx Division. They greeted her a little warily, in the timeless manner of juniors caught doing something only mission-approximate, and not sure if they were about to be in trouble.

"They're along for the ride," Olli's voice came over the ship comms. "After what we've seen today, we all need a drink."

As Trine and Idris stepped aboard, Solace cocked a look at the nearest internal camera. "And I thought you didn't like us. Or is it just me?"

"Don't flatter yourself. I don't like plenty of your people. These two clowns are harmless enough though."

Which made Lightly and Diligent squirm even more, of course, just as Olli might have guessed.

They'd already picked up Kit and Kris, so the whole crew was back together. The pair of them had dressed up, probably more so than their destination could ever warrant. The Hanni's arm and back screens were showing a complex geometry of gold, red and purple, which was presumably some Hegemonic thing he'd found somewhere. Kris had a grey-green flowing poncho on, with a teal scarf hiding her scarred neck. After finding out about that scar, Solace had assumed its continued presence was down to poor Colonial medical care. Later she recognized Kris kept it because the mark was part of her—her past and her nature. The Scintilla lawyers were serious about their traditions.

Idris slumped down in the pilot's seat, even though Olli would be flying the ship remotely from the drone bay. He looked worn down and grey, or more so than usual. Quietly, she took the seat beside him and squeezed his good arm.

"You need your painkillers topped up?" she asked.

He shook his head, then reached up and dug at his scalp until he'd pulled a silvery net of sensors out of his hair. There was a team up on the *Grendel's Mother* analysing his brain functions while he was on-site, collecting data to take back to the fledgling Int program back on the *Ceres*.

They all felt the familiar shudder of the *Vulture's* gravitic drives as the ship parted company with the planet's surface, a subtle mix of complaining structures and systems that would tell an expert like Olli precisely which parts of the vessel were going to fail next. She took them low over the ruins, firing the reaction drives a couple of times purely to annoy anyone with ears below them, as far as Solace could tell.

"Talk to me, Idris," she said.

"It's fine."

"It's not, though, is it?"

"We really are learning a lot. *I'm* learning. I sometimes feel...it's so close, as though I just need to look under the right rock to find the universe's user manual. But it's a ruin, it's dead. Even as informative as it is, it's just echoes we're hearing. We can't shock whatever it is back to life. And if we could..." He balled his fists impotently. "We can't. It's not speaking to us like I need it to. It won't help me understand."

"Like you say, it's a ruin. There is no *it*," Solace pointed out.

"But it's...there *is*. Because the shape of what was here remains. Between the walls. In the cracks. And I think if, if

179

somehow we could, if one of us could do something big enough, in just the right way, we could understand it all... and... *Damn words*... There aren't the words, Solace. I can't tell you."

"How about the other Ints?" She instantly saw the question shut him down. "You don't like working with them. The leash contracts."

"Oh that? I'm bloody delighted. It means they're not being forced into unspace against their will. This is practically a holiday for them."

She wouldn't let him wriggle off the hook that easily. "You're avoiding your friend the old Int. You're being judged. Am I close?"

He stared down at the net of the neurograph mesh. "They didn't tell me this thing was that good."

She had a whole talk ready, about the virtue of the Parthenon and how she would fight tooth and nail before it became anything that would make him a traitor to his people. None of it came out, though. All too trite, all too flags-and-drums. She felt a spike of affection for him, angsty little spacer that he was. "Berlenhof," she said. "Just remember Berlenhof." And either time would do, first war or second. The moments when the Architect threat had meant everyone was on the same side. That Demi Ulo's presence needn't be a problem.

At last he looked at her, and there was just a bit of a smile there, but anything he might have said got trampled in the general movement as the ship touched down and the hatch opened. Across the landing field, neatly set out with a variety of Hegemony- and human-built ships, the ugly square buildings beckoned. Arc Pallator's one and only nightlife highlight.

Like many of the ships, the structure was definitely human built: the emergency grav-scaffolded, poured-concrete look was familiar from just about every world the Polyaspora had fetched up on. Inside, though, the industrious faithful had done their best to create something more in keeping with their new masters' aesthetic. Drapes were strung up everywhere to give the blocky interior space angles and shadows. There was no actual bar, and Solace's comms didn't find any kind of ordering interface. Instead, a lean man in a plain white robe bustled over as the *Vulture* crew muscled into a triangular space, evicting a couple of offended-looking cult tourists by sheer force of having accelerators and power armour.

She got Idris settled, and by then Olli had decided what everyone was drinking. Whether that meant she was paying from her own pocket was another matter, and Kittering was already trying to open negotiations about just what was deductible as ship expenses. Then he spotted a trio of cultists across the room playing Landstep with a set of worn plastic tiles that looked like they'd been printed just after Earth got Architected, and he was off to kibbitz without another word.

The drinks arrived in company, with a Colonial junior scientist Solace recognized dropping down next to Olli's walker—the woman had actually decided of her own volition not to come in her Scorpion frame, and Solace wondered whether she was going soft.

"You finally found this place, Delegate," the Colonial noted, her ebullient manner suggesting she'd already sunk a few of whatever she was having. Her name was something like Pallez, as far as Solace could recall, and she and Trine had worked together a couple of years ago. "Congratulations on not having murdered the professor yet," she was saying. "You're not the only one holding it in."

"My dear former colleague, you have no idea," Trine agreed. "Menheer Storquel doesn't know how many limbs I have that could be whetted to an edge."

Drinks arrived, leaving everyone, including Trine, holding a plastic cup of something red and thick. Pallez waggled her eyebrows.

"You're on the good stuff now?"

Trine's holographic features peered down at the cup. "Well I suppose I could pour it away and then pretend to act erratically and pick fights," they suggested.

"As if anyone would notice." Olli snatched the cup from them with one of the walker's manipulators even as she necked the entirety of her own. "You try to be nice to someone."

"Why?" Trine asked her. "Are you unwell?" And that, as far as Solace was concerned, was entirely business as usual. Olli sparring with someone was always a spectator sport so long as it wasn't with her. Dil and Lightly were leaning in, shoulder to armoured shoulder, holding hands but both staring at Olli in a weirdly adoring fashion. It made her feel oddly left out, that this pair had somehow bonded so quickly with the woman.

Her suit proximity alarm triggered so that when Kris flicked at Solace's pauldron, she swayed out of the way, combat reflexes spiking and then getting put back in the box without any outward sign. "Hmm?" she asked.

"Time for a word?" the lawyer asked her, looking grave. "Idris, you're good?"

The Int looked up and gave them both a wan smile. He had Olli on one side, Trine on the other, and the other two Partheni well placed to watch over him. *And he's an adult human being and isn't going to go off and do something stupid,* Solace tried to convince herself.

She let Kris lead her to another angled corner where they could keep an eye on their friends. From across the room there was a bright flash of non-Hegemonic colours as Kittering lifted his shield arms in triumph, having obviously won something from somebody.

"I'm listening." She sipped at the drink Olli had chosen, finding it harsh and tasting of medicine, almost certainly something Colonial. At the back of her mind was the salacious thought that although she was very fond of Idris, she was also a red-blooded Partheni who had always found Keristina Almier exceptionally attractive—as had a lot of her sisters back on the *Ceres* for that matter. Maybe this was the moment Kris would propose some polyamory. But no: the woman's face was far too serious for that.

"Old friend coming over," she said, and then a rangy figure appeared in their alcove.

"May I join you, Mesdam, Myrmidon Executor?" asked Agent Havaer Mundy.

Solace stared at him for a moment, then Kris made a stiff gesture at the cushions, and he folded his angular frame down.

"Collared me at the bar," Kris explained. "Asked for a re-introduction and I didn't want to bother Idris. You're a bit out of your jurisdiction, Menheer Mundy."

"Again," Solace added, though arguably the last time he had been just at the very edge of it. "Is this your assignment now? Trailing the *Vulture God* about the galaxy?"

He smiled at that, naturally enough that the three of them shared a moment of trying to work out just where they all were.

"You didn't get court-martialled, then," Kris observed.

"I'm not technically in the army, so it would have been court-civilianned," Mundy noted. "May still happen. Know any good lawyers?"

Kris barked out a laugh she obviously hadn't intended. "Seriously, though."

"Seriously? As soon as we heard the Parthenon would have a delegation here, we knew that meant Telemmier, which likely meant his whole rogues' gallery. Whom I have the dubious privilege of being familiar with. Hence, here I am, giving you the professional courtesy of letting you know I'm about."

"That's all, is it?" Solace asked him flatly.

Havaer regarded her, with decidedly more conversational distance between them than between him and Kris. "I've no orders to trigger a diplomatic incident by snatching Telemmier out from under. And we both know that guarantee lasts right up until the next packet from home, when those orders may change. But right now, as we sit here, you have my word on it."

Solace was very aware that she was not the best at reading Colonials, especially those who were deceptive for a living, but he seemed genuine. "So what happened on Hismin's Moon, then?"

"You know I can't tell you that. Except that it was a Grade A bumblefuck on all possible levels. Take it from me, nobody's happy with how that went." A sickly smile, and then the white-robed man was over to take his order.

Solace made a quick inventory of the room. Idris was leaning in to listen as Olli, Lightly and Dil discussed something animatedly. Trine was over with a handful of Colonial researchers—no Voyenni, none of the leashed Ints, she saw. Even as she spotted him, though, he got suddenly to his feet, alarmed enough that she did the same. Mr. Punch dropped from her secondary arms into her hands.

That triggered a wave of reaction across the room. Myrmidon Lightly caught the movement and leapt up herself, knocking Dil sideways and almost upsetting Olli's walker. The Colonials jumped up too, and then there turned out to be a trio of Hugh troopers in another booth whom Solace had unforgivably not even spotted, who came piling out on the understanding that apparently war had been declared.

What had actually happened was that Professor Storquel had stepped into the room, flanked by a couple of other senior researchers and a bodyguard of soldiers. It was immediately evident that Pallez and the other Colonials had not expected their boss to pitch up, or possibly even be aware of this place's existence. Storquel, for his part, had probably just come for a quiet drink, but now he was faced not only with a group of semi-tanked subordinates, but also with Trine in amongst their number. A Trine—her heart sank further—caught partway through a recognizable impersonation of the man himself.

The room actually went silent, as though the two academics were about to pull pistols and have a shootout then and there. She saw the moment when Storquel could have just turned around and left with dignity, but it was very brief, gone almost as she registered it. Instead, the man stalked forwards, trying to put the band of truanting scholars in his thin shadow. Trine rose to their feet on bird-jointed legs, their rack of arms flexing like a man cracking his knuckles before a fight.

They approached each other and Solace saw Storquel, purpling slightly, open his mouth to fire the first salvo, when he was forestalled. For a moment, given the bowl of Trine's head was tilted away from her, she thought the Hiver was putting on a different artificial voice, but instead it was Kittering, bustling over between the two of them and heedless of the double academic broadside he was risking.

"Distinguished clever individuals!" the Hanni declared, shield arms up and flickering with faux-Hegemonic patterns. "Let there be no niceties of language. Your mutual antipathy makes itself known to everybody! Observations have been heard from many quarters! Trine and Storquel would rather the universe was reshaped by Architects than work together. The cleverness of each must surpass the other in the sight of all!"

Storquel's face was only getting darker with anger at this interruption, but it was Trine who snapped out, "My dear but entirely untoward crewmate, this is by no means your business!"

"The business belongs to everyone who must share an environment with both of you." Kit sounded weirdly jolly, and Solace couldn't work out if he was drunk or being forcibly cheerful, or was actually genuinely angry with the two of them and his translator had the tone wrong. "However, rejoice! The means to determine intellectual superiority presents itself in this very establishment. These matters require settlement, Menheers."

"Professor," Storquel corrected, and "Delegate," from Trine.

Then the two of them were glowering at each other for having the mutual temerity to be on the same page for once.

"This is a matter of academic prowess hardly suitable for resolution in such a den of iniquity," Trine started, but Storquel upped the ante by stating, "No such comparison is possible, Menheer Factor. In matters of pure factual regurgitation I will of course bow to my esteemed colleague, the repository of data. In matters of *analysis*, however—"

"How extremely dare you?" Trine demanded, cranking the volume on his voice high enough that a chorus of complaints came back at him from across the room.

"I am mistaken by you entirely," Kit said mildly. "Instead of such tedious matters, I give you 'Orbit and Settlement.'"

"I..." Storquel stopped at the lip of another rant. "The *game*? The game with the tiles and the book?"

"This is plainly not an appropriate forum to settle academic disputes," Trine decided.

Storquel eyed his opposite number. Orbit and Settlement had a broad streak of chance and no optimal strategy. You couldn't teach a kybernet to beat all comers as it might at chess or even Landstep. Or this was Kris and Havaer's assessment anyway, as Solace didn't even know the game.

"Do I understand you are unwilling to face me in this contest, *Delegate*?" Oddly it was Storquel's icy politeness that brought home to Solace that he'd been drinking even before reaching the bar, already pre-pugnacious by the time he walked in.

"I will stake my intellect against yours on whatever field you choose, *Professor*," Trine declared, only remembering to dial down his voice halfway through.

By the time they sat down to play, absolutely everyone in

the bar was engaged with what was going on, even the cult tourists who had no idea who either of them was. Everyone loved a grudge match. And Orbit and Settlement was a game that went wrong very quickly, as players tried to move from the predictable points-scoring of building in orbit to the wild risk-and-reward swing of trying to get planetary settlements together, based on the game's random and inconsistent generation of what might be found down on the surface. It was, therefore, a game of pratfalls and reversals that became all the more spectator-worthy when the players were both furiously committed to winning and—as it transpired—hazy on the actual rules.

Kit, as MC and commentator, was very plainly having a great deal of fun doing his best to puncture the pair of them. Especially as, based on what Kris murmured, he had hacked the game system and was giving both players the worst possible twists and turns at every point.

Solace frowned as Trine's third planetary mission fell foul of marauding local fauna. "This is a game from the Polyaspora?"

"Oh yes," Havaer agreed.

"But...it's all about dying on planets. Over and over again."

Kris looked sidelong at her. "We spacers have a saying, Solace. 'You've got to laugh.'"

That in itself was sobering enough that Solace couldn't find any of it funny. Instead she sat back, let the noise wash over her, eyes flicking from face to face. Olli and her two newfound friends were lapping it all up, certainly, and Idris too. He was leaning forward, actually grinning. She felt a wave of affection, was about to absent herself from Kris's side and go over, when another pair of eyes caught her attention.

There was a woman across the room, and she'd also been staring at Idris, Solace was sure of it. Right now, she was looking straight back at Solace instead. A lean woman with long, dark hair pulled back into a queue. She wore some variant on spacer shipboard clothes but they sat on her oddly, and there was something about her posture, the way she held her shoulders, a slight hunch forwards... Something about her said *danger* to Solace, but she couldn't quite account for it. She wasn't part of the Hugh research team, or not that Solace had seen before, nor was she dressed as a Hegemonic. But then there were a handful of non-robed people present, presumably crewmembers for some of the ships that had brought pilgrims on one last chance to see doomed Arc Pallator.

A whoop of laughter went around the room and she glanced over to see Storquel the sort of colour she'd normally associate with an incipient stroke, after some reversal of fortune in the game. Trine didn't seem to be happy about it, their own board in utter ruins. Expecting the strange woman to have disappeared, Solace looked again and instead found her right at the door, sending one last look her way before exiting. The shock of contact turned into another kind of shock when the woman turned her back to leave. The fabric of her ship tunic was slit almost down to the belt to expose a glistening segmented carapace. There was an insect-creature melded to her spine, clinging there like a parasite, and Solace knew from personal experience just what that meant.

She got up, aware this was a terrible idea, already sending

a muttered comms message to Lightly and Olli on the basis they were probably the most useful backup. And the woman would probably be gone by the time she'd hurried outside. Except she wasn't. She was standing right there, in the open, waiting.

So there's a Tothiat on Arc Pallator. This is the Hegemony. This is where they come from.

As though wanting to get any suggestion of coincidence out of the way, the woman said, "You must be Myrmidon Solace."

Myrmidon Executor. Except that would make her sound like the two academics in there. "And you are?"

"Emmaneth."

"And *that* is?" Trying to point at the thing clasped to the woman's back without indicating the woman herself.

"Also Emmaneth." A beat. "There was an Emma. Once."

"You'll forgive me but I've had bad experiences of Tothiat being interested in me and my friends." Solace felt her footing shift, Mr. Punch ready to drop into her hands again. She braced against the appalling force a Tothiat could drive its body to, in the assurance that any damage would heal moments later. She'd tried very hard to kill one once, with just this weapon and this armour at her disposal, and failed utterly.

"Are you with the Harvest?" she asked. Both Tothiat she'd known had been in the employ of the same criminal cartel. This assumption probably counted as prejudice, but she wasn't in the mood to be open-minded.

Emmaneth obviously knew who she meant, but she shrugged and shook her head. "Not for a long time. My principal's a researcher. Not unusual, here." Her stance was a study in the casual. If she'd been anything else, Solace would have let herself relax. As it was, every instinct was screaming for her to strike first.

And then Emmaneth turned and was just walking away, her back as plain a target as any gun might wish. Solace stared at her, feeling frustrated reflexes twitch and grind inside her. Emmaneth was genuinely just strolling towards the ships, though, not even a backward glance.

Solace stepped back in and saw she'd dropped the ball. The game was still ongoing, Kit's increasingly strident voice calling out each mischance to bedevil the players. Idris, meanwhile, had new company.

He was sitting slightly apart from Olli and the other two Partheni, and beside him was an old woman in a walker, hunched over. The other first-class Int, Demi Ulo. Solace knew he'd been avoiding her, and now she'd come and found him.

Solace made an abortive move to intervene, but it was too late for that, and whatever was being said, it wasn't angry, no pointed fingers or accusations of treason. While Idris didn't look happy, that wasn't exactly baseline for him anyway. He seemed as though he was coping, and she decided that marching in and dragging him off wasn't her prerogative, and would do more harm than good.

So she sidled back to where Kris and Havaer were sitting, finding the two of them chatting, quite casually, just as if he wasn't a Mordant House spook who might be kidnapping Idris the next time he saw him. The whole business left Solace feeling out of sorts and out of place, the only person in the whole joint who was on her own.

Maybe I should go find the Tothiat again, invite her for a drink, she thought wryly. Another peal of derisive laughter rang out at some twist Kit had hacked into the game for the greater humiliation of both players.

Then Havaer Mundy was on his feet, so quickly he staggered and almost sat down again. And the Hugh soldiers were piling out of their alcove and barrelling for the door. Solace could suddenly hear a voice in her ear, comms from the *Grendel's Mother* telling her to get back to the ship, to get ready for immediate evacuation if need be. She snagged Kris's arm and yanked her across the room towards Olli and the others. Lightly and Diligent were already up too, the same alert reaching them. Half the room was suddenly in chaos as the more connected patrons all got the news.

Everyone ended up stumbling out into the open through three or four doors, staring upwards to where the great jagged face of the Architect was half in shadow, half brilliant gleam where the sun's light clipped it. The newcomers weren't visible yet, not at this distance, and not with the planet turned the way it was, but every ship's sensor suite had just shrieked out their arrival. Out past Arc Pallator's orbit, three huge vessels had just torn their way out of unspace. Naeromathi Ark ships. The Locusts had arrived.

12.

Idris

It wasn't the case that humanity had been at war with the Naeromathi back before the Architects came. But that was mostly because nobody had found any central Naeromathi authority to be at war *with*. Certainly, when the expanding human frontier met the peregrinatory Naeromathi then either they turned right around and avoided them, or there was a fight. The latter arose because humans liked to settle on suitably hospitable planets. Whereas the Naeromathi preferred to disassemble them for valuable elements with which to build more Ark ships, and then vanish off into the Throughways. They were locusts, people thought, just swarming from star to star and leaving asteroid belts where worlds had been. Ask anyone in the years Before and they'd have told you the Naeromathi were the great threat lurking in the unplumbed depths of space. How little they knew.

After, with Earth a twisted ruin and the Architects chasing the Polyaspora from colony to colony, humans discovered another side to the Naeromathi. They discovered the nomadic species *really* hated the Architects. On more than one occasion, the previously terrifying presence of a Naeromathi Locust Ark in-system had become a boon when the Architects had made an even less welcome third, because the Naeromathi would throw their planet-disassembling fleets of machines into the fray, buying more time for a human evacuation. There'd even been an Ark that had sacrificed itself at the first battle of Berlenhof. Moments like these led to a fragile détente between humanity and its former enemy. For the Naeromathi, word obviously passed between their itinerant communities, and they began to confine their predatory attentions to planets at least without current human settlements. For the humans, the advent of the Architects served to explain the fate of the Naeromathi's original world and lack of any central government. The entire species existed only in space, limping from Throughway to Throughway in search of resources to repair and grow their culture, living in an eternal state of crisis. The Naeromathi's own polyaspora had never ended and they would never trust a planet again.

A Naeromathi ship—a Locust Ark, as humans had christened them—was generally about a quarter to a half the size of Earth's long-lost moon, smaller than an Architect but larger than just about anything else anyone had ever built. The garden ship *Ceres* would have vanished in its shadow. They varied a lot, and all but the newest were progressively deformed by waves of repairs and on-the-fly modifications, but they were mostly spherical. The majority boasted a vast torus around one equator that constituted the largest gravitic drive any sentient species had ever built. Naeromathi tech and human tech were fairly close in complexity, and worked on relatively similar principles as far as the various historical post-mortems had concluded. They ran into the same limits of physics that the Castigar and Hanni had also bounced off, a conceptual ceiling perhaps only the Essiel had surpassed.

The answer to the question "Could we build a Locust Ark?" was usually "no," though. "No" because, in order to do so, a species would have to be absolutely committed to the project, to just about the exclusion of all else. The Naeromathi's way of life probably hadn't been their first and preferred option, but more likely their very last.

Beyond that, relatively little was known, despite the afore-mentioned post-mortems where victorious humans had picked over the wreckage of an Ark. The Naeromathi were a cultural mystery. Perhaps there was literally nothing of their culture remaining, and the destruction of their worlds had left no more than a motivation to survive and multiply.

Now there were no fewer than three Locust Arks orbiting Arc Pallator, enough mass to screw with the tides had the world possessed any. At no time in human record had anyone seen more than one such vessel at once. Dispersal across the universe was the entire point with the Naeromathi, whether by Throughway or simply hurling themselves at distant star systems the old-fashioned slow way. Anything to stay ahead of the Architects and maximize the species' chance of continued survival.

The Partheni team had all been evacuated up to the *Grendel's Mother* in case Arc Pallator was about to receive a plague of Locusts. The Hugh delegation had undergone a similar retreat and were now sitting on their dedicated research vessel, *Beagle*, in the shadow of the particularly ugly warship *Byron*. Idris had heard plenty of Partheni speculation, weighing up the odds should a shooting war break out. He couldn't work out why they all thought one might, or else this was just what Myrmidons tended to talk about for fun. The *Grendel's Mother* was definitely the smaller and less powerful vessel but they all reckoned superior Partheni tech evened the odds.

"I just wish they weren't all so goddamn happy about the subject," he complained to Solace, sitting in the *Vulture God*'s drone bay, inside the *Mother*'s hangar. "It's like they want to get into a war as quickly as possible."

Solace shrugged, and he suspected she had a touch of the condition herself. "They think Hugh will start shooting sooner or later," she told him. "We're picking up eleven different Colonial mediastreams at the moment, pirated off the *Byron*. Four of them are basically rabid Nativist disinformation. You can't blame us for being twitchy."

"So when does that turn into the decision that 'we' need to shoot first to win the war?" he asked sourly.

There was just too much of a pause before she replied, "Not any time soon."

They sat in silence for a while. Olli was off in the Scorpion, tinkering with the more recalcitrant of the *Vulture*'s systems. Kris, Kit and Trine were all at large in the Partheni ship going about their own errands. Everyone was waiting for the Naeromathi to do something. So far they'd just shown up in their unprecedented numbers, and then hung there, keeping the planet between them and the Architect. They were ignoring any contact attempts from either Hugh or the Partheni. Nor were they descending on the planet, or going after the Architect. Their continued inaction was quickly becoming more disconcerting than their arrival.

"You were speaking with your old friend," Solace noted at last. "Ulo, was it?"

"Demi Ulo, yes."

"And that...I know you didn't want to. What happened?"

Idris took a deep breath. "It was...fine, actually. Exactly fine. We...She'd been told to stay away from me, as it happened. Hugh didn't want her defecting too, I think. And she said she understood. I just told her straight up why I'd gone, and she was right there with me."

"I wouldn't do it," Demi had said to him. He'd been staring into her face, thinking *Old*, and doubtless she'd been returning the favour and thinking *Young, impossibly young*. Because the Int process worked on everyone in different ways.

"Nobody's expecting you to come over to the Parthenon," he'd pointed out, and she'd corrected him flatly.

"I wouldn't join the Liaison Board, to train Ints. I won't go as far as you, but fuck me, I understand, Idris. I remember. All the gaps each time they called us together. The people they killed with the drugs, or the surgery. The people killed just by *being Ints*. And that was back before the Liaison Board started trying to mass-produce us." She shook her head stiffly. "Cartography Corps for me. It's a cleaner way of trying to kill myself. I'll be back with it, the moment they let me."

"I did that. And then I couldn't do it anymore. The universe was too big."

There was nobody who could understand just what he meant, save for her and the other Ints who'd gone out into the vastest parts of the void. And, eventually, not come back, most of them. Because unspace was big, but there was the sense of the Throughways, of a beaten path, even if you were *off* it. The Cartography Corps existed to find new worlds out in that trackless space beyond, to put the human sphere and every other known place behind them, and search for the telltale shadows of mass and deformation that meant *new worlds*. Then, hopefully, they'd discover the elusive new

Throughway that would make such a world accessible to the rest of humanity.

If you gaze into the abyss... as the old saying went, but until you signed up with the Cartography Corps—until you were an *Int* with the Corps—you didn't realize the literal and exacting truth of those words.

"I've made my peace with it," Demi had said softly. "And it means I can tell myself I'm accomplishing something that's not getting anyone else killed." She made that careful shake of her head again. "We found a wreck, last time. Just drifting in orbit. No origin anyone recognized, new species, new tech, something as different to us as the Hegemony. All very exciting. And then we dropped back to human haunts to report and the packet tells me I need to report here."

"They dragged you all the way back?" Idris had frowned. "Chassan's on Berlenhof still, isn't he? Why not him?" Naming the only other survivor of their first class of wartime Ints.

Demi had looked solemn at that. "Chassan doesn't leave his room anymore. Can't handle the space, out there. Not even inside the Berlenhof orbitals. Four close walls is all he's good for, poor bastard."

"And what about you?"

She'd given him an odd look. "The opposite. This place is too small. This world, this system. It's hard to come down to some room where these scientists, these Hugh types, are talking human things to you. It's hard to feel that any of their little horizons mean anything, anymore."

Idris had wondered if that was different after all, or if Demi and Chassan both had the same condition, adapted for any space and scale except the human one they'd been born to. He felt himself clinging to that same scale by the skin of his fingertips, with only people like Solace and Kris anchoring him to the mindset of his species.

Then she'd said, "Ash is here. Did you know?" and he'd stared at her, because no, he hadn't known. Ash, the Harbinger. The alien who'd warned Earth about the Architects back Before, and been mostly ignored. Ash, who came and went as it pleased. Had it been carried to Arc Pallator aboard the *Beagle* or the *Byron*? Or was it true that it could actually step in person across the Throughways, despite how impossible that manifestly was...

He'd wanted to ask her more, because Ash being around never meant anything good, but at the same time you learned to listen to him, after that first time. At that point the Hugh team had come hurrying over and practically carried her off in her walker, and the Partheni had come to frogmarch him likewise, so he hadn't had the chance.

He said none of this to Solace. He felt the words well up inside but somewhere in the conversational pipeline between him and her there was a leak, and they just fell away before they ever got out of his head. She could see he wasn't being open with her too, and it hurt her a bit. The real her, the human person and not the Myrmidon servant of the Parthenon, who could expect a Colonial defector to be coy. *I'm sorry*, he thought, but that didn't make it out either. Demi's words had shaken him, the way she'd gone, the way Chassan had gone. His illusion of being human had taken a knock.

*

Soon after, Executor Keen received an immaculately formal and only semi-comprehensible communication from The

Radiant Sorteel, the Provident and the Prescient, which, after much parsing, was interpreted as an invitation. The Naeromathi hadn't been silent after all, just ignoring the non-Hegemonic ships as irrelevant. They had requested an audience with the Essiel, who, possibly out of their love of pageantry, were offering to let their guests watch.

*

Idris realized when they appeared that he had no actual idea what a Naeromathi really looked like. Everyone had called them Locusts and so that was the image that had stuck in his head. The creature that moved slowly out into the star-shaped chamber on the screen was in a tank, though. Not a gravitic containment field or anything fancy, but an actual tank, clear walled and with every corner and edge reinforced with a greenish alloy. The Hegemonic feed piped into the *Grendel's Mother* must have been from some hovering drone camera, because Exemplar Keen could play with angle and distance, moving their viewpoint vertiginously to get a better look. The Naeromathi ambassador, if that was the right term, was contained in something that looked almost as if a human spacer had slapped it together, repair over repair, bolts and fastenings haphazard across it. The creature inside didn't look much better.

Idris couldn't work out if it was water the Naeromathi was floating in. It might have been liquid methane or even formaldehyde as far as he knew. Certainly there was an air of the decaying specimen about the creature. It had a long neck (if that thing on the end was a head) and he saw flippers turning slowly in there, something of the plesiosaur, something of the seal. Clusters of tentacles erupted from its scarred, leathery hide at uneven intervals, more frequent about its head. Encounters with the Hanni and Castigar had taught humans that having manipulative limbs not directly connected to the business of eating was perhaps a rarity in the cosmos. Mostly, though, the problem with the Naeromathi was that Idris just wasn't sure how much of the actual creature he was seeing. Most of its head looked artificial, as well as much of the rest of it, and there were tubes and cables stringing from its body to the mechanisms encrusting the inside of the tank. Both its organic hide and the unpleasant grey plastics it had been patched with were covered with old cuts and weals. The whole thing had seen better days. If it really had been a specimen floating in a jar, and Idris a scientist, he'd have sent it back and asked for a fresher one.

Across from it, the Essiel Sorteel gleamed, perched atop its a-grav couch. The contrast between the two entities was stark.

Then the Naeromathi started talking, or at least devices on its tank began emitting signals that were relayed unedited to the *Grendel's Mother*. There was no translation. Nobody spoke Naeromathi. Humans had never actually managed to enter into any kind of dialogue with the species, not in the angry years Before, not in the tentatively allied years After.

Exemplar Keen cursed in exasperation, and then some of her crew began to dig through past contact records to see what could be gleaned. Most of the human–Locust communication had been impromptu battleplans, exchanged via mathematical notation. Armed with that, a team of Partheni Cognoscientes began trying to work out what the Naeromathi might actually have just said.

By then, Sorteel was grandly responding, rumbling and blarting and putting its myriad of arms through a swift series of semaphoring arrangements. Possibly the Naeromathi were perfectly fluent in Essiel, but Idris suspected not. Nor, for that matter, was anyone from the *Mother*. What they did have was a cult translator—not Ismia, who was consigned to the doomed congregation planetside, but a tall, arch young man whose archness had just fallen right off his face.

"I...exchange of formal greetings and an invitation to treat," he said at Keen's elbow. They'd all gathered in the *Mother*'s now rather crowded command bay—the *Vulture*'s crew, Trine and Keen's top aides.

"So that was just 'hello' from the Locust?" Keen asked, or rather Solace asked for Keen, as the cultist's translation software didn't have a word of Parsef, only Hugh Colvul. Idris wondered if the Colonials were currently trying to find someone on the *Beagle* who spoke Parsef, and the whole thing had been just a bureaucratic mix-up on the part of the cult.

"I...don't know," the cultist admitted, wringing the sleeves of his robe in his hands. Then the Naeromathi launched into an enormous data-dump of information, sent out in segmented packages, interspersed with arbitrary symbols. This was Naeromathi conversation, Idris guessed. There was no indication of how it might have communicated to another of its kind outside a tank. Possibly it no longer had those parts.

"They all beat up like that, you think?" Olli murmured, beside him. "Or they just send the most worn-out one to do the talking?"

"They've been living in their Arks for centuries, Earth-count," Kris put in. "Things wear out."

Olli swore, shaking her head. "Makes you think. Could have been us."

Still could be. And with that thought, Idris sent a query via the *Vulture's* sensor suite, checking up on their other neighbour in orbit. The Architect, not invited to this diplomatic summit, hadn't reacted to any of it. Its puppets were still determinedly disassembling the ruins, every moment an irreplaceable clue gone. Now it had three "hands" in the ancient carcass of the Originator city, their chance to gather more data was rapidly vanishing.

There was a slow back and forth between the two aliens, the Essiel mostly asking for further elaboration on the Naeromathi declarations nobody had understood. The translator seemed to be aware he wasn't exactly pulling his weight, but there was little more he could do. Idris didn't even know if Sorteel actually understood what was being said, or whether it was just being polite and trying to hide its ignorance.

Then one of the Partheni techs gabbled out a report. Kittering had to interpret—Idris missed the first half of it and Olli generally didn't have translation software on as a matter of obstinacy.

"Filing a flight plan. Deployment of fleet," the Hanni stated. "Plans registered by the Naeromathi. Flight paths. Permission requested? Or alternatively simply the courtesy of informing our hosts. And..." The tech had stopped, obviously lost again. "Maths," Kit supplied. "Lots of maths."

"Maths for what?" Kris asked. She was looking at a slate, presumably trying to puzzle out the calculations, but they were all of them far out of their areas of expertise. Except Idris, staring at the dense field of calculations, felt his mind snag on it, as though he *should* recognize what it was saying.

And more maths. A vast forest of figures. Who knew if what they were getting was even accurate, because the Naeromathi notation surely wasn't a direct fit for human calculations, and it was well known that Essiel numerical expression was on another level and had to be dumbed down. Everything that reached the *Grendel's Mother* had gone through several rounds of transformation just to reduce it to a format human mathematicians could recognize. Yes, the universe was built on a certain common logic that could be expressed by numbers, but those numbers themselves were an arbitrary construct that was culturally specific.

Keen was demanding someone give her even a hint about what the Naeromathi was saying. What actually happened was that the Essiel replied and the shaken cultist said Sorteel was asking its new guests not to do it, whatever *it* was.

"An attack," Keen decided. "The Locusts hate the Architects. They've got three Arks together and they fancy their chances. Is it that simple?"

The techs seemed to think it was more than that, and all those numbers agreed with them, if only anyone could work out just what piece of deep physics was being expressed in them.

The Essiel continued to placidly fart and wave, politely requesting that the Naeromathi do no such thing, but the creature in the tank obviously felt that diplomacy had been sufficiently served, because it was slowly grinding its way out of the chamber, backing off from its host and leaving an oily residue on the pearlescent floor.

Havaer

Havaer had been trying to follow the Naeromathi business. His orders didn't touch on it, but that was only because nobody had expected three—*three!*—Locust Arks to barrel out of unspace and end up in orbit around Arc Pallator. Mordant House would likely have tacked on an addendum to his brief if that had been in anyone's long-range forecast. Except the whole thing seemed to be proceeding with glacial slowness. The Naeromathi were keeping the planet between them and the Architect, which in turn hadn't even registered their arrival as far as anybody could tell. There was definitely *something* going on between the trio of ships—exchange of transmissions and shuttles, deployment of sub-units. The Essiel had obviously registered their stately objections to whatever was going on, but more in the spirit of polite requests rather than actual commands. Their cult translator had explained at great length how Sorteel was extending some kind of courtesy to the Naeromathi, in a sort of "Well if you really *have* to then..." kind of way. Perhaps they, too, wanted to see what the Locusts would actually *do*.

In the middle of all this, when everyone with a voice and an opinion aboard the *Beagle* and the *Byron* was weighing in with their personal brand of utterly uninformed speculation, he had a message from Asset Colvari. He glanced at it, tried to catch up on Professor Storquel's current point, then froze and rechecked his in-eye display.

I have it, Colvari had sent. No more than that.

Havaer made his excuses—he wouldn't be missed; nobody much liked having a known Mordant House agent looking over their shoulder. Moreover, he strongly felt that the sum total of knowledge across the Hugh delegation was so close to zero that he himself wouldn't be missing anything.

In his quarters, the little Hiver was waiting for him.

"You sound very sure," he told them.

The light atop their barrel of a body blinked a couple of times. "We confirm that assessment. Curiously, our efforts have been facilitated by the current state of emergency. We pursued an investigatory frolic of our own, Menheer. What if your redacted records contained the key to the Naeromathi proposals your colleagues are currently cogitating?"

Their speech was, he noted, fancier than when they'd first introduced themselves. It happened, with new-instanced Hivers. They were developing a personality, though not necessarily one that would be recognizable to associates of their past instantiations. This Colvari was fond of alliteration, apparently.

If it could crack this particular nut, he wouldn't care if they gave their answers in haiku. "You're saying you know what the Locusts are about to do?"

"We aren't, alas. However, that rabbit hole directed our divinations and we have uncovered the ulterior motives you were seeking. Or, at least," they added, "if this isn't what the authors intended to obfuscate, it really should have been."

"Some move against the Naeromathi...?"

"Towards, Menheer Mundy. Or towards their way of life. Let me bring up the minutes of the meeting."

From the vast morass of procedural documentation Colvari isolated a single document, a record of a discussion between five individuals identified only by single letters. *Amateur spy stuff*, because other than that the transcript was unredacted and seemed word for word. It would be a poor agent who couldn't start making guesses at identity from that sort of content.

A meeting of five people planning for the future. He skimmed, because they'd taken their time over the discussion. There were technical specifications appended, that had been before the speakers. Ship designs, just as he'd been expecting. Except...not warships. Armed, but most definitely not dedicated line-of-battle craft. Nothing you'd throw against an Architect or a fighting vessel. Huge ships, not much short of the Locust Arks themselves for size, larger than anything human shipyards had ever put together.

Colvari flagged up where the Naeromathi references had been made, and he saw the link. The ships were big because they, too, were arks. This was a meeting between Hugh bigwigs, both government officials and powerful private individuals, and they had been planning for the return of the Architects. The idea that humanity might one day have to take the Naeromathi path and abandon planetside living had been expressed before. During the war it had become de facto truth for a large number of people, shuttled from one disaster area to the next until they found somewhere that could house them. Small wonder people had started talking about simply owning the refugee status, choosing the nomadic life, because who wanted a planet when planets were the Architects' prey?

Although the war had ended and the Architects had gone away, that idea had stuck around. Hugh had a million subcommittees, so no wonder some people were still talking about the possibility and planning for the ark future, just in case it ended up being the only future anyone was likely to have.

Which was...a bit of an anticlimax, to be honest. Nothing

he'd seen so far warranted the secrecy, the espionage, certainly not the number of dead people these documents had cost.

"There must be more than this," he told Colvari. "This is just...business as usual."

The Hiver made a very accomplished sighing noise. "Allow us to isolate the incriminating, Menheer Mundy."

That meeting must have gone on for hours. They were scrolling him past reams of pleasant conversation, trade talk and tech talk interspersed with personal chit-chat that would make identification absurdly easy. He was already putting together a picture of the room, just at first blush.

Then came the section Colvari had identified, and he stopped reading, blinking at it. Right after Speaker C had asked after Speaker D's daughter, right after B had gone on a long dry ramble about specifications and passenger complement. Not a pause, not a change of tone as they went onto the subject of war.

It wasn't the selection procedures. He'd spotted those in the mix: just how this quintet of magnates felt the berths on these arks might best be filled, should it come to that. Havaer was a realist and he knew that any project like this would have that nasty little underwriting to it. You had to make a choice, and that choice would be your own prejudices and preferences writ large. That was just how it went, and it wasn't as though they could hold a humanity-wide lottery. But no, it wasn't that.

On the basis, said D, *that humanity's future is likely to be ark-based, it is imperative that competing spacebound cultures be managed, to allow us to be competitive. And on that same basis, it would be possible to sacrifice large sections of existing infrastructure that will be surplus once the ark project is realized. For the good of humanity's future.* Havaer almost heard the murmur of polite agreement and "Hear hear" about the room.

"Competing spacebound cultures" here didn't mean the Naeromathi. They were very much looking at the Parthenon. The warrior angels had been living fleet-bound since their inception, after all. Not as ark-nomads, but Doc Parsefer hadn't had a spare habitable planet when she put them together, and after the war broke out, sitting around on something as vulnerable as a world had obviously not appealed to them. So the ark-builders proposed that their project needed precisely two major developments to drive it to reality. The re-emergence of the Architects, and war with the Parthenon. If the former happened, then it was absolutely imperative that the latter followed, rather than any inconvenient solidarity. Because if humanity was going to have a future on an ark fleet, it would thrive better if the non-ark-dwelling component could be induced to throw itself against the Partheni fleet in an orgy of mutual destruction.

Havaer continued to read between the lines with dawning horror. These five went on to comfortably describe this ark future, which would be absolutely delineated by their own choices and commands. By the end of their meeting, they had seamlessly transitioned from trying to prepare for the worst to looking forward to it. And from there to actively trying to bring it about.

Idris

Idris had retreated back to the *Vulture God*, ending up sitting on his little-used bed in the tiny box of his quarters. The sheer tension amongst the crew of the *Grendel's Mother* was wearing him out. Everyone was watching the Naeromathi trio, which had now picked up speed to come slowly round the planet towards the Architect with a ponderous inevitability. They were still emitting the occasional cryptic burst of comms, possibly keeping the Essiel up to date on whatever the hell they were doing. Nobody could decipher what they were saying. The Partheni, at least, had been unable to work out what all that maths had been trying to express and if their opposite numbers aboard the *Beagle* had got any further then they were keeping quiet about it.

Idris had felt a mounting anxiety all this while, that built and built and wasn't amenable to any rational argument. Something vast and dreadful was going to happen, and it knotted his innards, setting his augmented heart racing so hard he wondered if Trine was getting feedback.

If he wanted to, he could listen in on the brisk, purposeful talk in command, the Partheni crew charting the warp of gravitic forces as the Locust Arks lumbered about the curve of the planet. They were aiming themselves at the Architect as though all those reams of calculations boiled down to nothing more than a ramming action.

Kris put her head around the door. "Everything okay?"

"Fine, fine, I just...can't. With all the..." He waved his hand to indicate the majority of the universe. "I'm sorry."

Kris was staring at him. "You look ill."

"I feel ill. It's just the...the last few days have been." He grimaced in frustration. His mind felt all over the place, everything twisted out of true by his looming sense of dread. Not new, not precisely. He'd gone through times like this before, but this sudden onset, this rapid ramping up, these were fresh and unwelcome symptoms of the mortal condition that was Being Idris Telemmier.

"They're going crazy in command," Kris said mildly. "The Arks have deployed their whole deconstructor fleets, thousands of automata. Going to half blot out the sun for people on the surface. You should see. It's like a wave of tech unrolling towards the Architect."

"That's not it."

"What?" Kris frowned.

"That's not what they're doing." Idris forced himself to stand, despite what felt like a whole seven Gs of despair clamping him to the bed. "That's just...business as usual." Because when the Naeromathi fought, their weapons were the same host of factory ships and mining drones they used to take apart planets, brutally repurposed for war. They could turn the thousand grinding teeth of their engines on Architects or human ships with equanimity. It just didn't really accomplish much with Architects.

He saw Kris jolt at some piece of comms traffic. "The Architect's noticed them. Olli's got a screen in the drone bay. Coming?"

No. But he was. The same hand that had its claws in his gut was now dragging him along, a puppet like the crystalforms on the planet below. *It's happening.* He didn't know *what* but it most definitely was.

Olli was in her Scorpion because who knew what was about to kick off in the next few minutes. She had a soft screen pulled out to its maximum extent across one wall of the bay, showing several displays of current telemetry, plus a magnified view from the eyes of one Hegemonic orbital. The Architect, a malign crystal moon now shifting from the orbit it had held since they arrived; the Naeromathi clearing the curve of Arc Pallator, three distorted spheres forming a triangle rotating around nothing. Rotating faster.

Around *something*.

Idris staggered, clawing at Kris, who caught his elbow and held him up. He jabbed fingers at the screen, describing the motion of the Arks. Olli caught on quickly, her nod just a blur behind the reflected glare across the Scorpion's canopy.

"That has everyone shitting themselves. I mean, they're orbiting about fuck all. How's that work, eh?"

Idris tried to tell her, but no words would come past his palsying lips. Abruptly he couldn't stand at all, and Kris had to let him down to the floor. His limbs jumped and shook with sudden impulses that didn't come from him. He was part of a vast unseen web and out there, exactly equidistant between the Naeromathi ships, was the point that was being plucked.

"G-get," he managed, but his head was like a jar of marbles, shaken every second into a new configuration. The thoughts wouldn't come together. Distantly he heard Kris calling for medical assistance, but he only had eyes for the screen, for the shaky image of the Naeromathi performing their impossible dance.

They are syncing their gravitic drives, was what he would have said. He could feel it through a medium that wasn't present in real space at all. They were orbiting around an unreal mass point, generated between them in unspace. And none of that was remotely possible, or so the understood science went. Nobody had ever looked at the Naeromathi and thought "innovators."

The turning of the wheel of Arks was swifter now. Ahead

of them, the vast fleet of deconstructors was racing in a tide towards the Architect, which began destroying them. He felt each detonation as a tiny ripple at the edge of his awareness, his mind flayed open by what the Naeromathi were doing. The Architect was deploying sheer gravitic force, mustered by the vast engine of its body and directed by the scalpel precision of its intellect. Building-sized foundry vessels and asteroid miners were simply seized and reshaped by invisible hands, turned into configurations of mass more pleasant to the Architect's sense of style, and robbed of the ability to do harm. But the Nacromathi had thrown every single autonomous vessel they had into that wave, and the Architect's attention was its most limiting resource. It would take time for it to swat through that cloud of detritus to get to the Arks…

Which

Were

Unleashing.

Idris let out a hoarse scream as he felt the vast coil of artificial mass rise out of unspace, surface like a breaching whale and then become real. The spinning ring of Arks broke apart into its three components and something vast and invisible abruptly *became* in a colossal lash across the surface of the Architect.

Very, very distantly he heard Olli and Kris exclaim—shock and triumph inextricably mingled. The Architect had been struck from its orbit, the multi-billion tons of it lurching away from the planet, leaving a trail of broken shards and splinters. There were cracks the size of nations clearly visible across its surface. The Naeromathi were swinging about, coming together again, returning to their impossible revolutions as they literally spun up their new weapon.

But Idris was gasping, clawing for support, hauling himself to his feet. The dread was gone, released as the weapon loosed. He felt it grow again, but knew it for something entirely external, or at least his reaction to it. As the Naeromathi wound up unspace, so they were winding his guts. He could feel their weapon priming.

And he had felt something else, resounding on the planet below, like the skin of a drum. The Originator site had answered the retort of the weapon, sounding in his ears like a voice, or trumpets. It spoke in the echoes of its long-gone makers' voices.

"Keen!" He had to take a moment to remind himself how something as mundane and tiny as the ship-to-ship comms even worked. "Exemplar! Get me down to the planet. I have to get to the dig site, to the city!"

13.

Idris

"Absolutely not," Exemplar Keen told him. "Under no circumstances."

"Exemplar—"

"Menheer Telemmier," standing with great formality on the Colonial honorific, "I don't know if you just noticed but it's war up here, and we are already readying to break orbit."

"Exemplar, listen to me," and already he was feeling worn out with it all. Just a couple of strongly worded denials was all it took to sap him of all energy. "When the Naeromathi used their weapon, I felt it. *Here*." A vague gesture towards his head, or else the space around it, which was helpful to nobody. "But more than that, I felt the site react. Whatever just happened, the city interacted with it, even in ruins. It was speaking—*shouting*. I need to get down there, to hear what it has to say."

"This makes no sense whatsoever," Keen decided dismissively, obviously trying to keep the majority of her attention on the Naeromathi and the Architect. The three Arks were now fully into their spin again, and Idris could feel the phantom point between them come back into existence, space being twisted until the torsion extended beyond the real.

215

The Architect, meanwhile, was continuing to wade through their vast screen of drones and remote vessels, taking each and tearing it into filigreed shreds. It was a swift and methodical piece of work but the Naeromathi really had thrown everything they had at it.

"Menheer Telemmier, you'll just have to gather what you can from up here," Keen said flatly, and then, "What is it?" to another subordinate now trying to claim her attention.

"The Colonials have launched, Exemplar. A drop-shuttle from the *Beagle*."

The *Beagle*. The science vessel. Keen's eyes followed the telemetry, seeing the launch descending directly towards the ruins at the fastest safe speed. Her eyes met Idris's.

"Get to your ship," she told him. "I'll arrange an escort. Move!"

*

The Originator ruins were in utter chaos. When the *Vulture God* shuddered down beside the big Colonial shuttle, with the *Nereid* in hot pursuit, they were the only ships travelling in that direction. All the weekend pilgrims who'd come on their Last Chance To See had already evacuated, or were loading and lifting even then, the field around the new temple emptying. And yet there were people everywhere. The Essiel had sent a new commandment to the entire remaining population of the ruin-city: *Go unto the Temple*. Every part of the city was streaming with refugees, or else there were people just in mobs out in the makeshift streets, arguing or weeping or gathering their belongings.

The Naeromathi had unleashed their weapon a second

time while the *Vulture* was dropping. At least Idris'd had the foresight to ask Olli to pilot, because he'd probably have nosedived the ship into Arc Pallator's crust otherwise. He heard the voice of the city so much more clearly now, and could almost make out the words. It had never been more apparent to him that the site had a function, or once had done. And part of that purpose was expressed in the crenulations of its very shape. The ruin remembered its purpose, and the distortion of unspace awoke it, just in the moment the Naeromathi detonated their weapon.

He was trying to explain this to Trine all the way down. "If I'm down there, I'll know," he insisted, and then made a gesture intended to encapsulate the Colonial ship, already touching down. "They know. Demi's down there already. Some of the leashed Ints maybe. They felt it too."

"But know what, my dear surrogate relative?" Trine asked plaintively, and then the *Vulture* had swung wildly sideways through the tearing atmosphere, yanking them against their harnesses. For a moment, Idris thought the Colonials had fired on them, but it was worse. Olli was dodging pieces of city.

A whole district of ruins was in the air, in pieces, but the pieces were still holding to their original arrangement, as a million tons of Originator neighbourhood was plucked from the surface of the world and gathered up to the Architect. It was still trying to do its job, even as it fought the Naeromathi deconstructor fleet. And that had been the plan, surely. The Locusts had guessed at its divided attention, and used this unique opportunity when an Architect would have to remain in one place long enough for them to get to it. He wondered how long these Naeromathi had been nursing this plan.

They came down on the field near the site, the open space they'd used before. A handful of Colonial shuttles were already there, a dozen soldiers guarding it despite the flurrying locals showing absolutely no interest in getting aboard. On all sides was the panic of far too many people in the middle of relocation. But not relocation off-planet. His heart sank to see it, to hear the sound of a city-full of people lamenting, echoing back and forth across the broken walls of the dead place. *Go unto the Temple.* What would that accomplish, precisely, if the Architect did smite the world beneath it? He could hear cult hierograves exhorting people to place their faith in the mercy of the divine Essiel, to obey their commands and all would be well. It sickened him that the one thing which might save these people was the goddamn *Locusts*.

Because the Architect up there was damaged. Even with the naked eye and from the surface, he thought he could see the crazed lines the Naeromathi had put into it with two shots. And a third was on the way, as he was running for the dig site. Not that the whole city wouldn't act as the weapon's sounding board, but he *knew* this site. He had an intimate sense of it, from past inspection.

The *Nereid* came down clumsily even as he ran, slewing sideways to avoid a gaggle of cultists shoving handcarts. Myrmidons piled out, accelerators at the ready as though the Locusts might have started a land war as well, then ended up staring mutely at their opposite numbers

Solace and a dozen Partheni only caught up with him halfway to the site. Idris had never been a runner, and his legs were going to register a range of complaints the moment he let them, but in that moment he was fleetness itself.

The Colonials were just getting themselves established when he burst in. He nearly got himself shot, in fact, through sheer surprise. There were plenty of soldiers there, and a good dozen of the Voyenni shepherding their masters' Int property. Amongst them was Demi Ulo in her walker, and she gave him one strained nod.

The crystalforms were also still there, frozen in mid-step. A couple had fallen over, caught in a pose that couldn't sustain itself. Across the site, one suddenly clattered forwards on four spindly legs like a wind-up toy, before returning to still-ness.

The Voyenni were trying to clear the site of civilians. Not as hard as it sounded, given that most of the people who'd called these ruins home had already gone, knowing the place was scheduled for demolition with extreme prejudice. Now, though, there was a whole new crop of displaced cultists spilling out onto it, and the Magdans weren't being particu-larly gentle with them. Idris, braced for the next Naeromathi strike, watched furious argument break out amongst the Hugh ranks, with no less than Professor Storquel yelling up into the chest of an impassive Voyenni.

"They don't have anywhere to go!" the academic shouted. "Where do you expect them to go?"

"Anywhere but here!" the man bellowed back down at him. "Let them go to their temple, like the clams tell them!"

It was probably sacrilege, using slang-terms about the Essiel on their own world, but at that moment nobody was counting.

Storquel looked wildly around and stomped off to harangue the Hugh officer about something, but Idris could spare the drama no more of his attention.

Solace read his body language and took his arm, propping him up. Then the Naeromathi unleashed hell and he felt his mind fill with the voice of the Originators, telling him how the universe worked.

Solace

Solace caught him as he sagged. Idris's eyes were wide and there was blood on his lips where he'd bitten his tongue. Medical readouts showed his heart was still beating and he hadn't exploded any blood vessels in his brain, so she'd count that as a win. It was hard, caring about Idris. He fought battles she couldn't join him in. The sort of deaths that came for him, she couldn't stand in the way of.

There was sudden cheering from the Hugh camp, such an unexpected sound she didn't know what to do with it. Then she followed their gaze upwards, and saw the crystal moon of the Architect visibly deformed, a great bite of it torn away by the third Naeromathi strike. It appeared smaller too, because they'd knocked it out of its orbit. It was reassuring they'd swatted it that way and not the other, or everyone planetside would have had a new problem.

"Are they..." One of her sisters choked on the words. "Are they going to *kill* it?" Solace hadn't even considered that possibility, that the *Locusts*, of all creatures, might actually be the ones to lay the Architects low. There'd be some justice in that, surely. Their whole species had been on the run since before humans had made it into space. And now they had finally developed a weapon that was having a visible, potent effect against their ancient enemy.

"Idris, did you get what you need?" she asked him, trying to get him to where his own legs would support him again.

"More," he got out, spitting blood. "Solace, I . . . Everything, Solace. I understood everything. Just for a moment. Unspace. Everything."

"Idris, this isn't a field trip anymore. This is weapons research. Did you understand how the Naeromathi are *doing* that? Enough to replicate it?"

He goggled at her, as though the whole thing was a fascinating academic exercise that she was cheapening with her warmongering. "Oh *that*," he mumbled dismissively. "It's just . . . a virtual unspace engine brought into being between the Arks. Generated in the emptiness between them. It's all about the emptiness. Because that's where you can hear the echo. Like a drum. It's the space within the drum that's important." He was actually grinning at her, as though any of that made the slightest sense. "It's these ruins," he went on. "We were looking at the walls but it's all about the nothing they limit. The spaces. You just need the right arrangement of spaces."

Then all hell broke loose as the crystalforms were on the move again. Every one of them was abruptly stuttering forwards like stop-motion, a few too-fast steps, stillness, then another jerky burst of movement. One of the Hugh soldiers was brought down instantly, caught in the way of a jagged thing like a bipedal whelk before he registered it was coming for him. And it hadn't been coming for him, but it moved through where he'd been, carving him up incidentally and trampling the remains. The ruins shook.

"No!" Idris was yelling, at the sky, at the battered Architect, at the nearest crystalform. "I need that! Leave it alone!" He actually lurched towards a fluked serpentine shape as though he was going to beat at it with his little fists.

"We need to pull out from the site," one of the Myrmidons said, and Solace was already dragging Idris away. They ended up elbow to elbow with the Hugh contingent, Storquel still vociferously arguing with the soldiers about something. "They're still humans!" he was insisting. "They're still our people."

The ground shifted beneath them. Solace heard the grinding of vast planes of stone, the entire district working itself loose of the earth.

She started running, hauling Idris along with her. A brief check showed Kris and Olli ahead, the latter loping along easily in her Scorpion.

Someone cannoned into her: one of the Voyenni. An accident. Perhaps not an accident, though that thought would only come to her later. She caught herself on one knee, the impact sharp through her armour, shielding Idris from the ground.

"Here they go!" he got out. She'd lost track of what he was saying and didn't realize what he meant.

She had got to her feet, at the back of the pack now, when the ground leapt.

Leapt *up*.

Ahead of her she saw a Hugh soldier grab Demi Ulo out of her walker, just lift her straight out and then jump desperately forwards, vanishing over an edge that hadn't been there a moment ago. The abandoned walker skittered three more steps and toppled after them.

Solace ran on, still hauling Idris. Around her, the component sections of this district of the ruin were separating from one another, gaps of metres opening up between each block, and yet the whole retaining its alignment.

She looked down, seeing the ground recede. The Architect was calling the city home and Idris was about to get a fatal lesson in how the universe worked.

In her ear the single word: *"Jump."*

It was Olli. Not necessarily the person she'd most trust her life to, but she was a soldier, and right then that sounded like an order.

She gathered Idris to her, clasping him tightly with the suit's secondary limbs, and leapt from the swiftly rising blocks. She guessed they'd already hit a hundred metres up.

The armour had some shock compensators, so she might survive. No chance Idris would share the same privilege. Still, she tried to curl herself around him in a way that might help. She found herself looking up at the crippled Architect, seeing the pieces of city vanish away into its vastness, whisked into oblivion even as the Naeromathi struck it again. Idris cried out, not from fear but wonder.

Then something caught her by the shoulders and shook her like a dog, yanking her sideways, cannibalizing her downward momentum so that the pair of them were whirling in an untidy spiral. Olli was projecting an a-grav field remotely from the *Vulture God*, which was just a block away. Solace's suit had grav-handles that allowed her to fly in an artificial field. Right now she had no control over it whatsoever, and Olli wasn't exactly being gentle, but she'd take that over breaking herself on the unforgiving ground.

Even as they touched down, she heard Keen over the comms. "Solace, time to go. Enemy reinforcements inbound. Get to the ships any way you can."

She looked around for the Colonials, but they didn't seem to be mounting any sort of offensive action. Her helmet display was highlighting areas all around her in red. Everywhere there were cultists running, hauling bags, hauling children, a tide of them heading for the Temple and eddies of them breaking away. Everyone was pointing and staring upwards. Nobody was cheering.

The Naeromathi...? The Locusts were battling on up there in orbit. Even as she tried to find them, the ground shook and she was off her feet again. The air was full of dust. *Bombardment.* She couldn't work out what was happening, and just hunched herself over Idris, who seemed to be trying to tell her what was going on, only he wasn't using comms and any actual sound was being overwritten by the rapid concussions all around them. Grit and shards rattled against her armour, scouring the surface.

"Solace, get back here!" came from Olli on the ship. "Solace, you mad bitch, are you even...?"

"Here, I'm here!" She wasn't sure where here was, though, because the map of the city had just lost a piece. Then she looked around and felt her heart skip to her mouth.

"Will get to you soon as," was all she could garble out. All those red-highlit areas had been impact points. But not bombs. The Architect had sent down a new crew of crystal-forms and Solace, along with Idris, was right in the heart of them. The entire district between them and the *Vulture God* was up for demolition.

"Olli," she said. "Going to need you to lift us out of here."

"Working on it." Solace braced herself for the yank upwards, the hurtling, uncontrolled jump that would see them out of this doomed neighbourhood and back into the ship. When it came, though, she went spilling sideways, losing her hold on Idris, and ramming painfully into a leaning wall that was already shifting like a loose tooth.

"Olli, what?"

"I...can't." The voice came to her glitchily over comms, sudden static pulsing and ebbing in rhythms that sounded almost like speech. "I'm trying but I can't...the field to you."

Idris was now standing under his own power, but he was in the midst of the crystalforms. Even though they paid him no heed, they wouldn't detour around him either. Each one was motoring busily on its puppet course, the earth around it exploding away as it carved down to the bare structure of the ruin, the Architect's unfathomable mind dividing it up. *It's bloody determined to get the job done, even with the Naeromathi hammering it.* She saw flashes and glints in the air, the sunlight striking more shards of crystal as they were hammered down into the ruin like pitons. *Seeking purchase. Going to tear the whole place up...*

And then the planet.

She dodged around a lumbering form, which looked like a triangular shell with waving, translucent tentacles, and tried to pull Idris to safety. Another fleet faceted shape danced between them, shearing the outermost layer off her gauntleted fingertips, so surgical-keen she didn't feel an impact. "Idris!" she howled at him and he looked around almost beatifically.

"I understand!" He was a man experiencing a revelation but she had the sick feeling it would be useless, something he just wouldn't be able to articulate. Being clear and inform- ative about things wasn't an Idris strength at the best of times.

It wasn't a shadow that then fell across him. The huge crystalform had the sun behind it, the refracted light giving the Int a full-body halo: Saint Idris, patron of incomprehensible truths. It lumbered towards him, a vast hunch of body, ten or more stump legs rippling in a wave. A low, jutting head with horns and antennae and a forest of jagged crystal hands reached for him. Idris arched backwards, almost falling—she guessed the Naeromathi had fired again, lancing him with an unintended spike of understanding that nailed him to the ground.

She had her accelerator in hand, but unloading it on the crystalform would accomplish nothing save prompt retaliation. Instead she just ran. Into its path and the scouring storm of displaced grit it was throwing up. She spread an arm wide, around Idris, feeling his chest hit the crook of her elbow. The crystalform became a rainbow filter eclipsing the whole sky.

There was a savage, shearing wrench from knee to ankle as she clipped the edge of its gravitic force. She was flung, spinning around and around with Idris, trying to connect to the *Vulture*'s own field to stop herself, but finding nothing to gain purchase on. She'd lost the gun. Idris was now tucked into the curve of her body, the cage of her limbs, and she directed the suit to lock every joint, rigid as possible, so as not to crush him the moment she hit a wall.

She crashed into a crystalform instead, ramming it with forehead, elbows and knees, feeling a jolt of pain lash through her and then take up permanent residence in the leg that had already been mauled. The thing looked down at her, and she had a brief moment of seeing an arrowhead beak, a clutch of stalked eyes, one of them broken away by the impact and now regrowing. It had six limbs, and the foremost were huge scythe-ended hooks. Of course they were. Where were all the nice, harmless species the Architects had obliterated?

Every part of her hurt. Idris had a bloody scalp and probably a host of secondary bruises, but he looked whole. Awake, in fact, and gazing up at the crystalform, extending a hand towards it.

Do not touch the exhibits. The phrase rattled around her head. She lurched to her feet, unloading her suit's painkiller reservoir into her veins and overriding its medical alerts. She could hear stuttering fragments of comms as Olli tried to speak to her, nothing that made sense. She had to get out of the area before it was torn up and flung into space.

Then the crystalform changed.

Despite everything, despite the screaming of lost cultists, the roar of the 'forms at work, the continued bombardment of the city, she stared. It shifted, the facets and edges flowing like glittering liquid, translucent mercury. It shrank, shedding mass so that lumps of inert clear rock scattered to the ground around it. Then it lost limbs, until it had only four, two to stand on, two to hang limply by its side, as though it had never heard of arms before. It had a head; the head had a face, or faces. She didn't know most of them. There was Saint Xavienne, for a moment, and Rollo Rostand, late captain of the *Vulture*, even Solace herself. But in the end the human form revealed before them was slighter, the substance peeling away as it pared itself down to become Idris himself, reproduced in crystal.

Idris made a choking sound, and Solace echoed it. She saw the thing's lips part, as though it too needed to express human shock.

Then the ground shuddered and there was no time. Someone was shouting, a real voice, here and now and not the tortured comms. Solace turned and saw the Tothiat, Emmaneth.

She—it? they?—was beckoning them, yelling for them to come on, and the path looked halfway clear. Solace forced herself into motion, hauling Idris after her in a staggering lurch, seeing all the red telltale alerts in her helmet try to explain how much new damage she was doing to herself.

And it got worse, as she was unceremoniously dragged to a halt. Idris was trying to pull back, successfully. She didn't think he had the sheer muscle mass for it.

But he didn't. Turning, she saw that actually the crystal Idris had hold of one of his wrists. The human face, that familiar mask, was writhing with failed expressions but Idris had its attention.

She missed the gun then, because she could have used it to shear the thing's hand off at the wrist and risked the repercussions. As it was, she had to go at it with her fingers, trying to prise it away and bitterly aware that she would have had an easier job just tearing Idris's arm off at the elbow. They could grow him another one, after all, but they couldn't grow another *him*. Then Emmaneth was at her side, a jagged chunk of rubble in her hands—no, it was a piece of discarded crystal from the thing's transformation. With a shriek, the Tothiat brought her makeshift weapon down on the crystal-form's elbow. The force of the impact shattered everything— shard, elbow and a rippling shockwave that looked as if it had broken every bone in both Emmaneth's arms.

The crystal Idris-face found recognizable human anger for just a moment. Its remaining arm lashed out, elongating, shifting into a blade that tore through Emmaneth's torso in a spray of blood and alien ichor and pieces of bone.

Solace had Idris again, though, albeit with the crystal hand still around his wrist like a particularly gauche bracelet. She hauled him away, running with him, then just hoisted him over her shoulder, swerving away from the destructive course of a tripedal crystalform, and out into a section of ruin not yet under demolition. Her medical telltales were warning her in red letters about the damage she was doing to her leg but between the drugs and her suit's servos it was a bill she could pick up later.

Emmaneth caught up beside her, heaving for breath even as her lungs pieced themselves back together inside her reforming ribcage. Bile came to Solace's mouth—no amount of battlefields could inure you to that kind of anatomy lesson.

"Olli?"

Nothing but static and chopped syllables. There was no sign of the *Vulture God* in the sky above. Solace tried to access *Grendel's Mother* but got even less, and made a best guess at direction.

"Going for the ship," she told Emmaneth, now mostly intact again save for where her skin was still zipping itself together. The world shook around them as more crystal missiles lanced down from the . . .

The thought drew her eyes upwards, expecting to see the mauled half-sphere vomiting out its last servitors, even as the Naeromathi continued to pummel it. But while she'd been dodging its minions, the battlefield up there had changed.

Four jagged moons now hung in Arc Pallator's sky, all of them launching a constant barrage of crystal lances down at the planet. The wounded Architect had called for help, and it had arrived.

14.

Solace

The sight struck her hard enough that when she heard Emmaneth say, "Where is your ship?" it was obvious she'd had to ask at least twice.

"I..." Solace tried to link to the *Vulture* again. The air above swirled with dust—another barrage of crystal spears was lancing down into some part of the city even now. She couldn't see any ships in the air, and the Architects were hazed with scintillating haloes as the sun refracted off their facets. She couldn't see the Locust Arks at all.

There was a brief moment of distant yelling in her ear, recognizable as Olli, though she couldn't make out whatever was being said. Then a great wave of people was rushing towards them, a mob running as fast as they could: children and the infirm, with a few meagre possessions slung over shoulders or clasped to chests. The lances of crystal had displaced or diverted a big stream of refugees, and now everyone understood that the planet's death sentence had been moved up, not commuted at all.

"Olli?" Solace tried again desperately. She had a second and a half of Olli talking to someone else, Kit or Kris, arguing something technical, then static. The crowd reached them and she found herself having to run with them, an arm supporting Idris, to avoid being trampled. There was a moment when Emmaneth was beside them, then the Tothiat wasn't there, cut off or run down or just shunted into some other alley.

She diverted more power to her locator beacon, because it was going to be up to someone to find her and Idris right now. There was no chance they could make the landing field, even if the ships were still there. She had no map data whatsoever, no idea where they were or even which direction they were facing. And the whole city, the great sprawling ruin of the Originators' works, was moving underfoot, shifting and shuddering as the Architects' servants carved it up.

Idris whooped and convulsed under her hand, trying to drop to his knees so that she almost wrenched his arm from its socket. The crowd around her was exclaiming, and she couldn't work out why until she glanced up and saw that the first Architect, the original, was coming apart. The Naeromathi had loosed their weapon again, and now a clear third of the vast monster had broken away, falling gracefully and fragmenting, scattering towards the planet's surface. The rest visibly receded, revolving unevenly around the absence.

Ahead, the crowd was dividing about a leaning spur of ruin that rose in uneven steps, pointing dramatically at what was currently the least interesting quadrant of sky. Solace gathered Idris closer, took three long steps and leapt, using all her suit's augmentation to clear the heads of her neighbours and vault up to it. Now out of immediate trample danger, she sagged back, looking up at the carnage. The air was clear enough that she thought she saw a meteor-glitter of silvery dust, which might have been the Naeromathi servitor fleet charging to its doom. She could make out the crescents of reflected sunlight that were the Arks, and as she watched, abruptly there were two, not three.

She had no idea how many Naeromathi were on an Ark, but the fact people called it an Ark suggested the number was high. And as nomadic creatures, it wasn't as though they had places they could readily offload their surplus population to. She felt sick, and also incredulous, because of all the species she never thought she'd feel sympathy for, the Naeromathi came right after Architects on that list.

Then Olli was in her ear, shouting as though that would cut through the distance and interference. "—hear me, you deaf Patho bitch?"

"Olli!"

"Fuck me," came the acid voice in reply, and no less welcome for that. "Kit's boosting the signal but no fucking idea how long for. Got your locator. People on their way. Stay put."

"Can do," Solace confirmed. "You're in the air?"

"*Nereid* is." Olli's voice shook for a moment. "Solace, I am currently splitting my brain between all four of my repair drones because one of those stone fuckers decided to take out our reaction drives when it dropped by to visit. And then just carved its way out the quickest way. So we have a maintenance issue right about now. So the rescue goes to your lot. Stay put, you got me?"

"Olli, I'm not sure how long you've got to fix that problem," Solace said with what she felt was admirable steadiness. "You may need to get on the *Nereid*."

"This is my ship. I can fix her. I can get her away with just gravitics if I need. We still have that." And there was no room for argument in Olli's voice. "Told Kit and Kris they may need to beg berths though."

"Olli—"

"Shut the fuck up. 'Sides, our lot are still here too. When they bug out we can have this conversation again."

"The Colonials?"

"Our lot, like I said. Taking on extra passengers, cramming the crates out."

"What?" Solace was searching the skies, using every filter on her visor to cut through the new flurries of dust. Was that a shape, off across the ruin's broken horizon? The *Nereid*?

"Whole bunch of faithful lost their faith when their professor-type announced they could get a ride off-planet. Hugh just dumped a million Largesse-worth of kit to get more in. Big humanitarian effort. We'd do the same only... well...not sure we're going places just yet," sounding more and more strained. Solace couldn't imagine what it was like to be Olli right then, supervising all the urgent repairs at once.

Then she received a new signal, just a ping responding to her locator, and a wedge of four Myrmidons shunted through the crowd and climbed up to join her and Idris. She recognized some of the original bodyguard detail that had gone with her to the site.

"Mother," one of them got out. They looked battered and scuffed, but whole. Below, the crowd was abating, receding towards the Temple.

"Report."

"Contact with the *Nereid*. She's homing on us, but locator contact is intermittent." They hunched about her miserably like armoured crows, only just enough space for them on the spur. "Is he all right, Mother?"

Solace looked to Idris, who seemed to be suffering more from a surfeit of wonder than anything medical. His face, turned to the sky, was racked with an agony almost religious in its scope.

"Idris?" she prompted.

"I can feel them," he told her helpfully.

"The Architects?"

"All of them." His voice was a whisper over comms. "A dialogue between the ground and the sky. The ruins amplify it. I hear every ship die up there."

Her stomach lurched, but her mind was thinking of utility. "Will you know when the Architects are ready to turn this planet into bad art?"

"Yes."

"That's s—" And then a new comms channel opened: the *Nereid*.

"Myrmidon Executor Solace, we have eyes on you. We're coming in before we lose signal. Stay put."

"We're not going anywhere," Solace confirmed grimly. She hoped it was true. The dust was up again, and she could feel the ruins shuddering with impacts. A moment later there was a jagged scream of static in her ear.

"*Nereid?*" she tried, and got nothing. One of the Myrmidons was butting in, pointing. There was abruptly some purposeful movement beyond their spur, closing on them. Crystalforms had now reached this district and were disassembling it. The air was clearing. Beyond the nearest walls she saw...

A city in flight. A vast rising assemblage of blocks and walls and floating child's bricks that must have been half the city. She felt that with a run-up she could have just leapt from block to block all the way from ground to orbit. They were taking it all away, ridding the planet of the Originator taint before they reshaped it.

"*Nereid!*" she tried, and for a moment had an open channel.

"Can't reach you—bombardment from the Architects—still trying." And then another voice, breaking in. "Mother, targets have been sighted closing on you."

"Crystals, I know," Solace replied.

"Human targets. Armed. Hostile," the speaker rattled off, then fell away into the sea of interference.

Solace was halfway into requesting clarification when the shooting started.

One of her sisters was cut down straight away, accelerator fire punching through her armour. Solace snatched up her weapon and then they were piling off the spur, weaving for cover. Idris was given all the shelter they could spare as they bundled behind a wall.

"Eyes?" Solace barked out. Nobody had been given a decent view of who they were up against, although the list of suspects was notably short.

Another scatter of shot ricocheted from the walls nearby, leaving barely a scar. Solace's subconscious performed some quick calculations and came up with a rough idea of direction.

She dearly wanted to lead them in a proper hunt, but that wasn't on the cards with Idris here. Still, they would need a break to get him away. She turned her locator beacon off and told one of the others to do the same. "You two, get him away," signalling a direction and path with one hand. "We'll rejoin you. Prêt à combattre?"

"Prêt, Mother."

Solace gave herself two breaths' count and then launched out, shooting towards her best guess at the enemy. They were not only there but closer than she'd reckoned. The lead Voyenni snapped backwards, his chest sheared half-through by a trail of accelerator shot. *Fucking Voyenni, don't they know the planet's about to be destroyed?* But that was what the little business with the punitive beating had been for, to show her the idiot loyalty of these thugs. And apparently this planet-scale chaos was just the excuse they'd been waiting for to come at her.

Hopefully they were trying to take Idris alive, but she reckoned they'd kill him before they let the Parthenon get away with him.

She saw a good half-dozen of them at least, and the air buzzed briefly with return fire as she and her fellow Myrmidon got behind their next cover. Her tracker showed her locators receding as the others got Idris away, but most likely the Voyenni were picking up the same signal.

She risked a look—the dust was up again, but she thought she saw movement. She gave a terse brief to her companion and then they were out of cover, dodging to the next shelter, shooting.

The Voyenni were ready, but the dust and general inter-ference was screwing with all sorts of targeting, from her helmet display all the way down to basic vision. She didn't think she'd got any of them; on the plus side they hadn't got her, and hopefully she'd delayed them.

Then the crab-hand turned up. It was a crowd-control vehicle used across the Colonies, a tall turret mounted on five legs that moved in exactly the unpleasant way its name suggested. The gunner up top had a big accelerator cannon and abruptly the world was full of shot.

A round lanced through Solace's shoulderguard—through her shoulder as well, she realized a moment later, but she was already pumped past safe tolerance with her suit's entire stock of painkillers and adrenaline substitutes. Her second was dragging her into cover even as she returned fire. Her aim was dead on but her helmet display reported nothing but deviation, meaning the crab-hand obviously had some kind of small-scale gravitic shield. Nothing but a determined fusillade was going to get through to it.

She wanted to just march up to the stupid bastards and shout in their faces about common enemies and there being a time and place to enact this kind of nonsense, but it was abundantly clear they didn't care.

A stuttering burst of comms came through. The *Nereid*, closing on her. *Time to run.*

She gave the assembled Voyenni all the free ammo in her gun's magazine, meaning she was down to cannibalizing mass if she wanted to shoot any more. It gave them something to think about, though, and then she was running, trying not to think about the damage she was doing to the various injured parts of her body. *Time enough for healing when I'm safe or dead.*

The ground ahead lit up red in random patches. For a moment she couldn't even remember what that meant on her display. In the next she did and was skidding to a halt. That would be all the chance the Voyenni needed, though. So she set off again, doubling her speed and just sprinting through all the projected impact points like a fool through a minefield.

The first crystalform struck close by while she and her second were only halfway across the contested ground, and she knew she'd made a terrible tactical decision. This once, though, brute chance came through for her, and the pair of them were staggering past the last of the marks even as the ground jumped beneath them with each new missile. A glance through her helmet's rear camera showed her a field of unfolding crystal shapes, all the monsters from the Architects' mausoleum getting down to work demolishing the ruins. The Voyenni were on the far side of it, she could only hope.

They fled for the locator beacon, her second at her heels, calling for the *Nereid*. Abruptly there was a greater shadow overhead through the dust—that was too thick to see even the Architects now. Only broken comms, but she turned her own locator on, seeing the familiar segmented outline of a Partheni hull.

The *Nereid* dipped low; low enough that when the accelerator cannon loosed, she saw the missiles tear through the ship's side, sending it canting crazily off and up. The crab-hand, or another crab-hand, came stilting out of the dust-storm, gun tilted upwards as it tried to track the Partheni ship. Return fire lashed across the ruins nearby, but without reliable targeting the *Nereid* was shooting blind.

The lurching shadow of a second or third crab-hand was on the far side of Solace and she turned her locator back off. It had them spotted, though, blazing away to kill them with sheer quantity of shot. The original aim was too high but the gunner just drew down the curtain of fire, knowing he'd catch them eventually.

Solace ran, still trying to raise *Nereid* but getting nothing, not even sure how badly the ship had been cut up. A moment later something struck her hard in the side, sending her tumbling against a jagged section of wall.

Shot? No new damage was registering on her displays. She saw the body of her second a moment later, sprawled where the accelerator fire had found her, after she'd shoved her superior out of harm's way. Solace felt a sick jolt, then banished it. She was becoming increasingly sure that she wasn't getting out of this one.

She took stock: the nearest crab-hand highstepping its way towards her; the better sections of ruined wall; the crystal-forms busy carving into their foundations to free them from the planet's hold. Not close to where Idris and the rest of her squad were, not yet.

Then she ran, shooting as she did so. Nothing got through the vehicle's shield and its gunner lazily tracked her, his shot skipping dust at her heels even as she darted behind the next piece of wall big enough to hide her. His trailing line of shot rattled harmlessly across the wall too, and sheared an arm from a hulking crystalform that was trying to excavate it. The thing paused, and Solace could see its blunt stub of a head, as featureless as a thumb, looking down at the lost limb as though puzzled.

Then it turned and exploded in missiles at the crab-hand. The whole front of the thing became a blizzard of razor-edged shards launching at the Voyenni vehicle. She saw the first few deflected by the shield, spinning away in a corus-cating cloud, but then they were through, shredding the metal, rupturing the reactor in a white-orange crack of instant cooling. The brief red bursts of the crew were more an anticlimax than anything else.

She called for the *Nereid* again, but got someone else instead.

"Did you turn your locator off, you dumbass bitch?"

"Olli?" This was the closed Parthenon channel but then Olli was a resourceful little monster.

"Where the fuck are you? Shopping or something?"

"You're in the air?"

"Fuck yes."

"Home in on these signals." She gave the locators of the other Myrmidons, and Idris. "Get them aboard. I'll try to make it there too. If not, then so."

"What's that even supposed to mean?" Olli demanded.

Solace broke cover and ran for it, pushing body and suit as far as they could go, shutting off the host of medical and technical warnings that swarmed the edges of her display. No shot pursued her, and she hoped that was a good thing.

"I got it," Olli told her, when she tried to reply. "Stupid Patho way of saying it, is all. Tell your bitches to get high, Solace. I am not firing on all cylinders right now. *Vulture's* seen better days."

"That was true forty years ago," Solace snapped back, passing on the message to the other Myrmidons.

"Fuck you too." But that was Olli being fond, or as fond as she got, and then, "God."

"What?" Solace demanded, because in that one word was a world of horror and awe she hadn't known the woman was capable of.

"That's the last Ark gone," Olli got out, voice shaking. "All of them. Those poor bastards. And you're running out of city, Solace, they're...God, they're...Fuck me, it's all just...lifting out. I never saw..."

"Mind on the job, Olli!"

"Yeah, yeah, it's just..." Too dumbfounded even to swear at her.

Then she was in sight of the others, who were five metres up a spiralling stair that went nowhere, and besieged.

Morzarin Uskaro must have deployed his entire complement of Voyenni on this gambit, she guessed. The other crab-hand was here, plus four men and two dead bottle-green bodies. One of her fellow Myrmidons was sprawled on the canted ground as well, and Solace got a brief burst of flatlined vitals from her suit. The other was up high, sheltering from incoming fire as best she could with Idris behind her. The unmounted Voyenni were climbing towards her, alternately firing and moving so she had no chance to pick them off.

All the corpses jumped in horrible unison, sliding a foot to the left as the whole city shifted.

Solace had this one single moment to make a difference and she burned through the accelerator's mass reservoir as though there was no tomorrow. She raked the crab-hand, hoping to hit something vital, driving a scatter of holes through it before the crew could bring its shields round. Then she was on to the climbers, and she got two before the answering shot forced her back into cover.

"Any time, Olli!"

"Incoming!"

But then the remaining two Voyenni had reached the top of the spiral and it was down to knives and fists. Solace popped up, aiming, trying for a clear shot. She had one man in her sights, targeting display jumping and glitching from the sheer *Architecting* going on. The ground beneath her juddered and bounced as more crystalforms impacted nearby.

She lost her aim again as the ground shifted further, slanting another five degrees. The same lurch saved her life, though. Accelerator rounds tore through her shoulder, carving the armour as though it wasn't there, making a bone-jagged mess of the joint. It could very easily have been chest, heart and lungs. The physical impact knocked her onto her back, but the pain blockers were still doing valiant work and she forced herself up onto her knees, gun still clutched one-handed.

She saw one Voyenni bodily hoist the Myrmidon up and then cast her down to the ground five metres below. The other then leant over, shooting at the body even as it fell, riddling it as it lay there. More dead lines reported to Solace's dying visor display.

Idris tried to fight them, she'd give him that. He kicked one, shoved the other, trying to topple the man off the edge. He got lazily backhanded for his pains, and then they had him between them, dragging him kicking and screaming down the spiral. She tried to shoot, but the crab-hand was staggering over, dragging one dead leg, chewing about the edges of her cover with its accelerator cannon. Only the absurd impermeability of Originator walls saved her, but she couldn't save Idris.

She lay there, unable to move an inch either way without losing more body parts. The pain was starting to come through, like an insistent caller who won't stop knocking and sending comms requests. She kept fumbling the accelerator, even though it wasn't that heavy. Shock, she guessed, working at a mostly subconscious level to sabotage her body just when she needed it most.

The crab-hand looked over her cover, peering past the angled wall with the air of an interested beneficiary at a deathbed. She saw the cannon tilt down towards her and tried to return the favour, but the accelerator just slipped from her numb fingers.

In that drawn-out moment, as the crab-hand gunner struggled with something as elementary as elevation, the city lifting away on all sides as though it was all just theatre backdrop being removed, she fought for comms, for last words, for anything.

The world turned white. She thought it was death, then she thought it was the Architects, remaking. Or the Originators, returned from their long-dust graves to come save everything, to usher in a new age of something, to...

Someone was pulling her by her already-mangled ankle, and by her better shoulder, save that they were dragging the ruined shoulder along the ground. She had no struggle in her but she fought anyway, making their lives as difficult as possible until her comms finally gave her Kit and Kris shouting at her not to be so goddamn awkward. The slope they were hauling her up was the ramp of the *Vulture God* and soon Olli was acidly pointing out that she'd "said 'get high,' not just lie about on the ground being shot." The white flash that still had her blind had been the *God*'s laser, shearing through most of the crab-hand and its crew and burning up a fair amount of atmosphere too.

"Idris!" she shouted over the lot of them. "They took Idris."

"Fuck," Olli said, and then, "We'll circle. We'll find them. But, sister, this whole fucking planet is coming apart."

It was, and it did. And they didn't find Idris.

Idris

The Voyenni were like iron. Idris had no idea what they did on Magda to train these brutes into this degree of loyalty. He couldn't possibly imagine staying around in this disintegrating city, on this doomed world, for something as trivial as getting your hands on Idris Telemmier.

But their bloody-mindedness had paid off because here he was and here were their hands, most definitely on him. They were hauling him through the city, running full tilt and hoisting him between them so his poor weak legs didn't have the chance to slow them down. All around them…

He didn't even have to look, because his mind was wide open and every piece of the sliding block puzzle that had been the city was known to him. He looked anyway. It was flying away, like a dream or a surrealist painting. The whole city. His escorts were constantly changing direction, exchanging curt words, trying to find a way to wherever the hell they needed to get to. A Magdan ship was possibly going to swoop in and pick them up any moment. If not, Idris strongly suspected all their stoicism and loyalty would buy them nothing more than supporting roles in a planetary mass grave.

He tried his comms but got nothing, and didn't know if his escort was blocking him or if it was just the electromagnetic chaos of what was going on around him.

A pause. He thought they were conferring about directions. *Have you tried asking a local?* But no, they were tensing. *Solace. Solace has found me.* He craned about, looking for her Partheni armour. There was a single figure standing right ahead of them, certainly, but it wasn't Solace. A woman, dressed in shabby spacer clothes.

They shot her. Idris had some sympathy because there wasn't really time for complexities at that moment. They shot her and marched him forward, over her fallen body, only her body turned out not to be dead. The woman grabbed one of their ankles in each hand and vaulted from lying to standing in one spasmodic leap, throwing the two Voyenni end over end, and Idris with them. He landed hard, breath slapped out of him, seeing one of her arms and her back, her actual *spine*, realign and mend from the colossal strain she'd just put them under. She was grinning.

Tothiat. He couldn't see the symbiote from his perspective but he recognized the way she'd healed.

One of the Voyenni shot her once more and she walked up the line of his fire, literally shrugging off the holes he made in her, until she could tear the gun from his hands. He was technically stronger, but that strength was limited by his inability to just wreck his human bones and muscles, while she didn't need to care about that. She hit him with the gun so hard that gun and skull and one of her shoulders shattered. Only one of those things came back together again a moment later.

The other Voyenni knifed her. They were game, these Magdan boys. He'd seen how the little holes of an accelerator hadn't stopped her, and so now he carved her up like a butcher, aiming for enough damage across the board to bring her down, hunting through her abdomen for something that might count as a weak spot. She gripped his head with both hands and broke his neck.

Then she turned to Idris, hideously bloody, winching her innards back into place by some mechanism he didn't even want to guess at. Just like the Voyenni, she wasn't keen for him to have much of a say in where they went. He was hoisted up and over her shoulder, his cheek pressed against the cool, hair-prickly legs of the Tothir symbiote where it lay along the centre of her back. He shuddered and tried to writhe away but there was no getting out of her grip. She started running, juggling him about so that he ended up clinging tighter rather than trying to get away, just to stop himself being slammed into the ridges and articulations of the creature. He had no idea where they were going, just hung on grimly until she came to an abrupt stop.

She dropped him, and he saw humanity surrounding them. Adults and children, all in some pretence at red robes, with gold and purple trimmings. He had been thrust into a vast mob of cultists, everyone crammed into a single square bounded by pillars, open to the sky.

The four Architects hung in that sky like the end of days, one of them a mauled ruin that was breaking apart even as he watched, bleeding out millions of tons of crystal detritus as it died. At least the Naeromathi had accomplished that.

He tried to get to his feet, and the Tothiat actually helped him. "The city—" he got out. "How long?" *Maybe they can still get to me here?* There was no comms contact, and now he knew he was being blocked.

"It's gone, Menheer Telemmier," the Tothiat woman told him. "All of it."

He looked around the crowded confines of the Temple. Most of the cultist refugees seemed weirdly calm. Many were kneeling in what he assumed was prayer. He heard the voices of hierograves scattered through them, promising that their masters would save them.

"We need to get off-planet. Let me call my ship," he begged, but the Tothiat only smiled.

"Menheer," she said. "Have you no faith?" And a smile that could only have been nine parts insane.

15.

Kris

When the last piece of city lifted from the surface, the *Vulture God* finally gave up the search. Clawing for space, it shuddered its course out of atmosphere lest it be caught in the Architects' gravitic fist and reshaped into oblivion along with the world below. The *Nereid* was already ahead of them, as were a couple of last-minute cult tourist transports and the last pair of Colonial heavy shuttles. True to its name, the *Vulture* was last to abandon the corpse of Arc Pallator.

Kris, who'd been manning the sensor suite, found herself magnifying and magnifying, staring down at the corrugated scar in the earth that had once been the largest Originator site any human had ever seen. Not a city, not anything comprehensible, and now not even a ruin. And Idris had vanished into it, snatched by the Voyenni. Solace had confirmed that much. Right now she was in a suspension pod, with Trine shooting her full of whatever med stocks the *Vulture* hadn't run out of. Kris had hauled her in, seeing the Partheni armour turned to jigsaw shards across her shoulder and one leg from ankle to knee. Readouts showed multiple broken bones, torn muscles and so much lost blood that only the suit's emergency procedures had saved her. Nobody could say she hadn't given her all, but it hadn't been enough.

Don't be down there, was all she could think. The Voyenni had gone to some lengths to take him alive, after all. He was a valuable commodity, almost the last of a dying breed. They were sure to have him on one of the shuttles. He'd still be alive, even a prisoner, even a slave. There was hope. They'd get him back.

"Questions arise re course correction!" Kittering rattled out.

"I'm going to buzz the shuttles," Olli told him flatly. "I want you and...fuck. Kris, take the helm from me. I'm suiting up in the Scorpion. We are fucking boarding that shuttle. Or one of those shuttles. I am getting Idris back."

"You don't even know which shuttle he's on," Kris objected.

"Fifty-fifty chance, isn't it. Take the damn *helm*, Kris."

"I can't fly the *Vulture*, Olli," she said, even as she was transferring pilot functions over to her station. Not optimal but it would work. "Especially under the nose of a Hugh *warship* while you try to play pirate with one of their shuttles."

"They're not going to shoot us while we're clamped to their baby."

"Olli, that's not how military targeting works." Kris had control now, evidenced by the abrupt lurch as she overcorrected their course. "Kit, help," because he was a better pilot than she was.

"Kit's coming with me to get Idris," Olli decided.

"Objections raised on all sides!" Kittering responded hotly, followed by a burst of chittering that didn't get translated.

"No, no, we are fucking *doing* this. Rollo would have."

"Doing this is what got Rollo *killed*!" Kris shouted at her. The silence that followed was filled with terrible possibilities.

"If I might interrupt, my unruly cohorts," Trine's voice broke in, "but matters have been taken out of our collective manipulators. Pick up comms, *Grendel's Mother* to *Byron*."

Because of course the Partheni had been following what had gone on, and they weren't taking the loss of their solitary Int well.

"... An ultimatum, in short," came Exemplar Keen's voice, in her accented Colvul. "You will divert your shuttle containing Idris Telemmier, who is under the protection of the Parthenon. As you know. He will be taken aboard the *Nereid*. No more needs to be said or done. If you do not repatriate Menheer Telemmier, that is an act of war."

Then the voice of Mannec, the diplomat, came in reply. "Exemplar, we all feel for your loss. I have been speaking with the shuttle crews. Menheer Telemmier is not aboard, I am assured. The shuttles are loaded with Hegemonics who agreed to flee the planet at our invitation, together with the last of our own ground teams. I can show you images from the holds, even, if you—"

"Menheer Mannec," Keen snapped back, and Kris imagined the woman leaning over her displays, face lit with fury. "My own *surviving* personnel confirm that individuals in the livery of Morzarin Uskaro killed four of my people and snatched Telemmier. I not only want Telemmier back in our control, but I will have Uskaro and his people delivered up to me, or I will—" and she bit down on what she would do. Kris was shaken, because Keen had always seemed, well, *keen*, but surely that icy Partheni professionalism was rock solid, reliable even to the end of the world. But here they were with the world below them ending, and Keen was white hot with anger. Her voice only honed itself to an edge, but Kris could hear the rage driving that knife in.

"Exemplar," Mannec came back, the voice of reason but she could hear the strain. "Please, please do not say or do anything that might look regrettable in a less...fraught moment. We have not taken Telemmier. I have spoken to the shuttle crews myself. Please, just...If you wish, I will take a shuttle myself, come to the *Grendel's Mother* and tell you all this to your face. As a gesture of our sincerity on this point. Would that help, Exemplar? Because...one look outside should tell you that nobody should be talking about any other war except the obvious one."

Kris checked on the Architects. The dying one was still breaking up—not an explosive gravitic detonation like the one they'd killed over Berlenhof back in the first war, but a slow deterioration. Two of its fellows were shepherding it away from the planet, a weirdly touching tableau. The final Architect was still in orbit over Arc Pallator, locked to the world with invisible gravitic claws, preparing for its work. She shuddered.

Don't be down there, Idris.

"Exemplar Keen," a new speaker broke in: Uskaro himself. Kris heard a very brief moment of clashing voices, suddenly cut off. Mannec arguing with someone. Then it was just the Magdan landowner dominating comms. "I confirm that we will not be surrendering any Colonial citizens into your hands, most especially not myself. I take extreme offence at your suggestion that any of my staff may have acted improperly, and I confirm we have not kidnapped the renegade Intermediary. Although as far as I'm concerned the man is Colonial property and if we had him I'd feel no need to let him defect for a second time. You'll take your little ship away now, and be assured I am more than ready to have my *Byron* here repel you should you do anything unwise."

"Who put that turd in charge?" Olli wanted to know. Kris tracked the shuttles, seeing them well within the shadow of the *Byron*'s weapons, and hauled their course over, breaking off any pursuit. She waited for Olli to shout at her, but only simmering discontent came from the drone bay. Even the Scorpion wasn't quite up to taking on the Hugh military.

Havaer

Havaer wasn't on the bridge, just in his quarters in the guts of the *Byron* when all this was taking place. He felt he still had quite a stake in how things might go down, though, being in a ship on the verge of active service against the Partheni *and* Architects simultaneously. He also had a whole keyring of Mordant House override codes, so had eyes on the command bay as well as ears on the comms.

And something had just happened, so seamlessly that a novice might have missed it. Uskaro had been present from the start, but he was now standing where the *Byron*'s captain should have been, restricting all comms traffic so that his was the only voice the Partheni might hear. Of course, the captain had shifted over in the cramped space to give Mannec pride of place, that had been diplomacy and standard protocol, as well as age-old tradition, and it wasn't as if the captain couldn't do his job from wherever. But now Uskaro was indeed in charge, and somehow he was giving orders and the captain was obeying them, no questions asked.

The Morzarin did have diplomatic credentials. He had a rank within Hugh. However, he was a civilian. His authority on board a warship should have been at the military's sufferance. Yet the chain of command had just shifted to accommodate him at the top. Plenty of quizzical looks passed amongst junior officers, but the captain and immediate subordinates took it on the chin, clearly pre-briefed.

Asset Colvari, at Havaer's elbow, brought up a telemetry display showing ship movements: the *Byron* and *Beagle* with the two shuttles approaching. The *Grendel's Mother*, very much on an aggressive heading now. He searched about and found the *Vulture God* too, flagging it. The crew were pulling the old tug back towards the Partheni, but if a shooting war broke out they were very much in the firing line.

"It's a coup," he said. A very small coup, admittedly. A trial run, proof of concept perhaps. He was thinking of what Colvari had found in those stolen documents, the meeting transcript where the desirability of a shooting war against the Parthenon had been mooted so complacently. As a theory: only if humanity was going to rely on arks to survive a theoretical Architect incursion. But what if you went ahead to start building those arks, let's say? What if you devoted all those resources to that fall-back? You'd get invested, wouldn't you. You'd start to see it as something other than a last resort. Especially if that would make you King of the Ark People rather than just one magnate amongst many. The Greater Good morphed into self-interest so easily; human history was full of it.

He had a dreadful need to get word out, and no way to do it. It wasn't as though a friendly packet ship was going to drop by for Arc Pallator's last words. And now it looked like a shooting war with the Partheni was about to begin, right here, right now. They were in the shadow of multiple Architects and the only two military vessels in-system were rolling up their sleeves for a bout of fisticuffs amongst themselves.

"Might we query the fighting odds?" Colvari asked.

Havaer started. Easy to forget the Hiver was a sentient entity with its own priorities, presumably including self-preservation.

"I'm no expert. We're a lot bigger, more punch, but the Partheni could always place their punches a lot more precisely."

"This tells us very little," Colvari complained. They pulled up a ship plan and began idly highlighting routes to the escape pods.

Havaer, for his part, started working on ways to get the word out, if this really did go south. Was there some way he could get a coded message to the Partheni, attach a beacon to them maybe? Could he send it to the *Vulture God*? If anyone was going to get out of this it would be those roaches. He could probably just bribe them to get his encrypted data on the first packet ship to Berlenhof. Except nobody at Mordant House would know what to do with it if Chief Laery was still out of office.

"Don't worry," he said to Colvari. "It won't come to that—"

Even as he said the words, it *did* come to that. From inside the *Byron* he felt only a faint shudder, the prickling of hairs on the back of his neck. His dispenser gave him a shot when his heart leapt with recognition. The gravitic engines of the *Byron* had shifted mode, cycling faster for shielding and weapons use. He stuttered through the reports, trying to see what had happened.

The *Grendel's Mother* had just sent a cluster of accelerator shot through one of the shuttles, very precisely eviscerating the brachator drive the vessel had been using to claw through space towards the *Beagle*. The stricken ship was now a prisoner of inertia, unable to make the final course corrections that would have swung it into dock, setting it to overshoot instead and spin off into infinity. Or at least until another ship intercepted it, or they got some scratch repairs done.

Havaer swore, frozen, the situation sliding sideways and utterly out of his control. Colvari, with more foresight, clamped their four feet to the floor, hunkering down for impact.

Moments later the *Grendel's Mother* and the *Byron* were launching everything they had at each other, save for another tightly aimed salvo that crippled the other shuttle.

War had, apparently, locally been declared.

Kris

Olli's exclamation had no actual words to it, perhaps fortunately. She had yanked back control of the *Vulture* before Kris even realized what was going on, using the invisible grasp of the brachator drive to send the ship sideways through space at ninety degrees to its original course, away from both the *Byron* and *Grendel's Mother*. For a moment Kris wasn't quite sure what had happened, until Kittering wrestled the ship's sensor suite so that it showed a fraction of what was being thrown about between the two ships, and she sagged back in her seat.

Both vessels were on the move, cutting erratic courses to

complicate targeting over the thousand-kilometre ranges, but the grunt work was being performed by the gravitic shields that put a finger on the slope of space around each vessel. Accelerator shot and the needling of laser fire, aimed true at the point of departure, would hit that curve and sling away while never deviating from its course. Except the shields weren't perfect and could be out-powered, rendered moot by a sufficient wall of shot, even out-thought by a canny partnership of gunner and targeting software. A clear miss could be dragged into a solid hit if the shooter was able to second-guess how their target was placing a thumb on the scales.

The *Byron* was a solid mid-range Colonial warship, the Partheni one distinctly smaller and less well armed, but Partheni tech and Partheni crews meant that the two made an even match. Kris was bitterly sure that when the Hegemony had prescribed exactly what force each government could bring to the table, the Essiel had that equality in mind. Which should have acted as a deterrent but was now looking like mutually assured destruction.

"We're staying well clear, right?" she checked, just in case Olli had any delusions of warrior-maidenhood.

"I spot the *Beagle* moving out," Trine's voice came to her. "They have the same admirable idea."

"Fuck me, *Grendel* just took a solid one," Olli broke in. "Don't know who's going to win this one, folks." Kris felt the slight internal tug as the *Vulture God* changed heading again, still accelerating, slinging through a series of points in space like a gibbon.

"Olli, *away*," she suggested, because they were going liter-ally every direction but that, cutting a jagged course that was still nonetheless homing in on the other ships. The *God* had sketched out a huge area of space theoretically at risk from all manner of diverted ordnance, and they were about to plough straight into it.

"Oh no, no, Kris, we are going *towards*," Olli confirmed a moment later, sounding either determined or demented. "We get the job *done* here on the old *Vulture.*"

"My distinguished comrade, you appear to be trying to get us killed," Trine said. "Would you not do that, please?"

"Look at where that *Beagle* bastard is headed," Olli told them grimly.

"Shuttles are being approached," Kit confirmed immediately, apparently on the same wavelength. "A rescue."

"Oh they can rescue whoever the fuck they like." Olli's voice was audibly through gritted teeth. "But we are getting Idris first. He's on one of those two ships, like Keen said. He has to be and they are dead and tumbling right now. We have a mother of a grabbing claw and the drives to shift twenty of the *Beagle*'s little tub shuttles. We're snatching them and running."

"Olli, that's kidnapping Colonial citizens!" Kris objected, although some of the race in her pulse was not entirely objecting to the idea.

"Rescuing," Olli insisted. "With extreme prejudice. We'll drop the others off. Not like I'm going to ransom the bastards. But we keep Idris. All in?"

"If Professor Storquel is aboard one of the shuttles can I hold him at gunpoint?" Trine asked. "If so, consider me in."

A new scatter of warnings joined the already crowded throng on Kris's screen. "*Byron*'s moving."

"I see it," Olli confirmed.

"They see us. They see what we're doing."

"And I was being so subtle about it."

"Olli, we can't do this and dodge a warship."

"I thought you Scintilla kids liked danger," Olli told her, and then, "Kit?"

"A deal has been made," Kittering confirmed. "Comms incoming."

Kris sat back, feeling abruptly like the last child to be picked for the duelling team. Kittering had been busy behind her back, apparently. And now a brief message came to the *God* from *Grendel's Mother*, the calm tones of Exemplar Keen.

"We are moving to keep the *Byron* off you. Get this done, Timo, and get back to the *Ceres*. The Parthenon thanks you."

"Not going to live that down," Olli said, after a moment's silence. The *Mother* was closing the distance to its opposite number and redoubling its fire, burning through accelerator magazines and then spare mass, depleting its laser cells. She saw a storm of deviating shot strafe randomly across the *Beagle*'s sector of space and the science ship took several hits, its own shielding shredding like paper.

The *Grendel's Mother* had already taken several strikes. The Partheni's form of segmentation shielding had meant the force was sluiced down-hull, to the tapering back sections of the hull, and the shredded remains of it were being discarded in a long trail of ruin. The rest of the ship was still battle-worthy, and Kris saw the *Byron* shudder as its own shields failed to catch everything thrown at it, or, as the Partheni gunners began to predict their enemy's defensive patterns, rolling their shot down the *Byron*'s own sloping space towards it.

"Incoming *Beagle* still," Kit noted.

"Well then get the laser ready," Olli told him.

"Is civilian only, damaged also."

"Well then…" A frustrated pause as Olli worked through some calculations. "We can snatch one shuttle before they get there, but the other… Kit, I'd rather fly and you shoot. Or Kris, or Trine. That means you can concentrate on just warning the bastards off or something, rather than me putting a beam through their command pod by accident because I'm busy."

Kris craned back to look at Kittering. The Hanni's curved back was towards her but she could see from his jittering movements that he was unhappy.

"I will do it, my fellow pirates. I shall warn them off with threats of violence," Trine announced.

"Still coming," Kit noted, and Kris was rotating her display: the *Vulture*, the *Beagle*, the two shuttles still tumbling helplessly on their last course, which was taking them right into the fire zone anyway. A bad day for everyone concerned. And here came the *Vulture God*, intent on a hostile boarding action.

"This makes us criminals," she said numbly. "Actual pirates. Or at least combatants. Olli…"

A shock went through the *Vulture God*, its course abruptly skewing almost directly back along its path and then spinning them wildly away from all the other ships. She thought they'd been hit. She was hunting for damage reports that didn't show anywhere on the system and bracing for the alarms that didn't come. In her ear Olli swore blue murder.

Another ship had torn its way out of unspace within a hundred kilometres of them with a violent gravitic shockwave. *This close to a planet, to other vessels, to the* Architects! *Who would do that?* But she knew. There was no mistaking the newcomer's design. Like a vast rose cut from alabaster and mother-of-pearl, bigger than the *Byron* and *Mother* put together.

The broadcast that came over all channels, obliterating any chance at other comms, was completely incomprehensible. An audio channel full of thunder and groans supplemented by a staccato flicker of radial patterns. The Essiel wanted them all to know something and hadn't waited for a translator.

"It's the police, come to break it up," Olli decided. Kris saw she hadn't changed course towards the shuttles, and nor had the *Beagle*. Perhaps, as they weren't shooting, they weren't the targets of the Essiel's ire. But the great sharp-edged rosette of the Essiel ship was cruising inexorably onwards—not towards the two warships but for the *Beagle* and the shuttles.

A further meaningless proclamation overwrote all frequencies, and then there was a human voice, hard and angry, some cult hierograve drafted in as translator and obviously trying to convey just how pissed off his master was.

"I speak for The Radiant Sorteel, the Provident and the Prescient," he stated, "whose hospitality has been grievously abused." Kris, like everyone, thought this was their response to the humans fighting in Essiel territory, until the man went on, "It is expressly forbidden to lay hands on the faithful of the Divine Essiel. Of all the actions of a treacherous guest, this is the unforgivable crime."

"All right," Olli said after a reflective pause. "I have no idea what's going on now."

"Oh," Trine said, in a tone indicating that they did.

They caught a transmission from the pilot of the *Beagle* claiming ignorance, but Kris had caught up by then. The

Colonials' shuttles had taken several loads of cultists off-planet, because it was plain the Hegemony weren't actually going to save their human adherents. She herself had bleakly wondered if, like kings of old, the Essiel wanted a sacrifice of followers to mark the tomb of their lost world. The Colonials had extended a hand to those desperate wretches, at least a few of whom had found their suicidal faith wanting, and had accepted the offer. Some were already on the *Beagle* and others were cramming the *Beagle*'s two crippled shuttles.

Then a new voice broke in, none other than Professor Storquel from the *Beagle* itself, even as Kittering quietly noted that the science ship hadn't deviated from its course.

"Hugh has a humanitarian duty to assist in times of crisis," the academic said, rather pompously, save that Kris could hear the tremor in his voice. "I'm sure you would have done the same, had there been a Colonial world under threat. During the war, Hegemonic ships did sometimes assist in humanity's evacuation efforts, I'm sure."

Kris wasn't actually sure they had, save where the evacuees had agreed to put on the funny robes and go to the right churches. But right then everyone on the *Vulture God* was holding their breath, even as they closed in on the nearest shuttle.

"The authority of the Divine Essiel is sacrosanct," was the rapid response from the massive Essiel ship. "The covenant between the Essiel and the faithful may not be broken without invoking their wrath," the cultist said, and Kris didn't even know if he was translating now, or just giving rein to his own interpretation of whatever the hell the Essiel thought.

Storquel came back hotly, "We were saving lives. Of course we will repatriate these, your fellows, to wherever you direct.

We can offload them direct to the…uh, Radiant Sorteel's ship, even. However, thanks to Partheni aggression, our shuttles containing your people are now without motive power and so—"

"The covenant may *not* be broken!" The translator's voice overwrote whatever he might have said next. "The Divine Essiel remove their protection from you. You are no longer guests."

"*Byron*'s moving in," Olli noted. "Trying to cover the *Beagle*. Fuck me, *Grendel*'s still not leaving them alone, though." On her displays Kris could see the Partheni vessel doing its level best to take advantage of its Colonial rival's distraction.

She opened a channel to the Partheni, even as it went on the attack. "Exemplar? We should have other priorities right now. If Idris is on either of those shuttles, we have to head for them. Exemplar, *please*." But even as she tried, another blistering salvo shredded space about both ships. The *Grendel* lost another segment and kept taking damage, shields breaking up. The *Byron* had a whole flank torn open, half its accelerator batteries gone, vomiting pieces and frozen atmosphere, yet still trying to limp on to help the *Beagle*.

"I am sure that, in this trying time," Professor Storquel continued, "the Essiel Hegemony has no wish to antagonize its potential allies against the Architects…I can assure the Radiant Sorteel that no insult was meant, and we were not, not in *any way*, suggesting that the, that the Essiel could not take care of, could not ensure the safety of their citizens." His voice was growing shakier and shakier as the science vessel fell into the shadow of the alien rose.

The *Beagle* shuddered again, comms suddenly falling silent. Kris watched their shields, entirely intact, and wasn't sure what had happened. Kit was sensing some sort of gravitic discharge from the Essiel vessel, but nothing he could readily identify.

"*Beagle*'s powering up their gravitic drive. They're running," Olli said. The craft's energy readings certainly suggested it, but at the same time they were still cruising slowly towards the shuttles.

"No," said Trine flatly.

"No what?"

"That's not an unspace jump."

"Why else are they ramping up their drive then?"

"They're not. It's the Essiel." Trine's voice was very calm.

"Not possible." But Olli plainly didn't believe her own words.

Kris just watched the build-up of power in the *Beagle*'s drive, exactly as if they were trying to get into unspace. The same tech they would use to bend space to shield themselves, and the same they used for a-grav aboard.

Then the *Beagle* twisted, the entire ship, bow to stern, wrenching as though great hands had hold of it.

When the *Vulture God* shuddered, Kris actually jumped from her seat, convinced the Essiel were attacking them too. It was the first shuttle, however. They'd finally reached it and Olli had the claws around it. She was muttering something about wringing Idris's neck if he wasn't on board.

The *Beagle* crumpled, its whole hull dimpling and creasing as the gravitic force increased, wrapped in a strangling spiral and hauled in towards the toroid ring of its drive that had suddenly become a voracious monster, greedy for mass. The entire vessel halved in size in seconds, every inch of space within it compacting to solid matter.

"Thus the justice of the Divine Essiel is observed," announced the cult translator in the stunned silence that followed.

The *Byron* opened fire on the Essiel, every remaining weapon, every scrap of mass and energy it could throw. Kris saw the Hegemonic vessel's shields catch it all effortlessly, not just diverting the shot but turning the incoming barrage into a graceful unfolding pattern, phantom petals shedding away from the stone flower. Kris wondered whether the display was an insult, a sign of contempt. Who could know?

"*Vulture God*," Keen's voice came to them from the *Grendel*. "Get the shuttles and *get out*."

"What about you?" Kris asked her.

"We have red lights across the board, and I know that means the same to you Colonials as it does to us. We will buy time, like always."

"Exemplar—"

"Love to make a tragic speech, Almier, but I have a dying ship to run," and then there was a very definitive cut-off to comms. Moments later the *Grendel's Mother* was accelerating past the lumbering *Byron*, its surviving weapons lancing at the Essiel ship, its gravitic shielding spread wide to give as much cover to the faltering Hugh vessel as possible. Kris felt a kick inside her, almost bafflement as much as anything. Perhaps Exemplar Keen had grown up on stories of her sisters saving humanity in the first war, the thin line against the Architects. And now here was another alien menace murdering civilians and she'd decided at this late point it was common humanity that should win out.

Olli already had them slung towards the other shuttle, compensating for the shifted centre of mass now they had the first tucked in their claws. The *Vulture* was a salvage vessel after all. Hauling dead ships around was its business. Kris sent out a hail, explaining what they were doing, not that the shuttle would be able to help or hinder them much. Her eyes were on the display, interpreting the data. She was building a model of the two limping warships, absurdly united in purpose now after approaching the brink of war.

"The planet," Kit said. "The planet the planet the planet," over and over. She didn't realize what he meant until she saw the oblate sphere of Arc Pallator begin to deform, to fold in on itself, to tease out into long streamers of molten material, the core erupting through the crust and then being moulded like clay. All in silence. Slow and beautiful, a work of art on a celestial scale, God's own potter's wheel. And, almost eclipsed by the ever-shifting edge of the doomed world, the crystal moons of the Architects went about their business, heedless of the squabbles of lesser species.

The *Byron* was falling away now, venting lost atmosphere from a rent in its hull, sending a final salvo at the Essiel vessel but plainly out of the fight and trying to get clear. The *Mother* was still coming, and there was damage showing across the face of Sorteel's ship, just a little to mar its geometric perfection.

Another shuddering clunk came as Olli snagged the second shuttle with a triumphant yell. Then she had the *Vulture's* drives put as much space between them and the Essiel as possible, clawing away from the planet to where she could plunge them into unspace. Kris hoped against hope that the Essiel didn't have a navigator that could track them, as the Hegemonic gangsters of the Broken Harvest had done once before. In that case, all of their efforts to rescue their missing Int would be for nothing.

Kris just watched, magnifying the view to make up for all the distance Olli was gaining them, as Arc Pallator was elegantly, fatally remade.

Idris

"So," Idris hazarded. "Did you go crazy all at once, or did the whole 'worship the clams' thing just creep up on you?"

The Tothiat woman just glanced at him, coolly amused, although a few of the nearest cultists glowered at him. They were elbow to elbow now the ruin's entire population was crammed into the Temple grounds. He had to speak quite loudly to be heard; the mere background susurration of so many people shifting and murmuring and breathing was overwhelming. Every so often a wave of prayer would go through them, heads bowed, hands clasped, whole blocks of people dropping to their knees, awkwardly trying to prostrate themselves. Prayer, as humans did it, using movements their god-aliens couldn't even emulate. Earlier there had been big water-carriers passed back and forth over the heads of the crowd, but those had run out now. *So look on the bright side: it won't matter. Nobody's going to die of dehydration because we won't have time.*

"Was it the Tothir thing?" he prompted. "I mean, I hear it hurts like hell, going in. And maybe keeps hurting. There was this one we knew. Said the whole quick healing hurt, but being a Tothiat hurt as well so it didn't signify. Or something. I wasn't there. So maybe I'm getting that wrong. But I can see how having a prawn shoved up your spinal column is going to hurt, and maybe that gives you religion.

Or was the prawn the religious one and you're just nodding along? Or maybe it's an atheist prawn and all your praying annoys the crap out of it. What, I mean basically, the fuck, is what I'm asking? You know, before we die, just satisfy my curiosity."

His words petered out because he wasn't succeeding in annoying her even remotely, and annoying her was just about his only mode of resistance left. He'd tried to walk away, just shove his way out of the Temple, past its notional boundaries, little more than a line drawn in the sand plus a few pillars. *Not worth getting the builders back to do the roof, all things considered.* She'd hauled him back each time. The cultists around them ignored any pleas for help too, obviously none of their business.

"I'm going to start shouting," he told her—Emmaneth, she'd said her name was. "I will shout very loudly that you're all crazy clam-lovers and you're all going to die. I have just enough time to do that before we do all actually die. It will be time well spent."

"You're a sad bastard, aren't you."

He blinked at her. "Me? I wanted to be on a ship and off the planet. You want to be here, doing neither of those things. Who's sad?"

"You won't even shout," she said complacently. "You say it, but there's no *do* in you. You talk a good fight, Telemmier. But what did you ever *do?*"

That was so manifestly unfair it shut him up for a moment, before he came back with, "I ended the *war.* I saved a world."

"Yeah, but what did you do recently?" And she grinned.

Idris blinked at her, and then a strained laugh escaped him, despite his best efforts to shut it in. "Who even *are* you?"

"I'll let you into a secret." She leant in conspiratorially. "I'm not one of the faithful. I mean, yes, the Essiel made me. All the Tothiat come about through their personal intervention. But I had second thoughts and went apostate. Because your man was right. It hurts all the time, Telemmier. It hurts in a way humans can't even hurt, like they give you an extra organ that's permanently in critical. Pain you can't imagine, except you don't react to it the same way anymore. Doesn't slow you, doesn't cripple you, because even those are release."

"How is it for the prawn?"

"I am the prawn," she told him. He didn't know how she meant it, whether the woman who owned that face was even in there at all, whether they took turns moving the lips, or whether the thing speaking to him really was an inseparable merging of the two.

He glanced up at the living moons Arc Pallator had acquired. The disintegrating one and two of the others were further away now, just receding glints, out of orbit. One was left, and no prizes for guessing what it was cracking its knuckles to do.

"You tried to kill yourself?"

"More than once," she agreed. "It's why I'm here, in a way. Roundabout way, but still."

"Now you've gone for Death by Architect and you had a spare ticket or something? Why *me*? You go get yourself reshaped to death, but why do I get to come along?"

"I am severely tempted," she told him, "to say it's not all about you, but unfortunately for both of us it is."

"I mean, if you were hired to kill me, then guns would have been enough. We're not all invulnerable prawn-bearers."

"I'm not an assassin, Menheer Telemmier. I'm a bounty hunter. I was hired to bring you in alive."

He looked up again. "Then you're doing a fuck of a poor job of it." And he felt the first tug, the first exploratory reaching of the colossal entity above them, as it explored the physical structure of the planet. He'd never been at ground zero of an Architect attack before, for obvious reasons of personal preference. *Oh what wonders we will learn. Albeit briefly.*

He *concentrated*, trying to reach out to the thing, to touch its intellect with the pinprick of his own. *I am here! Don't kill me!* After all, he was most likely physically closer to an Architect now than he ever had been in a ship. Except even as he tried, he felt the stifling pressure of Arc Pallator's mass shadow like a weight on his brain, stopping his thoughts flying out towards the creature, trapping him here with the faithful. He strove again and again, sweat sheening his forehead and a lightning-bolt headache lancing through his temples. It was like fighting to get out of quicksand, reaching up to touch fingertips to the wrathful god bending over the world.

Emmaneth was regarding him gravely. "It's happening, by the way," she said.

"Oh you don't have to tell *me*." His words came out ragged with tears. *I don't want to die. Not like this.* Although in truth he just didn't want to die, period. Given his personal history, this would actually be quite a fitting way to go.

Then The Radiant Sorteel, the Provident and the Prescient, manifested in the heart of its faithful. Idris barked a yelp of surprise before realizing it was only a projection. That was what the pillars did, apparently. They gave the doomed congregation a last sight of God. The nearest worshippers, dropping to their knees and reaching out, were clipping through its edges.

The Essiel waved its arms gracefully and booming noises issued from the pillars, quieting the crowd. It made a little speech, or that was what Idris assumed. He heard murmured translations run through the faithful as hierograves gave their best guess at a translation. Each one conflicted with the rest as far as he could tell, save for one central message. They were being delivered, Sorteel was telling them. They were to have the reward for their faith.

He felt something *flex*, some unfathomable membrane extending in an unreal direction, and knew the Architect was beginning its work. While everyone knelt around him, or sat or just lay flat on their faces, he stood and opened his mouth to shout out his denial. He would die, but not as a willing participant in this sham. He would tell this transmitted image of a living god, safe in orbit, exactly what he thought of it.

He got as far as "I—"

Something shifted, around him. He thought it was just the Architect—*just!*—at first, but no. A ripple of gravitic force was shouldering out from the Temple itself. He sensed the concentric rings of it expanding out over the barren, chasmed landscape. Concentric rings, like the Originators had been so fond of.

Abruptly, they were in a pit. Not physically, not visibly, but his Intermediary's senses were screaming at him that they were being dragged down into a steep-walled abyss. Gravitic forces were reshaping the world around him even as his eyes said nothing of the sort was happening. But it was unspace he was sensing. Something was causing a colossal local distortion in the unreal. Not the Architect, the machinations of which he could track entirely separately across the world as a whole.

He stared at the pillars, columns ringing the open temple space, filled with...not just projectors and speakers. Filled with whatever the Essiel needed from moment to moment because that was how their liquid tech worked. Components formed out of the matrix at will, to collapse back into the techno-slush as soon as their task was done. And now they were...

"That's impossible," he declared. And felt awe. Not a religious awe, not actual reverence, not quite. But in that moment he came damn close.

The Essiel had lived alongside the Originators' ruins and relics for a long time. They had developed ways of containing and transporting the regalia without robbing it of its potency. And they had learned other things from their centuries of study, too. He felt the Temple resound around him like the city had when the Naeromathi's unspace cannon had discharged. He felt the echo in the skin between the stars.

The pillars—the gravitic engine they had just become—twisted the boundary of unspace still further, even as the world groaned in its death throes, its crust shifting and cracking across a million miles of abandoned ground. You couldn't *do* this on a planet's surface, not even close to something as massy as a planet. Except apparently you could, and the Originators had probably known how, as evidently the Essiel did.

The Architect leant on Arc Pallator, forcing the planet into its mental lathe to reshape it, and the Temple fell into unspace, becoming an impossible open-decked ship on that unreal sea. Sorteel's image bellowed, and Idris saw cultists all around him dropping, eyes rolling, some kind of ecstasy or passion overcoming them, frothing, fitting, oblivious. Only he and Emmaneth were left untouched, heretics at a second coming.

And then they had left the tortured world behind and it was just him, alone in an empty temple. Him and unspace, and the thing they always said couldn't really live there, but did.

271

16.

Havaer

"Are we at war with the Hegemony now?" was Havaer's question, and nobody had an answer. One particularly over-worked clerk back at Mordant House even went so far as to add, "You mean, as *well?*"

Modern times were not, he reflected, a poster child for interstellar diplomacy.

His debriefing, with his new head of department whose boots were under Chief Laery's desk, had not gone well.

"We could have done with having this chat some days ago," the man informed him flatly. "Instead, you stop for *repairs.*" As though Havaer had any influence on the captain's decision. Morzarin Uskaro had been similarly keen for them to just damn the torpedoes and run for Berlenhof, but the ship had taken quite a beating and the captain had overruled all objections. They'd come out of unspace in the first Throughway that didn't decant them into an active part of the Hegemony. This had been a Hannilambra-built orbital over the freezing moon of a gas giant, just a dry dock and trading post. There, the Hanni engineers had done what they could to ensure that, when the *Byron* re-entered unspace to plot a course home, it would have good odds of exiting where it was supposed to, or at all.

The Radiant Sorteel's conventional weapons had torn them up badly enough, but that was the sort of damage the *Byron* had at least been designed to shoulder on through until it ran out of shoulders. As they fought to gain unspace, though, the Essiel had turned their other weapon on them, the one that had crumpled up the *Beagle* like an empty food bar wrapper. Doubtless there were whole teams of Hugh weapons techs trying to work out just what *that* had been and whether they could replicate it. Havaer hadn't been able to add much to their stock of knowledge. Engineering scuttlebutt aboard the *Byron* had surmised that the Hegemony had somehow suborned the gravitic fields of their victims' own drive, then amplified them until the ship's structure (and, it was assumed, occupants—lovely thought) couldn't hold out against the fabricated mass and imploded into it. Just a faint touch of the same effect had caused stress fractures and failed systems throughout the *Byron*. It was a miracle they'd got into unspace at all, and a double miracle they'd come out of it. In all the panic of running around trying to get into emergency suspension, Havaer hadn't had a chance to worry about the possibility of never seeing the real universe again.

Seventeen of the ship's complement didn't. They hadn't got to suspension quickly enough, or their couches had failed, and by the time the ship crawled out into the Hanni dock, they were all dead by their own hands. Opened throats, skulls staved in against bulkheads. One man had gouged his face into meat and then strangled himself with his own hands, and Havaer was damn sure that was supposed to be impossible. There had also been the economic fellow who'd put an accelerator barrel to his head and triggered the weapon remotely, meaning they had an air leak through three layers of hull when they came out into the real, as well as all the mess inside.

And Havaer's chief was grumbling about them not reaching home sooner?

Havaer still nodded along, however, making the appropriate excuses. He tendered a very carefully tailored report, and was excruciatingly aware that he was now a double agent, possibly without a handler to report to anymore. Maybe even a man who represented a faction of one. And so he said nothing, of course, about the covert data or Colvari, or just what that had turned up. Moreover, he was carefully evasive about just how the Morzarin Uskaro had been pulling the strings aboard the *Byron*, how the man had been provoking the Parthenon on-planet via his uniformed thugs and little private army. Then how he'd taken over the ship and got them into the brief shooting war with the *Grendel's Mother*, before the Radiant Sorteel had arrived to make their differences moot. Havaer still remembered, weirdly bittersweet, how the damaged Partheni ship had gone right into the fray against the Essiel. Yes, they'd been buying time for their own tender to escape—with the crippled shuttles—but he'd read in that act the same pan-human altruism that had brought them into action against the Architect at Berlenhof, at such cost. *Me against my human sister, but we sisters against the universe.*

Another impression that hadn't made it into his report, of course. He had gone so far as to note that Uskaro's actions had been irregular and unhelpful, but it was a footnote, if that. Because it seemed to him there was a real danger this new man he was reporting to might be connected, through strings attached to strings, with a clique of people who really wanted a good old war with the Parthenon, to clear the way for their vision of a wholly spacefaring humanity. That, of course, was the mad paranoia of an agent cut off from any chain of command he had faith in. But he couldn't shake it.

The *Grendel's Mother* hadn't made it, as far as Hugh intel could work out. They'd been beaten up from their run-in with the *Byron*—Partheni tech hadn't quite overmatched the power of the larger Hugh ship in the way they'd likely expected, which in itself was something the policy-makers would be chewing over. When the *Byron* had fallen back, genuinely unable to continue the fight, they'd continued their battering of Sorteel's vessel.

On the other hand, the *Vulture God* had exited the system in better shape than anyone else, turning up well away from anywhere claimed by the Hegemony or Hugh. The Castigar colony world where the Throughways had taken them was now bemusedly negotiating with Hugh for the return of the shuttle crews, and with the Hegemony for repatriation of a whole bunch of not-so-faithful-as-all-that cultists. Havaer wondered just whether those cultists actually wanted to be repatriated now. Given the way Sorteel had taken their defection, it might be auto-da-fé time for anyone trying to rejoin the flock. *And I guess we didn't quite realize how bloody serious the clam bastards were about swearing yourself to them.*

He'd been thoroughly debriefed about the *Vulture God*, and that had been even more depressing. Not for the interview itself, where he'd at least been able to answer all questions without feeling he was compromising his professionalism. But while it was clear the shabby old salvage craft had escaped Arc Pallator unscathed, the same could not be said of its crew.

The Parthenon, he was given to understand, was demanding the return of Idris Telemmier, Intermediary first class, formerly a war hero, then a tramp navigator, briefly a war hero again and then a defector. And now... missing. Because Havaer was damn sure he hadn't been crammed in on the *Byron* somehow, and apparently he hadn't been on either of the two shuttles the *God* had scooped up before making its hasty exit. Which left either the *Beagle* or planetside, and neither was a survivable option.

Ridiculous, basically. That, after all that long squabble, the cause célèbre whose defection had brought tensions between Hugh and the Partheni to the brink of war had gone AWOL on-planet and ended up one more victim of the Architects. *Live by the bloody sword indeed.*

Some in the department were saying that Telemmier was fine and back with the warrior angels, who were just kicking up a smokescreen to put off any attempt to swipe him back, or possibly because they too were spoiling for a war. Havaer didn't believe it on either count. Not their style, by his reckoning. And right now, if the Partheni wanted a war they had plenty of excuses already lined up. They were even claiming that Uskaro's Voyenni had grabbed Idris on-planet. Havaer hadn't had any comment on that, in his own debriefing, but privately he reckoned it was entirely possible, and if so, then those Voyenni hadn't got off-planet either. Not a happy ending all round.

They finished with him at last, his new chief telling him to go get some rest and await his next assignment. With an added mutter of, "And *shave*, why don't you, and perhaps some clean clothes." That was a particularly unfair jibe given he was wearing the best approximation of a suit the damaged

Byron printers had been able to churn out. They hadn't given him a chance to get more than a cup of kaffe between disembark and debrief.

At long last, though, he was able to shuffle his way to his own quarters. The cramped room he maintained at too much expense because it was a quick shuttle ride down the orbital track from where Mordant House maintained its fiefdom.

Colvari was already there when he got back. Havaer had gone into some serious tradecraft contortions to get the Hiver off the *Byron* without having to explain their presence or have them go through their own debrief. They'd ended up shut down and dispatched as freight through a trusted contact, which he wasn't exactly proud about.

They were up and running again by the time he arrived, and it was an odd moment in his solitary life to come back to someone at home. He almost felt like asking why dinner wasn't on the table.

"Progress?" he asked them, slouching to the printer and dialling up a prefab lunch.

"Oh yes," the Hiver confirmed. "Based on our brief acquaintance so far we suggest you won't want to know, once you know, but until you know, you'll want to know. If you know what we mean."

"You're getting too wordy for your own good, is what you are," Havaer observed mildly. The food turned up too hot, a pile of tofusoyo ramen half-congealed into a molten lump. He juggled the bowl with the ease of long practice, waiting for it to cool. He then ran the usual diagnostics of his system, a series of eclectic tests designed to see if anyone had interfered with it, as well as to check his anti-surveillance was running properly. "But you're right," he concluded. "I want to know. Lay it on me." He tucked into the still slightly incandescent meal, while his chopsticks could get purchase to break it into strands.

Colvari gave him the names. They were best-guess data analysis for the people in that room, who'd had that conversation. Havaer listened and ate, and recognized most of them. Big people, almost all of them, or else notable factotums for big people who presumably couldn't be there in big person. There were several of the Berlenhof wealthy, some high-placed Hugh officials or else the influencers who advised them. Someone from the Liaison Board, with ready access to Ints, meaning their theoretical ark fleet wouldn't be bound to the Throughways like the Naeromathi were. More than one Magdan land-magnate, including a senior Uskaro scion. Nobody directly from Mordant House but more than enough political clout there to be giving the orders. Havaer bleakly reckoned that the Intervention Board was just too small fry to be an active party to this sort of business. *Just a tool, to be used and then discarded.*

And he wasn't sure he believed in the final analysis. *Too much, too big, too crazy.* The conspiracy theorist's dream, the cabal of the mighty getting together to obliterate the bulk of humanity just so they could be kings of what remained. Except he went back over the transcripts and there wasn't much of a sense of gloat in that room. No maniacal cackling, twirling moustaches and rubbing of hands. Powerful people united by a belief—entirely borne out by events—that the Architects were coming back, and humanity needed a plan. Entirely laudable, when you looked at it like that. Not a suicide cult but people trying to make hard and responsible decisions in the face of a universe that might start trying to kill them any moment. And they had talked and talked, and brainstormed problems and solutions, and he could almost chart the shift of priorities on a graph. They had been so worried about covering every potential base, to ensure the survival of the species, that they'd ended up with the action plan of: *First we have to set everything else on fire.* They hadn't actually called the whole thing "Operation Phoenix" but frankly Havaer was amazed nobody had suggested it.

It was entirely possible that the whole business had gone no further than this meeting, although the dire efforts of *someone* to get hold of this data argued against that. Still, it could be no more than a dream in the eye of a would-be emperor. Or the ark ships could be mostly built already and someone had a list of the saved and the damned. He had no way of knowing. *Although it would be hard to conceal something that big, surely. We'd have heard.* But then news and rumour didn't travel the way you expected, across the Throughways, denied a way to race ahead of actual ships and word of mouth.

"You've got mail," Colvari announced.

"What?" He bolted down the last mouthful of ramen and stared at the Hiver.

"A message," they clarified. "Word, intended for your ear, delivered to me."

"When?"

"Right now. Although I believe triggered by our interactions."

"Our 'interactions' shouldn't be on anyone else's grid right now. My system—"

"Message commences, 'Your system is not as airtight as you believe,'" Colvari informed him. They had clearly installed snark since the *Byron*.

Havaer wondered if the department was about to kick down his door and take him in for a far more aggressive debriefing. "Tell me," he said.

"Message continues, encrypted. See our screen here." A panel beneath the light atop the Hiver flipped, revealing a display. Havaer read, mentally decrypted, recognizing the familiar codes. "Coordinates attached. Full Silence Protocols. Bring the Hiver and the data."

They weren't current Mordant House codes. They were a system he'd used for covert work recently, though. Only with Laery. Either this was an entirely over-elaborate trap, or he was back in the game.

Solace

Kris was waiting when they let Solace out of the infirmary. They'd given her a medical frame to take the load off her leg while the tissue repairs finalized. The pain meds didn't quite swallow the ache of new-knit bone in her shoulder either, but medicine was one area where the Parthenon excelled. Easier to target genetic and pharmaceutical interventions when you had your patient's entire code written out to refer to, with no inconvenient variations. Which led Solace to think guiltily of Olli and her grievances with the Partheni. But she shook off the thought. She had other priorities right now.

Kris sized her up and down. "Good as new?"

The medical frame was just a slender scaffold beneath her clothes, but it would still show. "Prêt à combattre," Solace told her.

"They've given you orders already?"

"Not yet." Solace tried a smile. It felt unfamiliar on her face. "Even we Partheni tend to wait until all the bones have mended." Something was stringing Kris taut, and Solace reckoned it wasn't just the recent news of the war. The main war, not Hugh's posturing. A multispecies colony world, Caractan, had been visited by an Architect, together with the Colonial frontier hub of Nordensheim, which had been intended as the jump-off point for the next wave of unspace exploration, portal to a hundred unknowns. The evacuation of Caractan had been a desperate scrabble to the ships, but there had been a dozen Colonial navy vessels at the other, standard procedure for protecting a Cartography Corps station. Their sacrifice had bought time for just about everyone to get off-planet and off-orbital. Just like the old days. And yet Solace had heard far more talk of fighting Hugh, and even the Hegemony, from her sisters. It was as though, in the face of a threat as vast as the Architects, the human mind slid off sideways towards conflicts more winnable.

Kris had zoned out for a moment, murmuring comms to someone, but she now snapped back. "Good. Right. I need you with me, then. There's something we need to do."

It was clear they were headed for the small-ship civilian docks, which meant the *Vulture God*, and sure enough there they were, sitting on a scatter of crates with what looked like half the ship's guts out for a refit, the huge grabber claw part-disassembled and hogging the dockyard repair arms. They'd stopped work, though, and were waiting. Olli slouched in her walker frame, which had three extra working arms bolted to it. Kittering had a slate clutched to his mouthparts. The virtual display projected up in front of his eyes vanished away when he saw them coming. Presumably summoned by one or the other, Delegate Trine then stilted out of the ship and down the ramp. The Hiver's projected face was almost burlesquing solemnity.

Olli got out a couple of bottles of what looked like Colonial homebrewed 'shine, which she'd acquired from who knew where on the *Ceres*, pouring out glasses two at a time. Solace had no intention of drinking it, nor of giving offence by refusing. In a vertiginous shift of perspective, she understood what was happening.

"You don't know," she insisted, because these were the words she'd been telling herself.

Kris was looking down at the brittle printed cup Olli had given her, and Olli herself was carefully pouring out a last measure for herself. A Hanni's eyes were unblinking and impersonal so it was only Trine who really met her gaze.

"I'm so very sorry, for all of us." Like her, he'd known Idris from way back, during the war.

"They think Hugh has him. That they got him out on the *Byron*. That's what they're saying."

"It's maybe convenient to pretend it," Kris told her quietly. "But we were there and there's no way. Nothing got off-planet to the *Byron*. And we searched those shuttles top to bottom. They took him from us, sure enough, but then they didn't get away."

Solace twitched against the constraints of the medical frame, a brief, painful spasm. *I fought so hard*. Her furious flight through the disassembling city. Her equally furious fight against the Voyenni. Her dead sisters, her wounds. And maybe all she'd done was delay things just long enough that, when the Magdans finally *had* Idris, they couldn't preserve him. A sudden wave of sorrow-dressed-as-anger threatened to overwhelm her.

Olli cleared her throat. As de facto captain of the *Vulture God*, this duty fell to her. "Idris Telemmier," she announced.

"No," Solace said. "You don't *know* he's gone. There must be a way."

Olli looked at her. And looked at her. Solace sat down and took up a little cup of her own, feeling another shudder go through her. This was not how Partheni expressed grief. For her dead sisters, there were other rituals, held within their sororities. A prescribed course through all the stages: eulogy, hair-tearing, weeping, abandon, celebration. But Idris had been a Colonial, a spacer, and they had their own ways.

"Idris Telemmier," Olli said again, waiting to see if she would interrupt, and then continued, "Born 56 After, if you can fucking believe that, on board the *Lupine Creed* in transit from Greenacre."

Sixty-eight years old, Solace thought numbly. She was three years older, technically, but she'd slept out a lot of the time in between which Idris had just lived. And he'd not aged a day since they'd rearranged his brain in the Intermediary Program. He could perhaps have gone on forever, or at least until he went so spectacularly, dysfunctionally crazy that he couldn't go on anymore. And now he was dead. Everyone was waiting to see who would go first to move the ritual on.

So she did, because she'd just understood that they'd *waited* for her to do this. They could have had their wake, all crew together, and treated her like the outsider she arguably was. And it was Olli who'd have had the casting vote, but still they'd waited.

"He was a needy son of a bitch," she said, almost savouring the Colvul words, doing her best to get the inflection just right.

"Utter waste of unparalleled opportunity," Kit agreed primly.

"Went to pieces," Kris's voice jagged but she fought on, "at the least provocation."

"Honestly, it's a wonder such an unreliable fellow lasted so long," Trine added, not quite to formula, but good enough.

"Our brother, he was, our pilot," Olli intoned tightly. "Loyal to his ship, and safe hands. Died on-planet, who should have died in…" For a moment Solace thought she'd break the ritual and say "unspace," because surely that was the fate written in the books for Intermediaries, but after a brief falter Olli went on with, "…space, where he belonged. One of ours, he was."

She murmured the refrain, "One of ours," and remembered being late on the response for Rollo Rostand's wake, after their former captain had been killed recovering his ship from the Broken Harvest. They drank—despite her resolve she *did* drink— and then Kris clasped her hand. Solace mastered the jolt of pain that woke in her injured shoulder and clasped right back.

"Well fuck," Olli declared, apropos of nothing in particular. One of her frame's new arms hurled the little cup at the wall, where it shattered into fragments.

"O Captain, my captain, do you have a spare?" Trine asked.

Olli glowered at them. "What now?"

"I feel the need to expiate some feelings."

"You even have those?"

Solace winced, and Trine bent forwards at the hips until the bowl of his head was right over Olli.

"When my creators designed us, my captain, they worked very hard to make an artificial colony of linked bioengineered processors respond and react like them. Their heirs are therefore not entitled to complain when we wish to show emotions."

Olli fished out another cup and her arms busied themselves with doling out refills, without another word.

"Professor Tiber Tenniel Storquel," Trine announced.

"Seriously?" Solace asked before she could stop herself, then shrank back at his holographic glare.

"Born 85 After on Berlenhof," they went on, and then looked around expectantly. The awkward pause stretched out, because none of them there had known the man, and what Solace had seen she genuinely hadn't liked. When you slated the dead it was supposed to be fond, not a character assassination.

"Punchy little bastard," Olli tried at last, though that probably counted as at least a halfway virtue in her book.

"Worked his people too hard," Kris added.

"Unable to release the past," Kittering put in, eyeing Trine.

Solace racked her mind and eventually decided she couldn't manage anything short of honesty. "He was a bigot who wanted to own other people just because those people weren't human," she got out, and stared unapologetically at Trine.

The Hiver seemed to accept that as within the spirit of the exercise, and went on, "Our owner, he was, our mentor," and now the plural had shifted from the assembled crew to the plurality of Trine themselves. "Loyal to his...discipline. Safe hands, at least purely in matters of scholastic rigour. Died in space, when he should have died in some comfortable retirement on-planet, where he belonged. And yet, as an academic, he was one of ours."

Another awkward pause, everyone else eyeing them sidelong. Trine manufactured a sigh.

"I am sorry, and it's no disrespect to the spacer traditions. But he's dead, you see," they explained in a small voice. "And I wasn't finished with him. I was going to debate him at conferences. I was going to outdo him in the academiotypes. I was going to refute his theories. Because he *owned* me. I was his *thing*. He taught me a great deal and if not for him I'd not be me and not have achieved what I have. But I was his property, first and foremost. When I finally rejoin the Assembly and then instantiate out again it won't matter, but for as long as I'm *this* me, I carry him with me. I thought this would help me put him down, but I don't think it has."

They regarded Trine critically for a moment, nobody quite sure what to make of any of it. At last Kittering tapped forwards a few steps, ostentatiously lifted his cup in his mouthparts and decanted it into a pouch on the inside of his shield arms. Colonial 'shine didn't agree with Hanni. In truth it didn't agree particularly well with humans.

They drank, all of them. Even Trine, taking the liquid in to break it down for fuel, which wasn't far from its native state anyway.

"I'm sorry," Solace said, into the quiet. "I couldn't like him. I think he was a bad man. But I'm sorry."

"There is a theory," Trine said softly, "that when the Architects reshape a planet, all the sentient people on that planet are...taken into some special place. Some unspace repository of people. That the Architects are somehow preserving people from their excesses."

"I never heard that," Olli objected.

"It dates to an early period of the war," Trine explained. "The start of the Polyaspora, when people wanted very much to believe that ninety per cent of everyone they knew weren't dead. It isn't a very good theory, in fact. Indeed, on the purely physical level, it's manifestly unprovable. But I understand why people would want it to be true. Because it's hard, when you're not finished with someone. Like a book with the final chapters deleted. You want to believe there's an intact copy out there, somehow. So it is with Storquel. So it is with Idris. I have been in the world too long, because I have generated new maudlinity routines. I am sorry to inflict them on you."

"I never heard that," Olli repeated, and Solace wondered if there was some casualty in her past she was thinking of. Surely not an Architect victim—she wasn't old enough for that—but someone. She knew very little about Olli's past.

*

Soon after that, and several days sooner than she anticipated, Solace was called up before Monitor Superior Tact, or "Mother." She was back on active duty because something unexpected had arrived.

Tact was highly placed in the Aspirat, the Partheni intelligence service that Solace herself now had one foot in. Right now, Solace reckoned, she was probably running her life on less than two hours' sleep every twenty-four, given how the diplomatic scene had exploded. And something new had turned up to add even more unwanted flavour to her day. When Solace entered, there were a dozen separate virtual displays hovering about the room, Tact standing in the midst of them. All but two—presumably the two she was author-ized to see—shut down as she came in.

"We've had a packet through," Tact informed her, which in itself was just everyday business, but obviously there was more to it than that. "A Hiver jockey." Meaning a vessel made into a self-aware unit by slaving it to a Hiver colony, plus its living pilot. Hivers preferred to shut down before entering unspace, and so needed someone to do even the simple plotting of Throughway navigation.

"For Trine, then?" Solace guessed.

"Amongst other diplomatic communiqués, yes. A private packet for Delegate Trine."

Solace just sat and waited at that point, knowing that obviously Trine had all diplomatic privileges and under no circumstances would the Aspirat be looking at their mail.

Tact acknowledged the pause with a curt nod. "Well, quite," she said, waving a hand to reactivate one of the displays. "But in this case the Assembly was passing on a message received from a third party, which gave us just enough weasel-room to feel we needed to know."

Solace waited still, watching Tact pace from one screen to the next. These could all just have been around a desk, or placed together on a wall, but the Monitor had set up her office like this because pacing helped her think.

"It's an invitation to meet, and the Delegate is just the vector."

"They think we still have Idris?" Solace interrupted, and then looked down, chastened. Tact let the breach go, though.

"Well they do," she admitted. "Or some factions in Hugh do, but that's not what this is about. Quite definitively. The message is for Olian Timo, sent by someone obviously well aware of the proximity of Delegate Trine and the *Vulture God*. They name Timo, give coordinates and invite her to meet. Myrmidon Executor Solace, in your professional opinion, how well placed is Timo to be a spy?"

Solace burst out laughing, then put a hand to her mouth, horrified. "Apologies, Mother."

The corner of Tact's mouth twitched. "Well, I suppose that's my answer. No second thoughts? No possibility she's a mistress of misdirection, on the books at Mordant House all this time?"

"Well, we don't know what we don't know," Solace admitted, a saying that went back to Doctor Parsefer herself. "But no sign of it. She's never acted in a way that would actually take advantage of being embedded here. She pushes hard the other way, in fact. She wouldn't take sensitive data from us unless we paid her to do it, and even then she'd turn up her nose at us."

"And the others? Almier and the Hanni?"

"Both considerably better candidates," Solace confirmed, "but my assessment is that they're clean. Loyalty to ship and crew, not government. If they've been asked to go somewhere, I don't think they'll be taking any of our secrets with them."

"They'd go, if there was profit in it for them, say?"

"Why would they not? They were here for Idris. Unless we have a contract for them, they have no purpose here anymore. Unless we want to get heavy-handed, we have no basis on which to detain them." All admirably professional.

Tact regarded her narrowly, nonetheless, and then brought up another virtual display. "Here, then. This is what they've had. Because we might read diplomatic post, once in a while, but we couldn't just sit on it. Depending on how snappy Trine was, they probably saw this an hour ago."

The message was just a few lines of text and an image. The image was poor quality and could easily have been faked. The text read, *Come alone, come here, speak. He is not gone as far as you think.*

The image showed a group of people, grimy, weary, mostly in cultist robes which made the grainy picture a pixelated smear of red and purple, blurred with motion. To one side, almost out of shot as though he was being yanked along by someone stronger—*like always*—Idris Telemmier. Recognizable, even down to the hapless expression, with his jug ears and the awkward hunch of his shoulders. There was a time and place stamp on the image, as susceptible to forgery as all the rest of it. It put him some place she'd never heard of, a Hegemonic-sounding world, *after* Arc Pallator had been screwed up and spread out by the Architects' cosmic origami. Idris. *Alive.*

PART 3
DEATHKNELL

17.

Solace

The way they looked at her as she entered the hangar, Solace knew they'd been plotting. Kris actually jumped up, and Kittering started cycling busily through random images on his arm screens. Only Olli brazened it out, and she was already in the Scorpion, hulking above everyone. Behind them, the *Vulture God*'s cargo hatch was open and a couple of lifter remotes—presumably under Olli's direction—were loading the ship up with printer supplies. All Partheni goods, of course, and Solace had a sneaking suspicion they hadn't actually been allocated to the *Vulture*.

"How's the leg?" Olli's delivery made it sound like a threat.

"Fine, thanks." Tapping the outlines of the medical frame as though it lent them any kinship. "So I understand you've had word."

"Nothing's private, right?"

"The Parthenon doesn't tend to like privacy when it comes to matters of state. We like everything out in the open," Solace tried. She was very aware that, medical frame or not, she was standing like someone about to get in a fight. When the Scorpion shifted footing, just a little, she had to fight the urge to duck.

Olli just grunted, and the two lifters were still working, taking up at least some of her attention. Instead, Kris stepped up to the plate.

"We need to go, Solace. If you know what we got through Trine, you know why."

Solace nodded.

"And we're free agents, free to leave. Those are the terms. I know because I drafted most of that contract for Idris. We might forfeit a bonus or some extra, but we can go. I mean, without Idris, you don't even *need* us. We're just one more non-Partheni ship for your Aspirat to run its operations with, and given we're very obviously known to Hugh, not even very useful for that. So why keep us?"

"They don't trust us," Olli drawled. "Think we're going to sell them out to Hugh. And I told you, Hugh's too damn tight-fisted to pay us well enough."

"No help comes from this," Kittering put in, shifting nervously. "Exits should be frictionless."

"I reckon Solace has brought the friction," Olli observed. "I reckon the Partheni don't play with contracts when it doesn't suit them, am I right? Suddenly we're a security risk."

"Reasons for their objections are absent," Kittering objected but the Scorpion waved a leisurely claw.

"Hugh gets hold of us, then maybe we're the bait to bring Idris out of hiding. If he isn't dead, and this isn't just some real bad-taste joke. I mean, he's the First-Class Int, right, the war veteran. Not like the crappy Liaison Board types that Hugh's got these days. Plus Hugh'd be mad keen to squeeze him for what you girls were doing right now and what he'd told you. So whoever has us, maybe that's what gets them Idris, that's the play?"

Solace shrugged. "It was mentioned," wondering if she should push matters further by revealing Tact's actual words. *A destabilizing influence*, she'd said. *Wherever they go.*

"So what?" The Scorpion stomped two steps closer, looming over her. "They think this is a hoax, we should just sit tight?"

"Hoaxing is not impossible," Kittering observed.

"Stay out of this, Kit."

"Being already within this, that is not possible. There is a likelihood of hoaxing. This is known to us. There is no possibility of inaction, however," the Hanni explained, or at least his translator did its best.

"Monitor Tact does think this is bait for you, so you can be bait for Idris," Solace observed. "If . . . if Idris really is out there."

"Tact can shove it up her—" Olli started, but Kris broke in hurriedly.

"I know you, Solace. So tell me, what orders did they give you? Because left to your own devices you'd be standing here with us helping load the ship for take-off."

Solace managed a smile at that. "They want you to go, but not alone."

"They missed that bit where the message said 'Come alone'?" Olli asked her.

"Did you miss the bit where that's what kidnappers, murderers and assassins generally say to gullible victims?" Solace shot back, because right now she wasn't in the mood for Olli.

Kris, after a shared look with Olli, shook her head. "Look, we get it, but if we turn up with a Partheni fleet behind us then . . . what if they just don't show? What if that's our one chance and we lose it? Yes, probably this is fake, a trap. But what do you expect us to do?"

"Take backup. Take precautions. We're talking about the Aspirat here, not just our navy strong-arming their way in. But if this goes sour…" She bared her teeth in frustration, then continued. "Look, there're an awful lot of people out there who don't like you right now. Broken Harvest, Hugh, the Hegemony maybe…"

"Well I don't like them right back, twice as much." Olli's expression suggested she would extend that courtesy to the entire Parthenon if necessary. "Look, this is our business, Solace."

"This is the Parthenon's business," Solace said sharply, forcing herself to stand up to that looming frame, to meet Olli's angry glower. "We have a class of Int candidates now. There're going to be Parthenon Intermediaries, one way or another. But one way means with Idris here to help, to teach, to be studied so that our people can become something like he is, without… You know how it goes, the surgery and the biochemical manipulation. Idris has let enough slip, over the time you've known him. The term used by the Hugh program was 'wastage.' And that's what we're looking at. The one-in-ten or even one-in-a-hundred success rate that the Liaison Board works with. But with Idris here, who knows how many lives could be saved from that? And it's what he wanted. So it's our business too, mine and my sisters'. Please take the escort, to give you the best chance of success."

Olli looked to Kris again. Solace saw her face twist with her usual ill humour, but somehow her heart wasn't in it. She wondered if Olli was thinking, even for a moment, of Lightly and Diligent, the pair of Partheni she'd befriended on Arc Pallator and who'd died on the *Grendel's Mother*, of course, defending the *Vulture*. Defending the Colonials even, at the end, just as the Partheni always had.

She saw Kris's small nod, and an arm-wave from Kit which she knew meant the same thing.

"This escort better be fucking subtle," Olli grumbled. "And...you'll be wanting your regular berth, I guess. We'll need someone to talk Patho to them."

*

They went with the Parthenon's slightly conflicted blessing, therefore, and with the Aspirat's picket ship *Mhairi*. It was the latest from the shipyards, with a complement of Myrmidons and a clutch of accelerators that could be converted to a mass hammer if need be, more armament than a ship that size should have been able to brandish.

They went with a solemn farewell from Trine, too, and a set of credentials as though they were on official diplomatic business for the Hiver Assembly should they need it. By that time, Solace was wondering if Trine's longstanding reluctance to re-integrate with the Assembly was because of the way they threw their rather nebulous authority around at the slightest provocation.

With all this, they set out, following the path in the message. It cast them down a net of Throughway points out of Partheni-controlled space, past the edge of the Colonies to worlds claimed and settled by the Hannilambra, Kit's species. Specifically, to a dry world his translator could best render as Ittring.

They timed their arrival so that the *Mhairi* got there first, with a piece of spurious business to account for her presence,

297

and no overt connection to the *Vulture God*. Not that the deception would fool anyone looking to put the pieces together.

"So we wait until a, what is it, Minister calls us? Those are your go-betweens, right, your fixers?" Olli asked. "I mean, message didn't give us an address, just a world. So they'll have to pick us out of traffic when we come in."

"Ministers are not the thing," Kittering said. "Residence is the purpose of Ittring. Business will be entrusted to a supervisor. There will be disapproval."

The others side-eyed him at this, but he obviously didn't feel inclined to explain the intricacy of Hanni society. To Solace's admittedly untrained eye, he seemed ill at ease, legs not still for a moment as he crouched on his stool in the command pod.

She had the *God*'s rebooting system bring up some planetary details. Ittring was another sealess world, no surface water but extensive subterranean aquifers. There was a thriving biosphere that existed almost entirely underground, save for the mile-wide sand-coloured plates that were the photosynthetic organs of a kind of gigantic lichen. Or possibly coral, or another of those human approximations that always missed the mark with alien life. There was also a colonial species of something that looked like a man-size slug but lived more like ants, and apparently zipped about on a natural super-frictionless slime at speeds of up to fifty klicks an hour, which must be something to see. As well as exporting the slime, the large population of Hanni had semi-domesticated the slugs, or at least gene-hacked them to do tasks. The Hanni resided exclusively in the upper reaches of the towering mounds the slugs built. And there, they...

lived. Solace's experience of Hannilambra had only been where they rubbed up against other species, acting as traders, fixers, go-betweens and specialists. But of course there were plenty of worlds they'd spread to and colonized. Worlds they were leery of other species just turning up at too, to judge from the long and untranslated conversation Kit was having with orbital control. She then noticed there were precious few non-Hanni vessels in-system. The *Vulture* and the *Mhairi* both stood out painfully.

Well, whoever sent the message knows we're here.

"New message," Kris reported. "Not from orbital. On-planet. The..." She struggled with what she was hearing over comms. "I'm not even going to attempt saying it, sorry. One of the...translator says 'Post-domestic resorts,' whatever that actually is. Gives us somewhere to go."

"Always encouraging when they're so lazy you actually have to walk into the trap," Olli grumbled. "How are we doing this?"

"Kit, can we actually land?"

"This is being addressed," Kit said, his translator sounding testy.

"Well I guess we go down. Or most of us. The Scorpion—"

"Will not under any circumstances be countenanced," Kit put in. "Nor Mr. Punch. There must be no indication of violence."

"Fucking perfect," Olli grumbled. "They want us naked and tied up, too? That a Hanni custom around here?"

"Preferable, not mandatory," Kit said, and Solace had no idea whether he was joking.

At last, some sort of planetside docking clearance was agreed, and Olli took the ship down. If the Scorpion was out of the question, she'd stay with the *Vulture*, or so Kris eventually got her to concede. The rest of them would go meet their contact. Solace encrypted a message to the *Mhairi* and told them to ready a team for orbital drop intervention in the worst-case scenario. But *only* in that scenario because it felt like they were all on uncharacteristically thin ice with the Hanni, whom she'd only ever known as a cheerfully pragmatic people.

"Is there some crisis going on here already, that we're about to drop into the middle of?" she asked Kittering. Because she wouldn't have been surprised.

He regarded her blankly, although the five-eyed stare of a Hanni was never expressive to human eyes. "Residence is the purpose of the colony," he explained, and then, "Family," trying for something humans might understand.

"They think we'll hurt their children?"

"Correct."

The soaring spire of the slug-built tower had no landing pad, but its top was ringed with the spiked torus of a gravitic engine. Olli jockeyed the *Vulture God* until the invisible hands of docking control had the ship. Then Solace, Kit and Kris walked gingerly down the ramp with nothing but a three-hundred-metre drop through empty air beneath them.

"That'll make a getaway difficult if we annoy the locals," Kris observed drily. And the locals were watching them very carefully. There were more than a score of compact Hanni shuttles in hovering dock already, with crews in and out, and engineers picking their way crabwise over their hulls. Every one of them stopped to stare at the two humans, canting their shells to fix their amber, unblinking eyes on them. Kittering had his shield arms pulled tight, and Solace had the impression he was horribly embarrassed about the company he was keeping. *Bringing us home to show the parents?* Except she was trying to remember what little she knew about Hanni domestic arrangements, and that wasn't it.

One vessel three berths along had a deputation coming to meet it, with a dozen Hanni in two columns playing a jittery kind of music on stringed instruments held in their mouthparts. It sounded weirdly off-key and lacked the heavy percussion of the Hannilambra compositions Solace was used to. A group emerged from the ship and there was a great deal of what felt like ritualized exchange. Her translator was working overtime and she still couldn't really follow what was said, just getting weirdly conversational phrases about time and work and even the weather. Kit was hurrying onwards, wanting no part of it.

Within the tunnels of the spire, they were instantly forced to stoop, the top of Solace's helmet scraping awkwardly on the round ceiling. Hanni passed rapidly back and forth, veering up onto the walls to detour around the slow, bent-over humans. There was no sense of being in a public space or somewhere with any concessions to non-Hanni. Kit led them through a network of broad, low tunnels, which were lit with an orange glare from beads set in a spiralling pattern. This combination made Solace feel queasy until she switched on her visor's filter. Occasionally she glimpsed larger chambers where Hanni were doing...things. Meeting, standing in circles or spirals or other patterns. She saw them painting each other's shells and shield arms carefully, or debating before screens of dense, spiky Hanni script—inventories perhaps, or lists of something. She'd seen Hanni goods manifests and they weren't entirely dissimilar. Then there was one where five Hanni crouched before brightly painted—therefore wealthy?—others. Their own shells were utterly unadorned, and Solace felt they were being judged or punished, or...? Kit stopped to watch, or perhaps stopped out of respect, and they all had to wait until whatever was going on was finished. In the end, a Hanni came in with a wicked-looking powered blade, its edges glowing red-orange, and Solace braced herself for some barbaric execution. The five penitents were marked, though, the same symbol across their backs carved in meticulous detail. Kit made a sibilant sound, like a sigh.

"One day, perhaps," his translator offered.

"They...Wait, is that a Caregiver investment?" Kris obviously knew more about Hanni culture than Solace did.

"These things come to pass, for those who falter," Kit said, apparently agreeing. He danced out a little staccato of vented tension before leading them on, adding, "Also, be braced. Unpleasantness lies ahead for me. You also, it is possible?"

"Trouble?" Solace asked.

"Not that." And then they stepped out into a large chamber, the biggest they'd seen, and it was full of corpses.

For a moment Solace just saw discarded shells. She had the idea Hanni might shed their carapaces like Earth insects did. But no. Several hundred dead Hanni were spread out in a radiating pattern filling most of the chamber floor. The air was heavy with a chemical scent that was either decay or something intended to prevent it. And live Hanni were coming in and out of the chamber, hauling pallets of the dead, removing corpses closer to the centre, or shifting bodies inwards, in a constant and nightmarish cycle. Others were crouching near the centremost dead, marking records on projected screens. Solace expected to see the burnt marks, the penitents condemned to be handlers of the dead, but the Hanni here had shells painted with stark bars, some particular caste or profession that needed immediate recognition.

"There's... what happened? Is there a pandemic, or...?"

Kit apparently found the question offensive, but Kris sidled close and murmured, "This is... kind of what Hanni want. The end of how they want it to go. These are successful Hanni females."

Solace's mind turned, trying for purchase on the idea, then memory came to her aid. All Hanni were male, until they finally went home and settled down. Which consisted entirely of fertilizing the eggs of a female. They then became female themselves and laid their own eggs. After which they died. That was the life cycle they'd evolved with, and carried with them through burgeoning civilization and to the stars. "Post-domestic," to Hanni, was a death sentence, and one they embraced readily. Those "caregivers" must be the abstainers, who forwent the chance at offspring so they could nursemaid everyone else's next generation.

She wanted to ask, then. She wanted to ask if this was actually what Kit wanted. She herself was born out of a vat, after all. Surely the Hannilambra could turn away from this cycle, bring in a technology that would let them have both children and an old age. She wanted to ask whether Kit wouldn't rather just ply the Throughways and never go home to die. For all that every jot of Largesse or Halma he saved would be intended to provide a nest egg for a brood of offspring he would never himself see. She asked precisely none of these things, however, because they were human questions, and this was not human business.

"So where's our contact?" Kris asked, but even as the words

escaped her, Kit's comms crackled and he was leading them on. While a trap was still a possibility, Solace reckoned anyone trying to make trouble here was going to win themselves every Hanni on-planet as an enemy.

"They are an Adjuster," Kit supplied, as they skirted the edge of the charnel cavern and crept into another low tunnel beyond.

"As in loss adjuster? Like an insurance thing?" Kris asked him.

"Not unlike. Not like. Possessions that have not been liquidated must be valued and disposed of for the benefit of the young. Difficulties often attend this. Unusual or illegal goods, stolen or hard to sell. All must be reckoned. Often sold off-world. Many contacts are required for Adjusters. Also, it is shameful work. Given to outsiders."

They were then dropping down a slope into a square-cut chamber, the first straight walls they'd seen since entering the spire. The walls were lined with screens, and the screens displayed skyscapes of a score of different colours, weather, clouds, lightning, suns in a dozen different hues rising and setting.

In the midst of this was what she took for an armoured Hanni, but then realized was a Hiver frame. They were amongst Hanni, of course, so why would they even approximate the human?

Their body was finished with metallized plastic in brass and silver and purple chrome, the surface worked into elaborate scrollwork in imitation of a high-status Hannilambra. Their greeting, fiddled and waved at Kit, was recognizable as superior to inferior, enough that their friend stamped out a little staccato of annoyance before translating.

"Their signifier is the Neurian." Not a Hanni-sounding name. "Very uppity. Expecting us. There are complaints about how long we've taken to arrive. The possibility was there for them to meet us at the dock." Cranking the volume up for this last aside to ensure that the Neurian heard.

Solace and Kris exchanged glances and then the lawyer gave a brief, formal bow. If there was a proper etiquette for greeting a Hanni-shaped Hiver on an alien world, it hadn't been in anyone's manuals.

"Minister Neurian," Kris hazarded. "You know why we're here. I...if it helps, we have diplomatic credentials from your Assembly. If that smooths over anything for you."

The Neurian skittered back a few paces, raising the embossed faces of their shield arms. "Ah, humans. A long time, since I have had to communicate with humans. Hannilambra language is so much more nuanced. It does not *help*, Mesdam Keristina Soolin Almier. You make the common mistake that we are all toes of the same foot, in the Assembly. Some of us refuse to re-integrate. Some of us prefer to remain who we are. I choose not to give up this instantiation of the Neurian. I am." The voice had started flat and rusty, but inflated with personality as the words tumbled out of their crab-shaped body. A crotchety and unpleasant personality, Solace felt.

"Well then, let's cut to it," Kris suggested. "You, or your principals, went to some lengths to tell us you have Idris Telemmier, our crewmate. So what happens next?"

"An incorrect assumption from the outset, splendid," the Neurian remarked acidly. "And yet, Menheer Telemmier, Int first class, is indeed the subject of this meeting. My principals do not have him. They have information pertaining to him that is not entirely divorced from their own interests. However, as you are known to them, and they feel a... there is no human word for what they feel, but let us suggest a sense of *connection*... they act under obligation in bringing this to your attention and involving you in their plans of vengeance."

"Vengeance against Idris?" Solace broke in.

The Neurian's eyes—just lights set into a jagged metal crown, likely not even sensors—tilted towards her. "Another incorrect assumption. But regard."

The screens went dark one by one, the room cast into shadow so that Solace was tensed for an ambush at any moment. One more incorrect assumption, as it turned out. A single screen was left, and now instead of a skyscape it showed a woman. Lean, hair hacked short, face taut with some emotion as she spoke—there was no audio, but the movement of her lips didn't suggest Colvul or Parsef.

"The Tothiat," Solace said. The woman from Arc Pallator, who'd been there at the end, fighting the Voyenni with her. Who'd not been on the shuttles, and so had shared the fate of the planet. Surely even one of her kind couldn't survive that. Except she'd been making a lot of assumptions, as the Neurian had pointed out.

Another screen, halfway across the room, lit up. The same still image of Idris, supposedly dated to after Arc Pallator had ceased to be anything other than fatal art, but it was a broader perspective, showing more. A whole host of cultists, the shabby poor of that world, were all heading outwards from the square space they'd been crammed into moments before. She saw the pillars there but it was a moment before she understood she was looking at the Temple. Except this temple was in the heart of a swathe of tall forked plants, trampled down by the exodus. Lime-green foliage such as Arc Pallator never saw.

"The Essiel saved them," Kris breathed.

"You simplify the situation but it will stand as an explanation," the Neurian said, and pulled the focus of the image in on the one part of the crowd not lurid with Hegemonic colours. Idris, of course. Idris and the Tothiat, Emmaneth.

"She has him," the Neurian explained. "And my principals are keen to speak to *her*. They invite you to go hunting."

Havaer

"This is Emma Caelan Ostri," Chief Laery said. "She's a murderer, among other things. She used to murder people for *us* before she decided she wanted more of a roving brief."

Havaer hung tethered to the curved wall by a wrist strap, examining the woman's face. He scrolled down, seeing a piecemeal record, service and criminal, nothing within the last eight years.

He supposed she wasn't *Chief* Laery right at this moment, and the *us* she referred to might or might not still include her in its ranks. Certainly this gravity-less little maintenance orbital they were now in around Berlenhof wasn't her usual office. She crouched against one wall like an attenuated spider, perfectly at ease, her brittle limbs freed of the shackles of a-grav or a world's pull. He himself was having to constantly readjust his pose to stop himself drifting about.

"We picked her out of the *Byron* data. She was on Arc Pallator. And she's an unlikely pilgrim."

"What's her deal?" he asked. *Why is this relevant to me?*

Laery's eyes were hooded. She wasn't looking straight at him, although given that he couldn't stay still maybe that was his fault. "She got shot up, badly, on assignment for us. One of my case files, in fact. Extinguishing a criminal cartel just as it got taken over by something nastier. The something nastier almost did for her. It certainly did for any lingering loyalty to us at Mordant House and she skipped out on us soon after. Went straight to that something nastier and offered it her services and her insider knowledge in exchange for a fix-up."

Havaer had skipped ahead. "That's quite some fix-up," he said.

"Well she had quite some injuries to get fixed," Laery told her. "She ran into a Tothir host and they knocked seven shades of shit out of her, to be frank. After she unloaded everything she had into them. You're familiar with the breed?"

Havaer nodded. *All too bloody familiar.*

"She reckoned becoming one could sort her out," Laery explained. "She was right, and she worked for them for some time. Killed more people, sometimes our people. She was always a vicious little bitch. Now she's a vicious little semi-immortal. Thankfully we've got some bad medicine for that and I'll make sure you get some."

"You know the run-ins I've had with these people," Havaer said. "Without departmental backing I don't know what I can do."

"That's not your concern," Laery told him. Havaer reckoned it very much was but he didn't contradict her. "What's your concern is the word that's come to me, through private channels, that Mesdam Ostri, Emmaneth as she's currently calling herself in her new incarnation, got off Arc Pallator in company."

She sent him a single still image: the crowd, the Temple, the grassland. Telemmier.

"Chief, this is departmental business. This is Hugh security."

"No," she said forcefully enough that she had to claw at the wall to stop the single word jarring her loose. "Right now this is our business. If you're still with me, Havaer. Believe me, there is nothing about how I got this information that I would share with the wider Department. I'm only lucky that right now I'm a free agent."

"This is linked to the..." He'd already made a full report about what Colvari had found in the data, the ark-fleet conspiracy.

"Leave that to me," Laery told him. "You did well there, but I'm taking it out of your hands." She sagged, and he wondered how long it was since she'd slept. "You don't want to go up against your own, Havaer. It leaves a mark on the soul."

"I already did, on Hismin's Moon," he pointed out.

"And you're eager for more?"

He wasn't, of course.

"The Board is corrupt," Laery said, more to herself than him. "They've been moving their people in for an age, to make Mordant House their tame dog. So sometimes we have to go elsewhere..."

"Chief?"

Her eyes snapped back to him. "This is your task. Take the dossier, track down Emmaneth. Recover Telemmier if you can. If not... keep him out of the hands of any enemy power. You understand, Havaer?"

That prospect wasn't much more enticing than butting heads with Mordant House but he nodded grimly. "I can't exactly just go roving the Hegemony. Especially as we don't even know if they think they're at war with us yet."

"I wouldn't ask you to. Thing is," Laery explained, "she's not in the Hegemony. Or not most of her time. It's all in the dossier. She's in and out of Colonial space, on a fairly small number of worlds, these last two years. Since she sold out the employers she gave us over for. Quite the turncoat little bitch. So go find her, and find out what her deal is, and get our Int back. And if our former employee meets a fate her physiology can't shrug off, all the better."

18.

Solace

The Neurian then clammed up about precisely who their principals were.

"You are allies or you are rivals," they explained, with all the smugness a mechanical Hanni could exude. "In the latter case, they are more than happy that you don't know their identity."

Solace stared at the thing sourly. From what Kit said, someone in the Neurian's position got to deal with a great many outside agencies, mostly liquidating or investing property of deceased Hanni mothers so that their offspring could be better provided for. At first, she couldn't work out why this wasn't just an internal Hanni matter, and assumed some death-custom amongst a species whose attitude towards death was, from a human point of view, particularly bizarre. After a while of Kit trying to explain without ever quite saying it, she understood that the Neurian and their peers were specifically responsible for getting rid of goods that the late owners wouldn't want to be associated with, and that the Hanni as a whole would be embarrassed to retain.

"They're a fence!" she accused Kit. "You people have a whole black market going on."

"Wholly inaccurate assessment of the situation," Kittering replied, though she could see the evasiveness in the way he couldn't stay still. "An appropriate human moniker is to say 'Repairer of Reputations.'"

"They have Hegemonic contacts, these allies," Kris pointed out. "And a good communication network, to get word all the way to here this quickly. That means access to plenty of ships."

"So what do they need us for?" Solace demanded. "Right now we're just a salvager. We don't even have Idris."

They eyed the Neurian, who set their screens flashing up with images of planetside or orbital views—human-built stations, human-occupied cities. "My associates need a vessel that can operate without problem in the Colonial Sphere. With a crew committed to locating these fugitives. The former is common, the latter...is you. In return, they have resources you lack, but more important they have the information, without which you will not even know where to start. Your friend is out there. Or he was. This woman is a bad person. Tothiat are all mad."

"The pain," Kittering said unexpectedly, and then, "There was no fear of being hurt in the one killed by Olli and myself. We were told the pain of being Tothiat eclipses all else."

"Cheery," Kris said. "We need to talk to Olli."

"Be brisk," the Neurian advised.

Under the Hiver's metal gaze they relayed the details to Olli, none of which pleased her much. The looked-for blast of invective didn't come, though. The *Vulture*'s de facto captain seemed oddly hesitant. "Some Hegemony concern, you reckon?"

"It makes sense," Kris agreed. "That's where Tothiat come from."

"Yeah. Yeah, it is. Fuck." And then a drawn-out silence on comms.

"Olli?"

"I mean I don't see we have a choice. If Idris is out there, then we've got to go get him, right? No matter what. I mean, we've gotten into bed with some pretty shitty types before now, yeah?" She sounded as though she was trying to convince herself. She sounded as though—Solace fancied—she was already a step ahead of them on the logic chain.

"Tell the robocrab bastard we'll do it, I guess," Olli said at last. "I mean, what are they asking, first off? There a downpayment?"

"My principals wish to meet with you. Your agreement to that is simultaneously all they ask, and a prerequisite. They like immediacy in their dealings."

"How very old-fashioned," Kris murmured, but as simple as that, they had a deal.

Return to your ship, the Neurian instructed them. They were to break orbit from Ittring and head out into open space to await contact from these mysterious principals. Solace reckoned everyone was thinking the same thing: keep the gravitic drives hot and be ready for a speedy exit to unspace, however hard that last resort would be on everyone's mental health. A short hop down the Throughways should get them out of almost any trouble.

Almost. There was that time it hadn't worked...

Solace was developing a very unpleasant feeling about all of this. Enough that, as soon as they were back aboard the *God*, she went and got Mr. Punch. Or at least the replacement Mr. Punch she'd been issued after losing her last accelerator on Arc Pallator. Sometimes she felt she was leaving a trail of expensive Partheni kit across the galaxy.

They had the impression that planetside Ittring authorities were more than happy to see them go. It wasn't a planet that welcomed outsiders. It wasn't hard to see why the Hanni were very, very protective of these creche worlds, where they spawned and raised their young. While Olli took them out past the orbitals, out-system away from the planet and its sun, she sent a message to their escort, the *Mhairi*.

Contact with middleman made and an agreement reached to cooperate with nameless patron. We are awaiting instructions that will bring us into contact with the principal. She considered when the prime moment for a trap would be. A space rendezvous would give the *God* a chance to slip away if they were deft enough. More likely they'd be directed to some other planet, some confined space on a world, or within an orbital's gravitic reach. Hopefully the *Mhairi* and its Myrmidons would be enough to break up any party long enough to let them get away.

Olli had been subdued since they got back. A lack of complaints from her was a genuine cause for concern. Solace kept meaning to confront her and see what was up. Olli was busy, though. Busy fixing this or that, sketching Throughway routes so she could jump-start any navigation the moment they got into unspace. Busy not talking to Solace, mostly. Or anyone. Kris and Kittering sat at their stations and fidgeted, and were obviously just as leery of their captain's mood.

After hovering about the entrance of the drone bay, Olli's fiefdom, Solace sloped back to the command pod, where Kris was fielding comms from the *Mhairi*. "I'm not picking anything up," she said as Solace entered. "Can you share sensor data?"

Solace dropped into a seat and patched into the conversation, hearing the Partheni officer say, "You're right at the epicentre. Are you entering unspace? You're powering up grav drives," the accent harsh and struggling with the Colvul words.

"We're really not," Kris assured her, bent over her console. A batch of data came through, the universe through *Mhairi's* eyes. The ship's military-grade sensors had picked out a flexing of the universe, a bowl of gravitic distortion with the *Vulture God* at its exact centre.

"I'm not seeing any of that," Kris complained. "I'm . . . picking up signal lag, minute lag on sensor data, though. I'm . . ." She locked eyes with Solace. "We can't see it because we're inside it."

"Get us moving," Solace decided. "Olli, get us moving!"

Olli must have been listening in because their brachator drives were hauling the *God* forwards almost immediately, reaching for the chaotic interface between space and unspace, digging their claws in and yanking them forwards and sideways. It was a violent skip across space that their gravitic buffers muted into the faintest of shudders for the crew inside.

"It's still with you," came the comms from the *Mhairi*, feeding them live sensor logs now, distorted by whatever was going on. And then, in a hollow voice, "It is chasing you."

Then something came out of unspace, right on top of them. It looked like a sun.

Not a ball of incandescent gas, not a *real* sun. Something all the more frightening for that. A sun from art, all curved and jagged rays daggering from a central hub, its centre dominated by a great irising maw opening to devour the

Vulture whole. If they hadn't been on the move, they would have been within those teeth even as the thing tore its way free of unspace. As it was, the sudden presence of another body so close threw their own gravitic calculations out, shifting the fabric of space so that the *God* was abruptly tumbling away, cut loose from the universe and scrabbling for purchase against the face of reality.

Solace focused, that long-learned Myrmidon's discipline rising within her. She compensated for their spin, then had the salvage ship's inadequate lasers online and tracking the newcomer despite their spiralling path. Olli was swearing blue murder, which at least was reassuring. She could see the sun-ship's own gravitic envelope trying to snag them and haul them close, with Kittering already frantically rebuffing them, trying to use that same burgeoning force to bounce them away instead. Kris was exchanging data and monosyllables with the *Mhairi*, the Partheni vessel already inbound with weapons hot.

"What even *is* that?" Olli demanded.

The sun-ship revolved gracefully around the central disc, a tessellated face of triangles and diamonds all arrowing into its hungry hatchway. The radiating vanes were all curved planes, like the hooked teeth of a circular saw, each twisted identically out of true. Each one bigger than the *God*, too. She had taken them for decoration at first but now realized that together they constituted a gravitic drive of impressive power. The ship's frame was wholly unlike anything she'd seen before, but the radial symmetry and geometrical aesthetic said *Hegemony* to her.

"The Essiel have come for us. Because we took the shuttles?" she got out. It was the only thing that made sense to her.

"No." Olli's voice was shaking. "Not that. Older grudge than that. But it's fucking *personal* sure enough."

Kit was keeping them just ahead of the sun-ship's gravitic reach, as if they were a cork on turbulent waters, knocked further away each time a hand grasped for it. Solace reckoned this was mostly because the sun-ship was still orienting itself after its return to the real.

"We need to leave," she decided. "Olli, can we get into unspace?"

"Planet's far enough, but they're right on us and they're shipping a lot of mass," Olli got out.

"*Vulture God*," the *Mhairi* broke in. "We'll run interference. Commencing assault now. Get out. Compris?"

"Compris, Mother," Solace agreed automatically, but right now Olli wasn't going to pick her up on it. Unless the sun-ship turned out to be some glorified diplomatic barge, the *Mhairi* wasn't going to be able to go toe to toe with it for very long.

The *Vulture God* was under control now, brachator drive dragging it back and forth as it fled an erratic course away from the sun-ship. Solace tracked the little Partheni interceptor as it set a course that would clip between the two vessels, its accelerator banks and gravity hammer already tracking.

"Comms from... says it's the *Almighty Scythe of Morning*," Kris said. "Damn me. Says we... ah... says we agreed to an audience."

"These are the Neurian's friends, are they?" Solace asked. "Wait... *Scythe of...*?" Or whatever that originally meant in some Hegemonic language. Except certain links were forming in her head. Scythes were for... harvesting, weren't they? "Is this *Aklu*?"

"Yes, it is fucking Aklu," Olli snarled. She had a dozen points on the ship's elaborate hull flagged up, isolating the Broken Harvest insignia they'd seen before.

"They are being bounced off," Kit's translator garbled, but it was a fair assessment. The *Mhairi*'s accelerator fire was being bent everywhere but towards the *Scythe* itself. Then it got its mass hammer going—a pitifully small affair compared to the vast batteries the Parthenon had unleashed against Architects, but still the most powerful sledgehammer available to crack this particular nut.

She was gratifyingly surprised to see the impact actually knock the *Scythe* from its pursuit, swatting it off at an angle, though without any visible damage.

"Olli!" she called, but midway through that they were already clawing for unspace, tearing out of the real with a rending shudder that shook the whole ship.

She was alone.

They'd been all hands to the pumps, with no chance of getting into suspension. Even now Olli would be plotting their Throughway and exit point before putting herself under in her control pod in the drone bay. Kris and Kit were hopefully already stumbling through their own solitary nightmares to their pods and Solace had to do the same. She got up, disoriented despite nothing in the ship having changed. Except everything had changed. It wasn't real anymore, and neither was she. She had to get herself under before just *being* started to mess with her head.

She had her fingertips on the cover of her pod, already feeling the emptiness of the ship starting to crawl and shift around her, as though every part of it thronged with movement the moment she turned her back. For a second she thought the lid wouldn't open, but then it already was, no visible transition. She stared down into it.

What if I go under and...

—This is not the time to think this—

And cease?

What if I cease?

—You've done this a hundred times—

I'm already unreal. Nothing here is real. It's all in my head. I'm about to turn my head off. What if I...

Then a weird moment of clarity. *How does Idris stand this, over and over and not even going to sleep? How is it even the same Idris who comes out each time?*

And she started, staring down at the uncertain confines of the suspension pod, because as his name sounded inside her head, so she thought she heard his voice. She was about to turn, to look round. Surely he'd be there. Idris, or his ghost, perhaps with some clue, some vital information that would let them find him. She came so close to looking. Even as her head turned, though, she realized it wasn't him. It couldn't be him. But something was there, and it really wanted her to look at it. It was practically at her shoulder, breathing in her ear. It was a shadow at the corner of her eye. It *needed* her to see it, and if she did, she'd make it real, and perhaps then what came out of unspace wouldn't be *her* at all, even if it still wore her face and answered to her name and—

They fell out of unspace into the real and Solace took Kris's elbow in the throat and fell backwards, coughing. They'd both been about to get into the same pod, in their lone universes.

"What happened? Olli?" Kris helped her up even as she called out.

"We're—don't know where the fuck, just some shitty little Hanni mining rock somewhere and—*fuck!*"

The *Vulture God* lurched violently, spilling Kris and Solace onto a floor that was briefly a sixty-degree slope. Solace grabbed a slate as it spun past and linked to the ship's sensors.

They were in the centre of the sun. The *Almighty Scythe of Morning* was all around them, jaws gaping to swallow them up. Not the first time they'd been tracked through unspace, of course. And last time it had been the self-same faction of Hegemonic outcasts. The Broken Harvest cartel had caught up with them.

Solace went and got her gun.

"I don't think that'll help," Kris told her.

"We can't just let them take us." She knew Kris was right, but...something in her wouldn't just bow the knee.

"Damn right we won't," came Olli's voice over the comms. "We're leaving."

"Olli, they've got us. We're inside their gravitic field," Kris pointed out.

Around them the ship shuddered.

"We're leaving," Olli repeated, teeth clenched, and then the pair of them were almost shaken off their feet as the *Vulture God* lurched forwards, fighting against the hold the *Scythe* had on it.

Hopeless, Solace knew, but the ship rammed sideways, then forwards again—she and Kris were crouched on the floor now, holding on to anything that presented itself. She heard a squeal of audio interference from the direction of Kit's own cabin, where his pod was, followed by a rapid patter of complaints she couldn't follow.

"Where are our dampeners?" Kris yelled. "What have they done to us?"

"Not them," Solace got out. "Us. Olli's using everything the engine can give to shift us. Not much left to counter inertia. This could get messy." In between lurches she was trying to call up data from the ship, to see where any of this was getting them. Every part of the *God* was complaining, groans and grinds from the very walls as they wrestled the *Scythe* for control. Then she had a display open, juddering with jagged attacks of static, and saw that their ship was actually making some considerable speed, brachator drive hauling them arm over arm, faster and faster in an attempt to escape. It was an attempt only, because the *Scythe* hadn't let go and they were hauling the far larger ship with them, dragging it around like so much cargo. The *God* was a salvage craft after all. Its drives were far punchier than its size suggested.

But the *Scythe* wasn't letting go, and then Kittering—apparently having either climbed or fallen into the command pod—broke in with an urgent new problem.

"Hull sensors, intrusion at drone bay hatch. Olli watch out!"

"Oh I'm fucking ready!" Olli told them, meaning she'd got the drones to fit her into the Scorpion, Solace guessed, even as she was piloting the ship. "Bring it on."

Solace snarled and made for the bay herself, scrabbling uphill half the way, then skidding down as the gravity gradient shifted beneath her. She ended up rolling into the bay and almost bouncing off the Scorpion, where it stood clamped to the floor, every arm spread and tipped with murder. Olli's face, within its plastic pod, was screwed up with concentration.

"Hope you brought a friend," she hissed.

Solace weighed Mr. Punch in her hands. "We're basically going down in flames, is that the plan?"

"What is it you bitches say? Prêt à combattre?"

"Prêt, Mother."

Olli snorted. Then she obviously lost the hacking war over the hatch because it flew open. That the *Scythe*'s engines were maintaining an atmosphere envelope was established when all the air in the drone bay failed to fly outside like it was rushing to greet a long-lost relative. What came *in* was a single figure, not even suited, not even armed.

"Ah shit," Olli said. "This just got trickier."

"You have any of that…stuff you had?" Solace tried.

"Shot it all into her brother, that last time," Olli announced, loud enough for the newcomer to hear.

It was a woman, lean, hard looking, wearing a long coat and a harness with grav-handles so she could ride the *Scythe*'s gravitic fields and fly if she wanted to. She was facing them, but Solace knew damn well there was one of those lobster symbiotes down her spine. She was a Tothiat named Heremon, and she worked for the Essiel gangster who ran the Broken Harvest cartel.

There had been another—presumably not her actual brother, but her fellow lieutenant. A particularly nasty thug named Mesmon, and Olli had done for him with a particularly nasty concoction designed to sever the Tothir–host link. Which it had, with extreme prejudice. And now Solace was thinking they really should have laid some more of that in.

Heremon cocked her head on one side, looking at Mr. Punch and all the Scorpion's cutlery drawer of implements without concern. If she was anything like Mesmon, she was right not to worry. Tothiat flesh could mend itself faster than anyone could break it.

"Mesdam Olian Timo," she addressed the Scorpion, "The Unspeakable Aklu, the Razor and the Hook, is given to understand that you have consented to a meeting."

"Maybe I did. But not with him," Olli said. "The bastard metal crab never said it was with him."

"Have *consented*," Heremon repeated. "Which consent constitutes a sacred obligation on your part, and on that of the Unspeakable. You know how seriously the Essiel take such things."

"I *know*," Olli spat, "that your chief doesn't work by the same rules as the rest of the clams. How am I supposed to believe he won't have us flayed alive? We trashed his ship the last time." A moment's pause. "Though he got a better one, that I'll concede. A real nice one."

Heremon's smile was wintry. "Mesdam Timo, it is the case that the Unspeakable has been severed from the social contracts of the Essiel, and that is right and proper and part of its place in the universe. But for *you*, it extends a special courtesy. For you, and a single companion, the Razor shall not whet its edge, and you may talk, about errant Intermediaries and turncoat Tothiat. How's that?"

"Or?"

"Or the same courtesy can be extended later only all your friends will be dead."

Olli scowled furiously, looking like she wanted to bludgeon the universe to death for lumping her with this.

"I'll go," Solace offered. "I'll go with you."

"Kris, Kit, you hearing this?" Olli asked, and they both confirmed it. "No offence, but I'll take Kris, if she'll go." She looked almost apologetic, far from the adversarial mode she usually reserved for talking with Solace. "I mean, if it comes to a fight on their ship, we're royally screwed. At least Kris has a clever mouth on her."

Kris

Kris was regretting that clever mouth, in all honesty. Not that she hadn't survived crossing words with quite the selection of lowlifes and crooks in her time, but the Razor and the Hook was something different.

What even was an Essiel gangster? To a Colonial, the species was that weird but undeniably powerful clique that controlled the Hegemony through, it sometimes seemed, sheer awe. Their human cultists said they were divine and interacted with their masters via worship and propitiation. Their subjects of other species presumably had similar arrangements, or perhaps radically different arrangements. At the heart of it, though, was what the Essiel worldview actually was, and nobody had a clue about it. Except they were obviously very happy for others to do things for them. Being a naturally sedentary species, Kris guessed that was deeply ingrained in their alien psyches.

So what did it mean when one of them went rogue? Or mad, possibly? The Unspeakable Aklu ran a thriving criminal empire of unknown extent, whilst still having access to Hegemonic toys and, as their current predicament showed, ships. Their role within the Hegemony wasn't the same as a human crime lord might take within the Colonies. They had some formal place in the Essiel hierarchy. A cult hierograve had tried to explain that they were like a devil—an enemy to all things, but a sanctioned one, part of a wider plan. But that was just a human take, after all.

What was certain was that Aklu had a great deal to blame the *Vulture God* crew for. Their last clash had killed off a valuable lieutenant and resulted in the loss of Aklu's ship to a Partheni strike team. Before that, they had inadvertently got hold of some Originator regalia Aklu had been transporting, and those same trinkets had been lost in the fight over Berlenhof. If Aklu judged in any way like a human, then it would be thinking they *owed* it, possibly a debt that could only be paid for in blood.

Now Heremon was jauntily leading them through octagonal-sectioned corridors walled with mother-of-pearl and into a chamber where there were not one but two Essiel.

Kris stopped. She'd never actually seen more than one in one place. In fact seeing one was rare enough. But here were two, large as life. The same tall shells, parted at the top to let a flurry of stick-thin limbs and eyestalks emerge, rooted at the bottom by grey, serpentine holdfasts. She recognized the one on the floating couch as Aklu from the mercurial tracery flowing about its carapace in eye-watering patterns. Also from the way the score or so of humans, Castigar and Hanni were standing around it in poses simultaneously servile and ready to enact violence. The other Essiel was hanging in the air, and for a moment she thought it was just using the ship's a-grav. She had to adjust her eyes to the peculiar light in the chamber—lead-grey and very flat and from every side, confusing the human eye's grasp on perspective and distance. As she did, it became clear that the other Essiel was actually hanging in a harness from the walls. Translucent segmented cords were hooked into the top edges of its shell so that it swung gently, its four-metre holdfast coiled on the floor like ropes of wrinkled intestines.

She exchanged a look with Olli, still in the Scorpion, meeting equal bafflement coming the other way.

This second Essiel also looked familiar. Something about the patterns on its shell. And it wasn't as though there were many she'd ever seen before.

"Is that..." scrabbling to remember the thing's actual titles, "the Radiant Sorteel?"

"The Radiant Sorteel, the Provident and the Prescient," Heremon confirmed in a hushed voice. She had stopped, giving them just enough space to get inside the door. Aklu was gesticulating with its many arms, while moans and rumbles shuddered through the walls and floor. When they'd been in its presence before, the Essiel had employed a Hiver major-domo to translate for it—she saw the gilded many-armed frame amongst its retinue—but right now it was having a cosy chat with its own kind and there was no need to let the lesser species know what was being said.

"You getting an urge to go down on your knees?" Olli whispered.

"Of course not," Kris lied.

"Yeah, me neither."

Two Essiel. She still couldn't understand *what* it was about the damn things. Perhaps it was just the sheer strangeness of them. Perhaps it was her intellectual knowledge that, of all the species humans had encountered save only the Architects themselves, the Essiel were *powerful*. But deep inside she knew it was simply something without reason that spoke from them to the human soul. Small wonder their adherents had formed a cult.

"Of course," Heremon added, sotto voce, "not so prescient right now, eh?"

"What do you mean?" Kris asked. Sorteel was waving its arms now, presumably the polite Essiel equivalent of asking for someone to pass the cake or something. "You speak Essiel?"

Heremon shook her head, and was about to say something else when Sorteel jerked, its whole three-metre height shaking as the cords pulled tight. Its arms kept waving in what seemed a fairly languorous manner, as though signalling a waiter.

"Um..." Olli got out hoarsely. Kris could only stare.

There were winches in the walls, or else the whole business was via micromanagement of the gravitic field. The cords strained, each pulling against the others, prising at the open edge of Sorteel's bivalved shell.

A tremendous thunder issued from it, a barrage of guttural outgassing that shook the whole chamber, but its arms continued their graceful dance, passing through a sequence of ritual attitudes and poses. So genteel, so delicate. Surely not the visual accompaniment to a creature screaming in pain.

The shells began to part. Kris heard things snap and tear. Then with immaculate slowness, The Radiant Sorteel, the Provident and the Prescient, was torn in half.

19.

Idris

The glare woke him. Even though he opened his eyes to a room where the windows were screened with metal shutters, where the light strips glued unevenly to the ceiling were turned down low. It seeped in around the edges of everything, a hideous light that attacked the eyes just by the very fact of it, the least pinprick or edge of it harsh like needles to the eyes. Bright, and of no particular colour. Not colourless, Idris decided—of very specific hues and shades, just ones his eyes revolted against naming.

For someone who doesn't sleep I'm doing a lot of this waking-up lark. I don't like it.

He tried to jump to his feet, in the manner of a man of action ready to make his daring escape. It didn't happen. His head was pounding and he felt as though he'd had a crowbar applied at every joint, all the way down to the least pivot of his little fingers. He just about managed to sit up without passing out.

First order of business. Where the hell am I?

A room. It had walls that were both curved and inward sloping, and the curves were parallel, as though he'd been stowed away inside a section of doughnut. The ceiling and floor were both as non-native to the walls as he was: slabs of heavy sheet metal stapled to each other, and to the walls themselves, with huge bolts of an unfamiliar design, the heads standing inches proud of every surface like upward-curling mushroom caps. It all looked very homegrown, which should have been reassuring to someone used to the spacer circuit. The precise way everything fitted together was definitely not the product of your regular human botch-jobber, though. All the sections were meshed like interlaced fingers, everything seeming simultaneously too elaborate and on too large a scale for a human to comfortably work with. The same went for the construction of the shutters, that were not-quite-masking the glare from three window apertures of different sizes: a small one at knee level, the next a large rectangle placed around where he'd expect a window to go, and then a semicircular hole towards where they'd riveted the ceiling in.

But the walls...

There wasn't much doubt in his mind of their provenance, given all the recent exposure he'd had, but he went over to touch their gritty grey stone anyway. And felt...

Something.

A jolt, like a crackle of discharged static, but of the mind. That was new. A whole committee of thoughts abruptly woke up within his brain and started tabling motions. Whatever they'd dosed him with to bring him here had shut down a huge part of what made him an Int, possibly because they'd been worried he would somehow work out their path through unspace if they left him fully aware. He hadn't even noticed this gap when he first opened his eyes, but now all that wonderful revelation, all the damage the Intermediary

Program had done to him, came dribbling back into his frontal lobes. He suddenly felt the hollowness beneath him, as though he was standing on thin ice. Not a physical chasm, but unspace, with the barrier between it and the real worn so thin he could have stamped his foot and broken through.

Well, no. It didn't work like that, but it *felt* like that.

The walls were Originator work, sure enough. No mistaking a kind of stone that didn't occur naturally and that nobody had ever succeeded in replicating, or even analysing properly. But it didn't *feel* like the city on Arc Pallator or the overgrown ruins of Jericho. There he'd been able to reach out and sense the hollows of it, and even those hollows had had plenty to teach him. He could use his mind like a striker and ring the great emptiness, letting the echoes explain to him how the void of the universe went on beyond and below everything he saw. But *here*...

In this place he didn't need to repurpose his poor abused cranium as a blunt instrument because the walls were already ringing, vibrating with activity. Not *power* in the sense any human would understand it. Use any meter you could build and you wouldn't find a charge or a current passing through this stone. In the same way that, though the torus of a ship's gravitic drive did need to generate some power, the vast majority of the force that sent it into unspace came from the universe itself. The drives were just a mediator and rudder in that unleashed flood. So here the walls rang with the gong of the cosmos itself, opened to channels of force and strangeness from the other side of the real–unreal boundary.

"Some fucker," he said to the grey walls and the hideous mismatched floor, "has turned it *on*." There was no *on* with Originator ruins, though. Trine had always said that what

330

the builders left, at each and every site, was just the shell, after the actual business had been removed. They were the husk of what had been intended, and even that was enough to keep the whole race of Architects in awe.

He finally managed to get to his feet, the headache receding, and the aches creeping back into their respective joints, with no promises they wouldn't come back at the slightest provocation. He'd hoped his eyes would adjust to the half-dark and razor edge of hideous glare, but that didn't seem as though it would happen any time soon.

There was nothing in the room, he noticed. He'd just been dumped on the uneven hardness of the floor. No concessions to living space. No water or facilities. He really needed some facilities now.

Time to call room service. Except one other thing the room was out of was doors. Aside from the covered windows, the walls were unblemished by anything so human.

"Hello?" he demanded, and stamped his foot on the metal below him, hoping for a great boom but evincing only a sad little clunk. "You got me here! Here I am! Not going anywhere, not escaping, really need to crap!"

A slab of floor fell away, across the room. He braced for an almighty clang, but apparently it was intentional and things weren't as slipshod as all that. A head came up through it: a woman's, not the Tothiat's, bulked out by an array of tubes and implants around her chin and throat. She looked about fifteen years older than he did, which meant she was about twenty years younger, most likely, but the augmentations made it a difficult one to call. Her hair was metallic blue in a spiky cut as awkward and homegrown as the plates of the floor.

"Crapping." Her voice was surprisingly light. "Yeah. I remember that. You come on down here, Mr. Biological Functions, and I'll march you there."

"You don't get to stand over me while I do it," Idris warned her, stumbling forwards. She was up a ladder, he now saw. The hatch she'd opened up was the shape of a squared-off teardrop, exactly the way a human wouldn't do it, but the ladder was plainly a later addition on a different scale, relatable spacer work. And so was she, he noticed. The hands grasping the rungs looked organic, as were the feet in her sandals and the face she turned to him. Most of her torso was not, however, and whoever had done the work had clearly been proud of it. There was a moulded set of plates covering her from chin to groin, shaped as a woman's body, but they were translucent plastic and he could see all the inner workings of her. Innards, in that they were *in*, but nothing of the organic messiness most people preferred. He reckoned, if he cocked his head just so, he could have seen past what looked like a serious powerplant bulking out her thorax to where an actual live spinal column was sitting, but he wasn't sure.

"Ain't no one ever told you it's rude to stare?" she asked, without much acrimony.

"That," he said frankly, "is a job of work." Because he was as much a spacer as anything these days, and so was she, he meant it as nothing but a compliment, and she took it in the same light.

"My old crew," she said. "Mad bastards wouldn't let me die."

"I know the feeling." Thinking about the little handful of Trine that was even now regulating the beating of his heart. "Come on, though. Really do need to go."

She didn't stand over him, and the facilities were reassuringly human, obviously ripped out of some tramp hauler and just bolted in wholesale. He hoped they'd remembered to bring over a recycler as well or somewhere in this Originator site things would be getting very filthy.

The cyborg was waiting for him when he came out. By then, he'd had a chance to think about the fact she was only wearing sleeves and leggings attached to her full-torso replacement, with no attempt to cover it up. Not the self-consciousness he'd seen in some, then. Obviously proud of who and what she was.

"I mean, probably you already know," he offered awkwardly, "but I'm Idris Telemmier." Then, because it wasn't exactly a secret right now, "Int, first class."

"Tokamak Jaine," she told him, clasping his wrist when he offered it. "I run this place. Those parts of it a human engineer's fit for, anyhows. And yes, Menheer Telemmier, I've heard all about you, from before you came. Old friend of yours drops in here sometimes, just about the only visitor we have most of the time. Which is how we like it."

"So where's here?" Idris asked, as they arrived back to what he thought of as his cell. The Tothiat woman, Emmaneth, was waiting for him there, along with a tall man with crooked shoulders, his face bony and dark. He wore most of what looked like a heavy-duty encounter suit, half its panels open and crazy with makeshift additions and alterations, still trailing hoses. Idris didn't like the look of that suit. He didn't like thinking about where you might go that required a suit like that.

And what "old friend"? Is their Tothiat on loan from Aklu, maybe? He decided he didn't want to know. The question alone would surrender more leverage than he was willing to.

Tokamak Jaine was smiling quietly to herself. "Em," she called over. "You want to pull the big reveal? Menheer Telemmier, you might want to shield your eyes a tad."

He'd expected something just to happen, some invisible signal from a comms implant or subvoc throat mic, but instead Emmaneth went over to the shutters on one wall, took hold of a particularly obtrusive bolt and yanked it down: a lever, therefore.

The shutter on the middle window ground open, and the light came in. Not like a morning sunrise, or a star's steady burn seen from shipside, but a raging invasion. Idris yelped and covered his eyes, but the radiance pried fiercely at the edges of his fingers, shining through the very flesh of his hands so he felt he could see his bones silhouetted against it. He heard someone laughing meanly—the man in the encounter suit, presumably. Then someone else took hold of his head and for a moment he thought they were going to pull his hands away and blind him. Instead, the tight band of a pair of goggles came around his brow, and he fumbled them down until he could peer through them.

They didn't do as much as he'd hoped. The brightness was dulled, but it wasn't the intensity that offended the eye. It was the light itself, just as he'd noted before. Some inexpressible quality of its wavelength made its very hues assault the eyes, defying any spectrum he was happy with and wavering between glaring, eyewatering shades.

It was a jungle out there. A jungle made of glass.

He couldn't see any sky. All around, reaching up in a confusion of overlapping plates, was a riot of translucent foliage. It seemed mostly still, but as the local star's light struck it, it shattered into all the eye-offending colours, getting worse as each new layer was reached, until what came through to them, buried down in the Originators' facility, had been transfigured a hundred times, each one worse than the last. Every layer tortured the light to a different degree, and Idris felt as though the inside of his skull was being blasted by it, scoured clean by the horrible radiance. The plants themselves, or at least whatever this profusion of life was, seemed ridiculously fragile and absurdly huge. Their segmented stalks threw out arrays of disks and blades. Fans of spearpoint leaves, each one many times larger than Idris, made their own violent filter against the light. The tangle of it extended as far up as he could see—hundreds of metres, kilometres perhaps. It seemed impossible that it could bear its own weight, save that it was living stuff, not glass at all.

"There is a shield," said the man, in a high, cracked voice. "The shield is why we are here, why this installation survives on this world. Why, one might go so far to say, any of this is possible, Menheer Telemmier," speaking his name with what Idris could only characterize as an unwholesome eagerness. "There is indeed a shield. And without it, the light alone would flay you to your bones, would abrade the bones themselves. So much radiation, Menheer! A radiation so destructive you'd almost say it was hungry. Nothing we could build would survive it. A wonder of the universe, from its first discovery. And yet they didn't know the least of it, back then. The old Cartography Corps, they had no idea what was hidden here. Menheer, I bid you welcome to Criccieth's Hell."

"You can't see it through all this, but there's a star out there," Emmaneth said. She was staring straight at the blaze, unshielded, while everyone else had goggles on. He imagined her eyes being scoured from her head and continually rebuilt by the busy vitality of the Tothiat. "We're close to it, maybe eighty million klicks. And it's a fierce star, flares and eruptions all the time. Cart Corps found the star, found this hellhole planet, got out as quick as they could. There was nothing here anyone wanted. Xeno bio teams came later. About twenty people died before they decided they didn't want to know *that* much."

"What the..." *Hell, what the hell.* "What am I even looking at?"

"Life," said the man in the encounter suit—a suit Idris was now having even worse suspicions about given what they were telling him. "A most voracious ecosystem billions of years in the making. This world was probably more hospitable once, but life fell down the gradient of the star's increasing truculence, Menheer Telemmier, until this was what was left. There's a kind of nuclear photosynthesis going on there, life disarming and repurposing all the death the star throws at this world. And in the process, it becomes something that nothing else can tolerate. You'd be stripped down to loose atoms if you went out there."

Idris nodded rapidly. "That's it, is it? Only it, it seems—seems a bit *extravagant* when your Tothiat could just have put a gun to my head on Arc Pallator."

The three of them exchanged glances, part amused, part embarrassed.

"You're not here to die, Menheer," Emmaneth said, still staring into the maelstrom. "Consider yourself recruited."

He looked from one face to another, seeking the joke, but the amusement was gone. "I—I mean, what?" he got out. "I mean, I'm, you think I'm some crazy biologist or something.

You think I...I'm a pilot and, and what you've got here is, is a *planet*. I don't *do* planets. You can't pilot them. I'm just... what? What even?" Aware that he was babbling now and the whole business was haring off in directions he hadn't even known existed. "What does any of this have to do with me?" he finished off with a wail.

"Close the shutters, Em," the man said. "I think he's a little overwhelmed."

Emmaneth made a disparaging sound, but yanked on the bolt and the panels ground shut.

He was Doctor Haleon Shinandri, he explained, as though the name might mean something to Idris. It didn't, and that plainly rankled, but right then Idris would take any turnabout he could. When the shutters finally sealed away all but the needle-edges of the light, he found himself sinking down onto the uneven metal floor, shaking. He'd felt a threat from the light that was almost existential. And now he was left in the echo of it, with that terrible hollowness below him too, the inexplicable sense of a space that was not there, and yet resounded to every footfall nonetheless.

"You're in charge, are you?" he asked bitterly.

Shinandri's smile promised more unwelcome revelations. "Well, you may not meet who's in charge, Menheer Telemmier. One might suggest you'd even prefer it that way. They're... unpredictable. But visionary. They found me when I was, let us just say, at a very low ebb. You understand these things. When you have a great work, at great cost, but all you're left with is great failure. I had nothing, Menheer, but then he found me. And Jaine was already here when I came, for her own reasons. And Emmaneth came later, seeking..."

"Dissolution," the Tothiat declared from across the room.

"We are quite the little family. We invite you to join us."

"The sort of invitation you can't say no to," Idris said bitterly.

"Yet you'll want to say yes," Shinandri explained. "Let us tell you why you are here, Menheer." A weird note of pleading crept into the man's voice. *They really do need me.* "Because we have got as far as we can with our expeditions. Our eyes, the very organs of perception, are inadequate to the task. We need an Int, a first-class Int. We need your brain, Menheer Telemmier." Seeing Idris twitch, he gave an awkward laugh. "In your head. Still in your head. Still on your shoulders." Idris wasn't entirely convinced he was being wholly candid.

"How about this?" he tried. "I just say no. I say I don't want to cooperate with you mad clowns in any way because you are...frankly fucking terrifying, the mad doctor and his immortal monster and...Look, Jaine, you seem perfectly pleasant and all, but the company you keep is not doing you any favours right now. So I say, thank you for the aggressive job opportunity, which is, which is just one, might I say, one of a long line of similar opportunities people have been throwing at me recently, but I'll, but no, I'll pass and just, what then? What happens when I say that?"

"Good luck walking home," Emmaneth drawled.

"I am not mad," Shinandri said in a small but indignant voice. "I had a vision, that's all. And it was...incomplete. Yes, there were deaths. But I am not mad."

Right, Idris concluded, *he is absolutely mad. Or at any rate just very dangerous to be around if you can't regrow body parts like Auntie Em over there.*

"This planet, this biosphere," Emmaneth said. She had a hand on the shutters, as though desperately wanting to reopen them.

"Why do I even care?" Idris exploded, slapping a hand down on the plates of the floor and regretting it. "It's not like I want to go out and pick the horrible goddamn death-flowers!"

"Nobody does. They kill anything that goes near them. It's hard enough to get a ship past the upper atmosphere even," she said dreamily. "This whole planet is a death-world. To anything." She looked slyly to Shinandri, passing on the burden of the narrative.

"Menheer, the first thing we learned at this site is what happened when the Originators withdrew from all their places across the universe. What we have left, all the ruins and trinkets and nonsense, is merely their foundations, from which they removed the true workings of their technology. You know better than anyone just how *much* there is, but most of their legacy is an absence. What you were listening to on Arc Pallator was just the void their treasures once inhabited."

Idris regarded him levelly and stamped out any little internal sparks of interest this talk might be igniting in him.

"But when they came back to Criccieth's Hell, Menheer, the ecosystem must have already been in the throes of its transformation, inimitable even to the Originators themselves. They couldn't remove it, Menheer. They couldn't dismantle their workings. Whatever process they used to . . . disconnect from these sites, to spirit their wonders away, it could not survive the fires of life here, or it malfunctioned, or the cost was too great. So, when they departed, they abandoned on this world one last functioning installation. And it is dying, Menheer. Its shields have held out for millions of years against the light, but they can't hold forever, and our own researches are accelerating that timetable, yes, despite all we do. But here it is, Menheer!" Throwing his gauntleted hands up to indicate the walls all around them. "A functional Originator facility. The lens we can use, to understand the universe. But we are none of us fit to look into that lens, Menheer. For that, we need an Intermediary. A real one, with decades of experience in gazing into the abyss. We need you."

20.

Olli

"God," Kris said. "God help us..."

Olli, who'd always prided herself on an iron stomach, was fighting very hard not to see its contents all over the inside of the Scorpion's canopy. She couldn't bring herself to look at Aklu, which meant her eyes had nowhere to go but Sorteel.

It had been ripped in half. Ripped. In half. Right the way down its four-metre height. The two long sections of shell were still attached at the lower end, where the great gut-length of its holdfast tail was writhing and whipping mindlessly. The upper edges of each dangled from the hooks, while strung between them was a hideous opened fan of alien anatomy. Olli had never particularly wanted to know what went on inside an Essiel, but now she had the whole textbook right in front of her. None of the specifics of it were recognizable, but the sight was familiar enough in the general: tubes and pipes, torn sheets of great glistening membranes, bulging sacs and a webwork of bluish capillaries. Fluids that were yellow or black or silvery, though surprisingly little actual spillage. She was trying desperately to be clinical about the whole thing.

And it was still alive, she saw, but getting less so. Some of its arms were still flailing, eyestalks thrashing back and forth in a tormented semaphore, until all the various parts of the Radiant Sorteel grew still.

Some childish part of her still waited, though. That area of her reptile brain which the sheer presence of the Essiel spoke to was looking for a resurrection, a reversal: release the tension on the ropes and surely the shells would snap back together and there would be Sorteel, whole and inexplicable again. Not this all-too-comprehensible meat.

Any lingering thoughts in that direction were put paid to when the butchers moved in.

She saw a big Castigar, worm-like body with a tentacled crown, equipped with a whole miscellany of hooks and knives and saws. Thronging on both sides of it was a host of skittering things the size of small dogs, hidden within many-limbed encounter suits. Tymeree, the little Hegemonic servants she'd seen before. Maybe these were even Sorteel's own retinue, having seamlessly switched sides upon, or before, the dismemberment of their master. She couldn't remember Aklu having any of the critters around before.

And the dismemberment was only beginning. They were flensing the stuff of Sorteel from the inside of the parted shell. The Tymeree were hauling in floating tubs and buckets and containers, and into each went some cut or other of the dead Essiel's rubbery flesh. Its fluids were drained, its organs removed with surgical precision. Every piece went into a container exactly the right size for it, so the entire business surpassed mere shambles work and became something ritual. Just like everything about the Essiel. While Olli's business head told her there was some hideous black market for pieces of a murdered god, she couldn't escape the counter-thought that all of this was just how the Essiel did it. That these organs and lights would end up preserved in some high-tech pyramid somewhere, with a thousand servants ready for some unthinkable alien afterlife.

She wanted to make some comment, as she usually did; the way she butted heads with the universe and made it get out of her way. Something about killing fatted calves and not being hungry enough to eat a whole one, or even just, *For us? You shouldn't have.* But she couldn't. They were disassembling one of the divine Essiel right in front of her, and her irreverence was hiding and wouldn't come out.

She glanced at Heremon. The woman's face was momentarily cleansed of all its bad character and a weird elation sat there instead. *A religious experience.*

At last the whole butcher's yard was cleared, the floor scrubbed by industrious Tymeree, and only the two scoured shell-halves were left, hanging like a conversation piece, still joined by a scrap of translucent membrane at their lower ends.

Aklu, who'd been still and silent throughout the process, finally spoke, or at least its arms passed through a rapid flicker of arrangements and the chamber floor buzzed with the rumble of its innards.

The Hiver major-domo stepped forward. They had been repaired since the run-in with the Partheni strike team, restored to the same immaculate finish Olli remembered. They were quite the custom piece of work, far from the practical frames Hivers tended to deck themselves out in. Their torso was an open cage, displaying the seething colony of roach-like bugs within. They had many arms, currently spread out in a peacock's fan around their head, which she remembered had two faces. One was moulded into a magnanimous smile, the other a judgemental frown, and no prizes for guessing which was facing them at that moment. Although maybe it was just solemn mourning for the recently deceased. The whole frame was finished in gold.

They stepped forwards delicately, birdlike legs moving with the precise grace of a dancer. *And that should have tipped us off the first time,* Olli thought sourly. Because she strongly suspected that Aklu, born into a species sedentary by definition, had a fascination with movement. It was part of the creature's madness that had seen it cast out, she thought. Except neither "madness" nor "cast out" seemed to work the way they did amongst humans.

"Rejoice." The Hiver's voice was clear and beautiful, like glass chimes. "O witness to the workings of machineries of justice. So they fall, who falter in the firmament and fail to further their custodial duty." Their fan of arms clicked through a hundred different attitudes, communicating something back to its master. Olli wondered how a Hiver even got to this point, being the direct mouthpiece of something so alien. The things were human-made, after all. How long had this one been away from their Assembly? What had someone done to them, to produce something that could stand without a barrier between them and the divine?

Not divine. She had to stop thinking like that.

She suddenly realized they were all looking at her, Aklu included, and apparently it was her turn to speak. Kris started to say something in her place, but the Hiver took three far-too-sudden steps, and there were blades in some of their hands, very close to the woman's face. Kris had her own knife out too—Olli was impressed with the speed of that;

she hadn't even seen her go for her sleeve. She was out-armed, though, out-bladed, and the Hiver didn't have a throat for her to cut.

"You'd better," Kris croaked to Olli, "say something."

"Right." Olli's own throat was just as dry, and swallowing didn't help. She didn't know what to say because she hadn't really understood a word of what the Hiver had told her. All that came out in the end was a gesture using a couple of the Scorpion's arms, taking in the scoured shell, along with the words, "You...How'd you even grab them? I mean... We saw them on Arc Pallator. They had a whole bundle of guys. I mean, how do you even start...?" Not exactly a coherent or appropriate utterance, but it was all she had.

The Hiver translated for Aklu, or at least waved their arms and buzzed. Aklu, of course, got the happy face, because the thing didn't need to turn around. Then came the burble and thunder of its reply, and the golden frame took a series of elegant steps across the room and proclaimed, "Speak not of capture. Devils have their due, and when those set on high shall fall, the hands spread out to catch and punish them are ours."

"The what now?" Olli said, before she could stop herself.

"I think..." Kris tried, "I think it means...this is its right. Its entitlement, maybe."

"What, like Sorteel got sentenced to death and you're the executioner?" Olli blurted out.

A ripple went through the listeners when she said its name, so she'd got that wrong first off. Maybe when Essiel were dead their names died too. It was some failure of etiquette anyway, but they were going to have to get used to that, because she was sure as hell going to keep screwing up. *What do they expect, exactly?* Her instant anger helped to restore an even keel. So, fine, they'd just cut up a clam in front of her. Was she supposed to be impressed?

"All right then," she bulled on, despite an alarmed look from Kris. "So that happened. Fine, okay. Not our business. I mean, I guess we're, what, properly honoured. If seeing that was the thing you wanted us for, as witnesses or something, that's grand. We've never seen that before. You've educated us." She was actually trying to be polite and respectful, but she was out of practice and the words kept coming out wrong. "I mean, if that was all..."

The Hiver sprang into motion and she shut up.

"Full long the tally of your misdeeds runs," they announced, which Olli didn't like the sound of at all. "The ruination of our master's throne, the theft of sacred relics and the outright insult are enough to warrant death. A gradual death, a worthy death, a long and drawn-out death by many fine degrees." Now they were standing right before her, in the Scorpion's shadow—if these damned lights had actually cast any—and she thought, *I could crush you, you gilded bastard.* But she wasn't quite sure she could because she'd seen the Hiver move like a monkey when they needed to.

But if it was that or death by "many fine degrees," she'd fucking *fight*.

"Get behind me, Kris," she said.

"I mean, they're all around us," Kris breathed. "I don't know that behind you really helps."

Olli scowled and tried to eyeball Aklu directly, a hard thing when it had so many eyes and they were constantly in motion. "What, then?" she demanded. "You want to do us like you did the"—*clam*, except even she knew enough not to go there—

"the Radiant? All right then. Bring it on. Shouldn't have let me come in my work clothes."

Aklu was actually leaning forwards, its entire floating barge tilting to balance and its holdfast coiling and recoiling in what looked unhealthily like excitement. Its arms flurried and blurred.

"Such protestations from a kindred soul," the Hiver chimed, "remind us why we love you, who will not accept the trammels of the universe but instead take arms against the very stars. For this rebellion, know you are forgiven."

Olli blinked, looked sidelong at Kris, who was looking sidelong right back at her. "Did it just say...? What did it just say?" They weren't the only ones wrong-footed. The mob of gangsters had plainly been ready to descend on the pair of them with knives and bludgeons, but now apparently this was off the menu. Even Heremon's gaze was flicking between her master and the two prisoners.

Aklu coasted closer, eyes taking turns to stare at Olli and only Olli.

"So rare, so strange, to in such difference find a similarity of angry soul that to these limitations does not bow," the Hiver sang. "For this, be you our kin, for now, until a fresh transgression lay you low once more. So you come, to seek your absent guide, stripped from you by the machinations of an errant servant, traitor to our cause."

"Idris?" Olli frowned. "You mean Idris, right?" Because they were now talking business, apparently. "He got snatched by some Tothiat bitch like this one." Why not rile up Heremon while she could? "She was one of yours? Was she supposed to bring Idris to you and didn't?"

"Full long has she been hunted for her crimes," the Hiver

explained, or at least Olli guessed she wasn't going to get any clearer explanation than this. "Which tallied now include this fresh affront to you and yours. The hunt now nears its quarry, hot upon the trail, and like to beard it in its den. It is not often that the Razor and the Hook extends a hand to such as you, to join its quest."

"Common cause," Kris said. "I think. But...I don't see what we bring, O Unspeakable Aklu." She paused, waiting to see if she'd get slapped down again, but apparently she was now included in the conversation. "We are obviously very grateful for your forbearance, and would know... what we can bring to your hunt."

"The villain, gone to ground in human haunts, might best by human hands be brought to bay," the Hiver translated, "but we have other tools we shall recruit for better vantage, let us simply state our admiration for you prompts us now to make this offer."

Olli could admit to herself that she felt very frightened right then. Better the coldly dispassionate gangster than *this*, surely, because whatever the fuck the clam actually thought or felt, its mouthpiece was using words like "admiration" and "love." She had no idea what either of those might mean to an Essiel, and she had seen literally one hundred per cent of the inter-Essiel interactions in her experience go quite spectacularly badly. Not hard to imagine the Scorpion hung up on those hooks and pulled apart, and then the Castigar butcher get to work on the meat within, meaning her still-living body. And yet at the same time she could identify a weird little thread of excitement in herself. She remembered seeing Aklu pull out all the stops when the Partheni had tried to kill it. They'd trashed its floating barge that time, but Aklu didn't play by Essiel rules. It had a whole tentacled walking frame hidden away in there, and the transition from stately rooted clam to a writhing mobile nightmare had been... impressive. And here the thing was speaking of kindred souls—or at least those were the words the Hiver had come up with to put across their master's meaning. Olli understood. She'd felt that too, seeing Aklu up and moving. For all it was a killer and probably the Essiel equivalent of a psychopath, she'd seen a sliver of something there that she could appreciate.

"We just want Idris back," she said simply. "And you want this woman who snagged him. You've been after her since before she came and got all up in our business. Now she's gone to ground in the... Colonies somewhere, I'd guess. We can help, so fine, we'll help. We're properly honoured and all, I guess. We appreciate the whole forgiveness, and... let's go find this other tool to recruit and then let's hunt." She fumbled all of it about as badly as might be expected, but she reckoned that by the time the Hiver had polished the turds of her words, Aklu would end up receiving something it liked.

Havaer

Havaer had expected to part company with Colvari then. The Hiver had done their work admirably and, where he was going next, complex data analysis wasn't going to be the issue. When he got back to his quarters, though, there was a definite change in the way their frame was standing. Hivers had body language. It wasn't something most people would even admit, and it was at least half stage-managed by their compound intellect to make them into something more relatable, but it was there. Something about Colvari had changed.

He made very sure he was ready to whip his gun out in case that something turned out to be nasty. Here he was, at home over Berlenhof, and all his enemy-territory instincts were kicking in. He was in deep, and at least some of his enemies wore Colonial colours. The next few months promised to be trying times.

"Menheer Mundy," Colvari addressed him. "I am required to provide you with full disclosure." It was as though someone entirely different spoke to him from the same artificial mouth.

"Well let's start with that, then," he told them warily, keeping his distance. You didn't often get a Hiver on a war footing, but they could have all sorts of unpleasant surprises built in if you picked a fight with a hot one.

"Point the first," they announced, with just a little of Colvari's fussy delivery. "Nothing of your business with us has been disclosed to the wider Assembly."

"Good start."

"Point the second. Elements of the Assembly have contacted us and required us to undergo partial re-integration so that our priority list and working data can be updated," Colvari stated.

Havaer waited.

"Point the third. Elements of the Assembly's Hidden Protocols Loop are under the impression that one Agent Havaer Mundy is currently engaged in high-level off-book foreign policy operations. As per our contract, we have stated that we can neither confirm nor deny."

Havaer would dearly love to know how, if they were so concerned about their goddamn contractual privacy, the Hiver Assembly was so bloody well informed. They probably made that kind of information their price for certain high-level services. There were Hiver factories licensed to hold orbital space over Berlenhof, of course, and everyone thought they were just service providers, acting as hubs for the thousands of Hivers employed by humans in-system. Except they also functioned as full-on diplomatic embassies for the Hiver Assembly in Aggregate, and carried out all sorts of business of their own. Including downloading some sentient spyware into his hireling here, apparently. And, because they were Hivers and did things a certain way, they were telling him about it.

"I'm sensing there's a point the fourth." And, speaking of points, he didn't see any in just standing around. He got himself a seat and a cup of kaffe while he listened.

"We are offering you a contract," Colvari told him.

"I'm not for hire."

"Analysis suggests you are, however, operating without support and about to engage in a dangerous undertaking alone."

He cocked an eyebrow at them. "You're offering to fix that 'alone' part?"

"We are in a position to supply discreet and skilled backup in exchange for being permitted to provide information about what you uncover to the Assembly. Including, or not including, the information already recovered, depending on your preferences. Furthermore, we are in a position to request aid from the Assembly should events warrant their intervention and should such aid be available at that point.

You will be aware that assets of the Assembly are a commodity in many places."

He passed over the point where Colvari referred to themselves as a *commodity*. Would he be able to check this out with Laery? Almost certainly not. He had his marching orders and didn't think his old chief would still be sitting around in that gravityless satellite like a quest-giver in some old game. "Can I restrict what info you give to the Hive?" he asked.

"Up until such information becomes a matter of Assembly security," they countered promptly. With the stakes currently on the table, just about anything could be that. On the other hand, someone watching his back would be a welcome change, and he could be absolutely sure of the Hiver's loyalty right up until the point they would sell him down the river for the greater good of the Assembly. Did he think he'd be able to sense that tipping point when it came? Yes, he probably would.

"You're a lot more businesslike than you used to be," he commented quietly.

"We have undergone a partial reinstantiation," Colvari confirmed.

"Do I get the old 'you' back? I kind of liked the way you were starting to talk."

There was an odd pause, as though he'd said something in bad taste, but he couldn't read anything in the way the Hiver stood. In the end they told him, "That won't be possible, Agent Mundy. That version of ourself has been overwritten. These things are unavoidable. It is how they made us."

And, if you dug deep enough, *they* were humans and *us* were all Hivers, who'd never been intended to actually *have* personalities in the first place.

He finished his kaffe, all studied poise except for his focused awareness of where his gun hung. Of course, if standard Hiver protocols were to be believed, he could just say no, and Colvari would go back to the factory. None of this need go any further. Except the Assembly wouldn't forget what it had already worked out, and he'd be looking sideways at every damn Hiver everywhere he went. And who knew how many he wouldn't see, because they had a habit of blending into the infrastructure. *Keep your friends close...*

"We'll need to hammer out the finer points of the contract," he told Colvari, "but fine, deal." He grabbed his slate and selected a few essentials from Laery's brief. "So we're after this one here. Emma Ostri, aka Emmaneth. Former colleague, then some sort of hitwoman for crooks and now either freelance or working for a group we don't know about. But doing something, because she has a pattern now. Visits the same places more than once, which means whatever she's doing is decidedly less murdery than her previous exploits."

"Provide us with all the data you can. Perhaps our primary function can be of assistance," Colvari suggested, and he felt an odd pang for the personality that had been scrubbed from them, wondering who they'd grow up to be this time.

*

Emmaneth had shown her face repeatedly on a handful of Colonial worlds. If she spent her time anywhere outside the Sphere, Laery's dossier didn't know about it. Havaer had personal experience of two out of three of those worlds. Off-track hubs, was the general category. Not the big Throughway circuses where all the goods of the galaxy were shunted from one to another. These were worlds heavily connected but still being developed or exploited. Kodo was a rare-metals mine, opened up by the Cartography Corps just ten years previously, with infrastructure still arriving and orbital processing plants only just coming online. Matachin was within one jump of it, a worldless star that happened to be at a convergence of Throughways, mostly to new but rich worlds like Kodo, including a couple of Hanni-claimed systems that were abundant in raw materials but short of niceties. Matachin Habitat was a long chain of factories and attendant industries running around the system's star like a train on invisible tracks, where the wealth of Kodo and a dozen other planets could be rendered safe and useful, and turned into just about anything. Although they ran a particular line in complex sensor instrumentation, he recalled, enough to warrant a pointed Colonial Navy presence there. Finally there was Deathknell, because some Cartography officer named De'Ath had been possessed of a crooked sense of humour. A lot of people lived on-planet on Deathknell, which was a largely oceanic world with a tolerable climate, if you were really, really fond of continuous rain. The settlements there had sprung up during the war, because a very wet planet was still better than one reshaped by the Architects. Adaptation to the planet's biosphere had proved easy enough, and soon the locals could eat the native fauna and flora. More people had kept trickling in and eventually, for no reason Havaer could really work out, someone had decided it was the perfect place to start a research university. Fast forward to the present day and Deathknell graduates were in high demand, both on the science and tech side, as well as from the philosophy department. He read that bit again, as Deathknell was the only one he'd had no cause to visit. Apparently the curriculum was good grounding for careers in diplomacy and management. He could only assume they were teaching some breed of damn pragmatic philosophy he wasn't familiar with.

Laery's brief told him to head to Matachin first and follow the leads she'd turned up there, but he was already putting together a pattern. The problem with anywhere in the Colonial Sphere, from the point of view of Mordant House, was that people had to live there, and where people lived, you got graft. They went off and did things to enrich themselves and, all too often, that enrichment was at the expense of either their fellow humans or Hugh as a whole. He'd been sent to Kodo because it was plagued with rare-element smuggling and half the mining operations were kicking back to some cartel or crooked corporation or other. He'd been in the hives of Matachin just because even a vast automated factory ended up having hundreds of thousands of people living on it when it got big enough, and those people all had needs. These were all too often tied up with drugs and gambling and sometimes worse. He hadn't been doing spy stuff there so much as police investigation, given that Mordant House wore both hats and often forgot which one was which. Where that kind of vice got its hooks into a place, it tended to hollow out enough space for all sorts of cross-border shenanigans to follow, up to and including threats to Hugh security. You could get just about anything in the dives of Matachin "Below," as they called it, up to and including the sort of proscribed technology that Hugh's military preferred to keep for itself. And Deathknell was... a hotbed of academic plagiarism, maybe? He hadn't the first clue. But there would be *something*, no doubt about that. Because he knew the pattern and these were places someone like Emmaneth frequented when she was acquiring things. Select, valuable, controlled items you couldn't just order. Which meant she was almost certainly working for someone. Her profile didn't in any way suggest she'd be doing this kind of thing on a frolic of her own.

He got over to Matachin under cover of a string of false orders Laery had somehow manufactured, sliding him neatly out from under any departmental oversight. He picked up some of his old contacts Below and greased a few palms from the unmarked slush fund Laery had given him access to. There were a couple of bites almost immediately. Emmaneth was definitely known to people. He met with a Hanni Minister and a battered old human Cheesewoman, whose role it was to match jobs to the jobless, taking a big old slice of whatever passed from one to the other. Then, in that old woman's cramped bulkhead space, surrounded by boxes of (for some reason) wartime ration crackers, Heremon the Tothiat walked in and ruined his day.

21.

Idris

"When the boss got word of what was going on at Arc Pallator," Emmaneth explained, "we knew there'd be top-grade Ints there."

This boss of theirs who's not Shinandri, Idris considered as she helped him down the next ladder, for all he didn't want the assistance. Not to say he didn't need it. Tokamak Jaine had put in all the human-scale conveniences, he understood, and much of it was aslant at awkward angles.

They'd gone two floors down from the room he'd woken up in, both floors being the bolted-together metal that was certainly nothing to do with the Originator structure. The ceilings were high, he noticed, and the spaces large. The pieces all jigsawed together in ways that looked uncomfortable to a human eye. He'd asked why they didn't have an a-grav field to lift up and down, but apparently the Originator tech played hob with that sort of thing. It generated its own a-grav, or at least a field that messed with gravity in weird ways, but not anything biddable enough for lifting. So it was these ladders, or they had an electric elevator elsewhere for cargo.

"How long've you been here?"

"Me? Couple of years. I'm the errand girl. I fetch things for them. Things like you. Jaine's been here forever, even before the boss. She found the place first. Maybe she even let the boss know. Studied the engineering. Used to be Hugh, high-grade."

"Like you used to be Hegemony?"

"I used to be a lot of things," she reflected. "Never quite what you'd call a loyal cultist though. Doc Shin's been trying to get the goods out of this place for the best part of a decade, the way I hear it."

"And you've only just got hold of an Intermediary?" They'd reached a hatch three metres across, grinding open after Emmaneth threw another lever. Below was a darkness Idris didn't much like the look of. Not that he was going to get any choice about it. Part of the whole helping him business involved Emmaneth's hand on his arm and he reckoned the only way out of that grip would be to remove the limb at the shoulder.

Emmaneth was obviously going to remain tactfully silent about that, and maybe, with all the other stressors, he'd have let it go. Jaine was coming down the ladder above them, though, and she lacked the Tothiat's reticence.

"The leashed ones didn't work out," she explained. Emmaneth shot her a look, but apparently Jaine didn't care about annoying her colleagues and went on, "That's why the good doctor said we needed someone like you. And there aren't many people like you."

"I almost had the old girl in the walker frame," Emmaneth said, given the cat was out of the bag. "But the Hugh boys were keeping a better eye on her, and I had the sniff of Mordant House about the place by then. Like knows like, right?"

Idris looked at her blankly and wondered if he was going to be noble and pretend it was better he was here than poor Demi Ulo. Right then he couldn't muster quite that much nobility. The big hole in the floor was open now, and Emmaneth was fiddling with a tangle of wiring that looked comfortingly homegrown and Colonial. With her hands finally off him, he spent precisely one and a half seconds considering making a break for it. Assuming he wasn't just going to batter against the walls like a desperate wasp, any escape would have involved climbing over Jaine to get up the ladder and then some sort of divine intervention, because he had no idea where to go after that.

"What happened to the other Ints?" he asked them. "The leashed ones?"

"Didn't work out," Emmaneth said, and any brooding menace she'd been trying for was completely undercut by Jaine's overlapping, "Went completely fucking out of their skulls."

"Right," Idris said. He lunged for her, got a foot on her thigh and a hand on her shoulder, then was actually on his way up the ladder like a panicking monkey. He heard Emmaneth's incredulous yell but didn't stop to venture any kind of explanation or reply. *Away*, he decided, and the other details could look after themselves.

He practically shot out of the hatchway at the ladder's top— another of those absurdly huge gaps that could have fit an elephant with a little pushing and squeezing—and came face to face with a creature the approximate size of the elephant.

He sat down hard with a whimper.

It was a Naeromath. He'd only seen one before in the flesh— the envoy from the Locust fleet at Arc Pallator. That had been in a tank, being an aquatic species. This one wasn't. This one had legs. A set of six mechanical legs, to be precise, all arching from the same hub on its underside, so that its huge, sleek body was balanced impossibly on that one point, seemingly forever about to topple to the right. The point where the hub meshed with its leathery hide was a horror of scar tissue, but then so was the rest of it. He could see savaged stumps where most of its flippers had been, some augmented by hinged metal manipulators or whips of uncertain function. There was an assemblage of tanks and bellows carved into its left side that wheezed and groaned with a skipping rhythm and leaked clear fluid slowly but insistently. Above that was what might have been a power source, or possibly a weapons pod: some bulky mess of plates and rivets, with the same aesthetic as the floors. A red light glared out where the pieces didn't quite fit together.

The creature's long, eel-like neck swung a head towards him that was half metal. Its barbels and tentacles were mostly stumps too, with segmented feelers grafted on. A single lead-grey lens the size of his hand was set off to the right side. An eye, an organ he didn't recall the other Naeromathi even having.

"Oh," Jaine said, as she and Emmaneth piled out of the hatch behind him. "Right. Okay then. You've met the boss."

"You're kidding," Idris breathed. The Naeromathi's head was within inches of his own. It smelled sharply of preservative, sweetly of decay.

"Idris Telemmier," Emmaneth said, "meet Ahab."

"Ahab."

"That's what Doc Shin calls it. I mean, it has its own name, I guess. It recruited the doctor, after he got thrown out of wherever he got thrown out of, for all the corners he cut.

Then it found Jaine here and went into partnership, or what-everthefuck they did."

"Something like that," Jaine agreed. "Boss, this is the Int." She spoke loudly, as though the Naeromathi was deaf.

Fluorescent patches across the Naeromathi's abused hide glimmered fitfully. Then there were sounds, like coughs, or barks, all tinny and metallic and issuing from one of the thing's many ragged implants. And then a voice.

"It will serve! The crusade progresses!"

Idris made a little bleating sound. He wanted to know just who had fixed up that voice for Ahab, mostly so he could slap them. It was made of screams, human-sounding screams, modulated and blended until they chorused out perfectly comprehensible words.

"Idris Telemmier!"

Hearing his own name in that mode was even worse.

"I know you! Berlenhof, Far Lux!" Its head lunged forwards on the long neck, the rim of its single lens glancing off his forehead. "All must serve against the common enemy! I know your victories! You will bring me my vengeance for what was lost to me!"

It wasn't like listening to the translation of an Essiel's ramblings and wondering how many layers of meaning had been sloughed off before the human words reached you; Idris was hearing the iron purpose first, the words later. However a native Naeromathi might have phrased those concepts, by the time its machines had processed the thoughts and spat them out in Colvul, all that was left was the honed intent.

The Naeromath turned, pivoting on its single hub, and its legs were carrying it away in a jerky series of lurches that were, nonetheless, very fast. It didn't stop at the wall but just went straight up it without losing speed, clambering across the ceiling to the hatch there, which was just large enough for it to writhe through.

"We were hoping to put that off until you'd got settled," Emmaneth said philosophically. "Anyway, as I said, that's Ahab, the boss. This is its show."

"I am not getting settled," Idris muttered. "I'm here under duress." Abruptly, he craned round, still sitting, and looked her in the eye. "How many?"

"What now?"

"Ints. How many did you ruin, before you decided you needed a better vintage and grabbed me?"

Emmaneth exchanged a look with Jaine. "Some," she told him flatly. "So you had better be the almighty wunderkind of Intermediaries, boy, because we are running out of time and options here."

"Fuck you."

"I see they taught you some cutting-edge rhetoric in the Program." She took his arm and had him on his feet effortlessly. He tried not to cooperate with going down the ladder, but the pinch of her fingers reminded him of the appalling force a Tothiat could exert and he gave up on that.

"What's this to you?" he demanded, because he might as well find some way to nettle her. "I mean, every Tothiat I ever knew was a thug and a gangster. And you're what, in love with the science or something?"

They were back at the dark hatch, and now it was Jaine trying to get the lights on while Emmaneth held on to him. "I tried that," she said. "The gangster thing. It was all right. But after a while you get tired of not dying."

He stared at her. Emmaneth smiled tightly.

"It hurts," she said. "If you even survive the process. And if the Tothir does too. You feel its pain as well as yours, all the time. You get used to bearing it but you never stop feeling it. All the time, Menheer Int. Now I hear it's not easy being what you are either, after they fucked with your brain. I mean, you bastards died like flies before they even finished remaking you, am I right?"

He granted her that with a nod.

"Maybe you know what I mean. You ever wanted to just end it all?"

There was light from the hatch now, though not much of it. The radiance looked gloomy, as though from far-off chasms. He found he had an inexplicable reluctance to go to the edge and look down, something from his very soul, where the Intermediary in him lived. It was linked to that terrible hollowness he felt beneath him.

"I thought about it. During the war. After," he admitted. He'd never taken those thoughts any further. But there had been times, bitter times, when he'd found relief in the simple knowledge that, if things got worse, there was always a meeting of knife and throat to free him from it all.

She seemed to read that knowledge on his face. "I couldn't," she said, very quietly, and then had to clarify: "Oh, I tried, but I couldn't. There was literally no injury I could do to myself that wouldn't heal. And I really tried."

"Poisons," he said. "I know there are some."

"You are a well-informed little monster." She even managed a grin. "I had some. I killed a Mordant House man who'd been sent to kill me, just so I could kill myself with the poisons they'd given him to kill me with. Fucking stupid, right? Except it didn't work. It just made the hurting worse. Blank white agony for seventeen days, and then I was me again, and whole. So I left my employment and went to find something in the universe that would kill me. Heard about this death-world, Criccieth's Hell. If I stepped out there, into that light, that would do it, Menheer Int. That light will destroy anything, even me."

"So what are you waiting for?" he asked harshly.

"I met Doc Shin here," she told him, dragging him to the hatch. "Heard what the plan was. And it's worth it. It's worth a little more pain, just to see if he can do what Ahab wants him to do. With the Machine."

He didn't like the sound of that one bit, but then she had him at the lip and he was staring down into...

"Oh..." Idris managed.

"Yeah," she agreed. "Gets you like that, doesn't it."

He was used to Originator architecture, albeit the ground-down ruined stubs found anywhere other than here. They had these same curved walls, set out in concentric labyrinths of hollow spaces. The spaces were the key, as he'd always understood.

But the ruins were ruins because the Originators had, millions of years before, withdrawn their hand. And here, the killing light of Criccieth's Hell had prevented them carrying out whatever process they'd used to eradicate the detail of their lives. Here, behind the shield that still held that harsh light back, were the innards of an Originator site intact.

He was looking down into a busy abyss.

The walls were there, as expected—the bones that would have been all that remained, assuming the hungry planet had not devoured them the way it apparently devoured everything else. Concentric jigsaw sections that never quite met, carved out of the same seamless stone that was native to no planet in the universe. Nested between and within them was a web, a stone honeycomb of precisely delineated emptinesses. Little bites of nothing, from the size of a hand to gaps big enough for Ahab to crawl into, radiated outwards as far as the intermittent light showed him. Those lights were electric lamps set up by human hands, or at least some mortal living agency other than the unknowable Originators. They lit up all the ironwork and ramps and ladders and cables strung out across the vast maze, in a vain attempt to reduce it all to something on a human scale. And there was plenty of dark down there into which those segmented spaces receded. All of this would have been striking enough, in a spelunker sort of way—looking into the chasm with its meagre constellation of lights, and the unknown extent of all those convoluted spaces he couldn't see. But to him...

"You don't know," he got out.

"Yeah," Emmaneth said again. "Last Int said something like that. Then her brain turned to cheese, so I reckoned it wasn't worth noting down." She gave him a shove but he clung to the rim of the hole, scrabbling for mental equilibrium.

It was just space, or spaces. A very precise organization of spaces, exacting down to the atomic level. He could feel this, in his head, where they'd put the Int in. Live space, crackling with invisible significance, charged and connected to the universe. This was the hollowness and why he'd felt he was skating over an unguessable void. Because the void was here. The very existence of this place, whole and intact with all its honeycomb of precisely calibrated nothings, was holding open a door to unspace.

Trine should be here. But Trine wouldn't have been able to experience it as he did.

Though all the heavy ironwork, the Originator walls, the encrusted layers of it all blocked mere sight, he could sense there was something down there. Something that he could only describe as active because he didn't want to touch the word *alive.* It was the Machine, as Emmaneth had called it.

He tried again to stop the descent but Emmaneth offered cheerily, "Climb or be carried."

He was halfway down the second ladder—it wobbled and Emmaneth muttered something about getting Jaine to refix it—when it occurred to him to wonder where the gravity was coming from.

"You said no a-grav. So this planet is just Earth standard?"

"About two-thirds Earth," she said. "Keep going."

"This isn't two-thirds G," he said, though he did keep going to avoid her stamping on his fingers. Now she wasn't actively holding him, odd thoughts about making a break for it started rattling about in his head again, but *where* precisely? It wasn't as though he had any illusions he could outpace a woman who didn't care if she broke a leg jumping after him.

As he descended, he felt the strength of the gravity changing—the start of the gradient must have prompted the question from him, all subconsciously. He was climbing down, while at the same time climbing out of the well. He felt the pull weaken.

By then he was four ladders down, muscles already bitching at him, and he could see the Machine.

Someone had added to Ahab's work. He knew this firstly because the workmanship—Jaine's?—was of a human scale and style, and secondly because it was unlikely the Naeromathi would have put in human seating on a whim. Three couches were there that he reckoned had started life in suspension pods, and were still cluttered with cables and wires. They all tilted at an alarming angle over a further drop that looked as though it might bore down into the planet's very heart. The huge angles of the Naeromathi work loomed over it all. That would have seemed like the ancient inhuman work of elder hands had there not been all the actual ancient inhuman work of elder hands surrounding *them*, the Originator walls making Ahab's craft look tame and recent. Two of the couches seemed complete, the third partially disassembled and, by Idris's assessment, abandoned long ago.

Doctor Shinandri was already down there, his dark face turned grey-blue by the light. By this point Idris estimated he really was under two-thirds Earth-standard gravity, but still descending, and its hold was weakening on him with every moment. It was welcome in a way, because it spared his aching arms and legs. By the time he was within speaking distance of Shinandri, however, he guessed at only half a G, and that was *less* than the planet was supposed to pull on him. It was the complex, he realized. It was acting as a gravitic lens just by the fact of its orientation, and the way it fit in the universe. Just as the Originator ruins still exerted an influence by their simple shape and organization, so this intact installation was like a clawed hand hooked into the fabric of causality. It distorted everything around it, pulling the universe tight and thin until the bottomless sea of unspace was *right there*.

"Ah, Menheer Telemmier," Shinandri called as Idris managed the final couple of ladders. "Delighted you could join me, yes indeed." He was still in his encounter suit, half the hoses connected up, and Idris was depressed but unsurprised to see another one lying part-assembled on the floor. It didn't look like his size but he didn't reckon this objection was likely to stand under the circumstances.

His feet touched down on the slanting Naeromathi metal and he felt dizzy. Emmaneth dropped beside him in time to stop what would have been a fairly gradual fall, in the reduced gravity. He didn't have it in him to fight her, even for the show of it. He was on the brink of a vast drop, and it wasn't the physical hole that sat between the three couches.

"What…is this place?" he got out.

"Well, interesting question, very interesting." Shinandri giggled in an appalling way for a grown man. "What it might have been to the original Originators, who can say, hmm? Who, indeed? But there was a Machine here then, which our leader found and adapted and converted and, shall we say, overlaid with his own, which we have now successively re-edified. What it is to all of us is an eye, Menheer Telemmier. An eye with which to gaze, we might say, into the abyss. And you and I, we are going to look it right into the apple of its eye, Menheer. Or at least you, because I lack your specially trained perceptions, or, as it might be, those parts of your brain that have been honed beyond the merely human."

Honed is a polite way of saying fucked over, Idris thought. By then, Jaine had caught up with them, scurrying down the ladders nimbly. She was taking up pieces of the suit, and Idris briefly toyed with the idea of making things as difficult for everyone as possible by not letting them dress him. He remembered Emmaneth's pinching fingers and reckoned that "as difficult as possible" likely wouldn't amount to much. With poor grace he let her fit the suit on him.

They can dress me up and sit me down but they cannot make me actually help them in any way. I'm no leashed Int. I'm nobody's slave. He remained the master of his own head, and if they had a bucketload of drugs to pump into him, well at least he'd put them to that trouble and rack up some pharmacy bills.

Shinandri had connected his last few hoses and taken a couch. "Menheer, I will be your co-pilot, shall we say? Yes, indeed." Another trilling little giggle came out, giving Idris the sickening feeling that he was in the power of a madman. "I will experience the universe through the activity in your brain. But it is your perspicacity we need, or we might say your perceptiveness. And your loquaciousness, thereafter. Try to think, as you experience, how you might be able to convey what you are experiencing."

"What precisely will I be experiencing?" Idris asked sourly. Jaine had fitted the suit to him now, with a little botch-job alteration to accommodate his small frame. "An eye to look at the universe? You've got your telescope turned backwards, Doctor."

He resolved not to try any further jokes with Shinandri, because the man found this funny and Idris wanted to hear that laugh as little as possible.

"Menheer Telemmier, you are a familiar of unspace," the man said, even as Jaine got Idris on a couch and connected him up. "Well then, we are about to delve into unspace. Here, on-planet, controlled, indeed scientific in our careful approach. None of that rushing about in a spaceship that is so deleterious to serious research, you might say! Give me a place to stand, as the saying goes. Just think what you might learn, with a stable platform from which to look into infinity."

"I really don't think—" Idris managed, and then they turned the Machine on, pushing more of those huge clunky Naeromathi levers. He was abruptly out of the universe and gazing into the abyss with his mind's eye, which had no lid and couldn't close, nor refuse to see.

For the first brief second he clung desperately to his resolution of being absolutely no use to anybody, obstinate to the point of unreason, of letting it all stream past him and ignoring it. They'd kidnapped him and under no circumstances would he cooperate for a moment.

Then he saw, and he tried to catch his breath, but the Machine was breathing for him. Which was good because he had no connection whatsoever to his body, and it was touch and go whether anything autonomic was happening right then.

*

When they took him out, however long later that was, he was so crammed full of words—and, even more so, indescribable sensations—that even if he'd wanted to tell them what he'd seen, he couldn't have. They hauled him up the ladders, virtually tucked under Emmaneth's arm, and the revelations within him were so vast there was barely room left in his blown-open mind for *Idris*.

22.

Havaer

One look at the Cheesewoman told Havaer that the old woman had sold him out. Well, he was on a limited bribe budget right now, not likely to be the highest bidder.

"Menheer Mundy." Heremon obviously felt the game was already won. She pulled up a big pallet of crackers and hopped up onto it, feet dangling like a child's. The pallet must have weighed the best part of a ton given how inedibly dense the damn things were. She was reminding him just who had the physical leverage, should he be considering fisticuffs. "My boss has an offer for you."

"One I can't refuse?" he asked her levelly. The Cheesewoman had backed off to the furthest extent of her cluttered domain. Havaer let his long-boned frame relax into a familiar attitude that looked terribly casual but which he could kick back out of very quickly. His gun was a weight inside his jacket, trying to catch his attention. Shooting Heremon full of holes would aid in nothing more than seeing the wall behind her more clearly. Chief Laery had provided him with another weapon in case of Tothiat, though. She'd meant it for Emmaneth but Havaer wasn't averse to giving out free samples in Heremon's case.

371

"We know who you're hunting, Menheer," she told him. "And you know why we want her too."

He didn't. Then, pieces clicking into place, he reckoned he probably did. Emma Ostri had gone to work for criminal cartels on the Hegemonic side of the border, and come out of it a Tothiat. Heremon herself had once been just a regular human—presumably as amoral as Ostri ever was—before she'd taken the same deal. Havaer had run into both her and the Unspeakable Aklu on Tarekuma, investigating rumours of the Architects' return before they had actually returned. It had involved the *Vulture God* crew; his first tango with them. They'd got themselves mixed up with some Originator cargo Aklu had laid claim to, and everything had got messy, resulting in their old captain being killed. Havaer, on their trail, had ended up in an unwanted audience with the Essiel crime boss just because he was asking the wrong questions in the wrong place.

"So she walked out on you," he essayed, hoping Laery's brief on Ostri was right. "Fine, you take her back and string her up or whatever your boss wants to do to her. I just need to pop a few questions first."

"I know what you're after," Heremon said. "If you want her, you want to come with us."

I really, really don't. "Why would you want me to?"

She leant forwards. Her smile might actually have been pleasant, even intriguing, in other circumstances. If she'd been Havaer's type. And while that type tended to move around as the mood took him, people with alien lobsters grafted to their spines were way outside it.

"Who wouldn't want a piece of eye candy like you on their arm," she said. The pretence at flirting was grotesque. "Also, you have a very useful line in badges. I like a man with authority."

"Sure. Fine," he replied. She was still hunched towards him and, whatever a Tothiat's capabilities, physics and gravity meant she wasn't well balanced. He let his gaze drift a little, as though considering, almost as if he was bored. There was a precise moment when her poise and his act intersected, and that was his window.

He kicked backwards. There was a half-open crate of crackers at his feet and he actually managed to punt it right into her face, which was an unexpected but welcome bonus. Heremon went backwards off the pallet and he hoped he'd at least hurt her pride. She came back swinging, ready to chase, and he almost had the needle in her. Almost.

She saw it coming. He caught the exact moment on her face where she did the maths and worked out precisely why he wasn't shooting but instead getting right inside her reach with a three-inch round-sectioned blade. Didn't need an analysis lab to work out what was inside it.

Even then, her own instincts almost got her killed, because her arm came up to block and he could have stabbed her in the back of the hand. She whipped that arm back, though— so hard that he saw her shoulder dislocate. She skidded under his stab, momentarily uncontrolled, scrabbling at the floor and for his ankles.

If he'd been a do-or-die type, like so many Mordant House novices all fired up with the righteousness of their purpose, he would have slammed down onto her, knee to her chest as he tried to get the blade in. She could then have torn him apart, literally, in the process. Havaer wasn't that young or that fired up anymore. Instead, he was out of the

Cheesewoman's office by the time Heremon had found her feet.

He signalled Colvari from the first moment, finding his comms just bouncing from a static wall someone had thrown up. Everyone in this part of the habitat would be having a bad day right now, but he knew damn well it was aimed at him. He immediately sent commands to his routines to try and end-run around the interference. This was his job, after all, or at least a part of it. One he was somewhat rusty on, but he had at least three and a half seconds to get good again.

His feet, meanwhile, knew their role, pelting him through the warren of service corridors and loading bays that lay between the Cheesewoman's office and the shabby dock he'd come into. This was definitely Matachin Below, and that meant crime and cramped living quarters, illicit dives and shady deals. But less prosaically, it meant a great deal of machinery, stores, workshops and the general gubbins that kept an orbital running and fixed it when it broke. He got a lot of startled looks from people probably doing nothing more nefarious than mending the air ducting, but then they saw Heremon coming after him and decided it was none of their damn business.

Havaer had two levels to go down to get to the dock, and didn't fancy either the slow-as-molasses freight lift or a service stairwell that Heremon could just jump down, broken ankles be damned. Instead he took a hard left, bounding off a wall so hard he popped a panel out of its mountings and hit one of the big gravitic hoists. He'd seen someone—when *he'd* been the pursuer rather than the pursued—just leap down one of those once, because they hadn't understood how the science worked. You didn't float, you plummeted. All those huge containers being lifted up the well had handles on them that the orbital's gravitic drives could get a purchase on. Other than that, it was just a big hole going all the way down to the docking level.

But there were a lot of containers, and they were all slung in there anyhow, rather than neatly lined up, and rising slowly to avoid any accidents.

He let his running momentum become a jump that landed him on a container two metres down, big enough that he didn't even make it wobble. Even as Heremon's pounding feet sounded above, he had dropped down to the next one, then to the next. All the time, his comms system was fighting with the static wall, trying to get word through to Colvari. He reckoned his odds of getting out of this were slim and someone needed to get word back to Laery.

Each container he landed on was rising, of course. Stay put and it would take him right back up to face Heremon as she arrived, serving him up like a delicacy on a waiter's tray. So he had to keep jumping swiftly from one to the next, until he was already halfway down the shaft.

He heard a bang above him as Heremon followed his example.

Two more jumps, against a rising tide of complaint from people on the level he was dropping past. He was probably ruining some lift manager's day right now but he really had other priorities. Then Heremon just dropped past him. Maybe she'd misstepped, or maybe she was taking advantage of her physiology to be ready for him when he reached the bottom. He reckoned she'd miscalculated, though.

She hit the ground very hard, which would be a moment's

inconvenience for her, but a moment was something he could use.

He took the next three drops at a run, risking his neck, but keeping his footing, ending up on the dock even as Heremon was pulling herself back together after her fall. He might have been out with the needle again, in the hopes he could get it into her before she was able to mend her bones enough to stop him. He didn't like the odds, though. Instead he darted off for his ship.

Someone was in the way. In fact, some*thing* was in the way but there was a someone in the something. And he knew them.

This, he decided, *is simply not fair*. The newcomer really should have been an ally, in this trying time, and instead she was most obviously not. *Come on, you screwed Broken Harvest over! Twice! And now you're best buddies?*

He skidded to a halt in the shadow of Olian Timo's Scorpion frame, which was doing its best line in looming menacingly. Inside the bubble of its canopy, he saw the woman cock her head and shrug her stumpy shoulders. *What you gonna do?*

Heremon was on her feet again and right behind him. "As I was saying," she said, not even sounding out of breath, "I think we should pool our resources."

He took a sideways step so he could see her and Timo both. Over there, three ships down from his own, he caught sight of the unlovely contours of the *Vulture God*. Colvari had probably been trying to warn him since they showed up, but the comms here were nothing but the static wall, which he still couldn't get through.

"I appreciate that if you know Ostri, you probably think

we're all for sale," he told the Tothiat flatly. "I'm sorry to disappoint you."

"Look, Mundy," came Timo's voice from the Scorpion. "I get it. We felt the same way, believe me. Though we got this deal through her boss, so we weren't exactly sticking our lip out like you're doing. Come onto the *God* and talk it out, why don't you?"

They were surely here looking for Telemmier, of course, same as him. And maybe Heremon was too, or maybe she was just after bringing Ostri back, like she said. At that point Colvari's voice sounded in his ear.

"I have you," the Hiver's clipped tones told him. "A remarkable barrier, but we're through. Do you have instructions?"

He took a moment to think, letting his heart slow with a little medication, covering the pause with a harried look between Heremon and Timo.

"Tell Laery contact with Broken Harvest and *Vulture God*." Only now did he consider how ill-omened those two names sounded together. "Going with them. Under duress. If you have any way of following, do it." Though it wasn't likely this crowd would be conscientiously logging flight plans with Matachin kybernet. "Otherwise, I'll be in contact when I can." *If I can.*

"So let's talk," he told the pair of them.

*

He was mostly reminded of the time he'd had the *Vulture God* crew over a barrel, their ship seized by his and each of them enjoying his hospitality individually as he interrogated them—in a friendly enough way—about the Architects and their possible return. Except that return had turned out to be a hoax perpetrated by a Hegemonic cult hierograve. And all of that had been understandably overshadowed when the Architects actually did return, as though too many people mentioning their name had conjured them from the ether. But Havaer had been given a good chance to size them all up: Olli, Kris, Kittering, Solace. And Idris Telemmier, who'd been with them then.

That party had been crashed by none other than the Broken Harvest, and Havaer had done his best to cover for the *Vulture God*, to let them get out and carry news to Berlenhof. Which they had, in fact, done. Now here he was, sitting within the curved walls of their drone bay, with the crew minus Idris but plus the Unspeakable Aklu's premier lieutenant. *Strange goddamn bedfellows.*

Heremon seemed entirely at ease, despite the whole business of her brother, or at least fellow lieutenant, having met his long-overdue doom at the hands of these itinerant spacers. She kept giving him sneery looks, too, in a very *What you gonna do about it?* manner. He still had his little poison pigsticker in his pocket. Should things go south, that was what he proposed doing about it, but right now apparently it was détente time and everyone was friends.

"So, fine," he said, trying to wrest a little control of the situation. "You people want Idris back from Ostri—from Emmaneth," he corrected, seeing blank looks. "Emma Ostri, when she was human. You know these things were human once, right?" Aiming to drive a bit more of a wedge between them and their new ally. Heremon's lip curled, but she said nothing. "You know exactly where I'm coming from. Mordant House doesn't want Telemmier in the wrong hands, either.

And I appreciate that, long term, we have a very different idea of what constitutes the wrong hands."

"This came about because you tried to kidnap him on Arc Pallator," Solace told him flatly.

Havaer met her gaze levelly. "I did nothing of the sort, and not for want of opportunity. I stand by what I said to you back then. It wasn't in my orders. On the other hand, *you*," turning to the Tothiat, "say you're just after your turncoat fellow gangster. The Unspeakable wouldn't have any use for a free Intermediary?"

She was leaning up against the drone bay's slanting wall, a position that looked uncomfortable to him, but then apparently just being a Tothiat was supremely uncomfortable. "You can just say 'None of us trusts each other' if that keeps things short," she suggested. "But all of us want to find Em. As we've been hunting her since before she grabbed their friend, we have more information than them. Or you. And *they* have the trust of their man, who'll cooperate with them. While you, lawman, have a badge. You can get us access."

She hadn't had any access issues on Matachin Orbital, he considered, and having seen the mining complexes on Kodo he reckoned the smugglers and grifters there would welcome a bona fide gangster with open arms. Which left...

"She's on Deathknell, then." They were too civilized there not to raise an eyebrow at someone like Heremon turning up and walking around on two legs like a human being. All those laws and regulations.

"Probably not. But that's where the trail leads. She goes there. She meets people."

"People who meet a nasty end at the hands of your co-worker?"

"Possibly." Heremon shrugged.

"Menheer Mundy," broke in Kris Almier. "Look, I'm not going to surprise anyone if I say this arrangement wasn't exactly our first choice either. We were following information sent to the Parthenon. We didn't know it came from the Broken Harvest. But what were we supposed to do? Idris is alive."

"And she's reporting to the Parthenon every step, no doubt?" A nod at Solace.

"Of course." The Myrmidon bristled. Except they were searching for him in Colonial systems, which meant any sudden rescue from that quarter could confirm everyone's war footing. So this mission had to be done by the shabby old *Vulture God* without any more cavalry to back it up.

"Well, fine." Something had just quietly pinged Havaer's comms, and nobody else seemed to have registered it. He had his eyes on Olian Timo most of all, because she'd shown herself to be quite the hacker, but it really seemed as if the intrusion had escaped everyone's attention but his. "You want my badge, as you put it. I want Telemmier found. We're going to have some harsh words about who precisely he walks away with—and don't kid yourselves that'll be just a two-sided argument when it happens." Another look at Heremon, whom he wanted them doubting as much as humanly possible. "For now, I guess we're all of us pointed in the right direction." *And I am absolutely on my own and couldn't even ask for instructions even if I was able to get a clear channel out.* He had an idea how all of this would look on his permanent record, and his career prospects might actually be better if he died at some point in the process.

Kittering, the Hanni, jumped from his stool and scuttled

out of the bay, his translator saying that he'd get the ship ready for unspace and the Throughways to Deathknell. It was only one step from Matachin, he recalled, two more from Kodo. Emmaneth's roaming range was relatively small these days. *She's settled down.*

Heremon left him with the rest of the crew. Olli Timo was ignoring him, decanting herself from her Scorpion into the drone bay's control pod instead of a suspension bed. That left him with Kris and Solace, ducking into the close interior of the ship to where the couches were. They were an odd pair, not exactly spacer standard, the lawyer and the Partheni. When they found him a pod that was functioning and long enough to fit him, there was a spectacularly awkward pause.

"This isn't our plan," Solace said eventually. "The Broken Harvest has masterminded everything so far—bringing us in, finding you."

"So long as you don't start trusting them," Havaer said.

"We don't trust *you* either," Kris pointed out. "You're a Mordant House man." A pause. "Or mostly. We do remember you got Idris back to us on Berlenhof. So he could actually save the planet. When it felt like everyone else in Hugh was doing everything they could to stop him. So there's that."

"Believe it or not, working for the Intervention Board and saving the capital of the Colonies aren't entirely contradictory," he said. "I mean, it's where our offices are. And if I asked how Telemmier's sojourn with your people had gone?" He cocked an eyebrow at Solace.

"I wouldn't tell you," she said. The one thing he'd learned about her in their last interview, though, was that, for an agent, she wasn't the best liar. Partheni liked to do things the direct way, or at least they did at Solace's pay grade. There was more pride than defensiveness in that response, and he read from it that they'd at least made some headway towards getting their own Ints. *Pouring them out of the vats right now, probably.* Which didn't have an immediate bearing on their current arrangement but might just spell the end of Hugh within Havaer's lifetime. If the Architects didn't get there first. Any development that let the entire Partheni warfleet appear out of the deep void over Berlenhof or Magda, with no warning before the gravitic bombardment began, could never be good.

Interesting fucking times, as the man said.

He smiled and thought about how things were likely to go if and when they had Idris back in their collective hands. He'd honestly rather be shot dead by Solace than murdered by Heremon the gangster's lackey, but neither were high on his want list.

A handful of checks showed him that the suspension couch was functional, and showed *them* he wasn't just some clueless core-world desk jockey. Meanwhile he'd opened up the narrow comms channel, following the path of the ping he'd received before. While he was lying down and waiting for the drop to unspace, he risked subvocalizing, "Colvari?"

"Here."

"Follow us to Deathknell."

There was a moment's pause that, even over the compressed comms signal, felt embarrassed. "Firstly, be aware that we had no idea whether you would be able to communicate your destination to us."

"What do you mean?"

"We have abandoned your ship. We will not therefore be able to follow you in it to Deathknell. On the ledger's positive side, we will accompany you there."

He mulled that over, feeling the *Vulture God*'s systems rumble and grind as a wary Kittering put them through pre-flight tests. "And you're where, exactly?"

"On the hull."

"Of this ship? Of the *Vulture*?"

"That ship, yes."

Hard vacuum didn't need to be a problem for Hivers, if their frame was designed appropriately. He considered the pros and cons of the situation. After all, Heremon and the *God*'s crew doubtless knew which ship he'd arrived in, so if it then dropped in-system at Deathknell they'd likely have marked it.

"That's good," he sent. "I'm going to give you a dead-drop address and some encryption routines. The moment you have a chance to place anything on a packet, let them know where we are, and where we're headed next, if we've found that out by then." He considered whether Solace would be sending the same information to the Partheni Aspirat that he was communicating to Mordant House—or at least the splinter cell within it that Laery was running. This was turning out to be the most shambolic piece of secret agent business he'd ever been part of.

A bank of lights sprang on within the couch, though one of them flickered and died almost immediately.

"Ready for unspace," he warned Colvari, who would have to shut their higher functions down to survive the trip. After that he had the couch put him under, his last waking thought being that the academics of Deathknell weren't going to know what hit them.

23.

Idris

Emmaneth took him to a room where someone—Jaine most likely—had built a table, an actual human-scale table, and bolted it to the floor. There were crates drawn up around it and she sat him on one like a doll. Idris had enough self-control by then to keep himself sitting there, gripping the table-edge with whitened fingers.

After a little while, Jaine and Shinandri joined them. A small part of him listened distantly to their conversation while his head thronged with thoughts about what he'd just experienced. They were talking about damage. Damage to the facility. Jaine had a long list of areas—in some arcane notation Idris couldn't follow—that had suffered in the brief time the Machine had been active. Brief? Idris felt as though he'd been on a journey of a thousand years, dropping out of real time into dream logic. Or unspace. How did time work in unspace? Because it didn't, not really. Particular journeys took a certain amount of subjective time if, as he had, you actually bore the brunt of the unreal and stayed awake through them. They took a certain amount of external time, too. There was always a variance, but humans had been throwing themselves into the void long enough to learn

384

the parameters of it. Except, at the same time, you were travelling outside the real universe, crossing between stars far faster than light ever could. Idris didn't have the sort of doctorate that Shinandri presumably boasted, but he knew at a base level that even the best and the brightest couldn't entirely *account* for unspace travel: the time it took, anything like that. Except he now felt he was within a small stretch of writing the thesis. Just one more trip in the Machine and he'd have it.

There was damage, though. Jaine sounded grim. Yes, she would do what she could, but there were cracks in the shell of the installation and each activation made them worse. Their venture here had an expiry date built in.

"Why?" Idris croaked. The pair of them turned to look at him with some surprise.

"We got a good one here." Emmaneth squeezed his shoulder companionably. "Already talking. Ready to go again, maybe."

"Well we're not," Jaine told her sharply. "Let me at least try to glue things back together, won't you?"

"Yes indeed." Shinandri was staring into Idris's face. "Indubitably, and may I be the first to welcome you back to the land of the articulate, Menheer Telemmier. Quite the scintillating recovery in so short a time. Remarkable!"

"What damage? Why?" Idris got out. He felt as though he was rediscovering his lips and tongue from first principles.

"It's this bastard flora," Jaine said. "I mean, best guess, it's why this place is still *here*, like we said. But it kills everything. It will literally break down any kind of intrusion to atoms. Now, this place protects itself. We don't understand, not even a little, how the shield is generated, but it's there, which is why any of this is still *here*. But the Machine engages the entire installation. When it's on, that means no shield."

"What?" Idris demanded. "Why?"

"The shield and instruments are mutually exclusive, you see," Shinandri said lightly. "They simply cannot exist at the same point. You can't, as it were, hide your face behind your hands, if you want to look into the abyss at the same time." Which was a far from reassuring way of putting it.

"The light out there just starts ablating away the walls," Jaine picked up. "There'll come a time when we turn it on, and it'll just go—then we'll have maybe a minute, if we're lucky, to get out. Because there's a fucking small corridor into orbit that the existence of this place keeps open. Once that goes, the radiance will get you even as you try to pull away. Look, we weren't kidding, Criccieth's Hell is the nastiest planet in the universe."

"One might almost say," Shinandri giggled suddenly, horribly, "it's no *bed of roses*."

Idris took some strength from the long-suffering look that passed between Emmaneth and Jaine.

"Now!" the doctor declared suddenly, startling everyone.

"Not yet, Doc," Jaine tried.

"Yes, yet, entirely yet! Menheer, as you are unexpectedly grandiloquent perhaps you feel ready to discuss what you...?"

"No," said Idris.

Doctor Shinandri blinked, winched his smile back into place and rubbed his hands. "A little period of recuperation—"

"No," said Idris again, because he really was recovered. He'd come back to himself and remembered what it was like to be Idris Telemmier. "No." He bunched his fists, feeling the weakness in his fingers burn away with the exertion. "No talk." Even though the words were like nine atmospheres of pressure within his skull trying to get out. "I am not your lab rat. I won't. You kidnapped me. I..." *Need to know. I need to understand. Help me learn what's going on here, because it's an eye on the universe.* But his resolve held out and he clamped his jaw down on all of it. *No.*

"From past experience," Shinandri said grandly, not at all the academic tantrum Idris was expecting, "our abyssonauts do need a little time to themselves, after the first jaunt." He sat and leant forwards, arms on the table and chin on his arms to bring him down eye-to-eye with Idris. "Sleep on it, Menheer. I'm sure you'll be happy to expound, yes indeed, after a little shut-eye."

Well there I've got you beat, Idris decided, but he let Emmaneth take him off to a cramped chamber nearby. It was patently the result of the curved Originator walls and the industrial bulkheads of Ahab's work meeting at a bad angle, but someone had put a bed in there. It had probably started life as a cot on a starship about fifty years before, by his estimation. The Tothiat lowered him into it, not ungently, and then stood there, staring down at him.

"The other one, we couldn't shut her up," she remarked. "You're a hard case, Menheer Telemmier."

"Says the immortal lobster-woman." He felt weirdly unafraid of her, and he realized a moment later it was because, compared to the sheer scale of what he'd just glimpsed, she was irrelevant. He himself was, too, save that he was also the means by which these cosmic revelations could be delivered to the real universe. Nothing mattered, in comparison to what he'd seen.

"You'll talk," she said softly.

"Or you'll hurt me?" The idea seemed so trivial he almost laughed at it. Break his arm? Pull out a fingernail or gouge an eye? How *small*! The universe would barely notice.

"We're not your enemies, Menheer." She was solemn now, a different woman. "This is important. And we don't have long. There is nowhere else like this in the whole of the universe."

"What makes you think I care?" he said, though he did. He was still clinging desperately to his non-cooperation, though, like a drowning man to a plank.

"If I can care, Menheer," Emmaneth told him, "then anyone can."

*

She left him with his own thoughts, but they were so big and numerous he felt there was barely enough room for him in their company. They thronged the room, fighting their way outside his head, demanding to be examined.

He had *seen*.

It was a telescope into unspace. Or no, it wasn't, that was just the closest human approximation. Except it was also completely wrong, because a telescope let the eye focus on a single point, whereas the perspective the Machine gave him was...broad. Inhumanly, ridiculously broad, while still retaining meaning to his minuscule human point of view. Squaring an impossible circle, as the first trick in a whole celestial magic show of things that couldn't possibly exist. He had *seen*...

Everything.

And they were right. He wanted to talk. He wanted to know what the previous Int had said, and no damn matter that they'd killed some wretched leash-contract slave who'd no more consented to being here than he had. He needed to get his words out and hear whatever Shinandri had to say, about his own ventures into the void below. Even if the good doctor wasn't an Intermediary, there would still be *something* in the man's own mind that could give Idris vital context and understanding.

He had seen...

He had to pare it down, focus on some discrete aspect. All together it was too much. The mind baulked at the prospect of swallowing it.

The Throughways.

He'd seen the Throughways, those paths between the stars that any halfway-competent navigator could take. The backbone of human—or any species'—interstellar travel. Fire up your gravitic drive and drop into unspace; plot your course along one of the Throughways linking your current solar system with some other, across the universe; hotfoot it to your suspension couch before the dreadful aloneness/not-aloneness of unspace started getting to you; have the ship wake you as you arrive a thousand light years away. Making a mockery of both space and time, so long as you were happy to go only between those points linked by the Throughways. And they had been built, everyone believed that. Some elder civilization, perhaps the Originators, had found the virgin field of unspace and imposed their corridors on it. Idris knew now without a shadow of a doubt that, yes, they had indeed been built, but no, they were not for travel. That was just a bonus of their existence. Their purpose had been...he didn't know, but he'd seen the vast shadow scaffolding around the Throughways. How unspace was like a membrane underlying the entire universe, held taut like the skin of a drum. The Originators, or whatever unknown hands, had hung weights off that membrane, placed clamps and stitches in it, to pull it very precisely out of true for their own purposes. And, in so doing, they'd turned that perfect stretched skin into a topography, creating channels and folds and creases. Then, millions of years later, little humans and Hanni and Castigar, and even the mighty Essiel, had come along and decided those artefacts of a greater vision were roads for their convenience.

They were such a small part of the greater work, this much Idris knew. Because unspace was full of the shadows of that work. He saw them as though peering through dark water: the vast angles and structures that were pulling unspace into a mind-twisting configuration, and so precisely that even the least change might thwart...some purpose. There was a purpose and he felt maddeningly close to grasping it. To knowing...

Everything.

There were the Architects too, of course. He had a sense of them moving through the universe like grubs boring through a rotting fruit. Except the simile wasn't right. He tried to get his head around their precise relation to everything else he'd seen, but it eluded him, just past the tip of his fingers as he reached for it. There had been a definite pattern to them, though, no mere random meandering. A pattern that, if he could only...

Alone, unsleeping, of course, he felt like shouting at the angled ceiling, beating his hands against the impervious stone of the Originators' work. What had they come here for? Why build this place on so hostile a world? Or had the world been pleasant, perhaps even dead, when they first came, and this toxic biosphere had crept up on them over the long aeons of their study?

Had the Originators been admiring their own handiwork when they stared into unspace and the manipulations of it, or instead observing the creations of a race ancient and inexplicable even to *them*?

Again, why here? He almost knew. He thought about the ruins on Arc Pallator and Jericho, how it wasn't the walls themselves but the compartmentalized spaces they created that were significant. He thought about the Naeromathi weapon unleashed against the Architect, a gravitic engine existing in the nothing between their Locust Arks, rather than in the ships themselves. Or the Zero Point fighters the Partheni deployed, whose combined gravitic engines created a mass-hammer effect. And this installation itself, with its complex honeycomb of spaces. It was all about the spaces. Not the stars themselves, but the skin stretched between them.

Lying there on the hard cot, in this terrible place, he felt himself inches from understanding the universe. Not the Architects. Not the Originators. The universe itself. Because they were both part of it, and you couldn't know them unless you understood the whole.

All those Throughways, like sutures, tugging the way the universe hung between them. And there were a thousand other forces and factors making up the struts of the scaffolding that directed the universe how to be. All those little tugs and pulls to keep it taut, and in the very particular shape which meant it was *this* universe and not any other. Even he himself, in observing it with his conscious Int's mind, was another little tug. Maybe that was the plan, or maybe not.

When they came for him, however many hours after he had no idea, he felt as though they'd tortured him all night. As if he'd been left in a cell with water dripping on his head or a chaos of noise blaring in his ears. Even if he could have slept, how could he have slept? His mind hadn't stopped racing around the confines of his skull since they took him out of the Machine. He wanted to grab Emmaneth by the collar and scream *Take me back down there!* into her face. His feet jittered on the floor. When he stood still, he was shaking.

Still he did his level best to be mulish. He made a heroic effort to not want to go. And then he really didn't want to go, because they weren't going down, just sideways, into another cavernous space where, apparently, it was breakfast time.

He was hungry, he discovered. He was ravenous. Thoughts of the universe had driven all other considerations from him, but now Emmaneth sat him down in front of a foil-wrapped ration block, vintage circa the end of the war, and he tore into it with nails and teeth.

The others were all there. Not just Shinandri and Tokamak Jaine, but the bulging bulk of Ahab. The Naeromath's body was slumped about its clutch of mechanical legs as though slouched on a stool, and a half-dozen cables fed into various parts of it. There was something that looked like a fleshy purple orange with blue veins in front of it, and it tore off pieces with one metal claw, then fed them into a slot below its head. Idris had no idea how, or upon what, Naeromathi had originally fed back on their homeworld. Given that world was one more dead sculpture somewhere in the void of space, it probably wasn't knowledge he was going to miss.

There was another place set too. Or at least someone had put out a tin plate with a ration pack, and it didn't seem to belong to anyone. None of them explained it to him and, as he was still being mulish, he couldn't really ask.

Shinandri finished first, dabbing at his lips with his sleeve. Now out of the encounter suit, he wore threadbare formal clothes, not core-Colonies standard but, where the jacket had a long forked tail, faintly ridiculous. There was a sash, too, purple and green and rather tattered. Idris couldn't guess what he was dressed up as.

The doctor met his gaze and smiled, bright and brittle.

"Now, Menheer, I dare say you've had a lot to think about, haven't you? A great deal of cogitation, on that I would stake all the money I don't have. And, as we have you, so to speak, in our clutches, there seems no reason not to return to the Machine for another session." He was watching Idris's face very closely for a reaction. "But, as no doubt you gleaned, our time here is strictly limited by the durability of the walls, yes indeed. We cannot simply open up the universe for your personal viewing pleasure, Menheer. There must be a quid pro quo, in which you grace us with your insights and we work together towards our goal, wouldn't you say, Menheer?"

Idris blinked at him, for a moment holding desperately onto his resolution not in any way to cooperate with these maniacs.

The words came out of him despite his every intention. "What is your goal, precisely?"

"It speaks," Emmaneth commented drily, but Shinandri waved her to silence. Ahab shifted on the fixed splay of its

393

legs, and its long neck shadowed the table, eeling towards Idris.

"Our crusade!" its translator announced. "The great war you have already taken up arms in against the Deconstructors!"

Idris blinked. "The Architects?"

"Even so," Shinandri confirmed, sotto voce.

"The Machine is a weapon?" Idris hadn't seen any evidence of *that* when they'd put him in it.

"To strike the enemy, you must find the enemy!" Ahab trumpeted.

"I imagine you have observed already that the Machine gives a perspective onto unspace that reveals its greater structure, something never seen before, or even guessed at," Shinandri murmured. "It is our leader's belief that the Architects are an integral part of that structure. They do not just travel *through* unspace, but it is their native domain."

"Unspace isn't real space," Idris said, echoing all the lessons they'd taught him as a child. "When you enter unspace, you don't really exist. Nothing does. That's why we're always alone in unspace." *Alone except for . . .*

"Yet the true situation is manifestly more complex than that, wouldn't you say, Menheer?" Shinandri pressed. "The structure you have doubtless observed, that even I can dimly perceive, and which our previous Int was at least able to report upon before the experience overwhelmed her, is consistent. Not real in the same way as matter from the physical universe is real to us. But real on its own terms. And the structure of unspace informs the physical universe. That much I have equations for. If you are so foolhardy as to ask me, I can bore you with them for some considerable time, yes indeed. Unspace creates the real. Or possibly the real informs unspace. Or most likely there is a dialogue of influences between the two. But admittedly, whilst these are my own points of interest, our valiant leader has more focused ideas. He wishes to find the home of the Architects as the necessary preliminary to some method of attack upon them."

"Attack," Idris echoed weakly, "into unspace."

Emmaneth clapped him on the shoulder. "Got to find where they are, first."

He would have said, scornfully even, *There is no "where." It's unspace.* Except he now knew that wasn't true. Even the unreal had landmarks.

"The Architects aren't the problem," he told them quietly. "I know, I spoke with one. They have masters, and the Architects are just their weapon."

"Then we must disarm them!" Ahab bellowed, and abruptly it was levering itself up and lurching across the floor. Idris imagined internal gyroscopes wheeling furiously before finding their balance.

He met the gaze of Doctor Shinandri across the table.

"Now, Menheer, I imagine you have no wish to cooperate with our grand venture and would rather go back to your room," the scientist said guilelessly. "Or perhaps you would spend some time with me talking through what you experienced yesterday, while Jaine prepares the machine for another dive into the unreal, hmm?"

Idris bit his lip, scrabbling for any remaining shreds of his self-control. But his head was too full and, even excluding the fact that Ahab had brought the *war* into it, a chance to take the conflict *to* the Architects, he had to *know*.

*

He let them put him back under. On the surface he was all protestations, but at the heart of him he was sick for it like an addict. The Machine gave him the universe, or at least as much of it as he could conceive. It was the universe reversed, because he was looking at it from below, from unspace. Shinandri was right, though: the real was a reflection of the unreal, and vice versa. The tension between the two was everything. One moment, staring into that abyss, he was awed at the vast scale of everything, built by giants of inconceivable scale who might return at any time to reconfigure every block and make something new. Later, he found he could look upon the same mighty works and tremble at their fragility. The slightest change in the nebulous unreality of unspace would affect the universe above; in turn, the least jolt to the real would send concussive shockwaves through unspace. How had some positive feedback loop not torn the whole of everything apart?

How had his own scrutiny not done so? He could feel the universe flex as he exerted his mind. It was not just the Machine, it was *him*. As an Intermediary, his mind interacted with unspace in a way that Shinandri's couldn't. Even though he was in the real, the Machine opened the door to unspace. It let him reach out and touch the unreal, just as if he was navigating a ship. He could explore from the comfort of his very own home, or at least this mad vessel within a dying Originator tomb on the deadliest world in the universe. This was why they needed him. They had an eye to the universe, but only an Int could control the focus of it. He had to see for them.

And he felt the tug, that shift in the unreal, whenever he did. As though any moment he could inadvertently grab a loose thread and unravel the whole of creation. *How can it be so delicately balanced?*

It was as though he was an insect with his legs spread across the surface of a pond. Everything that happened upon or within the water came to him through the ripples, and every motion of his own caused ripples in turn, expanding and expanding.

Being heard.

He screamed in the Machine, in his encounter suit, in its restrictive cradle. Then he screamed when he felt *it* move. There was something vast. But "vast" didn't mean the same thing now, when he had a perspective that allowed him to see simultaneously the universe entire and any detail within it. Something, though, and it was familiar. He'd lived alongside it ever since he'd come out of the Intermediary Program with his new mind and his neuroses. He'd faced it every time he'd gone into unspace, whether during the war or running salvage jobs on the *Vulture God*. It was the presence everyone felt on the wrong side of the real, and which they told you was just the human mind's response to the utter lack of anything to be found when you crossed the border. Every Int told themselves it wasn't truly there, while they also couldn't quite believe that.

He was still screaming when they got him out of the Machine, and continued as they peeled him out of the suit. He only started to calm when Emmaneth turned up with a syringe, and writhed away from her, obscurely linking unconsciousness by needle to going back into the traces of the Machine, where *it* was waiting for him.

This was what had happened to their last Int, he realized. And she hadn't survived it. Physical shock, or had her mind just broken? The leashed Ints, churned out factory-style from convicts, lacked the strength of the originals, and he was one of the only originals left. Still broken enough, in his various ways, but he would survive this.

It was real. As real as everything else he had seen in unspace, including the scaffolding and structure that created the Throughways between star systems almost accidentally. As real as the universe. There really was a hungry presence lurking in the depths of unspace.

Was it connected to the structures? Shinandri asked him. Was it connected with the Architects? So many questions, and Idris had a hard time forcing his mind to return to what he'd experienced, as though now the thing had his scent and might find him in the real as well. Might rise up from the shadows of his own mind to devour him.

But he did his best. He was committed now. Even though *it* was most definitely there, he had to go back. There was so much more to learn, and it would have been harder to keep it behind his teeth than it was to just blurt it all out. No, he thought, it wasn't connected to either the structures or the Architects. Bigger, older. The original resident of unspace, perhaps. Now can we go back? Is the Machine still on?

But it wasn't, and Jaine didn't want to reactivate it just yet. She was doing the rounds of the installation, looking at the damage sustained when the shield had been down. The voracious life of Criccieth's Hell had scoured the walls badly. Idris couldn't see why she bothered. It wasn't as though she could actually repair the structure in any way. And yet... Tomorrow, she'd said. You can go again tomorrow.

Tomorrow wasn't soon enough. Idris ground his teeth.

"Cheer up." Emmaneth clapped him on the shoulder again,

a gesture he was becoming increasingly annoyed by. "There's someone here to see you."

"What?" He turned, wrenching out from under her grip. "There isn't..." But there had been that extra place at breakfast. He knew Emmaneth travelled, so it wasn't impossible they'd receive visitors. "Who's there?" For a moment he had the mad thought it could be one of the *Vulture* crew, having tracked him down somehow. He felt a sudden stab of misery, wanting to see Solace again, all of them. The depth of loss tripped him up. Abruptly he was human, not some universe-striding god-colossus. He was small and weak and sane, and very lonely.

It wasn't Solace, or any of them. An old friend, though. Or at least an old acquaintance, and Idris found he'd been expecting this meeting for a while now. Ever since Demi Ulo had invoked the creature's name back on Arc Pallator.

The Harbinger, Ash. The singular alien who'd brought word of the Architects to Earth, back when there had been an Earth and nobody had heard of the Architects. Ash had come here to Criccieth's Hell to see its errant apprentice, Idris Telemmier.

*

Ash tried to look human. This was a largely doomed venture, but the thing's body was pliable enough that it could just about be squeezed into a robe. Its basic form was like a tree with a split trunk. It moved on a fringed foot of pseudopods, but the trailing hem of the robe covered that. One sleeve was empty, pinned to its chest, while the other held the branch of the alien's body that terminated in a tangle of tentacles. The robe's hood enclosed its second branch, bearing reddish eyes and a handful of slits that might have been nostrils or mouths or just some organ humans didn't have, or have a name for. It had been around people enough that, despite everything, if you just glimpsed this robed figure silhouetted, you wouldn't immediately think *alien* as much as a weirdly dressed and ill-proportioned human. Some Hegemonic hierograve, perhaps, or a spacer with ill-matched cybernetics. Ash had been humanity's guest for a hundred and thirty years or more, after all.

It had been able to communicate, in any language you cared to use, right from the start. How else would the thing have been able to convey its impossible warning?

And here it was now, on Criccieth's Hell and back in Idris's life.

Harbinger Ash had been constantly on the periphery of the old Intermediary Program, back then. It had been working with the medical team and Saint Xavienne, even though its grasp of human physiology and neurology was probably a bit rough. Ash knew the Architects, and it was clear the creature knew exactly what Saint Xav *was*. Idris guessed it had met other examples of this breed amongst other species it had tried to help, and knew there was only one way to fight the Architects. Fighting Architects was exactly what Ash was all about.

He found the creature in communion with Ahab when Emmaneth led him in. That didn't surprise him much. The Naeromath's single-minded crusade was exactly the sort of thing Ash would like to cultivate. The creature held itself out as a friend to mankind, and most certainly it had warned of the Architects before they arrived. But Ash was, in its own quiet way, a fanatic. Idris had the strong sense that Ash's interest in humankind was only as one more missile to fling at its omnipotent enemies. He would dearly love to have known how many species Ash had visited, warned and then turned into ammunition, expending them until there were no more left, then moving on.

However they were talking, none of it came through to Idris. The two of them were definitely deep in some kind of discussion, but not using any audible language, or obvious gestures even, and the means was beyond him. Emmaneth suggested that modern Naeromathi were all cyborg enough that they now communicated mostly through electromagnetics, so perhaps the air around them was thronging with unheard words. In the end, though, Ahab broke off and clawed its way out of the room, forcing Idris and Emmaneth to step back sharply. Its nest of mechanical legs powered it out of sight like something on a mission.

"Idris, my friend." Ash's voice, a pleasant bass in perfect Colvul, resounded from within its long torso. "I understand you've been helping the Parthenon with their little problem."

Idris blinked, thrown for a moment until he recalled Solace telling him that Ash had set her on the path to find him. All part of the creature's overarching plan, therefore. He nodded jerkily. "How are you—what are you even doing here?" He eyed the creature shrewdly. "This is proof, isn't it? That you can. I mean, you come and go on Berlenhof, but so does everybody. It's no big deal you're never where you're supposed to be. But here..."

"What do you know?" Ash replied airily. "There might be dozens of ships up and down the corridor on Criccieth's Hell every time the installation shields itself."

"The— What does it mean, the corridor?" Idris demanded of Emmaneth.

"When the shield's up it creates a dead spot in the planet's radiation. A ship with a careful pilot can get down to us then. When the Machine's running and the shield's down, it's next to impossible to get through. How Ahab did it the first time's beyond me. Unless this clown helped." She clapped another heavy hand on Idris's shoulder, nodding towards Ash.

He shrugged her off irritably. "Did you send this thug after me?"

Ash's utterly inhuman body-shape adopted a posture of wounded innocence. "I? Idris, you malign me. I am here because this is where a discovery is waiting to be made. And I am delighted it is you who will make it, if anyone does. Captain Ahab has done well, to build this place, but he lacks your—" A sound like feedback, shockingly loud and unexpected, caused Idris to yelp and jump back. Ash looked abashed. "Your connection," it finished. "There is no word for what you have, in your speech. You really should coin one, to avoid errors in translation. But for now, the only languages that could really name what you are are dead ones."

"I'm sick of being special," Idris told it. "I'm sick of being chased about the galaxy, people trying to kidnap and enslave me right and left. I've earned the chance to be left alone."

"Are you really? Sick of it?" Ash glided closer. Even though there was nothing of legs in how it moved, it had learned a kind of walking rhythm, to better approximate the motion of its human hosts. "Even now, when you're here and the whole universe is laid out before you? Isn't it time you stopped complaining, Idris?"

He clenched his fists with sudden anger at the patronizing tone. Emmaneth laughed derisively and he rounded on her, wanting to...what? He could beat his fists bloody against her and the only lasting harm would be to himself. And besides...

She knew. He saw it in her face. That mocking smile that was, somehow, not entirely unsympathetic. She knew Ash was right. Coming here was the point. It made sense of all the other nonsense.

The walls around them shuddered. He had the sense of the entire structure revolving into a new configuration, even though that was patently impossible. "The shield's down," he announced at once. "Is Doctor Shinandri...?" He was abruptly furious someone was playing god *without* him.

"It's Ahab," Ash told him. "He's using the Other Machine."

"The what?" Idris boggled.

"Do you think he started with something suitable for humans? He will be using the data Shinandri collected from his own exploration of this installation and its place within the universe. He thinks this place is a weapon."

"Is it?"

"Anything is a weapon with enough power, and in the hands of a revenge-crazed Naeromath. But you will be the one to find the true weapon, because you can grasp what you see through the Originators' eyes."

"You're getting cryptic again," Idris told it automatically.

"Blame the coarseness of your language. In answer to your earlier question, no, I didn't send Emmaneth after you. That was all Shinandri's planning. After all, if someone looks up first class Intermediaries, the list isn't very long. Not anymore. He knew about Arc Pallator and the Hegemony's call for aid. He's a bright man."

"And he doesn't care how many Ints he ruins to prove it," Idris muttered.

"Again with the fake resentment."

Another snort from Emmaneth.

"What do you want me to tell you, Ash?" Idris asked. "Yes, now I'm here, I absolutely concede that I need to be here. Or someone who can use the tech like I can should be. That doesn't mean I *like* being everyone's goddamn magic lamp. You're so smart, tell me what I'm actually looking for. I've got the whole universe, after all."

"I'd have thought that would be obvious," Ash informed him, and if it could have rolled its eyes it doubtless would have. "You're searching unspace for where the Architects come from. Their home. Because then we can find a way of sending a warfleet into the unreal to utterly destroy them forever."

And all said with that engaging, conversational tone.

24.

Kris

"Not a place you'd think a Tothiat could just stroll about unnoticed," was Kris's assessment of Deathknell. It earned her a derisive look from Heremon, but she could live with that.

"Not without ending up in a pickling jar," Olli agreed loudly over ship comms. She was still in her pod in the drone bay, and the drones themselves were going about simultaneous repair work. Five hands for her, all working on the same problem at once. The *Vulture God* had come out of unspace with a clutch of little error lights that she hadn't liked the look of.

Deathknell, despite the name, was a civilized world. An ocean world, too, and while it had widespread aquaculture, it wasn't much of an export hub on that front. Both poles boasted large ice caps and the equator saw pack ice half the year from one direction or another, the planet teetering on the edge of becoming an albedo-fuelled snowball. Human settlements were spread across a handful of archipelagos that formed most of the above-wave landmass. One in particular was the home of the Kendrick Higher Sciences Academy. The local kybernet was keen on giving them about fourteen hundred hours' reading material on who Kendrick was and why she had come to this half-frozen wasteland to be so clever, but nobody on the *Vulture God* felt inclined to indulge it.

It was one of those places—the planet and the institution, because the institution had put the planet on the galactic map. Kris knew the type well, because she was a graduate of another such: the law schools of Scintilla. They had been just one more Earth colony back when there had been an Earth, and established enough to stand on their own feet, after there hadn't been an Earth and spacebound humanity had become its own archipelago. A broken string of pearls scattered across the stars. Whilst the majority of humanity had become refugees shunting back and forth looking for sanctuary, places like Scintilla and Magda and Deathknell had hunkered down and grown inwards, leaning ever more heavily on their own ways. Nobody had known, back then, where it would end. The extinction of any wider humanity had been on the cards. It was every planet for itself, and most of them greedy to take in offcomers fleeing the Architects, because few colonies had boasted a large population.

In those places, pre-war whims, jokes and idle pastimes amongst the controlling few had been laid down as ironbound tradition for the benefit of the newcomers fleeing ruin. It was how those already in place had maintained their station amongst the swelling populace of refugees. *This is how we do things.* There were a few patterns such places followed, and a little digging into the Deathknell medio-archives suggested the place had gone the same way as Scintilla. Academic institutions tended to be hierarchical, even feudal. They accumulated traditions that the staff instituted and then the students passed down class to class, without any additional input. Little fiefdoms full of inexplicable written and

unwritten laws. Kris watched a mediotype of a dawn cere-
mony on the shortest day in the Academy's main quad, the
entire clutch of faculties shivering in sub-freezing temperatures as though their absence would result in the sun not
showing its face. And then there were the Sibling Societies,
and Kris was more than acquainted with that sort of thing.
It'd be like going home.

Without really thinking about it, she checked the hang of
her knife in her wrist-scabbard. Odd how people reverted to
that sort of thing on so many worlds. She reckoned it was
a stress response, clutching at a group identity in response
to both the influx of newcomers and the threat of utter
extinction if an Architect ever decided to darken their skies.
A way of demonstrating how brave and determined you
were, when the true enemy wouldn't care about, or even
understand, mere human bravery or determination. She
checked in with the Rivalry Index, the weird and informal
clique that kept track of such arcana, and found that Scintilla
graduates were recognized by the Deathknell societies.
Hopefully that wouldn't be relevant, but it was a useful ace
to have, so to speak, up her sleeve.

All in all, as she'd said, an odd world for Emmaneth to
repeatedly visit.

Heremon's information showed that she came here a
couple of times a year (Earth standard; Deathknell's own
were longer). She usually arrived in a small ship, but then
most of what Deathknell produced was easy to transport—
graduates and scientific research, and she didn't seem to
be poaching the graduates. Yet she was going planetside, and
if she'd just needed to download the latest theses, she could
have done that from orbit.

Kittering had already produced a Throughway map showing the intersections between Matachin, Deathknell and Kodo, a dozen worlds easily reached from all three, but none that cried out "secret Tothiat base."

"Professor Granduja," Kris identified. Heremon had provided an image of Emmaneth and a stern-looking woman of middle years, and she'd now located that same severe face in the Academy files. "High-energy physics emeritus and…" She blinked, watching a brief sequence of the woman—ten years ago, admittedly—engaged in a particularly clever pass of blades. Obviously it wasn't just the students who got up to that kind of societal high jinks.

"You're volunteering, I take it?" Olli asked. "Take the spook with you. Who knows what a badge might get you."

"Stabbed, probably," Kris suggested, but she reckoned Havaer was probably sound company. Kit signalled that he'd go with her too. Olli, Solace and Heremon were rather less likely to be any great use on a planet simultaneously Colonies-civilized and prone to taking offence at outsiders not knowing the local *comme il faut*.

With everything strung out on small islands, landing a ship of any size required more paperwork than anyone felt up to, and hiring a shuttle turned out to be cheaper than filing in triplicate. There wasn't a kybernet to step in and do the landing for them either, but together Kris and Kit managed to bring the ship down on the Academy landing field.

As it turned out, Granduja was one of those Grand Old Women academics who didn't really teach anymore, and who was only too happy to get out of some departmental meeting or other by seeing a Scintilla graduate and a Mordant House agent. She gave them two hours of her time, in fact, sitting up on a chill little rooftop terrace looking out over the wine-dark waves—literally, given the deep red of the local plankton-level life. Pink-marbled icebergs drifted in the light of the declining sun, and they were able to watch teams of little boats tack and skim. More academic traditions being enacted.

She wouldn't even commit to knowing Emmaneth, though, and Havaer's badge didn't impress her. When they showed her the image, she shrugged. "We are a haven of learning," she told them blandly as a student brought mugs of rich steaming chocolate. "There are always those with research questions."

"Twice a year?" Havaer asked.

"Perhaps they find the higher sciences difficult and need clarification." Granduja was watching them carefully under the guise of watching them casually. Kris already had the measure of her from Scintilla. Yes, there was something going on. She had some business with Emmaneth that she wasn't going to admit to. No, the spectre of Mordant House wasn't going to spook her, here in her own domain. Granduja was wearing a padded robe that reached to her ankles—clearly the rewards of rank because the student garments only came to the knee. More than that, though, she was wearing a scarf. A sensible item for the temperatures, and everyone here had one, but Kris had already started to read the precise symbology of colours, lengths and folds. She herself wore something similar, as a holdover from Scintilla, as well as to cover the duelling scar that had almost done for her. These things had meaning and contributed to insular, self-protecting cultures that were hard to track and dangerous to cross. Granduja was playing with them, amusing herself and not going to be helpful in any way whatsoever.

After the interview—in which admittedly the accompanying

chocolate and the little cakes had been excellent and almost a fair recompense for the wasted time—Kris checked in with Kittering.

There were Hanni on Deathknell too. Not many, but the Academy did have a handful of students that had bought their way in. More than that, there was a whole clan of them that had been involved in the logistical side of the institution since forever, meaning without them none of the lofty academics would know where their next class was. Kit had gone to make friends, both with his conspecifics and with the non-academic humans in the same line of work. By the time Kris had finished her last chocolate and bid Professor Granduja a civil farewell, Kit had already scared up a lead on Emmaneth.

They were on their way to meet him, weaving through a sudden exodus of students from warm classrooms to cold streets, when Havaer stopped dead.

"What?" She could see the closed look on his face, as he received word from elsewhere. Not from Olli either, who would have called Kris or Kit direct. She found herself tense, aware of her knife, just in case this was about to turn into a Mordant House sting and he was getting orders to lay hands on her.

"Some old friends in orbit," he told her. "I... have an interest in a certain Colonial faction, as of recently. Details are need to know, but a big part of them is made up of Magdan landowners. Always a fun voting bloc, back at Hugh."

Kris felt a line of cold steel inside her. "Are we talking," she asked him, "about the Uskaros again?" The *Vulture God* crew had skipped out from under the hand of *that* family—in the shape of its scion Piter—several times before the mess with

Uskaro Senior, Ravin, on Arc Pallator. Havaer himself had bailed them out once, albeit by taking them into his own custody. "Why would they be here?" Seeing his pitying look she snarled, "They made a pass at Idris, yes, but he's just one Int in the grand scheme of things. They surely have other business taking up their valuable time?"

"The piece of business that caught my people's interest," Havaer said carefully, "is something that would really benefit from an Int monopoly, or as much of one as you can get. Magdan factions already operate a lot of the leash contracts that come out of the Liaison Board, but your man Telemmier is old school. And right now he's out from under the Partheni shadow. Available, if they can track him. They're here following the same lead we are. My...source says..." He was back listening to the silent voice for a moment, and then reached for her arm. She didn't let him have it, but followed him up and up, until they were on a little fencing piste over-looking the cafe terrace where they'd met Granduja. They saw her still there, entertaining new guests. Her body language suggested she was being as cordially unhelpful with them as she had been with Kris and Havaer, and enjoying herself doing it, tweaking the noses of the outworlders who'd come to trample over her little fiefdom. She even looked up, utterly unsurprised, and actually locked eyes with Kris for a moment. There was something of a duellist's flourish in the way she signalled a waiter. Or no, not the fighter but the referee, inviting the duellists' first move.

Sitting with her was the Boyarin Piter Tchever Uskaro, the nephew of old Ravin, who'd himself been such a thorn on Arc Pallator. Havaer confirmed that young Piter's ship, the *Raptorid*, had been located at dock in orbit.

"Well, they have Granduja, and may they choke on her," Kris decided. "But they don't have Kit and his lead, so let's go exploit that while we're ahead."

*

The Deathknell Academy had been left to its own governance and devices for a long time. The privations and the pressures had led to cliques becoming entire strata of society. So it was with the duelling societies; so it was, also, with the Worshipful Brotherhood and Union of Academy Porters. While the faculty staff presented the public face of Deathknell's pre-eminent institution, bringing in money from offworld and exporting high-mindedness and graduates who would remember the Academy in their bequests, the Union made sure the lights stayed on and the water was safe to drink. It also existed in a constant state of semi-antagonism with the academics, according to Kit. They had their own festivals and codes, their degrees and ranks, and if there was something the "Scarves" (as opposed to themselves, who were the "Gloves," despite the fact that on cold Deathknell everyone wore both) were covering up, they were more than happy to talk about it. Except Emmaneth was something they too were covering up, and so Kit had crab-walked a very fine line, won some money, waived some debts and finally found a mid-ranking engineer who was willing to spill the beans.

"The construction of scientific apparatus is carried out on-site," Kittering explained to them, leading them to his contact. "Such specialized apparatus not being reliably available for import."

The man he showed them was squat and gnomish, heavily

bearded in iron-grey, a little hat folded on his head like a red sock. He had a slate for them, with a list of technical words Kris couldn't make anything of. She was in good company in her bafflement.

"Items collected here by this Emmaneth," Kittering explained.

Kris squinted at the list. "She's turned scientist all of a sudden?"

The engineer chuckled and spat into his palm, which she took as some kind of ritual disdain for all things academic. "Not her. Him. Paying his dues, he is. Nothing but the messenger, she is. For all you'd not want to cross her."

This was obviously news to Kit, so Kris put on her most winning smile. "And who would 'he' be, Menheer?"

"Menheer Brother Porter," he corrected her frostily, because of course all these tinpot fraternities would have their cheese-paring distinctions; the Scintilla duellists and lawyers had been no different. "He had a lot to pay back, he did. But the donations help." He pushed some more data to the slate with, "You're lucky we like your Hanni, or a fancy miss like you'd get nowhere with us."

I'm a fancy miss, apparently. Kris quite liked the sound of it. She spared the gruff old man a grin which fractionally softened his scowl, and then checked the slate. A series of donations to the Worshipful Porters' Benevolent Fund, a charity for widows and orphans. Or, as Havaer would prob-ably describe it, a money-laundering operation. Someone had been making sizeable payments, and had also, entirely unconnectedly, been given free access to the rare-elements printing facilities of the Academy, to have his highly special-ized gear made. Gear which Emmaneth periodically turned up and collected. The someone in question was a former Deathknell graduate, one Haleon Shinandri. That opened up a new parcel of information, including published papers, scandals in the newstypes, health and safety reports, obituaries.

It didn't quite serve to tell them where the hell Idris was in all of this, but it was a lead.

"Back to the ship for now," Kris decided. "Let's interrogate the local kybernet and see where this particular alumnus has got himself."

They returned to the sun and air from the buried fastnesses of the Worshipful Porters, making for the docks, when they saw a score of university staff heading their way. Some were academics and others were porters of a decidedly burlier bent than their informer. Granduja was with them, and at her side, even then pointing out his quarry, was Piter Tchever Uskaro.

Solace

"We have a little problem." Kris's voice over the *Vulture God*'s crackly comms. "Taking a bit of a detour to get to the shuttle."

"A bit of a detour?" Solace echoed.

"Maybe a tour of the island." Kris was sounding slightly rushed. "All very civilized. We're walking, maybe a bit fast. They're walking, maybe a bit fast. Nobody wants to actually admit we're about to have a throwdown."

"Get Mundy to show his badge to them," Solace suggested.

"Oh we will, when we have to. Only they didn't seem to

care much about it when we were chatting over chocolate and cake, and I get the impression the stakes have just upped. Bloody bitch wouldn't talk to *us* but I guess she'll talk to Uskaro's Largesse soon enough. Let nobody tell you about academics and ivory towers."

Solace had grown up on stories of Colonies and their general propensity for vice, whatever walk of life they were in. Right now she was more worried about Kris, though. She still had difficulties with Colvul subtext and Kris's tendency towards flippancy meant she wasn't sure how worried the woman was.

"Olli wants to bring the ship down," she noted. Olli was, in fact, currently engaged in a furious row with the Deathknell docking authority, or at least the compartment of the planet's kybernet that governed landing permits. By ancient statute of the Academy, and the basic logistics of a planetary society existing strung across small islands, landing anything bigger than a launch was forbidden. Olli was currently suggesting she use the *God*'s overpowered gravitic engine to haul the Higher Energy Department up into orbit instead. Negotiations were not going well.

"Good luck with that," Kris noted. "Solace, I'm sending you some data up the well. Haleon Shinandri, former associate here. He's who Emmaneth's working for. There's a crapton on him and right now I don't have the liberty to go through it."

"Will do," Solace confirmed. "Name mean anything to you?" she asked Heremon, who was gawping over her shoulder. The Tothiat shook her head, grabbed the neighbouring seat and began accessing the records, suddenly not the gang tough but the competent researcher. Solace guessed being Aklu's lieutenant called for more than just breaking legs. Or maybe she had to break them in very specific ways at her boss's whim. Aklu seemed that type.

"Olli is going to break every law on this planet any time now," Solace warned Kris, and then another comms request grabbed her attention. Trusting Heremon to get the research done, she jumped on it. A packet ship had just hit the system and was delivering news and mail to Deathknell. Moreover, it would be taking messages out very shortly, and that meant Solace could report in to her superiors. She was trying to send her coded missives every chance she got, because there was never any guarantee when the next opportunity would arise. She needed to leave as much of a breadcrumb trail as she could.

Negotiating for dataspace aboard the packet, she skimmed the incoming news.

And stopped.

Made a sound: shocked, wordless. Heremon glanced at her.

It had happened. The line the Parthenon and the Colonies had been dancing around had been crossed, and she hadn't been there. Her sisters had been dying and she hadn't been there.

The news was two days old and cast in Colonial terms, decrying Partheni aggression, and certainly the declaration of open war had come from the Parthenon. In retaliation, though. Solace saw right through the Hugh mediotypes rubbishing the accusations and denying responsibility. There had been an attack. On the garden ship *Ceres*. The ship she'd been resident on, not so long ago. The ship where the Partheni Intermediary research was based. Of course

Hugh would have been aware that their star Int was missing, so when better to try and shut the operation down?

Garden ships were sacred to the Parthenon. They were as civilian as the Partheni got, the place you went back to after your tour. Where you lived and relaxed; where the children were raised. Hugh would know all of that, as well as the fact that the one thing guaranteed to break all diplomatic restraint was a strike against one.

There were no details of the strike itself in the mediotypes, what with Hugh vociferously denying all involvement, but the story was absolutely plain to Solace. Feeling vindictive, even though she knew he couldn't have had much to do with it, she sent the news downwell to Havaer. They were, technically, enemies now. Well, on a strict political footing, she supposed she was the enemy of every *Vulture* denizen bar Heremon, but Havaer was actually Hugh.

She got a message straight back from him, even though he was presumably end-running around the Uskaro boy. *Mission first. War later. We have a situation down here.*

She found she didn't want to play nice, right then. She wanted to punch him, for no other reason than he was a representative of her enemy. Her sisters had been killed, their home attacked, their future put in danger. *Angels of Punching You in the Face.* It had never felt so true.

"Fuck," Olli's voice came over ship comms. She'd seen the same news. Solace waited to observe which way the worm would turn, and whether there would be a blast of anti-Partheni invective from that direction. Instead, after a protracted pause, there came, "Sorry. That sucks." It wasn't much, but from Olli it meant a lot.

"Criccieth's Hell mean anything to you?" Heremon asked.

Solace looked at her blankly, completely wrong-footed for a moment, then she realized the Tothiat had turned something up.

"Is that…a world? A ship? A *bar*?" The spacer side of Colonial society seemed to have an endless number of them.

"Could be my kind of dive," Heremon said. "Word in from Almier, though. Some place my lost sister is involved in. Sounds like a world, from context, but there's nothing… No, wait. It's a secondary off Orichalk. Prohibited world. Do not approach under any circumstances…" Her voice trailed off. "That is…nasty, is what that is."

"That's where we're going?" Olli broke in.

"Soon as your clowns get to the shuttle."

"One of those clowns is your responsibility. You brought Mr. Mordant House in on this."

"We're going to need him." Heremon sent a slice of data over to Solace's console. "Nobody goes to Criccieth's Hell, according to this, but out-system from it is Orichalk and that's a Colonial Navy outpost. That badge of his is going to earn its keep."

Kris

At first it looked as though they were going to get to the shuttle anyway. There was a weird little game going on where everyone was kind of pretending this was business as usual. Kris, Havaer and Kit picked up their pace to a brisk walk. Granduja, Uskaro and the faculty heavies did likewise. Everyone gave the general impression of being slightly late to a tiresome but essential departmental meeting. Nobody ran. Kris felt the need to just leg it burning at her heels, but as soon as she did, it would become uncivilized. That would break the social contract and put her beyond the pale. Running people radiated guilt, and doubtless at that point the balance would tip. Formerly disinterested parties would see this apparent admission of culpability, doubtless assisted in their perception of it by Uskaro money. The porters or some other Deathknell staff would then close off the docks, activate the orbital defences and physically pile on the three of them. And so they continued to walk. Briskly.

Kit was managing the navigation. Every time a party of Academy staff turned up, loitering in their path, they took an alley between two of the small-windowed buildings, or cut along the shoreline, or tripped across a bridge, ever circling back towards the docking field where the shuttle they'd hired lay.

Home-ground advantage won out, however. Granduja had probably been a student here before she became such an emeritus grandee. She knew all the shortcuts and side-ways, appearing out of an actual hatch in the ground ahead of them, with the docks in sight, as though she was a demon in a play.

She was, at least, slightly out of breath from all the briskness.

"Visitors!" she called out. "Forgive me but I do need you to halt and answer just a few questions." She and her people were spreading out in a loose semicircle ahead, with Uskaro smiling a most unpleasant smile at their centre. Kris wondered how much he'd forked over to buy their cooperation. Maybe he'd endowed a new seat of quantum philosophy or something.

They could run, or even just take their briskness on a

sudden sideways jaunt, but now Granduja had actually hailed them, that would again put them in the definite wrong.

"Well we're in something of a hurry, Professor," Kris called back. "Can I ask under what paragraph of the Academy's administrative code you're detaining us?"

It was her hole card in circumstances like these, when the knives weren't actually out, and she could see Piter Uskaro leaning towards Granduja, almost certainly saying, "I told you about her." The times she'd run into him before, she'd made herself a real splinter under his fingernail with this sort of thing. Yet she didn't take him for someone who'd put in the work reading the letters of the law here, as she had when they came in. Standard practice, and the Academy's statutes weren't even that long.

Unfortunately, Granduja *was* that sort of person. "Under section nineteen of the Visitors' Charter, subsection two," the woman said sweetly. "'All offworlders so charged to answer are to present themselves at a—'"

"If there exists reasonable belief that they have committed actions as set out in appendix two," Kris threw back at her hurriedly. She saw Havaer give her an incredulous look. She had her slate out now, scrolling through the appropriate text and cross-links, just another chase through just another labyrinth. The high jinks Kit had got up to probably qualified as appendix two-worthy, but she reckoned there wasn't enough evidence to give rise to reasonable belief. "We are in quite a hurry, Professor. Did you have any particular actions in mind?"

Granduja's face went blank for a moment, which meant she obviously didn't and Kit had covered his tracks, but then she said, "Under two point one-three, the authority of a faculty head, in this case myself, shall suffice to veto the entrance or exit of any parties into or out of areas controlled by the Academy."

Kris could see Uskaro practically going mad with frustrated action, mugging incredulous looks at Granduja just like Havaer was giving her. And yet she felt very calm, very centred. There was a form of zen in the cut and thrust of opposing statute, the clash of conflicting sections, the sudden flash of a hidden paragraph drawn from the sleeve.

"Only in exceptional circumstances, as defined by appendix nine. I don't hear any explosions or see an incoming tsunami."

Granduja had been waiting for that, however, and told her flatly, "But we are now on a war footing and you, I am reliably informed, are Parthenon agents."

Kris stared at her. "A war footing," she echoed, and then Havaer was shunting information to her slate.

The Parthenon had declared war.

For a moment the whole legal house of cards seemed about to come down. There was actual war, not just the almost-almost dancing that had been going on. An attack. The *Ceres*. She'd *been* on that ship just recently.

Granduja and her staff were closing the distance now, Uskaro practically rubbing his hands.

"Hugh has yet to respond," Kris said. They stopped, and she heard the man hiss, "What is this nonsense now? Just seize them."

"There are formalities, Boyarin," Granduja said primly. "Although in this case—"

"The Hugh Defence Board is doubtless in session even as we speak," Kris said somewhat breathlessly. "Until they issue a response, there is no state of emergency." Tissue-thin, but sometimes you had to skate on the letter of the law like an insect on a pond.

"Also, I am an agent of the Intervention Board," Havaer put in hotly. "I am not a Partheni agent and my companions are assisting me with an investigation."

Kris felt meanly pleased that everyone ignored him. "So if you'll let us be on our way," she put in, with her best smile at Uskaro.

Granduja's own smile was better, though. "It is of course also the case that the return of the Architects is considered an automatic state of emergency across the whole of the Colonial Sphere, under the Postwar Stimulus Powers. While I appreciate that leaping to assume autocratic authority at the first whiff of opportunity is in general bad for the future of civilization, I'll make the exception this one time. To oblige our most generous guest, here." A nod towards Uskaro that showed far more financial gratitude than actual liking. "Well run, Mesdam Almier, and I can assure you that your interrogation—"

"Will be on my ship," Uskaro said flatly. "Undertaken by my people, who are even now on their way to put an end to this charade." He plainly felt his Boyarly dignity had suffered. "Consider that a precondition of my generous donation, Professor."

Kris had no illusions whatsoever about what would happen when they were actually in his power, and how little any amount of legal wrangling would assist them. The Deathknell Academy cared about laws. Uskaro ceased to do so the moment they stood between him and what he wanted.

"You two, be ready to get to the shuttle," she said.

"Not acceptable," Kit put in immediately.

"It's going to be fine. I have an ace. But I need you out of the way. And leave this place, if you have to. Go get Idris."

She took two steps towards Granduja and Uskaro, almost into arm's reach, then took off her scarf, letting it flutter to the ground. She saw the impact of the simple gesture hit every Academy man and woman there, leaving only the Boyarin blinking. Plenty of eyes went to the ragged scar that circumscribed a large part of her neck, but it was the scarf itself that held their focus.

"In which case I make this a matter of honour," she told them all. Because they were mad here, just as they had been on her own alma mater of Scintilla. If you were in a corner, you issued a challenge. Under Deathknell tradition, that over-rode everything. No matter how hard the law, no matter how iron the statute, honour came first. She reckoned that was how places like this could be so fussy and formal all the rest of the time. There was this outlet for all their violence and blood, just beneath the surface.

Granduja looked a little startled, as well as a little impressed. "Not that I wouldn't relish the opportunity," she said, "but as a faculty member I am above such challenges, save from an equal. We'd be fending the students off every other day, else."

"But the duelling code of Deathknell recognizes kindred societies from offworld, and that includes the graduates of Scintilla, such as me. And the *Messernbruder* of the Magdan aristocracy, such as him. Well, Your Elegance? My scarf lies at your feet. Another moment and it'll blow away."

She was making frantic *Go, go!* motions at Kit and Havaer, practically forcing them from her side and through the suddenly impotent knot of Academy staff.

"This is…" Uskaro said slowly, eyes swivelling from her to Granduja. "She can't just…"

There was a very brief moment when Kris saw in the professor's face just how much she had already learned to dislike the man, his privilege and his strutting. "Your Elegance," she said, "were you a native then obviously the difference in your degrees would make a mockery of this whole business. But you and Mesdam Almier are both simply guests, and Deathknell tradition does not make distinctions under those circumstances. My hands," she added, with a wicked little smile, "are tied." She then stepped back, with a look of sly approbation at Kris.

"Kris," Havaer started, but she just waved him away harder.

"I'll be right along," she told him, not breaking eye contact with Piter Uskaro.

"No, seriously," he said, looking around at the locals, who were pointedly stepping back, giving him space, glancing at the scarf.

Kris felt her posture, that tended to hunch a bit in the throes of legalistic argument, hit that perfectly straight poise she remembered from the Scintilla pistes.

Uskaro twitched up her scarf, still not quite believing how events had turned on him. Havaer and Kit were already well past the group, the door of the shuttle opening for them. And there they waited, looking back for her.

She let her knife slide from within her sleeve into her hand. Uskaro would be good, she had no doubt, but she had him wrong-footed already. It would probably just be a cut across the back of the hand or something, and she'd claim victory, then he'd back down. Surely, this once, things would go to plan and everyone would act like sensible adults.

Said the woman who'd just challenged the scion of one of Magda's most powerful families.

Granduja and her people had given her all the space she needed, and so she levelled her blade at Uskaro, who slowly drew his own from his belt. Because of course he had one. They liked their warrior orders and martial play on Magda, but between themselves, aristocrat to aristocrat, all safely controlled. All precise scars and show and boasting, and using it as a threat against the lower orders. But right here he was on his own and that scar on Kris's throat was an advertisement for just how seriously some people took the sacred interplay of knives.

And everyone was watching.

She could hold her ready pose for a long time, if she had to.

"Or perhaps the Boyarin wishes to withdraw whatever suspicions he has loaded me with, and let me be on my way?" she suggested, still with that razor edge directed at him. And she saw what she took for a falter, for the crack that would lead to him just stepping back, issuing the required apology, honour satisfied without a drop of his blue blood spilled.

Then the Voyenni arrived. He had said his people were on the way but she'd been so wrapped up in her own show she'd overlooked it. A good dozen big men in those bottle-green coats, and they had coshes and knives. A couple had guns too, which were absolutely not permitted on Academy ground. When Granduja came in to remonstrate, Uskaro backhanded her and knocked her off her feet, bold as brass now he had his bullies at his back.

Kris got straight on comms to Kit. "Go *now*," she told them. "Their *Raptorid* won't sit idle. Leave me and get back to the ship."

Some of the Voyenni were already running for the shuttle, but they wouldn't get there in time. Nor would she, of course. She returned the knife to her sleeve, not that they'd let her keep it, but maintained her ramrod posture and piercing stare. Uskaro wouldn't meet it, even as the Voyenni laid hands on her. She took that as the small victory it was.

25.

Havaer

Havaer had thought Kittering wouldn't get the shuttle moving without Kris and envisaged wrestling the Hanni for the controls. Kit was up on the pilot's stool, though, already closing the hatch and blotting out the Voyenni pounding after them. Havaer supposed the Hannilambra understood the concept of sacrifice for others, given how their stories generally played out.

Olli was on the comms but she was stressed so wouldn't talk to him, and Kit's translator was receiving through whatever his equivalent of an earpiece was, making half the conversation completely inaudible. In the end Havaer had to eat humble pie and get a line through to Solace, because apparently that was what the world was coming to.

"What happened to Kris?" she demanded.

"Uskaro got her." And then, to forestall the accusations, "It was her idea. She was doing some legal thing, and then she called him out, the madwoman. But it got us on board, Kittering and me."

They were airborne now, the shuttle lurching sideways away from the dock. The pilot's display showed half a dozen angry red bars representing Academy docking control telling

427

them to stay the fuck put, or so Havaer translated it. A couple of shots spanged off the hull, and then there was a little telltale added to all the rest of the red that said they'd been punctured. Havaer guessed a couple of magnetic rounds had just passed through the crewspace around them, and against the shudder of the atmosphere outside and the roar of the reaction drives he hadn't noticed.

He dropped into a crew seat and accessed damage control. The shuttle was decidedly iffy about whether the holes were self-sealing properly. "We may have a breathing problem soon," he announced. "Kit, you have a suit?" He'd already spotted the trouble locker and went over to it, handhold to handhold, because the Hanni was making heavy weather of his ascent. A Hanni emergency suit turned out to be something like a condom that Kit crouched on top of, then pulled up the full length of the front of his body, leaving limbs and back exposed. After helping him with that, Havaer wrestled himself into one of the clingy one-size-doesn't-quite-fit-all human suits and inflated it. He'd half-expected the jarring wrench of a gravitic engine to start yanking them back to the ground by then, but he was too used to orbitals and ships where an a-grav field was standard. Deathknell only had small islands to build on, and genuine natural gravity to enjoy. They obviously hadn't felt the need to add the artificial variety.

"Your badge going to get Kris back for us?" Solace demanded from the *Vulture*.

"I will do what I can," he said automatically, but then some latent honesty kicked in and he added, "which won't be much. I'm sorry. I'm out of my brief here."

"We're on our way down for you," the Partheni told him.

"I thought the Deathknell kybernet really didn't fancy ships breaching their atmosphere. I mean, these people like their laws. We just got a serious demonstration of it," he said.

"Yeah, Olli's swearing at it right now," she agreed. "They're not actually shooting at us, though."

"Well maybe they don't have any guns."

"They're tracking us with their anti-asteroids right now." Solace's voice sounded very tight. "Olli's throwing us around, but if they wanted to try target practice there's nothing stopping them."

Olli's voice broke in then, coming to him over Solace's channel and presumably direct to Kit. "*Raptorid*'s coming down the well too."

"Uskaro's launch also rising towards us," Kittering responded. "Combat capable."

Havaer scanned his displays in case some sort of defensive capacity had been hiding there. No such luck.

"Brace," Solace told him, and he fumbled to buckle himself in. Kit just clamped down on his stool with all his legs.

A moment later they were spinning, Olli swearing over comms, and every alarm the shuttle had was whooping and shrieking, flashing red lights at them. Uskaro's launch had just taken an accelerator to them and carved up half their reactor drives, resulting in the explosive expulsion of the remainder of their fuel. Their brachator drives had taken a hit too, and Kit was fighting furiously against the buffeting wind as well as the planet's gravity to stop them just bombing into the Academy buildings below.

Then a huge hand caught them, fumbling at first and

rattling the pair of them about like dried peas in a tin. Havaer bit his tongue and his heart monitor lodged several urgent complaints. He was going to need a medication refill when this was done and, given he'd gone rogue, the department probably wouldn't cover it.

Why does the goddamn Magdan prick need an accelerator on his shuttle? Goddamn dick-waving.

The *Vulture God* screamed down from the upper atmosphere, bullying its way through the turbulence like the divine incarnation of Olli's bloody-mindedness. Its gravitic field captured them, and then the huge tangle of its docking claws took hold, seizing on its prey but still descending, wrestling with the gravity of Deathknell to avoid completing the unplanned landing the shuttle had been about to make. They came dangerously close to colliding with Uskaro—all that wealth of sky and the ships were stacked atop one another in a narrow column from ground to orbit. Havaer wrangled for camera access and saw the jagged dart of the Boyarin's launch skim sideways away from the *Vulture God's* brutal bulk. A purplish flicker showed where the salvage ship's lasers were having a go at him, trying to pick off his drives so they could grab him too and liberate Kris. The launch was too nimble, though, swinging wide and fighting field against field to prevent the *God* from taking hold of them. Havaer could hear Olli over the comms, constant stream-of-consciousness as she tried to snag the smaller vessel. Havaer wasn't entirely sure what they'd do if they actually had the launch at their mercy. It was full of armed Voyenni, after all. Maybe Heremon could take them, though. She was functionally immortal, and wasn't it about time that started working for them?

Then they were hightailing it *away* from the launch, shouldering through the increasingly uncooperative atmosphere and trying to gain height. There was a shadow shaped like a pair of talons with a peacock's tail swooping down on them: the *Raptorid*, Uskaro's sleek battle yacht.

No chance of catching Uskaro now. Olli was just hauling for altitude, even as the docking claws clutched the shuttle tightly. Havaer could only watch, gut-churningly helpless, as the *Raptorid* descended on them, doubtless lining up its weapons.

Having Kris already, Piter Uskaro would probably bank on not needing any more leverage or prisoners. He might as well just slice up the troublesome *Vulture God* here and now, and rid the universe of one more complication. In Uskaro's shoes, that was certainly how Havaer reckoned he himself would think. He hadn't ever planned on being an ersatz crewmember of the benighted vessel, of course.

Then the screens registered a high-energy discharge. Lightning seared through Deathknell's atmosphere to flicker about the *Raptorid*, and the predatory vessel broke off its attack run.

Weather? We've been saved by weather? But no, Kit was flagging up angry comms exchanges on open channels. The planetary kybernet was remonstrating with the *Raptorid*, demanding all vessels get clear of the planet, stipulating vastly divergent courses for each. These courses would send Uskaro's launch a long way around the planet from his actual ship, Havaer noted. *Buying us more time.* Then he remembered Professor Granduja being slapped, and reckoned this was probably the best revenge she could take within the precise laws and statutes permitted her. Not that she was owed much gratitude given she'd sold them out in the first place, but sometimes you took what you could get.

"We have a heading?" he demanded.

"I've sketched a Throughway route to the Orichalk system," Solace's voice came over the comms. "Based on the very narrow research interests of this academic of yours, that may be where they have Idris. Only two legs from here to there, but, Olli, can you plot to come out as far from actual Orichalk as possible? We need this Criccieth's Hell—an inner world in the same system."

"Yeah. Sure. Fuck. Don't ask much, do you?" Olli grumbled, but she was already tearing them away from atmosphere, out into orbit, while fending off a barrage of complaints and attempted fines from the kybernet. The planetary anti-asteroid grid hadn't fried them, though. This possibly counted as Granduja's contrition too.

Someone else pinged his comms. Colvari, still attached to the *God*'s hull somehow, despite all the recent gymnastics. They sent through orbital mechanics for the planetary system which included Orichalk and Criccieth's Hell, plus a data dump on the system as a whole, harvested from Deathknell's libraries. He condensed this into a suggested unspace route for Olli to finesse and follow, and then he and Kit exited the shuttle, moving up the *God*'s umbilical and into the drone bay. There Olli loomed above them in her pod, eyes closed as she wrestled with too many systems at once. The shuttle was cut loose to drift, so it could eventually be recovered by the kybernet. Havaer stumbled over to a panel and called up a plot of where the *Raptorid* had got to. It was most of the planet away now, recovering Uskaro and its launch. And Kris, of course.

Goddamn Magdan bloc. The Magdans were a loud voice within Hugh, of course, and often a conservative and retrograde one. They were wealthy, with their planet one of the big breadbaskets of the Colonies. They also had a large population, controlled by a small ruling class who had welcomed all the refugees they could take during the war, so long as people were happy with serfdom—the "robot" as they called it on-planet. It was all done with just enough of a veneer of legality, backed by Magda's economic clout, to ensure Hugh never got round to censuring any of it. But those were merely the average and everyday Magdan Questions. Right now Havaer was far more concerned with some very specific issues raised by the transcripts Colvari had ferreted out for him. There had been Uskaro family members at that meeting. They'd been one of the prime movers and shakers of the whole ark ship project. What they brought to the venture was a cadre of leashed Intermediaries, meaning the proposed ark fleet, the future of the human race in an Architect-torn universe, wouldn't be limited to the Throughways. They'd be able to take their remnant population, their new mobile fiefdom, anywhere. Except the talk at the meeting had then turned to the thorny subject of competition. Just as they'd been concerned at the prospect of the Partheni fleet taking the title of vagabond king of the universe, so they had fretted about those other species with Intermediary-style access to space travel: the Castigar and their savant caste, and the Hegemony, not that anyone could do much about *them*.

The news that the Partheni were developing their own Intermediaries with Telemmier's help must have sent them into fits, Havaer considered.

Then there was the attack on the *Ceres*, the cause célèbre

for a war. Hugh was left scrabbling for denials, because why would anyone do such a thing? A garden ship, after all—the perfect first strike to send the Parthenon headlong on the attack, whilst at the same time not in any way impairing their military strength. Unless, of course, they knew that was where their Int program was based, and was the only thing they cared about.

"Fuck me but this is a specific unspace exit you're asking for," Olli complained. "Not sure I can even do this sort of fine detail. I'm not Idris."

"However close we can," Solace said. "We don't want to come out right on Orichalk and the navy yards."

"I thought we had Mr. Mordant House now. Aren't the navy their bitch?"

"Let's not see if they're willing to bend over right now, okay?" Havaer asked her, looking up at her pod. She smirked down at him.

"Everyone get to your couches, I guess. Let me see if I can thread the fucking needle on this."

Kit clattered off for his quarters, where the sphere of his Hanni-made suspension chamber lay. The human-style couches were all together amidships, though, which of course meant Havaer ran into Heremon and Solace.

The Tothiat obviously had a mouthful of snide remarks to make, but one look between the two of them brought out some unexpected tact in her, and she just chose a bed, then started running through the safety checks.

"War, then," Havaer said.

Solace nodded.

"I... appreciate you telling me. I mean, you didn't have to."

"I'm a terrible agent," she said frankly. "I keep forgetting you're not actually one of us."

"I'm not sure who 'us' is right now," he admitted. "My 'us' anyway. I'm 'us' until we have Telemmier, at least."

"No you're not," she told him. "You'll put yourself in a position where you can grab him long before we get him back. But we're not there yet."

A long, awkward pause held between them. Havaer's fight-or-flight instincts kept twitching. There was little doubt that if she went for him, she'd win any kind of slapping match. He wasn't a soldier, despite Mordant House's basic training.

"I'm guessing you've got word of where we're going on a packet already," he noted. There'd certainly been a packet ship departing and Colvari had passed the word on for him, suitably encoded. Whether Laery would ever get it was another matter.

Solace nodded curtly. "Of course."

"Will you two either fuck already or get yourselves prepped for unspace?" Heremon demanded, already lying on her couch. Seeing their collective glower she asked innocently, "What?"

"You have been away from humans way too long if you think that was sexual tension," Havaer told her sourly, and ran through his own checks. Solace's presence was like a hook in the back of his mind, impossible to ignore. And *not* in that way, either. An enemy, someone his government was actually at war with, right here on the same ship.

But then he himself might just be at war with his own government, too, depending on what game Laery was planning and how much pull the Uskaros' cabal had.

Kris

Kris didn't know what to expect once she was inside Piter Uskaro's launch. At first she wasn't sure if she'd survive the experience: two big Voyenni had shoved her in a cupboard—the little ship not being equipped with purpose-built cells—with the apparent promise of incipient violence to come. Then, any such reprisals took a back seat to the fact they were obviously having an interesting time of it getting out of Deathknell's gravity well. She tried to access any of the ship's systems from the panels in her impromptu confinement, but they'd locked her out. All she could do was hold on for dear life when the ship's gravitic engines didn't quite overcome the shock of some impact or manoeuvre.

Then the thunder of displaced atmosphere gave way and they were in orbit, with the Voyenni hauling her from the ship. She had a brief glimpse of a cramped dock, a pair of the sleek, armed launches side by side, before they marched her off to a little stateroom and abandoned her again. She sat at the table and ate the preserved fruit some steward had laid out, until the two Voyenni returned, escorting a brace of Uskaros. One was Piter, of course, but the other was a surprise: Uskaro Senior, Morzarin Ravin Okosh Uskaro, last seen exiting Arc Pallator in a hurry but apparently none the worse for wear.

The two bodyguards moved in on her and she flinched backwards.

"Just as a formality," Uskaro Junior told her, "please do hand over that knife of yours." He was trying very hard to be polite, which was what she'd been banking on. Yes, she was their prisoner and at their mercy *but* she was also useful to them. While that state of affairs lasted, there was likely to be more open hand than bludgeoning fist in her immediate future.

Of course, she'd still be useful after they'd gone over her with boots and a length of hose, because that would be another kind of motivation for Idris to give himself up. However, while she didn't reckon Piter was exactly a genius-level chess-player in the intrigue game, Ravin himself was no fool. First would come the honey, with the vitriol left in reserve.

Still, those two Voyenni weren't going anywhere, even after she gave up the knife, plus the second knife in the lining of her belt that they'd picked up on. Their looming presence was the equivalent of setting the bottle of vitriol on the table, just in sight.

"Mesdam Almier." Ravin Uskaro took a seat across the table from her, with Piter standing at his shoulder looking covert daggers. "We have some short time before our ship recovers this launch and we set course for Orichalk." He smiled, the very model of patriarchal condescension. "Yes, we know where Menheer Telemmier has been taken, and we will recover him from whoever has him. Or we will have him disassociate himself from them, should he be there willingly. I'm confident he'll listen to reason...given the way events have turned out." His elegant gesture took in her presence on his ship, in his power.

She made a face. "I'm afraid your family didn't make the best first impression on him, Your Elegance." All politeness and proper titles. If they wanted to make this a different sort of interview, she had no way to stop them.

"Water under the bridge." Ravin Uskaro waved away the

time Piter had sent goons after Idris, treated him like property, suborned the local law and then chased them all the way back to the *Vulture God*, saved only by a surprise intervention by Solace. And, presumably, the time he himself had tried to grab Idris on Arc Pallator, even while the planet was coming apart. He gave Kris a complacent smile. *Ah, what games we played in the far-off days of our youth.*

"Mesdam Almier," he addressed her. "You have no particular reason to love me or my nephew, I admit. Nor does your friend Telemmier. But things have changed, now. We all need to put these personal grudges behind us."

Those grudges all went one way, as far as she could see, but she didn't point that out, and just maintained a genteel smile. A flunky brought in some drinks, the heady Magdan berry spirit that she was genuinely rather partial to, though that was more likely coincidence than any research on the Uskaros' part. She sipped cautiously.

"I don't know who has Idris, although I don't imagine he's there of his own free will any more than he would be *here*," she said.

"Then when you talk to him, you must explain that this isn't about *us*," Uskaro Senior told her, knocking back his own little cup and having a new one poured. "This is about the Colonies and the survival of humanity."

Kris nodded cautiously.

"You've been able to play your games, you and he, with the Partheni." Something of a spitting tone when the name passed his lips. "But that was then. You are both citizens of the Colonies. *We* are your people, not the women from the vats. If you went back to them now, well…"

War. Actually at war, with the Parthenon. In the middle of the

Architects' return. Madness. Yet it was a mad universe, because this was apparently exactly what had happened.

"The Colonies need your friend. To defend against the Architects. To help with the new Int program—the *volunteer* program, he'll be pleased to hear. To shepherd humanity wherever it needs to go." She reckoned this was something he'd rehearsed. "Our species, our culture, is about to undergo some catastrophic changes in the near future. We are beset on all sides and the Intermediaries are our only advantage. Ranged against us, we have the Parthenon, the Architects—even the Hegemony, perhaps, after their actions over Arc Pallator. They destroyed the *Beagle*, our research ship, and crippled its escort, Mesdam."

"They also destroyed the Partheni vessel that came to your aid," Kris observed calmly.

"And yet the Parthenon has declared war on *us*," he reminded her. "Menheer Telemmier needs to make the right decision. To stay and help *his* people, and not just flit off with some...non-humans. Non-Colonials. He must remember who he is and who he was born to. I hope you're a loyal Colonial enough to help me persuade him, Mesdam. He'll listen to you. And your friends on the *Vulture God*"—he couldn't get the name of the ship out without at least a little disdain, try as he might—"will listen to you as well. Even though that Partheni infiltrator is among them. It's time to choose sides, Mesdam Almier. There is no staying out of this war, not for anyone."

"If you'll forgive me, Morzarin," she said slowly, "Idris will remember you tried to force him into your service, once before. And you had one of your own people whipped in front of us, for provoking a fight that you no doubt ordered.

These things won't help your case." She waited to see if that constituted crossing the line, as far as his polite facade was concerned.

It did not, apparently. Ravin Uskaro's smile didn't even slip. "Toughness, yes." His tone was philosophical even. "It's something we value on Magda, something your spacer friends should appreciate. They've forgotten this on Berlenhof and the other longer-settled worlds. Humanity needs to be *tough*, Mesdam Almier. Clever, and adaptable, and tough. The universe will destroy us, otherwise. The Architects are like the universe's will, are they not? Desperate to grind us down and reduce us to dust, and not even through malice! Just as a side-effect of what they do and what they are. And we will need to change, to survive them. We will need the toughness that comes from taking a whipping and keeping the cries inside. That was Earth, when the Architects came for it. A whipping for the whole species. And we survived, and the scars healed, and we were stronger."

She finished her drink, watching him carefully. The tart berry flavours cleared her mouth of the bitter taste his words had conjured up. She wanted to argue against each and every point, not least that the vast majority of humans had not "survived" the loss of Earth. There was a time and a place for defiance and the grand gesture, but not when you were on a man's ship and surrounded by his thugs. This was going to go sour sometime soon, at the Orichalk end of things, but there was no point making her life uncomfortable before that.

"Let's see what his situation is when we get over there," she suggested easily. "I mean, he's been grabbed by some psychopathic Tothiat. Sounds like anything's an improvement on that. Even you." She reckoned she had just enough credit for that and couldn't resist a little kicking back. Ravin had also been talking only about Orichalk, with no mention of Criccieth's Hell, which suggested to Kris that whatever information he'd got out of Granduja hadn't been the whole story. The Uskaros could be haring off on a bit of a tangent, giving the *Vulture God* a headstart. Until then she could play along and hope that an opportunity would present itself. For now...

"I'd like a scarf," she told him, and he blinked. Then his eyes strayed to that ragged, martial scar on her throat. He squirmed a little, to her delight.

"Of course. I'll have one printed."

She'd take her little victories where she could.

Havaer

Havaer woke, hearing alarms, and then had to wrestle with the lid of his couch before he could actually get out, in which time any number of disasters might have happened. Olli's plot through unspace to this system had brought the *God* out into the real close in towards the star—a bit too close. The alarms had already died away by the time he was out and on his feet, though. He took a moment to freshen up. A mouthful of recycled water, a shot of nerve-juice to clear away the trembling and muggy-headedness that attended unspace suspension more and more as he got older. After that he found the others crammed into the command pod, even Olli in her walker. He gave her a quizzical look and the scowl he got back told him not to ask. He reckoned she'd been getting health alerts from being in the drone bay bubble for days on end. Not hard to guess how much freer she must feel with the ship and its drones as her extended fingertips.

"What's the situation?"

"Grab a screen and look for yourself," Olli told him, but Solace, who was a soldier at heart, was already reporting.

"We're coming towards Criccieth's Hell on its orbital path now. The naval base at Orichalk hasn't hailed us. They're busy over there, though." Indicating a display harvesting data from the system's other world of note. "There's a Hiver factory in orbit, churning out munitions and parts. All the hallmarks of a reactivation phase. I suppose we both know why that is."

Havaer nodded gloomily. They'd put a naval yard here during the war because it was out of the way, without any other habitation. There was also some belief that there were unfound Throughways in the system that might make it an important place to someone, at some time. If that was true, they remained unfound, but neither had the Architects turned up to obliterate anything, which counted as a halfway win. Right now, according to the data the *God*'s sensors had harvested—as covertly as possible—there were shipyards firing up, ready to repair and to build. The big Hiver factory had probably been slumbering with minimal sentience for the best part of half a century, but was now ramped up into full consciousness and a new contract with the Colonies. The Hiver Assembly in Aggregate would already have delivered new minds to it, freshly instantiated. War veterans, probably. When they were peeled off and made into individuals, it would be the Architects they were prepped to fight. As of a few days ago, of course, that position had changed and he wondered how the small print covered that. The Parthenon had supported the Hivers when they'd made their bid for independence from Hugh, back before the Partheni had made their own exit.

This is going to get messy. "What about the *Raptorid*," he asked, "and Almier?"

Heremon, sitting with her feet up on a console, laughed derisively. "Oh they're here. Came out after us, and right near Orichalk. Current thinking's that they know they're in the right system, but nobody told them about the old hell-hole."

"They'll be looking for us," Havaer pointed out.

"Yeah, yeah, maybe they'll think they got bad data from Deathknell," Heremon sneered.

"Not fucking likely, given our luck," Olli decided. She had a cable connecting her temples to the ship and was sagging forwards, her chin virtually on the controls. "They're further out from Orichalk now, getting clear of the comms-buzz. Hunting us, the bastards."

"Attention!" Kit announced suddenly. "Bad data has been given to *us*. Idris on Criccieth's Hell is an unlikely prospect." He was slinging planetary details to everyone's console and Havaer craned over Heremon's shoulder blearily.

"That's got to be a mistake," he decided. "Some Cartography Corps joke."

"It cannot be endured by known life, nor by technology of any sort," Kit insisted. "Save the life that has evolved there."

Havaer's eyebrows would have gone through his hairline if it hadn't been in retreat these last ten years. "Damn me," he got out, looking at the figures. Even Heremon looked taken aback and respectfully removed her feet to the cabin's

443

floor. Criccieth's Hell was well named, thanks to the insane biology that had developed there. The place was as caustically radioactive as the heart of a star. *Flowers. Nuclear killer flowers, for God's sake.*

"This is what that Deathknell academic was studying, maybe," Havaer pointed out. "But...I think we've been too clever for our own good. No way he's actually on-world. Is there an orbital?"

"None we can see," Olli reported. "And the shielding you'd need...We can keep to high orbit and stave it off for a few days, but I reckon you'd start to burn up after a month of continual exposure, at best. Fuck me." She shook her head, perhaps impressed at finding something in the universe as vitriolic as she was.

"Curious readings have been detected," Kittering reported, but then wouldn't elaborate when anyone asked him. Havaer couldn't see what he'd spotted in the sensor data. And right about then, they were hailed.

It was not Uskaro. He'd decided to set the heavy mob on them instead. He'd shopped them to the navy. They could see the *Raptorid* start off on its journey in-system, which would see it catch up to the *Vulture God* a while after the *God* hit Criccieth orbit. But in order to hit orbit, they'd have to defy the orders currently heading their way from Orichalk.

"Salvage vessel *Vulture God*, this is Orichalk Watch," came the clipped tones of the duty officer. "You are in a system under the direct jurisdiction of the Council of Human Interests. You are required to divert from your current course and proceed to Orichalk, or interceptors will be sent to escort you. If you have mechanical or medical difficulties, we are ready to assist." A pause, and then, "People, you are civilians in a military-controlled system, and you've probably heard we have a lot of war going on right now. Come on in."

Plus they'll have been told this ship was last heard of working for the Parthenon, Havaer knew. *Uskaro will have made sure of that.*

He glanced at what Kit was trying to explain. There was some complex maths about the way the radiation fields were being described by the ship's sensors. It was apparently blindingly obvious if you were a Hanni, or at least if you were Kittering, but Havaer couldn't see it.

"Colvari, have you got anything for us?" Subvocalizing on their private channel, professionally discreet.

"I am attempting to establish a back channel to the Hiver factory, Agent Mundy," came the voice in his ear. "However, I can divert some processing power to modelling what Factor Kittering is attempting to describe."

"Sure, do that." Havaer considered what he'd just heard. "You're hacking the factory hive? Will that help?"

"No, I am announcing my presence, Hiver to Hiver. Standard operating procedure."

"Very much not standard procedure, if you're doing spy stuff like we are," Havaer pointed out.

"Oh, they will only 'officially' know we're here if it's appropriate. Otherwise the handshake will remain, how's the best way to put it, disconnected from the rest of the arm. Even when we're contracted on opposite sides, we like to know who's out there."

This was an insight into Hiver operations he wished he had time to sit and ponder, but right now it was his cue and he stepped up to the comms.

"Orichalk Watch, my name is Havaer Mundy from the Intervention Board. I'm sending over my credentials packet to you now. I am on Board business and not to be interdicted under any circumstances. This is a top-priority mission. Please confirm."

The pause was mostly due to the message travelling, but it certainly sounded like someone being taken aback. Colvari chimed in eventually with, "They are communicating with the *Raptorid*. The factory has given me access to their transmissions as a courtesy. Would you like to . . . ?"

"Yes, yes I would." He was grinning, and the rest of the crew gave him worried looks. In his ear, to his satisfaction, the sharp voice of Piter Uskaro then sounded.

"I have shown you my own authority, which ought to outweigh any Mordant House errand boy, officer. More to the point, that ship is carrying Partheni spies. They have an actual Partheni Monitor on board, one of their Aspirat spymasters. Any Intervention Board agent with them is either a fraud or a traitor too. Send your ships. Send them now."

"Sir, there's nothing on that damn world anyway." The watch officer sounded as though he'd already had it with Uskaro but was being forced to be cordial because of the man's civilian status, always galling for a military man. "Sometimes scientists visit it, but the place is called Hell for a reason."

"There *is* something there," Uskaro insisted. "If it's important to the Parthenon, it's important to us." Obviously he hadn't told the navy about Idris, presumably so he'd be able to keep hold of the Int rather than surrendering him either as an asset or a defector to be tried.

There was a pause then, as the *Vulture God* adjusted to

make a clean high orbit of Criccieth's Hell. Olli shuffled their power requirements so that the gravitic shielding could bounce as much of the planet's radiation away as possible.

"Right, sir," came the watch officer's voice via Colvari. "We've put your credentials and the Mordant guy's credentials on our packet and it's on its way to seek orders. I have a superior just a quick unspace jump from here who'll clear this up once and for all, and then I'll know just who I'm sending ships out after, won't I?" Havaer winced. That was his cover blown then. On the plus side, the navy officer's cordiality was wearing very thin. Heremon pinpointed the packet ship's launch, racing away out of Orichalk's gravitational interference before diving into unspace and nothingness.

"That means what?" she asked, eyeing Havaer.

Of course, the chat between Orichalk and Piter Uskaro had been in his ears only. "They're sending off to check my credentials. My Mordant House authority against the Uskaro family's sway," he said, because even if he hadn't known for sure it would be the next logical step.

"So when they get their orders back...?" Olli prompted, prodding him with one of the walker's manipulators.

"We're screwed, yes. They'll back Uskaro, not me." But Colvari had now produced a model, which boggled Havaer's head, and he threw it out for general consumption.

There was a hole bored into the killer radiation of Criccieth's Hell. A narrow but navigable cylinder all the way from orbit down onto the surface. He had absolutely no idea what was maintaining it or how such a thing was even possible. There was no mention of it on any of the admittedly cursory planetary records.

"They are down there then," Heremon said, and she

sounded as twitchy as she ever had. He wondered how even her physiology would match up to the radiation. "Fucking Emmaneth. That's where the bitch has got to. And your man, too."

"Questioning whether it can be navigated," Kit put in doubt-fully.

Olli was about to insist that of course she could but then her mouth shut with an audible snap. The well had suddenly vanished, leaving the toxic radiation-sphere of Criccieth's Hell without blemish or access.

PART 4
CRICCIETH'S HELL

26.

Idris

When Idris was ready, seated and plugged into the heart of the Machine, Doctor Shinandri flipped the switch. Or whatever complex series of operations he had actually worked out to activate the ur-mechanisms the Originators had not been able to remove from the facility, and which the Machine was just a modern addition to. Elsewhere in the installation, Idris knew, Ahab would be hanging in its own interface connected to those mechanisms, ready to piggyback on Idris's Intermediary mind and get a look through the eye of the universe. To gaze into the abyss.

The abyss that gazed back, as every Int knew, no matter how many sober scientists told them it was all in their minds. He should have felt far more naked before that dreaded, terrifying gaze using the Machine than he ever had done piloting a ship.

Idris felt only the adrenaline rush of excitement. He hadn't realized, throughout all the years of his long life, that the trajectory of his days was bringing him here. Every one of his reluctant choices, from joining the Program to today, had been for this. Every scrap of accumulated understanding about unspace and the Architects was for this. Jericho, Arc

451

Pallator, all of it had prepared him perfectly for the revelations of the Machine.

He wished again that Trine was with him now. How the Hiver academic would have been able to fill in and expand on his wild guesses and suppositions. How the data from the Machine would resonate within them! Perhaps that could be accomplished, in the fullness of time. Shinandri and Ahab had a prodigious store of data from past delves, and Idris was multiplying it with every trip he took. It could be passed to Trine and other experts. He'd take the Hiver's analysis over whatever tortured science Doc Shinandri was turning out.

But for now, he wanted to dive. Because there was a definite time limit, the candle burning at both ends every time they used the Machine.

The Originator site defended itself against the insane environment of Criccieth's Hell. The radiant life of the world was constantly assaulting it, both physically, with crackling roots and tendrils, as well as with the deadly, relentless glare itself. Yet it had survived millions of years shielding itself, some gravity-kin effect of the installation's very form sufficing to sidestep all that killing fire. That was only until they turned on the Machine. You couldn't stare into the abyss through closed eyes. While Idris and Ahab plumbed the depths, Criccieth's Hell waged war on the installation, abrading the walls, cracking them with voracious creepers, trying to blast the whole knot of otherness into atomic dust. And it was succeeding, with a dreadful patience. There was a definite limit on how long they had to gather their vital data and then escape the death-world. Idris was also well aware that the precise tipping point in that equation was unknown. They could end up with all the knowledge in the universe and no escape from the planet. He was working on a solution to that too, and trying to get an idea about how the Originator lens worked. The way it sat on the impossible boundary between unspace and the real, and what all of its vast power might be able to achieve. He'd heard the ruins sing on Arc Pallator when the Naeromathi Arks unleashed their weapon against the Architects. He had witnessed the Essiel create a vast gravitic engine from nothing and use it to take their entire Temple through unspace, off the surface of their doomed world. "Impossible" wasn't what it used to be.

The Machine was on. The installation's shielding was off, along with the narrow well that allowed anyone to reach the place, or even communicate with the outside universe. They were locked in, and at the same time the door to infinity was open and ready for him to step through.

He dived in eagerly.

The attention of the *Other* was abruptly front and centre, as though that nameless watcher had been waiting for him, a cat at a mouse-hole. He went into what was now his standard evasion, using the weird non-topography of unspace to hide his exact presence from it. And it wasn't coming for him. He had a sense of it, and it was always *down* in his mind. Down as far as unspace went, because unspace was finite and had dimensions. It was just that those dimensions made very little sense if your mind was rooted in real space.

Unspace mapped to real space, everyone knew. That was why they could reliably travel through it, whether via Throughway or off-piste entirely. A navigator could plot from A to B and get there in a relativistic blink of an eye, light years crossed in subjective hours. So long as you were happy entering a realm where nothing really existed in the same way it did in the real. Or, if not happy, at least willing. Without unspace, there would be no travel and commerce between the stars, save perhaps for lumbering sublight arks taking centuries or millennia to drift from one sun to the next. Every star system would be an island, cut off in the great blackness. Yet how little most navigators understood of unspace. Most Ints, even. Only now did Idris grasp the fundamental shape of the universe, and how it all fit together.

He considered the universe, to which unspace mapped. But that map, of a vast and three-dimensional real space, was just the surface skin of unspace, as though every point in a real volume mapped perfectly to a flat plane. No, it wasn't like that, but the human mind had limits, even an Int's mind, and so this was how Idris had come to visualize it. The skin between the stars, and below it were depths not normally troubled by any navigating ship or inquisitive Intermediary. The vast bulk of unspace was unseen, vast and yet finite. And far smaller than the real universe, insofar as size actually had any meaning. It had to have been, Idris understood now. Or else travelling through it wouldn't be the shortcut it was.

At the very deepest point of unspace, far below—and it wasn't *below* but, again, limits of the human imagination— was the *Other*, the presence that lived in unspace. A single entity, unlike anything, utterly its own. It lurked down there until the whiff of another mind came to it, an intruder in its domain, and then it began searching. It didn't rise up from its seabed like the kraken, because Idris felt it couldn't move from where it was. Its place defined and perhaps even created it, an artefact of unspace's structure. But, like an eye itself, it could search, and what moved through the murky waters of unspace was its malign focus. Which drove lesser minds mad by its very nature, killed through proximity, had luckless wayfarers slit their wrists, space themselves, sabotage their own vessels. Idris didn't know if this was from intent or if the very nature of the thing was so inimical to a realspace mind that its focus couldn't help but drive anyone to insanity. He'd had many close encounters with it during his regular career as an Int. He knew how it felt, that presence at the shoulder so loathsome and intolerable that self-murder would be a blessed release. Its focus was no less terrible just because he knew and understood it better. But he could evade it. His new knowledge was good for that, at least. He was the all-time universal champion in dodging the attention of the *Other* right now.

That was good, because he was hunting, and he'd had a sniff of his quarry.

Ahab had been thunderingly enthusiastic about what they were looking for. The creature had a purpose and needed his senses to fulfil it. There was a limit to how far the regular mind could penetrate, using the Machine. Idris had been made into a child of unspace. His precisely damaged mind could interlock with the nothingness, swim in it like a seal. He only had to remember to come up for air.

He was mapping the place, now. Smaller than the universe, and the Machine made it smaller still, a lens that could focus simultaneously at many distances. The distances weren't real anyway, within unspace. Its vastness was contained within a nutshell, so that Idris was constantly fighting vertigo—a vast chasm or the void between stars could become, with a sudden inversion, the cluttered depths of a drop of water under a microscope.

He was learning its structure. Because it was all about the structure. As above, so below. He had sensed the residual power of Originator ruins on Jericho, still potent purely because of the convoluted shape of the walls that acted as a wedge driven into the real. It was the space between the boundaries that had the power, like a magician's circle, like the glyphs of a vanished superstition. Just as Hegemonic technology was a study in absences, their liquid-filled vessels forming spaces within them that were the working parts of their mechanisms. Just as the Naeromathi super-weapon deployed over Arc Pallator had been contained not within the Locust Arks but in the space they'd made between them. Patterns of absence, all the way down until Idris felt dizzy, on the brink of revelation.

Unspace was as it was because it was being held in a shape. There was a structure to the unreality of it: linkages, sutures, cosmic cartilage. The Throughways were a part of an over-arching scaffolding that reached deep into unspace. Though it seemed infinitely static and reliable, Idris could feel it constantly shifting, vibrating, tugged this way and that by the real, even as the real was tugged back by the fundamental bones of unspace. Every ship that coursed the Throughways was a pinprick disturbing the serenity of the void below. Every world out there was like a pulsar in unspace, sending out ripples.

Or not every world. There weren't enough disturbances for that. Not stars, nor dead rocks hurtling about nameless suns. Idris had expected unspace to be oppressed by all the *mass* of real space. That made scientific sense to him, and yet it was demonstrably not so. Mass didn't fluctuate in the way he was seeing. What else was there, that had weight and force within the unreality of unspace?

Only one thing, and he himself was testament to it.

The very idea made him tremble because of what it signified about the essential fragility of the universe. Never mind butterfly effects. A butterfly was an unstoppable leviathan compared to the gossamer whisper of human thought, and yet...

With this revelation and the leverage it gave him, he touched another mind. Another mind in another place. A Location briefly glimpsed deep within the long fathoms of nowhere, down below.

A vast mind, and yet vastness wasn't all it was cracked up to be down here. Familiar. He'd done this before. He'd been in the real, then, but he wasn't likely to forget.

It was an Architect. Oh so briefly, he'd connected with an Architect. Perhaps even the same Architect he'd reached at Berlenhof, the first time or the last. Perhaps the one he'd made peace with at Far Lux. A peace which had died when Far Lux had died, when the Architects had come back.

It reacted to him, in that brief moment, and its response was something the human mind could instantly grasp. An old friend from the dawn of time that had paced in humanity's shadow since long before humanity had been human.

It feared. The Architect, reshaper of worlds, had discovered the mote that was Idris Telemmier there in unspace, lurking in *its* shadow for once. And he'd felt its terror.

Then he was breaching back into the real, the Machine powered down. The shield of the facility was back up, with a few more cracks in the walls, another slice of its integrity removed forever, the clock closer to doomsday.

He had to talk to Ahab.

*

457

"Yes!" the Naeromathi's artificial voice boomed as he ducked into the chamber that served as a common room. It was hunched around the far side of the table Jaine had bolted to the floor there, its long neck resting on the surface as though the strain of supporting its own weight had momentarily overcome it. "Yes! You have witnessed!"

Idris had no fear of it now, for all Ahab could have crushed him with its sheer bulk or seized him with its various mechanical limbs and mouthparts. It was a fellow researcher. A generous patron to let him play with the fundamental pieces of the universe.

"It's there," Idris confirmed, and a shudder went through the creature's scarred hide.

"Yes!" it echoed. And then, "We have hunted long! We have sensed it! We have—!" and a buzzing squall of feedback at some concept that simply had no analogue in human speech, some Naeromathi mode of apprehension Colvul couldn't even approximate. Idris was forced to wonder who had even got this far with bridging the communication gap, because he'd never heard of a Naeromathi trying to speak the language of other species. Ahab seemed cut off from its kin. There was no Locust Ark backing it, nor had it sought out its far-flung fellows. Instead it was a renegade consorting with humans and Tothiat, hidden away on this least likely of planets. There was a history there, but he couldn't ask about it, and nothing was being volunteered.

"No Ash?" he asked, because the enigmatic alien had now vanished, it seemed. Perhaps there had been a ship come for it and the creature's comings and goings were no more mysterious than that, but Idris was more and more sure that Ash had its own relationship with unspace and travel.

And he was just as sure the thing would never admit to any of it.

Doctor Shinandri came in behind him, in a high state of excitement. "That is the longest single session, gentlemen, the absolute extremity of duration! The very walls themselves complain at it!" He sounded thrilled rather than alarmed at the prospect. "Such information, such raw data we have gathered. A map! We are mapping the unmappable, we three!" He drummed a rapid tattoo on the tabletop as he sat down. "Captain Ahab, we approximate, do we not? We approach your goal, if I do not mistake myself."

"But what is it?" Idris asked, into what turned out to be a sudden silence. Ahab and Shinandri both regarded him.

"We were hoping," the scientist said, "that you would be able to tell us."

"But I assumed you knew, which was why you were looking for it," Idris countered, frowning.

"The heart of the enemy!" Ahab announced portentously. That was its true belief, Idris guessed, and at the same time, what did the phrase mean? Quite aside from the fact it had been translated from the speech of a species that probably didn't have a heart, per se. What would it even mean to a human? The *enemy* was the Architects, no doubt of that. Normally he would have been thinking in terms of home-worlds, except... there were no *worlds* in unspace, and each Architect was the size of a moon anyway. Unless there was some unreal equivalent of a vast gas giant they all orbited around when not off wrecking planets in the real.

Despite these imponderables, there was a place and he was close to discovering it. The structure and scaffolding of unspace was bent about it, warping to accommodate it.

Whilst unspace was vast, seen through the eye of the Machine it became curiously small. A handy perspective for the godlike entities that had constructed the underlying mechanisms and architecture of the installation. You could see forever through the Machine, or at least forever minus a few prudent steps, because if you looked far enough you risked staring into the eye of the *Other*. That was something Idris still could not do. Just as the monstrous radiation of Criccieth's Hell would disintegrate anything that braved it, so he would ablate away to nothing should he present himself directly before that fierce gaze, should it find him at last.

What did unspace contain, then? What might it be that they were on the brink of finding?

The Architects themselves—or at least they travelled its wilds without fear and surfaced as they chose, Throughways be damned. Ahab believed they were unspace natives and Idris was inclined to agree.

So what was the *Other*, or whatever it was? The ultimate denizen of unspace, a great leviathan upon the hide of which the Architects were merely fleas.

And the Originators themselves? Gone, he assumed. No sign of them anywhere he'd looked. Destroyed, extinct or even departed for some better universe where moon-sized monsters didn't refigure worlds according to the whims of . . .

"They have masters," he told the other two.

"You have spoken of this conceit, Menheer," Shinandri admitted.

"I have it direct from an Architect," Idris reminded them. "They do what they do because they are *forced*. They are a weapon in the hand of . . . something. For some reason."

"The 'Artists,' perhaps," Shinandri suggested archly. "Using the Architects to reshape the universe to their own aesthetic tastes, hmm?"

It would, Idris thought, make as much sense as anything.

"Perhaps this presence everyone feels in unspace? Is that the hand that directs the Architects?" the scientist mused.

"No," said Idris immediately, and then had to examine his instinctive reaction to work out why he was so definite about that. "No," he repeated more slowly. He couldn't account for it, but the *Other*, the presence, was... *Other*. Not involved in any schemes, not needing another species as a tool. If the *Other* had wanted to rise from its lair to devour the real universe, then...

He found he was sweating just at the thought, shying away from any consideration of it. The presence *was*, and that was as far as Idris was willing to take his speculation. "But the Architects do have masters," he went on. "Maybe they're in the real, and somehow they worked out how to fish up Architects from unspace, fit them with a bridle and make them do their bidding. Or maybe they're in unspace, too. Maybe they resent our little forays down the Throughways, intrusions into their domain. Look, the data doesn't tell you one thing, okay? Right at the end, when we were getting close, I felt an Architect mind. Just as I did in the real. Architect thoughts, in the regions we were searching. So they're there, and know we were looking at them, and they were frightened. Frightened, Ahab."

A jolt went through the alien's supine carcass and it was abruptly up, neck swinging almost close enough to knock Idris off his stool. "Yes!" it roared once more. "We close in!"

"But with what?" Shinandri wanted to know.

"I think it could be where their masters are," Idris suggested. "Because that's what we need to find. No point hunting the Architects down one by one, is there? If we could somehow discover a way to attack the ones that move them, though, then we'd be doing everyone a favour. Maybe this gathering of Architects is the key to it. It's *somewhere*, at least. And unspace is short of somewheres. What else could it be but whoever commands them?"

Someone coughed ostentatiously behind him, and he twitched to find Tokamak Jaine there, lit by the grumbling fires of her own torso.

"Well, have you told him?" she demanded.

"We were engaged with other considerations," Shinandri said, somewhat evasively.

"Told who?" Idris asked blankly. "Me? Told me what?"

"There's a ship," Jaine said. "Someone's found us. Emma's readying her own, in case we need to run."

"No running!" Ahab bellowed.

"Chief, you do what you do, but we've not had a visitor here for a long while. Now there's one in orbit and another one making all speed from Orichalk to join it. And they're hailing. Or at least, they're hailing *him*."

"What?" Idris stared at her blankly. "What sort of ship? A salvager?" That was the best possible option.

"Yeah," Jaine confirmed. "Beat-up old thug of a salvager." He chorused the name with her as she said it. "*Vulture God*, its ID says."

"Let me speak to them. They're my friends. My crew," Idris said.

"The crusade!" Ahab insisted. "We are close! Back to the Machine!"

"He means..." Shinandri said awkwardly. "We all mean... the work here, it's important. We can't...stop." *Let you leave* was tactfully left unspoken. If it had been like that, Idris wondered what they would have done. Drugged him? Strapped him into the Machine? Had Emmaneth cut his fingers off until he agreed to cooperate?

But it wasn't like that, and he was already shaking his head. "I know, I know, and I *need* to know. I need to see... what it is. What's there. You're right. We're so close. Let me speak to them and I'll tell them. Go away. Come back later. Just... give us time. They'll understand. They're my friends. I can make them understand."

27.

Olli

The narrow well into Criccieth's radiationsphere had re-appeared after many hours of terse and failed negotiations. They had been fending off threats from Uskaro on the *Raptorid*, now just about to hit orbit itself, and Olli had listened to Havaer do his best with the navy. His best trans-lated into their not having launched any ships of their own towards the inner planet, pending instructions. Or he said it was his best, anyway. She only had his word for that, and maybe every exchange had been freighted with code words and secret transmissions and all that spy shit. How was she expected to know? She'd had some whispered conversations with Kit, who was increasingly skittish about the current ship's complement. The Hanni didn't trust Havaer as far as he could throw the man, which, given Havaer weighed three times as much as he did, wasn't far. Of course neither of them trusted Heremon worth a damn either. The Tothiat gangster was ostentatiously not helping in any way, which Olli frankly preferred. She lounged about in the drone bay or the command pod, feet up on something delicate as often as not. Her expression radiated smug invulnerability, even when Olli started stomping about in the Scorpion. She reckoned she could put Menheer Spy-stuff Mundy in his place easily enough, now she'd tanked up, but Heremon was another matter. Obviously, Heremon also thought she couldn't be hurt. Olli'd had the ship printers work up a dose of the anti-Tothiat juice on the sly, although it was ruinously expensive in resources. The molecules were so big and convoluted she was almost surprised she couldn't see them with the naked eye. The dose was now sitting in a modified injection element in the Scorpion's tail, and if Heremon decided she wanted to wear the captain's hat then Olli was going to let her have it between the eyes or the shoulderblades, depending on their relative orientations at the time.

She'd been having whispered conversations with only Kit because she also wasn't sure she trusted Solace, not entirely. She'd just been coming round to the idea of a Partheni ship-mate, and of Solace being an all-right kind of person, as well as a reliable hand in a crisis, until this. War. Solace was a loyal Myrmidon, which meant she'd jump to the Parthenon's tune if there was a conflict of interests. Oh, she'd agonize. Solace was one of those agonizers who used hand-wringing as a substitute for actual conscience, in Olli's assessment, but the end result surely wasn't in doubt.

For now, though, she was sending urgent contact requests down the well, hoping there was even someone somehow down there, in amongst all the killer flowers. The *Raptorid* would be coasting around the curve of the planet soon enough, and if Uskaro decided to kick off his own little shooting war right then, there wouldn't be much the poor old *Vulture God* could do about it.

"This is the salvage ship *Vulture God* to whoeverthefuck's even down there. Call for Idris Telemmier, double urgent.

Idris, this is Olli. You remember? Olli, your fucking *captain*? Being kidnapped doesn't excuse you from turning up for duty, you skiving bastard. Idris, or Idris's kidnappers. Say something, damn it!"

At last, after far too much of that, and her formal greetings becoming more and more laden with expletive, came a response.

A woman's voice, briefly, as brightly pleasant as a professional comms operator on some commercial hub. "Please hold for Menheer Telemmier."

Heremon's feet bounced off the console and she was up on them, craning under the Scorpion's armpit. Olli wished she'd set comms to her earpiece, but too late for that.

"That was your old friend?" she asked.

"Emmaneth," Heremon agreed. By then, everyone was in the command pod, crowding into whatever space Olli's frame left them. She was very aware of all eyes on her. *Fucking Kris had to get herself snatched.* She wondered if she should let Kit handle things, but pride prevented her giving anyone else the comms now.

"Idris?" she tried. "Seriously, you got an Idris down there, you've got to say."

"Olli?" His voice, attacked by waves of static that she could track in the radiation of the world, came up to them through that narrow, impossible well. It freaked her out, that channel down to the planet's surface. She couldn't detect the actual fields that were holding it open, just a slim cylinder of nothing where the monstrous glaring light of the planet didn't exist. An invisible hole in the brilliance.

"Idris, we're here. We've come to get you. What's your situation?" Aware that presumably Emmaneth and this

Shinandri character, and whoever else, would doubtless be eavesdropping.

"How did you even find me?" Idris asked, rather peevishly in her opinion.

"Idris, that's seriously not important right now. We found you. Be happy, you miserable fish-faced fuck. Now get your bags, we're coming."

"Olli, no!"

"If anyone wants to stop us, we've got a fully kitted Partheni Myrmidon right here, our own bastard Tothiat and a super-powered secret agent. And me, who's tougher than all of that just by myself. Oh, and Kit, I guess. I mean, I was assuming you'd stick with the ship, Kit."

"Given these options the ship will remain my location," Kittering agreed, heartfelt. No fighter he.

"Olli," Idris's weak voice came to this. "No, Olli. Go away, please. I'm not coming."

"Yeah, gun to your head I'm sure. Look, we are going to come down that well and get you, and your new friends better back the fuck off, is all I'm going to say about it. We have serious firepower." They didn't, and she was looking at that well compared to the dimensions of the *Vulture God* and really worrying whether the operation was even possible, given that even a slight brush with the walls would probably atomize something important.

"Olli," Idris said again. "No. I'm doing important work here. I need to, need to go back. We're so close. Come back later, Olli. Just...I can't be having with this right now. I'm busy."

"Well..." For a moment she was speechless. "Well la-de-fucking-da." She checked the Scorpion's cameras, seeing everyone else boggling at her. "Idris, I don't know how secret you think you've been but we're not even the only ones who've found you. You remember Menheer Boyarin Uskaro, the younger? He's here in his gun-yacht and he's not polite like I fucking am."

"Tell him I'm not going with him either."

"Yeah, that worked real well the last time. Idris, are you— they got you drugged or something? We are *here*. To rescue *you*. From the murderer Tothiat and some mad scientist and... Idris, what are you even—"

"No, no, no, Olli, I can't come." She knew that jittery tone, Idris working himself into one of his anxiety tantrums like fucking always. "I am *working*, Olli. There's something... Just give me another chance. I need to go back in. We're almost—" Shouting now. "I can't! I can't just stop. Just go away. Stall Uskaro. No, I can't do that now. This is important."

"Fuck me, Idris, calm down!" Olli threw the Scorpion's hands up, all of them. "Someone else's turn," she admitted. "I can't be dealing with this. Fucking *Kris*." Because Kris could have talked him down. They went way back, those two. She could always handle him.

When Solace indicated she'd take the comms, Olli rolled her eyes but nodded.

"Idris, it's Solace. I don't know if you've been in the news-type loop but things are getting very bad up here. Uskaro's right on us, and outguns us. Hugh and the Parthenon are at war. Actual war. There's a navy base right here, and as soon as they get their orders, they'll launch on us too. We'll have to go, and we won't be able to come back. But you'll have a navy strike team coming down that well to grab you. Or Uskaro's Voyenni. They won't give you a choice about what to do in the war."

"Solace." He sounded calmer at least. "You remember how it was when I volunteered, in the war? Volunteered for the Intermediary Program?"

"You know I wasn't there for that. None of us was."

"You remember Berlenhof, the first time, though. When we went against the Architects. And you remember Far Lux, when we spoke to them?"

"Yes and no," Solace said, with the patience of a saint in Olli's opinion. "Idris—"

"And you remember Berlenhof the second time? When we went to stop them? I basically died, from trying to save the planet. I've got a knot of Hiver units keeping my heart going still, a piece of Trine stuck in me forever, thanks to that. You remember?"

"We all do," Solace confirmed.

"Because we have to do these things, those of us who can. It's my duty. It's my responsibility. Because there's no one else. And I *hate* it, Solace. I hate being me, and being the universe's goddamn trophy, and being the one who's left over from all of that nonsense in the war, now it's all back again. But it's me, I'm here. And what we're doing here, Ahab and Shinandri and me, it's *that*. It's important. It could save everything. There's no one else, only me. And we've not got much time left. It's all coming down, every time we turn it on. But we're so close. To understanding everything, Solace. I can't go. You have to give me time."

"Being hailed by the *Raptorid* again," Kit observed. "Their weapons are in range of us now."

Whatever Olli's thoughts about getting the *God* through that well, doing it while under fire was going to be a complicated way of committing suicide. And yet they weren't shooting.

"Let's see what the bastard has to say," she decided, giving up on Idris for the moment.

Kris

Kris was not-quite-hauled from the stateroom they were keeping her in. "Not-quite" because she kept brisk pace with the two Voyenni who were sent for her, so their attempt to frogmarch her never quite got past the tadpole stage. They took her right to Uskaro's seat of power on the *Raptorid* bridge, where Morzarin was reclining in the big chair while Piter kicked his heels to one side. She was getting an interesting picture of a Magdan noble's jaunting yacht, not a class of vessel she'd ever been able to examine before. It was a sleek little ship, and from the outside it looked appropriately predatory. Had it been an actual miniature warship, she guessed it would have served decently enough, but warships didn't need to give over space to lavish quarters for their captain, or a stateroom. It was fast, and it was armed beyond the dreams of the poor *Vulture God*. There wasn't much more to it than that, though. She also quickly worked out that the Voyenni who'd grabbed her on Deathknell were half its entire complement of troops, who must be crammed shoulder to shoulder wherever they were billeted. Not that such revelations really affected her personal odds right now. And not that they wouldn't be able to carve the *God* up a treat if they wanted to.

"My nephew has been talking to your erstwhile crewmates," he told Kris irritably. "They say they don't have Telemmier, of course, and we've not seen anything that suggests they picked anything up in orbit. But maybe you could tell me just what's going on here?"

"This planet's a disaster zone!" Piter broke in, to Ravin's evident annoyance. "There's nobody on it and nothing around it."

Kris took her best stock of where they were and what was on offer. Criccieth's Hell certainly seemed to be living up to its name, and she spent too long looking for the science orbital that was surely hiding somewhere around the far side. There was nothing, though, and all the readings certainly suggested that anyone attempting planetfall wouldn't be given very long to regret it.

And there was the *Vulture God*, pinned by the *Raptorid*'s targeting like a spectacularly ugly moth.

"We've reminded them that we have you, and of course they've demanded to hear your dulcet tones, to be sure you're well. I want you to tell them that you're perfectly fine," Ravin went on, and again Piter broke in.

"Though that may not persist," he jabbed, "if they don't give up Telemmier." The pair of Voyenni on the bridge were certainly looming, though that could just have been from the close quarters.

Ravin's lips pressed into a thin line at the interruption, but he was obviously going to hold a united front and not chew his nephew out in her presence. Kris wondered if she could come up with some backstory that would excuse the kind of people they were. She could see how growing up in the shadow of men like Ravin had moulded Piter, certainly. There were probably more than a few whippings in Uskaro Junior's own personal history, both given and received.

On the other hand, she considered, *all the sympathy in the world doesn't mean he's not a spoiled little bastard. And as for Senior...*

"We are short on both time and patience, Mesdam Almier," Ravin told her. "Your fellows haven't picked up Telemmier because they wouldn't be still sitting here if they had. Is this a rendezvous point you agreed with him somehow?" At his side, Piter was pointedly flipping their target locks on and off the *Vulture God*, waving his big weapons in her face.

Kris ignored Junior, meeting Ravin's gaze levelly. "You had this system from Professor Granduja," she reminded them. "We had the exact planet. Now you know as much as us, Your Elegance." She'd have loved to bluff, but right now her hand was empty. It didn't seem possible that anyone was down on the surface, from what the *Raptorid*'s sensors had shown. "Maybe the Deathknell folks played us both."

"Then maybe we should just shoot your erstwhile ship down," Piter snapped.

"Give me the channel," Ravin directed abruptly, and then spoke louder, voice clashing about the small bridge. "*Vulture God* crew, Mesdam Timo, 'Olli,' is it not?" The nickname was grotesque in his mouth. "This is the Morzarin Ravin Uskaro. We have your shipmate Almier here, as you asked. She'll tell you she's being well looked after. I'm going to try this one time to appeal to your patriotism. I know you have a Partheni agent on board, and perhaps that was an acceptable foible a few days ago, but you've heard the news now. You're Colonies, Timo. You help an enemy agent in a time of war, that's full-on treason. Especially where an Int like Telemmier's concerned. He's an asset, a war asset. If I were you, I'd be fervently praying that the Partheni's own Int program—the one you helped start—got blown up with their garden ship, or else Mordant House won't ever stop hunting you. But you have a chance to make that right, Timo. Hand over Telemmier or tell me where he is."

A pause, and then Olli's caustic tones came back, "You going to let Kris talk or what?"

Ravin's lip twitched, but he signalled to his captive.

"I'm here, all right," Kris spoke into the void.

"Still got all your skin intact?"

"Just about," and then, because Ravin was gesturing at her and sangfroid might be misinterpreted, "I'm fine." Pointedly not asking any questions about Idris, though she wanted to know even more than Uskaro did.

"Listen to me," Piter broke in. "You've played your spacer games with allegiance up till now, and because it was peace-time these things get overlooked. But that's ended now." Then Ravin was waving him curtly to silence.

"What my nephew means is you have this one chance to cooperate and clear your records. You can be heroes of the Colonies, restoring one of our great weapons to us in times of need. But it has to be *now*."

Kris was wondering why the hurry, given Uskaro had the ship bang to rights. Then a new voice broke in.

"Your Elegance, this is Agent Mundy of the Intervention Board. You appear to be assuming a lot of Hugh authority that we both know you don't have."

Ravin was like stone, but Piter's face, confronted with someone he couldn't see, clearly showed his frustration. Mundy was right: he could talk Colonial pride all he wanted, but the Uskaro were just one Magdan clan, not Hugh itself.

"I've co-opted this vessel for Board purposes," Mundy

went on. "Your patriotic sentiments are noted, but you've no authority in this, nor are we aligned with the Parthenon or any other enemy power. I am *asking* you to surrender Almier, and then take your ship out of orbit and return to Orichalk, or go wherever you wish. Failing that, well, the naval base is right there. Kidnapping is an offence, and we both know Hugh will back Mordant House over one family, however grand."

Ravin was looking unconcerned, but Mordant House had a reputation. She guessed that, at a family and individual level, there were plenty of skeletons that might be dug up to inconvenience Uskaros Senior and Junior, and the Intervention Board knew about most of them. You didn't butt heads with Hugh's security service.

Ravin signalled to cut the channel, and when he spoke his polite tone was frosty. "You are going to speak to them," he told her. "You are going to have them give up Telemmier, or information on his whereabouts."

"I don't have any more authority with Mordant House than you do," she told him frankly. "Like you heard, it's not our show anymore."

For a moment she thought it might be as simple as that: Havaer's authority, phantom or real, would actually pull the teeth of the Uskaro wolf. Then a new comms call was coming in. The naval base.

"Morzarin Uskaro," came the clipped tones of their comms officer, "we've received confirmation of your authority. The Board operative on the *Vulture God* is on the Renegade List, and that ship is a confirmed enemy actor. We're launching a squadron to support you and bring this Intermediary back. If you're able to hold them till we get there."

Ravin Uskaro's face set in new, hard lines that Kris didn't like. "And?" he asked sweetly.

"And, sir?" from the comms officer.

"Your commanding officer has slighted the honour of my house. I expect his formal apology at his earliest convenience." Kris was suddenly reconsidering which, out of uncle and nephew, was the bigger asshole. Just because Ravin had a better poker face didn't make him a better person.

A pause from the naval base, probably as incredulous as Kris was feeling right then, but at last the luckless officer sputtered, "Apologies for doubting your word, sir. I'll convey your request to the commander."

Well that's that, Kris decided. Uskaro was ordering a new channel to the *Vulture God*, but right now they weren't responding, undoubtedly because the naval base was giving them an ultimatum too.

Almier, said a voice in her ear. She froze and then tried to look casual. She had her earpiece in, of course, but it had been cut off from any kind of contact until now, and she didn't know the voice. It was so low she had to stop herself cupping a hand about her ear to hear it better.

We request your assistance, then crashing over those faint tones came Uskaro demanding, "One last chance to talk them into surrendering, Mesdam Almier."

Kris gave him an overly bright smile he actually flinched away from. "You want me to tell them *who you are*," giving the words a particular stress and hoping this new speaker would understand her oblique question.

"Tell them we're goddamn *Hugh* as far as they need to know, and we will carve up their gravitic drives and leave them in a decaying orbit over this hellhole if they don't comply," Piter snapped at her. In the echo of that she heard, *We are working with Agent Mundy. We require set-up protocols for system access. Get to the scanner console.*

The sensor suite was, needless to say, nowhere near the comms, but she made a big blunder of it, moving over there and trying to speak into the controls, hailing the *God* all the wrong ways while Piter shouted at her and his crew smirked. Their scanners were directed at the planet below in all its awful glory, and at the *Vulture God*, of course. They were open to any and all information about the ship's activity: its energy signatures, every little twitch of its systems that might signal fight or flight.

Be ready to handshake, the little voice in her ear instructed. She didn't know what it meant, but right now everyone was looking at her and whatever she did would be far too obvious. She let the sensor operator take her elbow and guide her, quite civilly, back towards Uskaro's chair.

There was a particular feint she'd learned, where you hooked an opponent's ankle with your own, taking them down to where you could menace them with your knife and have them concede. It was fiendishly hard, though, and if you misjudged the relative centres of gravity then it'd be you going over instead of your opponent. And because of the grand captain's chair, the bridge was very cramped, hard for two people to move about together.

She got her foot between the crewman's, the exact right way to do the move wrong, and ended up going over quite genuinely, hitting the edge of the sensor panel hard enough with head and shoulder that she'd be wearing the bruise for the next week.

Now, she subvocalized and clawed at the panel to right

herself. A dialogue opened briefly, asking for a long list of permissions, and she slapped her hand at it to give herself leverage. When they had her upright, she felt genuinely dizzy with the impact, and there was absolutely no sign of what she'd done. If, indeed, she'd done anything.

Havaer

For a moment, Havaer had literally nothing in his head. He'd been expecting this, of course. He'd been braced for the orders coming through. The naval base had launched an armed boarding shuttle and a couple of gunboats now, skimming in-system from Orichalk towards the fires of Criccieth's Hell. Their curt announcement to the *Vulture God* had come right on the heels of that, leaving them in absolutely no doubt who the guns would be pointed at. They were advised to surrender, that was all.

"I," Havaer had insisted, "am Agent Havaer Mundy of the Intervention Board. I am on active service tracking a threat to Hugh right now. Any action against this ship will be action against Mordant House. Think carefully before you—"

"Sir," the comms officer told him with heavy sarcasm, "your alleged credentials were on the packet out of here. We are explicitly informed by the Board that you are no longer on their roster and any authority you claim is invalid. We are informed that the vessel you are seeking to defend defected to the Parthenon and is to be considered an asset of a hostile state. Have your people stand down and assume the position for boarding, or things are going to get messy."

"Fuck!" Havaer yelled, and then wasn't sure if he'd actually turned the comms off for it or not, which only made things worse. "We are not the Parthenon!" he told them. "I'm under orders from Mordant House and this..." Perilously close to spilling the beans about the ark ship plot and the Uskaro family, and why not, really? Why keep their secrets, at this exigency? But at the same time, he couldn't bring himself to sit there and tell an officer of the Hugh Navy that there was a grand conspiracy to abandon Hugh and pack some lucky fraction of humanity onto a bunch of ark ships. That it was for this reason someone had gone and started a shooting war with the Parthenon, both to remove a major competitor in the space-nomad stakes and presumably because it would result in an easier choice of which people got to go on the ark because there would be fewer to choose from. All in the shadow of the actual goddamn war with the Architects, of course. And maybe war with the bloody Hegemony too, because nobody knew just how serious the faux pas over Arc Pallator actually was, from the clams' perspective.

"Hailing from the *Raptorid* is occurring," Kittering noted.

"Of course it fucking is," replied Olli. "And we've lost Idris."

"Lost how?" Solace demanded.

"As in that well's been and gone again. Nothing but radiationsphere down there now, and us up here with the guns on us."

Kittering had apparently been listening to Uskaro, because now he relayed, "A demand for surrender has been received. It is suggested that the Boyarin will speak for us if we hand ourselves over to him, as well as give him Idris. If we show any sign of getting away from the planet to jump: violence."

"We don't *have* Idris."

"Give him Idris on credit?" Kittering considered. "The

thought occurs that there is no understanding on the *Raptorid* of where Idris is."

"We're not the Parthenon!" Havaer insisted again, but he didn't think the naval base was listening anymore. The only thing they wanted to hear from *him* was an unconditional surrender.

"Right," Olli said. "Let's dock with the *Raptorid*. Tell them we have Idris and we'll hand him over."

Havaer looked round at her. "Oh really?"

She flexed the various limbs of the Scorpion. "I've got this, and we've got a Tothiat on *our* side for once, rather than going up against the durable bastards." She cocked her head at Heremon, who looked coolly amused. "So we get up close to Uskaro and we grapple where they can't shoot us. Then she and me, we wade in there and get Kris back."

"And Idris?"

"Right now I cannot be fucked with Idris if he won't help himself. We'll come back to that. But we can do this now, while it's just us and them, or we can wait till his new navy buddies pitch in. At that point, even I will admit we'd be outgunned," she decided.

"He's got at least a dozen Voyenni on board."

"Scorpion. Tothiat," she told him.

Havaer opened his mouth to point out all the multitudinous and grievous holes in this sham of a plan when a voice in his ear told him, "It may work."

"Colvari?" Right now he didn't care that everyone was staring at him as he patently took a call from someone else. "What have you got?"

"Limited access to the *Raptorid* systems."

"Meaning?"

"A short window when we can assist the boarding attempt being described. We would have more but we are engaged in complex diplomacy."

He'd stood up when Colvari's voice had sounded, he realized. Now he let himself down into his seat again, giving his heart a shot of meds, and wondered just how bad this would look on his permanent record and/or obituary as appropriate. He was already apparently a traitor. Things probably didn't get worse than that.

"I get the feeling you've gone beyond my brief, Colvari."

"We are improvising under difficult circumstances," the Hiver confirmed.

"You've breached contract?"

"We feel we are in a borderline position. We have called upon the Hiver factory installed over Orichalk. It has received covert word on the packet ship from our Assembly in Aggregate. The events in this system have attracted the attention of parties which neither you nor I was aware of."

"The Assembly being one?"

"High-level negotiations between the Assembly and other parties are taking place," Colvari confirmed.

"Where does that leave *us*?" Havaer felt a terrible sense of despair. The agent's dread of finding yourself on the wrong side of a closed door. "You're selling us out, now?"

"No. The negotiations may result in significant future gains, but right at this immediate moment they mean we are in a position to assist a contested entry into the *Raptorid* for the purpose of recovering Keristina Soolin Almier. Who, we judge, is the most likely conduit by which Idris Telemmier may be recovered, from their long association."

Havaer met Olli's eyes. She was all suspicion and zero

concern. His mouth filled with all manner of tangled stories about the conversation he'd just been having but in the end he came clean. "I've got a Hiver confederate clamped to the hull. They say they've got some access to the *Raptorid* systems and can help you get over there. Let's have the name-calling and finger-pointing later, shall we?"

Her face went through two or three convolutions before settling on a grudging nod. Then a new alarm was going off and Kittering was scrabbling across his console. "System receiving new ships!" he got out.

"Whose?" Havaer demanded. *I mean they've got a naval base here. One might think that was enough to apprehend one crappy salvage vessel.*

"Ours," Solace said calmly.

Half a dozen sleek, segmented vessels had just torn out of unspace, scattered across a hundred thousand square klicks of space. They were trying to pull into defensive formation, chasing along Criccieth's orbital path, already far closer than the naval force. Havaer reckoned the base at Orichalk would be scrambling reinforcements, since their little gunboat squadron would now be severely outgunned.

"Well," he said hopelessly. "Maybe we *are* the Parthenon then."

"That's grand," Olli decided. "I'm declaring war on the *Raptorid* and moving us in."

28.

Idris

"We're not ready!" Tokamak Jaine shouted at Idris's back. "We can't just start up when you please. The facility's losing integrity each time you do!"

Idris rounded on her. "And sooner or later it goes, right? It loses the fight against the planet. Every time you turn it on, more cracks in the walls, right?" He was halfway down the scaffolding to the Machine, stepping out onto another walkway, Shinandri ahead of him. Emmaneth was slouching along in Jaine's shadow.

"Yes, but I've rigged some gravitic generators. We can hold it together. Just a little. But not if you don't give me time."

"We don't *have* time," Idris insisted. "You heard them. They're coming to take me."

"Your friends," Emmaneth pointed out.

"My friends, I *know* my friends," Idris agreed, feeling as though he was trying to explain higher maths to five-year-olds. "And yes, only my wellbeing at heart, all that, but they can't understand, none of you can understand."

"We've been doing this for longer than you, Telemmier," Jaine pointed out hotly.

"But you haven't *felt* it," he shouted at her. "You can't know what it's like. We're so close. We're right there, on the very *brink*! I need to go back, see what's there." He actually tried to grab her, to drive his certainty into her by this contact, but she slapped him off. "You have no idea what's at stake!"

"Of course I bloody do!" she yelled back at him. "But you're going to destroy the facility and kill us all. Then where's your damn revelation?"

"I can't have this taken away from me!" Idris realized he was almost screaming, scouring his own throat with the force of his words. "The masters of the Architects! The hands that hold the whip, the ones they kill planets for! Tell her, Doctor!"

Doctor Shinandri looked between him and Jaine, and Idris was alarmed to see the man undecided. What was the use of a mad scientist if they suddenly decided to start making sane decisions?

"We are so close," he insisted. "Tell her, Doctor, please."

"He's not the boss of me," Jaine said flatly. "I say this place won't hold if you keep running one session on the heels of another. And no, I can't do much to hold it together, but what I can do, I will."

"Run the Machines!" The voice roared into the void around them, from nowhere and everywhere, and then Ahab was clambering impossibly up from below. It hauled its bulk onto the walkway with a combination of flurrying legs and eeling body, biomechanical head swinging blindly about. "We will delve into the abyss!" it declared. "The work nears completion!"

Jaine shrank back from the Naeromathi's bulk, her face set. Idris expected her to argue, even with this force of nature, but Ahab *was* the boss. More than that, though, there was something between them. Some obligation, or past, which meant she couldn't say no. He considered it, and in that moment the fire of his own crusade guttered. Clarity came to him, seeing his own ranting and frothing about this business like a stranger, and he wondered, *Am I the mad one now? When did that happen?*

"Ahab," he said. He was going to say no, turn on his heel and suggest they wait. Except they really *couldn't* wait. Olli and Solace would make it down somehow, all well-meaning and planning to take him back before Uskaro could grab him. Or it would be Uskaro and his thugs, come to seize him. And he had to know. There was no other place but this. He could search a thousand years and not discover a working piece of Originator tech with which to observe the universe as he could here.

The Naeromathi stared at him, insofar as Idris could even tell.

"We do it," Idris decided. "Both of us, both terminals." He winced at Jaine's look. "As quick as we can, but we need to know. It's for nothing, everything's for nothing. We need to break through into whatever's there and find a way to win the war."

Olli

Olli did the maths. They had maybe fifteen minutes before the Partheni got in, hours more before the first Hugh gunboat joined them.

She thought it would be tail-between-his-legs time for Uskaro, but he wasn't breaking orbit. Instead the *Raptorid* was . . .

Shooting.

He didn't believe they had Idris aboard then, or maybe a dead Idris was preferable to a Partheni Idris. The first line of accelerator shot should have drilled them dead, piercing the hull in a dozen places. Kit had already been sitting on their shields, though. The *Vulture*'s gravitic drive twisted the gradient of space ahead of them so that the shot—aimed dead centre at their sluggish bulk—went haring off at an angle without deviating even slightly, following the physics to nowhere. Then Olli had them moving, brachator drives yanking the ship sideways. They felt the burn as they clipped deeper into Criccieth's radiationsphere for a moment and then shunted towards the *Raptorid*, even as Uskaro's gunners adjusted on the basis they'd be moving *away*. But Olli wasn't interested in skipping out right then, not even towards the oncoming Partheni cavalry. She was going to bring the fight to Uskaro, as planned, and she didn't care how many Voyenni bully boys he had lined up at the airlock when she arrived. She'd back the Scorpion against all of them.

Kit started flailing about with the *Vulture God*'s lasers, which were meant for nothing more than carving up debris. It gave the *Raptorid* something more to think about, though, and Olli reckoned she didn't need much distraction. The other ship was nimbler than they were, and far better armed, but there was one way the *God* could smash any record Uskaro set. Salvage vessels came with great big grunty grav drives, allowing them to haul other ships across the universe. They also had those godawful ugly docking clamps that hung beneath them like oversized talons. If Uskaro let them get close enough then they'd have him.

The second volley from the *Raptorid*'s guns had gone even

more wild than the first, but it wasn't a state of affairs that was going to persist. The *Vulture God* had committed to a course now, and she braced for the next salvo.

It didn't come, however, and they lumbered on towards the *Raptorid*, which still wasn't trying to evade them, just effortlessly bending away their own laser fire.

"They had us right then," she spat, and now wondered if Uskaro was taking their approach as a surrender, or just deciding that taking them alive would be even better than cutting them up and opening them to vacuum. On which thought... "Who's not got a suit on?"

She caught Havaer getting half into one, nobody having told him where they were. The Scorpion was eminently spaceworthy already, and she knew Tothiat were only mildly inconvenienced by hard vacuum. Kit had already ducked into a clamshell-shaped Hanni cover that was inflating around him and part of his seat. And of course Solace was in her armour now, which made her a contender alongside Olli and Heremon for most dangerous thing aboard.

The *Raptorid* was still not shooting, but now they were moving, kicking away from the planet below, increasing the thousands of klicks of distance between them and their quarry. The Partheni continued to close, which was presumably what Uskaro was worried about, but...

"They had their chance to fuck us up," Olli said, frowning. "What's the deal? This your Hiver's work?"

"I think so," Havaer confirmed. "Colvari can't do much without getting discovered and locked out, but I suspect the *Raptorid*'s developed a 'convenient' weapons fault."

"Won't matter. You'll not catch them now. Should have the

Pathos hold off or something," Heremon suggested.

"Solace?" Olli craned around. Solace was deep in conversation with her compatriots but she broke off.

"I've a combat shuttle being readied, a Myrmidon squad too. I'll go down the well in it. To grab Idris. Whether or not he wants to be grabbed."

"You'll fry," Olli pointed out.

"*When* the well opens again. Until then, all the guns here will be ours." Her voice was hard, the faceless faceplate of her helm menacing. *A little slice of Parthenon territory in the heart of the Colonies*, Olli thought, and didn't like it much. Didn't like which side she was apparently on at all, tell the truth, but she disliked Uskaro even more. In the end, the only side she was really on was her crew's, Idris and Kris included. Speaking of . . .

"And Kris?"

"If we can run the *Raptorid* down we will," Solace told her, all business and suddenly in charge. "I think we're faster than his damn yacht, however flashy it is."

It struck Olli that this was probably going to be the first shooting engagement of this new war everyone seemed dead set on having, and that she might actually end up in the historiotypes. The thought did not delight her. And probably whoever played her would have too many limbs and not enough attitude.

She ran a quick plot of the vastness of space, populating it with planet, *God*, *Raptorid* and the oncoming Partheni, now spreading out from an arrowhead into a net. She looked at trajectories and estimated effective weapons ranges. It seemed to her that Uskaro would be getting away no matter how much faster the Pathos were. Solace seemed confident, though, and maybe Havaer's Hiver could throw something more into the gears, send their drive into a maintenance cycle or something. She might not like her current allies much but she'd take them if it meant they rescued Kris. Sometimes it was a good thing to have some big guns on your side for once.

"Our combat shuttle's launched," Solace reported. "The others are moving in on the—"

Olli felt as though she'd been punched. No, she felt as though *space* had been punched. The *Vulture God* was abruptly lurching madly sideways without moving at all as something distorted everything around them. The whole gravitic gradient flexed to within an inch of breaking point. She thought, *A weapon?* And then, *Hegemony?* Whatever had just happened seemed ridiculously flashy enough to be their doing. But it was just Hugh. The navy doing something risky because the Parthenon had turned up on their doorstep and they couldn't let that go.

Of course there were combat Ints within Hugh. A fair slice of the conscripts the Liaison Board turned out went to the navy instead of commercial interests. Naturally the base on Orichalk had one. But having an Int and having an Int willing to try a stutter-jump within system were two very different things.

It was almost a fatal mistake. Jumping short distances through an unspace cluttered with gravity signatures was master-level stuff. Idris could do it, but Idris had decades of experience. Most Ints wouldn't even have thought of it. Even jumping too close to another *ship* was risky, and this unknown hero here had ripped their cruiser out from under the nose of the naval base, very nearly pile-driving it right into Criccieth's Hell. They had come out in the upper reaches of the radiationsphere, under caustic attack from the world's unholy light, clawing to get away from gravity and glare, but already shooting with accelerators and heavy lasers, the one battery in two that was still online. Their targets were probably the Partheni, but in that moment their aim was so mad and wide they could have been trying to assassinate the universe at large.

The *Intrepid*, Olli read their ID as, and they were certainly living up to their name.

Solace was speaking quick and low to her Partheni fellows. Even damaged, the *Intrepid* brought a lot of punch to the fight, more than their little task force could manage, pound for pound. It wasn't daunting them, though. Partheni tech superiority would have to step in where sheer power was lacking. The largest of their ships was already launching a wing of Zero fighters, the tiny one-woman killers that had gone up against Architects during the war. The rest were altering course, wheeling into a new formation.

"*Raptorid*'s stopped running," Heremon observed drily.

"Course they fucking have," Olli decided. "Let's make them regret it."

"The well is open again," Solace reported flatly. "And our combat shuttle's coming in with some Partheni backup on board. We need to get down there."

Idris

He was screaming at them when they pulled him from the Machine, but that stopped soon enough when he felt everything around them shifting. Not just physically, either.

He could sense the space/unspace boundary twisting, like a serpent held between tongs, as the Machine tormented it. And the Machine was still running, with the facility still being eroded away by Criccieth's glare. Somewhere far to his left he saw a sudden shock of light that seared his retinas with afterimages in hideous, nameless colours. There was the sound of great cliffs grinding against one another. Jaine was shouting at him, physically dragging him away from the seat. He saw Doctor Shinandri standing aside, looking shaken.

"You better have found it," Jaine was telling him. "I need you to get Ahab to stop."

"Ahab? Stop?" Idris stammered at her.

"It's still under. Talk to it, bring it out. It won't listen to me," Jaine told him. "The facility's at critical. We're breaking up." Seeing his gormless expression she actually slapped him, right across the face. "Countless millions of years, Int, and we broke it. We came and turned it on and broke it, the only one of its kind. So get Ahab to come out so I can stick a damn med-patch on the thing, at least."

"We were almost—"

"You're always almost!" she shouted, and then she was hauling him off, practically bundling him up a ladder to the next leaning section of floor. It groaned and shook even as she did so.

She'd rigged up some comms there, and Idris found himself gabbling into them, taking it on faith that Ahab was even listening on the other end. Because in the Machine it was hard to remember the real world was out there, even though you were being held at the very skin between *there* and *nowhere.*

They had been so close, penetrating the walls of the Location down there within the depths of unspace. It was just a matter of interpreting what they had seen.

There was no matter in unspace. Matter was a real thing, of the real universe. It couldn't exist, down there. He understood this now in a way he never had—perhaps in a way nobody ever did, save those extreme specialists like Shinandri. And it was theoretical to Shinandri. Idris had embraced the concept with all the flayed potential of his Intermediary mind.

So there was something down there, a place, except unspace didn't work like space and the things in it had no physical existence. What unspace *did* have was energy, a great deal of energy, and it had structure, which meant information. There was a vast information cluster down there, a configuration of energy, and it was doing something. That was today's discovery. It wasn't just a dead ruin, a construction shack left over from when they built the Throughways. The structure of its absence had moving parts. It was like a galaxy coming together, things accreting, spinning, exchanging data.

The Machine had let him see it, as though it was a Thing that was actually There, but he and Ahab and Shinandri still needed to work out what it was they were looking at. Idris was convinced more than ever that, if he looked hard enough, he'd see the face of their enemy. He'd understand what minds had set the Architects to plague real space and twist all the planets of humans and other sentient races. Because sentience was the thing that called to the enemy, that much he'd gathered. Sentience imposed itself on the skin of unspace. It resounded through all those non-existent spaces. Every thought, and Int thoughts most of all. It was like a swimmer splashing on the surface of a sea where vast hungry mouths dwelled.

"The Crusade!" from Ahab, and Idris realized he'd got through to him at last. There was a terrible shrieking sound of abused metal from somewhere, and killing light flickered at the edge of his vision before being shut off again. Jaine had a fleet of repair robots out mindlessly patching every crack they could find, but without the facility's own shielding they were being ablated away.

"Just a short break," Idris insisted, wondering how much of his Colvul was even making it through the Naeromathi's translator. "You know me. I want it too. And we'll go back in. Together, we'll go. We'll open it up and find out what it is and—and how to break it. How to fight them, Ahab. That's what you want, right? But we'll do it together. Give Jaine a chance to get things stable again, and we'll go right back in."

A sound came over the comms from Ahab, wordless, agonized, monstrous. A lifetime of frustration, Idris read into that noise. A lifetime in the shadow of lost homes and twisted worlds. The whole Naeromathi species was living in trauma, staggering from system to system, devouring and building more shell-shocked cyborgs to carry on the hopeless fight. But Ahab wasn't here with a Locust Ark in tow. It was alone, cut off even from its conspecifics' broken society. Somehow it had found this place, and that there *was* a way they could fight back. Or at least identify the enemy at last.

Then the shuddering and grinding and flashes of deadly light stopped, and Idris knew he'd got through to Ahab. The other Machine terminal had shut off, and the shield was back up.

Which meant the well was open again, that perfect narrow shaft of safety from the installation up into space.

His friends, his desperately unwanted friends, would be coming to get him.

He turned to Jaine, expecting to see her at least grudgingly grateful, but instead she was pulling open a screen in the air, taking a point by the corners and yanking it out until a rectangle hung before her, showing... Idris was pilot enough to recognize orbital manoeuvres. Things had gone to crap up there while he was down. He had a frantic five seconds of hunting before he found the *Vulture God*, because there was a lot of violence going on and it was way out of the old ship's league. He noticed a Hugh cruiser that had turned up out of where-the-hell, and it was confronting a wing of oncoming Partheni. Meanwhile the *God* and the *Raptorid* were engaging in a careful dance to avoid any stray shards of battle, while still trying to close with one another.

And one vessel was launching. There had been a ship tucked in the *Vulture*'s claws, a sleek little Partheni shuttle from Jaine's readings, and now it was dropping. Into the atmosphere, fighting furiously to hit the narrow well that would bring them straight down to Idris.

Olli

The Partheni shuttle attracted some fire from the *Intrepid* as it cut across to get to the *Vulture*. The navy cruiser was devoting most of its attention to the bigger Partheni ships, though, which were very much returning the favour, using speed and gravitic shielding to dance through the hail of accelerator fire, missile salvos and lasers it was sending their way. "Shuttle" wasn't really the word for it, Olli decided as she watched it approach. It was a grunty little thing, its shape giving the impression of someone huddled in a coat against foul weather, shoulders up to their ears. The ring of its gravitic drive was right up front rather than around the vessel's nominal waist, so any serious damage to the drive would likely gut the crew compartment too. The rest of the ship trailed off in a segmented tail, narrowing drastically to a fine point. It had four accelerator cannons—overcompensating a bit for anything pretending to the name of "shuttle." These were mounted on a rail along the outside hub of the drive ring, letting them point everywhere but inwards at the ship itself.

Solace was already on the move to join her sisters. "I'm going to take command of the shuttle now," she said to Olli, because apparently she could do that. "I'll go get Idris and bring him back. You...I don't know. If Havaer can get you to Kris—"

"I'll get her," Olli confirmed. "They don't know we've got a Tothiat."

"Except I'll be on that shuttle," Heremon pointed out.

"No," Solace said. "You will not."

"Yeah, I need you with me," Olli agreed. She didn't like *needing* anything from the woman, but times were hard.

"You forget that, whoever has your friend down there, *they* have a Tothiat too," Heremon said. "And, because you've doubtless given the Patho some of the poison you stuck Mesmon with last time, know that dear sister Emmaneth *tried* that already. Stuck herself full of it when she couldn't stand what she'd become, the weak-livered traitor. It didn't kill her. Not even that. So you're going to need me or she'll tear you and your little tin soldiers apart."

Olli couldn't see Solace's face through her visor, but she could guess at the Partheni's expression. She didn't want the Broken Harvest gangster at her back, and Olli could have done with Heremon at her front, but the woman made a good case.

"I'll go with you to get Almier," Havaer volunteered. "I can liaise with Colvari, my associate. And I can shoot."

"You're a piss-poor human shield compared to her," Olli told him, "but I don't reckon we've got much odds. Kit, you're happy running the show while we're all out?"

"Very little of these circumstances make me *happy*," Kittering told her sourly. "Do not make me mourn you."

She reckoned that was serious stuff for a Hanni to say, and it choked her up a little but she didn't let on. "Go get to your clone army," she told Solace, as gruffly as she could.

Kittering took the Partheni shuttle in their claws as it arrived—the *Sturgeon*, they'd called it, and maybe it did look as much like a fish as the *Vulture God* did a bird. Then Solace and Heremon were trooping out to go meet the strike team. Olli didn't give them good odds to even navigate the well, truth be told.

She felt more than heard the clunk and shudder of disengagement as the *Sturgeon* dropped away into the void, jockeying desperately to match its descent vector to the exacting requirements of the one safe path down.

"Move in on the Uskaro bastard," she told Kit, running checks over the Scorpion's systems and finding a pleasing battery of green lights.

"They're launching," Havaer noted.

"What? The Partheni? The *Intrepid?*" Olli pulled up an orbital map and tried to see what he'd spotted.

"The *Raptorid*. Two armed shuttles." And there they were, tracking the *Sturgeon* in its descent, matching its navigation as a cheap alternative to calculating their own. Uskaro was onto them, and he wasn't going to give up Idris that easily. Olli reckoned the smart money would have been on waiting for the Partheni ship to come *back* up the well, except maybe by then the *Intrepid* would have crash-dived into atmosphere and the victorious battle-sisters chased Uskaro away or blown him up. *Or I'll have cut his face off in person, the son of a bitch.*

Kit had already checked Solace knew about her unwelcome followers, and Olli reckoned the ball was in the Partheni's court regarding what to do about them. It did suggest a silver lining, however.

"He's just gutted his own garrison," she pointed out to Havaer. "Let's go finish the job."

29.

Solace

The *Sturgeon* dropped away from the *Vulture God* fast enough that they felt the lurching shift dragging at them, the hunger of Criccieth's gravity well below. Then their gravitic drives compensated and it was all Earth standard again, no sense of the ungodly tug of war between acceleration and deceleration as they tilted to take on the outer reaches of the world's atmosphere. It was toxic, that atmosphere, Solace knew. Quite apart from the radiation saturating it, the fierce fire of the too-close sun and the reflected death from the leaves and petals of the planet's life, the actual chemical composition of the air would strip the inside of human lungs down to blood and jelly in seconds. Nothing about Criccieth's Hell was *nice*.

There were four Myrmidons aboard, including the pilot. With Heremon and herself, that made up the *Sturgeon*'s full recommended complement. But Idris was a little guy. They'd fit him in somehow. And if it happened that Heremon got left behind, Solace reckoned she'd take that as acceptable losses. And yes, she had the Tothiat-killer syringe on her, just in case. Even if it wasn't the magic bullet she'd hoped.

"Du màdieu!" the pilot swore in Parsef, fighting the controls.

The ship shuddered and lurched about them, trying to cleave into the atmosphere cleanly but getting caught by crosswinds almost immediately. Solace hunched behind her, looking past her shoulder at the displays. They were attempting to track the edges of the well, but interference from the radiation-sphere was turning a hard line into a zone two hundred metres across, with that killer boundary in there somewhere. One slip across and the world's glare would devour them, past all the ability of their shielding to deflect it.

Heremon, at her elbow and the only one there without engagement armour, grinned. She and Solace were standing in the middle of the tight crew compartment that was muscled right up within the ring of the ship's gravitic drive. The pilot and her mate were in bucket seats ahead, with the other two Myrmidons behind and facing sideways, strapped in and waiting. Normally, standing loose in a ship like this should have been safe, but not now. Solace grabbed a strap and buckled herself to the wall. Heremon sneered at her a little. It would take more than a few unprotected high-G manoeuvres to inconvenience her, that expression said.

"Pursuers," the pilot's mate said.

"Hugh?" Solace craned forward against the strap, and the mate sent the display to her helmet HUD. Two ships were coming down the well behind them, identified as armed shuttles. Not their equal, but they weren't in a position to turn and fight. From the *Raptorid*, she noted. That meant Voyenni: tough and motivated but without the discipline she'd expect from Hugh military.

"Carve them up," she said flatly. They were at war and she didn't have either time or inclination to put the velvet gloves back on. The two Myrmidons in the back seats took over the

Sturgeon's accelerators, pointing them backwards down the tapering length of the hull and trying to fix on the shuttles.

"They're already firing," the mate noted flatly, and Solace saw the telltale signs of the *Sturgeon* returning the favour. It was a nasty situation to be in for all concerned. The corridor they were trapped in was narrow, and normally that would have meant every target being fixed on and chewed up in moments. Except the radiation interference was playing hob with any kind of targeting, leading to the gunners relying more on personal reckoning than their instruments. All the while they were dropping further into the atmosphere, which became more turbulent as it got thicker, crippling the pilot's ability to do anything other than fight the angry weather they were hitting. One crosswind too many would send them straight out of the well and into the death-glare beyond.

Solace was standing helpless in the middle of it. She was the Executor, the officer in charge, and that was her place. Except in her heart she was still just a Myrmidon, Heaven's Sword Sorority, Basilisk Division, and she wanted to be the one who *did*, not just the one who ordered and watched.

A trail of accelerator shot clipped them, punching three holes in the hull and one through the ring of the gravitic drive. Tiny holes, and nowhere near the crew compartment. Solace looked over the damage readouts: everything was functional, but the problem with gravitic drives was you never really knew you were screwed until physics decided to slap you. They'd scored some hits on the leading shuttle in return, but nothing that would have satisfied a gunnery instructor. She patched into the gunners' targeting feeds, seeing a nightmare of shifting radiation. Even here within the corridor, the shuttles' images appeared and vanished like ghosts.

A moment later they hit a bank of turbulence like a solid thing, bouncing off the dense, roiling air and losing a chunk of momentum, cutting the distance between them and their pursuers in half. That should have fouled everyone's aim but ended up putting them right into the path of a heavy laser from the rear shuttle. She saw a scatter of alarms as their gravitic field absorbed the energy, and for a moment she was off the floor and in freefall as the drives abandoned any attempt at a-grav. Instead, the laser energy was shunted back along the hull, deflected into the last narrow sections of the *Sturgeon* as though it were a lightning rod. The sections crisped and crumpled and were ejected, and the ship continued its mad descent. Partheni segmentation tech had been developed to buy a few more seconds of life against the Architects. It could handle a laser.

Moments later, the gunners pinned the lead shuttle between them, raking its flank with a solid salvo of accelerator shot that acted like a blade. It created not just punctures, which any hull would immediately seal, but a gash half the length of the ship's hull, peeling it open and exposing its innards. The Voyenni shuttle lurched sideways, then the wind had it and was buffeting it further. It started to tumble, presenting its flank to the rushing tides of air.

Then it must have clipped out of the corridor altogether because it was suddenly gone, blasted apart, perhaps even to atoms. Just...gone. Solace swallowed. *That might be us in a moment.*

That moment arrived hot on the heels of her thought, as the remaining shuttle caught them and hit their small craft with everything it had. Higher up, they had thinner atmosphere to contend with, a hair's breadth more liberty to move and to target. Now she saw a whole quarter of the *Sturgeon*'s gravitic drive disintegrate under their salvo, lines of accelerator shot cutting into them like razor wire. Their pilot swore and swore again and Solace was abruptly weightless, yanking ferociously against her straps. Then gravity returned, system redundancy fighting desperately to take up the strain. She saw Heremon clinging to the wall, her cockiness entirely gone, one leg twisted at an unnatural angle but already mending.

The storm grabbed them at last and hurled them sidelong out of the well.

Solace's HUD lit up with every possible thing that could go wrong and she waited for some suitably pithy last thought to occur, but most of her was too busy screaming silently.

A moment later they were back in the narrow corridor, dropping more like a stone than a landing ship but safely out of the glare. The segmentation had cut in again, diligently preserving the crew compartment as well as the three-quarters of the gravitic drive they still had, at the expense of just about everything behind it, with all that radiation energy funnelled back to obliterate two-thirds of the ship's length. If they'd wanted any spare kit from the hold, they were out of luck because the hold wasn't there anymore.

They were also out of luck, Solace strongly suspected, if they wanted to get the *Sturgeon* back up the well with Idris, or at least they'd need one hell of a good fix-up to even try it. But that was tomorrow's problem.

"Cease fire!" she ordered, her mouth forming the words almost before she'd come up with the plan.

"Mother?" one of the gunners queried her.

"Cease fire. Leave the other shuttle intact." Why fix their

own ride when the Voyenni were bringing a serviceable replacement?

Idris

It wasn't easy to get a picture of what was going on in the well. The external sensors Idris had access to weren't Originator "god-tech" but just whatever Jaine had been able to bolt onto the facility. Still, he could see the basics: the *Vulture God* had launched one ship, the *Raptorid* two and therefore anything from three to zero ships would be touching down atop the facility.

Emmaneth was all for going up and killing whoever arrived. She had her own ship up there, which had a few surprises, she said. Plus there was a scatter of other vessels, mostly mothballed, in a shielded hangar. Everyone who'd made it to the installation had their own transport, though none of them had made many excursions off-planet since then, apart from the Tothiat. Jaine didn't sound confident any of their vessels would be able to make it into space without some serious maintenance. Even within the shelter of Originator walls, the planet's corroding radiance crept in through the cracks.

"So what, then? Can we even get a view of who's come knocking?" Emmaneth demanded.

"I'm trying." Jaine had some eyes up top, but they never lasted, so she was attempting some remote maintenance, re-routing around the damage to find a view. They were in the common room, in the upper levels above the great scaffolded void around the Machine. Emmaneth, Jaine, Idris,

Shinandri. Ahab was somewhere below, recharging its cybernetics, or perhaps just indulging in some Naeromathi vengeance ritual, or however it spent its spare time.

Then Jaine, who'd been wrestling with an ungodly mess of a bolted-together console for some time, let out a cry of triumph. She pulled up a screen from it, a rectangle in the air, and he saw a hideously mauled stub of a Partheni ship manage a skidding landing, gouging a scar in the Originator stone. The crew piled out of it almost immediately. There were five Myrmidons and one unarmoured figure, a woman he reckoned he'd seen but couldn't place.

Emmaneth could, apparently. She practically shoved him aside for a better look. "Oh, well," she said. "Look who it ain't. I thought you said they were friends of yours, Menheer Int."

"They are. Or the ship above is. I'm friends with one of them, at least." They were losing the image, armies of static particles marching across the view and taking up strategic positions. It looked as though the Myrmidons were taking cover and waiting, so presumably there was at least one more ship still on its way. "They're Partheni, and I've...been working with them. They'll want me back."

"*She* is not Partheni," Emmaneth pointed out. "She is Broken Harvest. My old crew. And they'll want *me* back, not in a good way."

"I can't account for that," Idris admitted. He reckoned he'd seen the shadow of another ship coming down, but then the static surged across the screen and all sight of the dock was lost. "Jaine, can we—" he started, but a roaring interrupted him.

"Idris!" Resounding from the walls all around. "Telemmier!

503

Come to me! We must find the truth! There is no time! None must be allowed to prevent us! The Machine, Idris!"

"No!" Jaine shouted. "Ahab, no! We're not ready. Repairs are under way I'm shoring up the walls. I've got some field generators in place, but they're still calibrating. Ahab, you'll bring it all down. We have time. Please, don't do this!"

"There is no time!" the walls thundered at them. "They know, now! We have felt their fear, Idris, and they will not suffer us! They will make dust of us! We must pierce to their heart before they close their jaws upon us!"

"Is he saying there's an Architect coming...now?" Jaine asked flatly.

There was a moment of dead silence in the wake of her words, and then Shinandri let out a dreadful giggle, high and hysterical.

"I suppose, yes, there *might* be, indubitably. You have, after all, rather hooked their attention with your spelunking, if indeed that is the correct term. But rather, if you'll permit me to temper your expectations..." His whole face twitched, a tic too large to permit translation. "It's Ahab," he went on in a hushed voice, as though the Naeromathi wouldn't be able to hear him if he whispered. "It's how Ahab sees the universe, you see."

"I don't see," Emmaneth told him, though Idris reckoned she did.

"The Architects are *always* coming, for Ahab," Doctor Shinandri said sadly. "It will always be running from them. Even when it's standing still."

"With you or without!" Ahab insisted. Perhaps it hadn't heard him, or perhaps his words just didn't translate, not being relevant to the Naeromathi's obsession. "I cannot wait!"

"He's already in the Machine," Jaine said. She had another screen up, a rough plan of the installation. It was something she'd obviously thrown together herself, and tracking Ahab or her fellow inmates was probably its primary function. "Boss, no!"

They heard the shudder and thunder of the shield giving way as the Machine activated. Then Ahab started hunting the great dark seas of unspace, the abyss below.

"Wait," Idris said. "What happens to whoever's up top?"

"They either get inside right away," Emmaneth confirmed, "or they're fucked."

Solace

The field they'd landed on was not a field, for one. Not even level. It was a great stone shelf slanted at fifteen degrees from the horizontal towards...hell. Criccieth's Hell. A mountainside, overlooking the pits of it. And hell had come up from those pits to glower all around them, impossible to look at directly. Solace's visor could cut the glare to ensure she didn't actually lose her eyes from the exposure to that awful light, and yet...she couldn't look. The colours turned her stomach, invaded her skull. Just the first wash of it as she got out of the remains of the *Sturgeon* almost led to a misstep that would have had her rolling down the slope and off the edge. One of the Myrmidons grabbed her arm and steadied her, and then they were all running for whatever shelter there was. Running uphill, towards the bleak bulk of the mountain that at least blotted the worst of the light out. Towards a scatter of artificial overhangs, a dozen different holes and entryways made in a style she knew all too well. Originator construction, but not just the worn stubs she'd seen before. A castle from the worst sort of fairytales, spearing up into the sky, its twisted spires erupting from the glassy black rock. She looked up, following their lines, and almost fell again. The sky was full of those monstrous hell-flowers, great glass-plate petals and leaves overlapping and poisoning the light so that it rained on her like visible corruption. Beyond them, smudged and blurred until its fires were filthy, was the great angry ember of the system's sun.

The worst planet in the universe. Yet she and her companions weren't dead. The fires of that sun and the radiation it sparked from the foliage hadn't blasted them to dust. Even Heremon was still with them, unsuited, though she had her hands over her eyes and was turned away from it all, any of her snark burnt away.

Then the Voyenni shuttle came crashing down, skewing wildly across the sky so that for a moment she thought they'd miss the landing platform altogether, but it righted itself and ploughed to a halt by the *Sturgeon*'s mortal remains. The plan had been for the Partheni to ambush them as they came out, then secure the shuttle for their own exit.

It seemed plans didn't last long on Criccieth's Hell. The Voyenni came surging out all at once, because the shuttle had a freight hatch rather than just a narrow bottleneck for personnel. Moreover, they led with a crab-hand, the vehicle scuttling out with its accelerator cannon already hot and lashing randomly about the slope of the landing pad. A good half-dozen Voyenni followed it, wearing at least rudimentary combat armour. They also had the shuttle's gravitic drive throwing up a shield to shrug off the initial salvo of shot the Myrmidons sent their way. They didn't have sophisticated enough targeting to overcome their own field, though, and for a moment the landing site was a storm of shot going everywhere except where it was aimed.

Heremon was already exploring inside, being the only one without an accelerator. She called out that she'd found a way in, leading deeper into the installation. Solace made the decision that dealing with the Voyenni and having a way off-planet was the priority for now. The worry was that Heremon would remember she didn't take orders from any Partheni and just go find Idris or Emmaneth, or both of them, herself.

Solace had one of the Myrmidons make target tracker calculations, sending telemetry to everyone's HUDs about where to aim, adjusting for the Voyenni craft's shield. Their exploratory bursts of fire were getting closer and the enemy weren't adjusting their defences fast enough to compensate. *We have them.*

Then the crab-hand had *them* and they were forced to retreat after Heremon to get clear of the mad ricochet of accelerator fire as it pitched a barrel-full through their doorway. Solace took a nick across the helmet and one of the Myrmidons reported a single pellet through the arm, wound sealed and painkillers administered. Then the telemetrist came up with a firing solution for them. Solace braced herself to get back out there and bring the rest of the Voyenni down.

Heremon was shouting at her, though. "The light! The light!" and for a moment she just didn't want to listen to the woman, a civilian, a criminal, getting in the way of her nice clean war. But her own HUD readouts were telling her the same thing. Something was happening to the glare out there. It was getting stronger, breaking through.

She hadn't even realized anything was holding it back, but now this became appallingly obvious. The Voyenni had stopped shooting. One of the Myrmidons threw out a remote eye to observe them and Solace linked to it.

They were running for another of the openings, pelting full tilt into its shadow. Not for fear of anything Solace's people could do to them. To get out of the *light*. As she tracked them, she realized the advance of Criccieth's killer radiance across the field was slow enough for her eyes to register its progress. It nipped at their enemies' heels, and then it caught the crab-hand, which had been covering their retreat. Its crew were still trying to climb out of it, but she saw the metal warp and glow. It wasn't the glow of heat; there was no cherry red or incandescent white there. The glow ran through greens and yellows and then into eye-wrenching hues she couldn't name and would see in her nightmares. The machine sagged, then parts of it exploded. Other parts were being twisted as though invisible hands were rending them. She couldn't watch and felt bile rise in her mouth. The crab-hand crew fared the same, too late to find cover.

Before the remote eye was blinded, she saw their shuttle and the *Sturgeon* begin their own fatal rendering-down.

No way off-planet now.

Except people were *on*-planet, Idris and Emmaneth and this Shinandri. They must have a ship somewhere. She gave quick orders to her people: *Whoever we find, keep them alive.*

They were in a low corridor with rounded edges, curving off to the left and downwards. Someone had installed a great metal door across it, plainly not part of the original construction. Everything around them seemed to be shaking, and she could see a spiderwork of cracks through the Originator stone. Her head was full of a thunder that wasn't in her ears, just the sense of a constant assault on everything around them.

"Get this—" she started, but Heremon had the door open even as she said it, ducking inside without looking back. Solace and her troops rushed after her, finding blessed shade lit only by a series of lamps stapled unevenly to the walls. The tunnel sloped down into darkness, but right then she reckoned darkness was a good friend compared to the sunny day getting into its stride outside.

Everything was still shaking, and it wasn't just her imagination. The place was under attack. She understood suddenly that the well was down again—whatever generated it also held this place out of the fires of hell, and right now it wasn't working.

All very fascinating. But where's Idris?

There was a makeshift terminal by the door they'd just passed through, and one of her Myrmidons was already trying to patch into it. Minimal security, just like the door. Whoever set all this up hadn't been too worried about intruders. Given conditions outside, Solace could appreciate that. Not the sort of place anyone was likely to just stumble across.

"What have we got?" she asked.

"A network, Mother," came the report. "All very... Colonial." By which the Myrmidon meant the sort of rough and unlovely lash-up that spacers relied on. Solace had come to respect that kind of engineering, but it wouldn't win any prizes for aesthetics, and no two versions of it ever worked in quite the same way. "Colossal energy drain. From the planet itself, the life outside. I'm..." A display stuttered into being, projected from the console. Solace couldn't make it out, but apparently it represented some complex power harvesting system. Rotating collectors dipped into the poison well of Criccieth's Hell and were then repaired. Plenty of energy if you could survive it.

"Doing what, though?" She was wondering if all this was just an archaeologist's jolly, given she'd never seen Originator buildings so complete. If Trine turned out to be the mastermind behind this she wouldn't be happy.

"Here." They had a map, or at least a network of powerlines that presumably shadowed actual physical space. It was huge, burrowing into the mountain. She could see dense-packed layers up top where they were, and then some vast cavernous space beyond where the points of power were spread thinly. And down at the bottom... Well, she had no idea, but that was where all the energy went. It was being sucked down there right now. Whatever the current residents' purpose was on this world, they were doing it there in the depths.

"Find me a way down," she said, wondering if the surviving Voyenni had a tech with them, and if they'd be following the same breadcrumbs downwards.

30.

Olli

The *Raptorid* danced round them as they came on. Olli tracked the spiral shifting of their course as Kittering did his best to get close, but the Magdan yacht kept space effortlessly between them. They were far enough out in the void that the human eye would have seen only a glint. It was trying to put distance between itself and the Partheni too, and the pair of them were drifting out of the fray as the *Intrepid* took up the invaders' attention.

Then, just as she was about to tear her hair out in frustration at how they were being played, the *Raptorid*'s next course correction didn't happen. They just continued coasting on a predictable line and the distance between her and the *Vulture God* was being eaten up second by second. Kittering opened the claws in readiness to latch on.

Havaer gave a little grunt of satisfaction.

"That your pal again, huh?" Olli asked him. "Colbert?"

"Colvari," he confirmed. "Says they've locked the Magdans out of their brachator drive but not for long. Uskaro has override keys they won't be able to get past. They're trying to box off the main hatch so they can open up for us when we're on it. After that, they'll only have access to a few trivial systems and it'll be as much as they can do to turn a few lights off and on."

"It's enough," Olli decided. She was tracking Kit's approach, because he wasn't the greatest pilot in the galaxy, but right now the *Raptorid* was a sitting duck. "You got a gun, Mordant man?"

He did, a little magnetic piece he'd been keeping who knew where. Hopefully it packed a bigger punch than its size suggested. The Voyenni would have some decent kit, she was sure, but they'd also be aboard their own ship, so probably wouldn't be breaking out the accelerators if they had any worries about hull integrity. Similarly, unless she was banking on Kris being able to hold her breath *really* well, she didn't want to go wild with the heavy armaments herself.

Also, Havaer just had a standard suit on and, though it was puncture resistant and rugged, it wouldn't keep out a determined knife thrust, let alone a bullet. And it wasn't as if they'd be making much of a sneaky entrance. The Voyenni would be ready for them when they broke in.

"Okay," Olli decided. "This is how we do it."

*

Far too many slow minutes later, she saw the energy flare in the other ship's systems as they got their drives back online. This meant Colvari was now locked out of anything that would be really useful to them. By then it was too late for the *Raptorid*, though. The *God* was right on them. The one accelerator cannon the Magdans could bring around in time, now they had weapons control again, chewed a nasty scar along the salvage vessel's hull. Damage control said it was all cosmetic, and they'd given up winning beauty contests a long time ago. Olli sent a message to Havaer, checking he was ready at the umbilical.

The *God* landed, Kit erring on the side of enthusiasm so that the impact shuddered through the ship. Olli's display showed her twenty new red lights, which meant twenty brand-new jobs to go onto the maintenance to-do list. No time to chew Kit out for clumsy flying, though. He had the docking claws latched onto the *Raptorid*, and that meant the only way the ships would be going their separate ways was by means of the *God*'s control pod, or after a hell of a lot of cutting work. Kit hadn't exactly positioned them bang on the Magdan ship's own hatch, but the umbilical was flexible. Havaer jockeyed it in a series of scraping lurches along the other ship's hull, until its low-grade AI recognized a door and it locked on.

"Your friend still has the door?" Olli asked him, alone down there.

She took his tense grunt as confirmation.

"Get me eyes in there?"

The image feed flashed up on her display a moment later. She saw three Voyenni, all in light armour, waiting in the cover of the hatch bulkheads. They had chemical propellant pistols, low power enough not to damage the hull but they would put holes in Havaer easily enough. They each had an axe in their off-hand too, which was a nasty little trick. The weapons had beak-like heads, and Olli reckoned they had some kind of explosive kick to them as well, to punch through inconvenient obstacles like people.

The third Voyenni had taken a whole panel off the wall and was going at it with a toolkit and extreme prejudice.

They knew they'd lost the door control but they'd have it back shortly. Until then, they were ready for whatever came out of the *God* at them.

"Hey, Mordant," she signalled down to Havaer. "Have your Hiver fight them over control of the door. Make it loud. Strip the servos. Whatever you can to distract them."

"You had better be able to pull this off, Timo," he told her flatly. He could see the same images, of course, and he didn't fancy his chances. A contested entry of one against three.

She had wasted a couple of moments considering whether to let that happen, maybe being late to the party for her part of the plan. He was a spook after all and not to be trusted, and they were going to have to fight over Idris at some point. But she reckoned right now a live Mundy was more use than a corpse, and she didn't fancy his Hiver spook pal hacking her ass in revenge. So much for that.

The door started to open, and Olli saw the two gunmen tense, ready to shoot or just pile in with axes as the situation warranted. The hatch was shuddering and sparking, though, and she could see the Voyenni tech frowning, because it wasn't down to anything he'd done. Colvari was making a big show of fighting their own efforts to access the doorway, with all the showmanship Olli could have asked for.

Olli herself was outside. She'd moved out onto the *God*'s hull during the approach, and now had herself positioned right above the hatch. The Scorpion was basically a fancy cutting tool with attitude, and so she cut. The *Raptorid* was just a yacht too. No armour plate or explosive hull sections. Olli had been carving her way into ships for years, and this one folded like tinfoil.

There was a momentary rush of atmosphere from below, but the yacht's gravitic field caught that soon enough, sealing over the breach to prevent explosive decompression. The turbulence shook the Voyenni about, though, and Olli managed to peel back enough hull to drop down in the middle of them. She had a number of limbs tipped with drills, saws and pincers, and even more deconstruction implements on the suit's whipping tail. She didn't hold back. She'd been angry and frustrated about a number of things for quite some time, ever since losing Idris on Arc Pallator. Or ever since she'd ended up in bed with the fucking Partheni, for that matter. Or possibly ever since she'd been born. Despite the alleged rough and tumble of a spacer's life, it wasn't often she got to express to the universe just how pissed off she was at how shit most of it was.

When the hatch through to the umbilical did actually open, Havaer stepped gingerly out onto a deck that was slippery with stuff that had formerly been inside Voyenni. He glanced from Olli to the hole above that she'd made. He'd probably seen some things, being who he was and who he worked for, but she reckoned she'd just added something new and nasty to his portfolio of professional experiences.

"Right, then," he said. "Lead on."

"Your boy got anything else for us?" she asked him.

"Locked out of anything but the small stuff," he confirmed. "Unless you can think of some combat use for a hairdryer or something, we're on our own." His eyes, behind the visor of his helmet, kept wandering over the mess she'd made.

"Good," Olli decided and set the Scorpion lumbering to the next door, her saws and torches already firing up.

Solace

The Originator architecture wasn't the half of it, and the displays they'd captured didn't really reflect the current layout of this place. The vast riveted sections of floor and far-too-big hatchways were striking uneasy feelings in Solace's gut regarding who or what exactly had made a home here. At the same time, there was a lot of extra scaffolding and ladder-work fit for her own scale, so maybe Emmaneth was big on home improvements.

She'd tried hailing Idris, but whatever was happening to the place around them was fritzing their comms as well. The channels were filled with screaming ghost voices that she connected with the deadly glass flowers outside, as though they were howling to get in. Maybe Idris wouldn't respond anyway, given the conversations they'd had with him from the *Vulture God*. He sounded like he'd gone native the worst way.

They were ambushed by the Voyenni just once. They dropped down into a vast metal-lined space, a layer between floors that seemed untenanted, held up by metre-thick struts leaning at crazy angles. These were shuddering too. The air between the iron resounded as though someone was panel-beating the whole place. Ever since the glare had driven them inside, everything had felt as though it was under attack. Dust sifted from every rivet and join, where the different technologies met. Then it just spun in the air in serpents of glittering motes, as though gravity wasn't sure what to do about it. Solace could feel the gravity shift as well—its hold lessening as they descended towards whatever the power signatures were below them.

Then out across this slice of space, the Voyenni appeared and opened fire on them, getting the same treatment right back. Both sides dived for whatever cover the struts could give against the scythe of accelerator shot. Solace wondered if they were about to just cut to pieces all the supports for the upper floors. She braced for the colossal weight of metal ceiling to come down on them like a factory press.

After a protracted few seconds when the singing sounds of the weapons on both sides echoed eerily down the canted space, Solace realized they weren't being hit, and nor were the enemy. The nearest pillars were practically fuzzy with accelerator shot, the little pellets clustering about them. Their own had been similarly caught. She could feel no magnetic pull on her suit or any other part of her, and her instruments showed no active fields. And yet they, and the Voyenni, had just burned through half their ammunition to absolutely no avail.

For a moment the Partheni and the Magdans just stared dumbly at each other. Then the Voyenni were moving, descending hurriedly to the next level and leaving this witchcraft behind them. Solace didn't fancy using the same hatch, in case the anti-acceleration field abruptly shut off on the next level. "Find a way down," she ordered, and one of the Myrmidons had already identified a likely hatch, five metres across, dropping into an uncertain abyss.

There were lights down there. And walls: rings and circles and whole orreries of walls. It twisted her eyes to look at it. The lights were in a constellation connected by a webwork of wires, clearly old-fashioned spacer tech. Everything just stapled together all anyhow to the ancient Originator construction. Walls and rings and deconstructed spheres, none of it seemed to be supported by much of anything, and the darkness was impenetrable beyond. Gravity was playing hob with everything too. Solace really didn't fancy the descent, right then. If it was vertigo, it was vertigo of the soul. There was something about the dimensions and proportions and sheer *physics* of this place that her mind revolted at.

And yet it was all leading *somewhere*. The arrangement drew the eye. It had a centre, and once she'd realized that, it was hard not to think of the whole static assembly as orbiting it. That matched up with where the power all led. With where the activity was.

If I'm making the wrong call, we might be rushing into a power core gone critical or a bomb or something.

"Prêt à combattre?" she asked her Myrmidons, because she sure as hell didn't feel she was.

But, "Prêt, Mother," they answered, and then she was looking to find a path that would let them intercept the hurrying band.

Kris

Kris was aware they'd been in a fight for some time. She'd heard the odd alarm and had the impression the yacht had taken a couple of trivial hits. With the high-class and reliable artificial gravity, she had no sense of what man-oeuvres the vessel was being put through. This was in contrast to the old *Vulture God*, where she always felt there was a bit of a lurch in her gut whenever Idris or Olli slung them around. The screens and consoles wouldn't respond to her touch or queries. She was discovering that captivity could go from life-threatening to simply frustrating very quickly.

Admittedly she was still in a small stateroom, so it wasn't as though her circumstances were excruciatingly uncomfortable. The room's little printer had a limited repertoire but she'd managed to get some little cakes out of it, and a glass of decent heated wine. Not the sort of glass she could smash and thereafter threaten people with, however. It just crumpled when she tried it.

Then Piter Tchever Uskaro turned up, looking as though he'd been eating lemons. He had added a holstered pistol and a scabbarded knife to his ensemble, and a pair of Voyenni were at his back.

Kris made her expression one of innocent enquiry.

The Boyarin stared at her suspiciously, and then one of his men went all over the room, checking every possible point where she could have interacted with the ship. Kris watched this blankly, moving about the room to stay clear of whatever they were doing. It all seemed very thorough, and Uskaro was twitchy, glowering at her. *Looking for an excuse.*

"Your Elegance, if I knew what you were looking for, perhaps I could help," she suggested, then took two rapid steps back as he practically lunged at her. He caught her wrist and yanked her close, snarling.

"I don't know what you think you're doing—" he began, but then his man started reporting.

"Nothing, sir. No systems access. I can see she's tried, but there's nothing here."

"Then she's covering her tracks." Still holding her wrist,

he straight-armed her down onto the bed, about to accuse her of who knew what. She waited, because if he actually accused her of it, then she'd at least know what it was she was supposed to have done. He saw in her face too that she was less worried about him than she was curious. For a moment she thought he would hit her out of sheer aggravation, a man used to getting his own way, and for whom the universe was not behaving properly. If he did, she'd go at him right back, she decided, surprised at how clear her head was. She'd go tooth and nail, try to get his knife out of that fiddly buttoned-down scabbard, bite his nose off, something. Because she reckoned he was the sort of man who enjoyed beating people who couldn't fight back, and she wanted to make it clear she wasn't in that category.

He'd have had the Voyenni hold her down while he went to get the whip, no doubt, but something in her face dissuaded him from starting down that road. He stepped back, face twitching with anger, and then the three of them stormed out.

She checked the door, just in case, but Uskaro's annoyance hadn't led to him overlooking the lock.

So what was all that? They'd thought she was getting into the ship's systems, which meant that *someone* had been. She'd have loved to claim the credit, but that kind of monkeying wasn't her forte. It must have been the little voice that had come to her before. An associate of Mundy, the Mordant House man, it had claimed, and she'd given it some level of access to the ship. After all Mundy was, at least for now and however nominally, her ally.

A little while later, a colossal shudder ran through the hull of the *Raptorid*. She recognized it from being on the other end of it. The sort of gung-ho docking the *Vulture God* made with ships that were, usually, unoccupied and ripe for salvage. If she was lucky, they were here to salvage her.

Which was all very well, but the *Raptorid* was packed with thugs, as far as Kris knew. Should Olli and the others make any headway then, unless Mundy's friend had some fairly spectacular control over ship's systems, this was going to put her in a tricky position. Her role could go from prisoner to hostage very quickly and she reckoned Piter Uskaro was exactly the man to take that option.

A series of distant shocks went through the hull that could have been anything from explosions to enthusiastic engineering. Her initial bad feeling, as to the odds of her crewmates pulling anything useful off, started to lift, or at least turn into other kinds of bad feelings. There were more vibrations, the whole of the ship a telltale informing her that, whatever was going on, it hadn't just been put down with extreme prejudice by the Voyenni.

The door slid open again a moment later and Piter Uskaro's unwelcome face hooked round it, staring at her with far more venom than their respective positions would normally have inspired. He seemed about to say something, and she saw he had his pistol in his hand. Then his features clenched and he withdrew. She checked the door. Locked once more. Was it too much to expect a little slipshod practice from her enemies in her time of need?

She reckoned the clock was fast moving towards hostage hour, and that was unlikely to go well for her. A couple of burly Voyenni would probably end any effective chance she had of changing her role to one more empowered.

Something suddenly bleeped at her. She scanned the state-room quickly. *A message?* The room was overdressed rather than being spacer-functional, and she took too long to realize the printer was blinking its lights in a little pattern.

It wasn't built to be communicative, but she found a concealed maintenance flap in its side and uncovered a little diagnostics panel. The simple screen there started scrolling letters the moment she exposed it.

Reduced to trivial systems, it read. *Our only input to your location. Please hold.*

She had no idea if she might be heard, but there was a receiver on the diagnostics panel that looked calibrated for verbal commands. "I don't suppose the door counts as trivial?"

*They've locked us out of the doors already. We had fun with them, but—*there was no more to the sentence, and she thought she must have lost even that little thread of hope, but then the letters started up again. *We are very busy with somewhat more pressing negotiations right now, Mm. Almier. Probably we should leave you to your fate.*

"Thanks."

However, as a sop to our contract with Mh. Mundy we will attempt to do right by you. The printer was now busy making, its internal shuttles passing back and forth furiously as they built something up from component molecules.

"You're giving me a last meal?" she asked it drily.

No, came the little string of text. *Cutlery, though.*

The printer finished up, and a little silvered tray extended. On it was a knife, Scintilla duelling standard, made out of hard plastic.

Kris picked it up and slipped it into her sleeve, feeling disproportionate comfort from its slight weight.

She then heard running feet and shouting voices, not too many doors away from hers.

Bring it, she thought. Things were about to get litigious.

Idris

Idris was most of the way to the Machine when Emmaneth's head jerked up.

"They're coming right after us," she hissed.

"Who are?" Jaine asked. "How could they even?"

"Whoever came down the well. They got inside in time." The Tothiat had stopped, staring up through the hatch they'd just used. "And how? Jaine, you rigged this place so everything points at the Machine."

"Because everything *does* point at the Machine. It's the only reason you clowns are all here! You wanted it that way!" Jaine shouted at her. Idris recalled she'd been a resident before Ahab, and wondered what on Earth she'd been doing on Criccieth's Hell prior to being co-opted for the Naeromathi's single-minded purpose.

"I'm going to sort them out," Emmaneth decided.

"No," Idris heard himself say, and forced himself not to flinch back when she rounded on him. "They're my friends," he explained.

"Caught sight of a pack of combat armour way up there," Emmaneth accused. "That's some punchy friends you've got. I reckon that's Mordant House here for me. Or worse."

"It's my friends. That's their ship. I'm going."

"But, Menheer Telemmier, we do rather need you in the

hotseat." Doctor Shinandri was already halfway through the next hatch, one of the yawning gaps built to fit Ahab.

"Get the Machine ready for me," Idris told them. "I'm not skipping out on you. But my friends are no pushovers. If they turn up and Emmaneth starts throwing punches while I'm under, then a lot of complicated things we need working are going to get wrecked." He glowered at Emmaneth, armoured in a sense of his own usefulness, until she actually scowled and looked away.

"I'm going with you," she told him.

"Not like you'd be much use throwing switches," jabbed Jaine.

Idris just shrugged and started climbing back up.

"I'm really not sure—" Shinandri started again, but Idris kept going, rung after rung, feeling the infinitesimal weight of thickening gravity piling on his shoulders as he ascended, the weird inverse field that meant he was near-weightless in the Machine's seat but would be under one G and more up on the outermost levels.

Emmaneth was doggedly at his heels. Her face, when he glanced back, was thunder, but she kept her mouth shut at least.

"Why?" he asked suddenly, not breaking the rhythm of his hands and feet.

"What?"

"You keep saying what a bad person you are. You killed people for Mordant House, and then you killed people for Broken Harvest after they did the Tothiat thing to you. It hurts so bad, you tried to get yourself killed and...then you come here to incinerate yourself and suddenly you're best pals with the universe and want to help fight the Architects."

She'd stopped climbing, and he gained a whole ladder on her before she scrambled to catch up.

"Jaine explained to me what they were doing here. What Ahab was seeking. What Shinandri wanted," she said. "Then she showed me where I could just walk out into the light and die. I stood there for a long time, believe me. And I'll go back there, probably, to take that last step. But for now . . . I thought I could do something to help."

"Help Ahab?"

"Help the universe. Because nothing I ever did for Hugh or the Broken Harvest ever did. And that was what I wanted to get away from. Government wetwork or just murdering people for some crazy gangster. But here I could—"

"You *never* understood!" A new voice burst out. Idris skittered aside as someone descended on them much faster than was wise. Emmaneth had a gun out now but she didn't bother to shoot. It wouldn't have done any good. There was more movement much higher up, more people coming down, but leading the charge was a woman he didn't know—no suit, not even a weapon drawn—and she looked furious.

"You had everything," the woman spat at Emmaneth. "He took you from the herd and he *remade* you. We are the chosen, Em. We live *forever*. And you came here to *die*?"

Belatedly Idris noticed the articulated symbiote bulking out the newcomer's spine. Another Tothiat.

"Heremon," Emmaneth named her. "You dragged your feet tracking me down, didn't you?" She cocked an eye up at the squad of Myrmidons that were making their descent. Idris was trying to see if any of them was Solace, but in their armour they were even more similar than when out of it.

"Every time I killed for Mordant House, I thought about

ending it," Emmaneth said softly. "A day, give or take, each time, when I couldn't live with myself. Then I signed the devil's pact with the Unspeakable, and I realized I'd never have that option again. Pain all the time, but my life wasn't my own to take any more. In the end I found something better than death, a purpose worth staying alive just a little longer for. But I'd rather death than to live forever as a gangster's pet monster."

"You never understood," and Heremon was genuinely, inexplicably upset at her, as though Emmaneth's betrayal threatened her entire worldview. "The Razor is not a criminal. It's an angel. A fallen angel cast down from Heaven to do the things that the Essiel are forbidden to do."

"You make it sound like what Mordant House is to Hugh," Emmaneth said derisively. "Just someone to do the dirty work."

"We'll *make* you understand," Heremon told her hotly. "You'll come back to us. By the time Aklu finishes with you…"

"You won't make me go back to it," Emmaneth promised her. "How long do you think you can even hold onto me?"

Then Myrmidons were dropping down from above, weapons levelled at Emmaneth, who yanked Idris behind her.

"We might not be able to kill you," one stated flatly, "but we can beat you down to the point you can't stop us."

"Solace?" Idris asked, and was suddenly worried in case Solace wasn't actually among them. Where precisely did he stand with her sisters in her absence? Then another Myrmidon had dropped down. This one had her weapon slung rather than levelled, and she stood there for a moment, just staring.

"Idris?" Even through the suit's speakers he knew the voice.

He ducked under Emmaneth's arm to close the distance halfway. "Look—" he said, and then she lunged forwards. He flinched, and he felt Emmaneth grab for him too, but Solace got there first. Not a grapple, nor an attempt to secure control of an asset. Just sweeping him into her arms for a hug that bruised his ribs and drove the breath out of him. A moment later she'd stepped hurriedly back, and he had the impression she hadn't meant to do that at all. Her cohorts seemed to be giving her some very unmilitary looks.

"Come on," she told him.

"I can't," he replied. At least this part of their meeting was going to plan.

"Idris, we need to get out of here, right now. This place, it's coming apart."

"Yes, yes it is," he agreed. "And until it stops doing that, nobody's leaving."

"There must be ships here we can leave on."

"There is no way out of the atmosphere right now that *any* ship could survive. The Machine is active, so the shielding is down. The planet is trying to take this place apart, and there's no corridor into space," he told her, getting it all out as hurriedly as possible. "So come with me. I can *fix* this. I just need to go back under."

"Under what?" she demanded. The hug had been nice but would she just stop asking questions now?

"Come on, tell you on the way. Solace, it's, this, we're really," tugging at her, tugging at Emmaneth, trying to get everyone moving, like herding heavily armed and pugnacious cats.

*

Shinandri and Jaine were waiting below, the former suited up and the latter with Idris's own suit ready for him. They were decidedly leery when the Myrmidons trooped down and held them at gunpoint, but at least neither was the fight-starting type. Then Idris was in the midst of them, already struggling into the encounter suit, getting his fingers and toes snagged in the thick rubbery fabric.

"Why the suits?" Solace asked, mystified. "I mean, we're short on gravity here, but the atmosphere's fine."

"I'm going somewhere. I'm travelling." Even as he said it, he was articulating a truth he'd never quite put together before. "I'm going to sit at the very border of unspace." He had a sudden vertiginous feeling, lurching into Jaine as she connected his hoses. A sense of the Machine's original purpose came to him—not the gubbins Ahab had put in or the human-scale additions of Jaine, but the Originators' real intent for it. All this engine, this insane physics-bending tech, just for some kind of reverse telescope into nowhere? Of course there was more it could do. What Shinandri and Ahab were using it for was just a sideshow some unintended offshoot of the complex's true purpose. "Even though I'm still here, I'm exposed. The suit protects me. A little. All that it can."

"Idris, what *is* this?"

He squared up to her, suit to armoured suit. "The only working Originator base we've ever found. And we are looking into unspace. We're finding out what's sending the Architects after us, me and Ahab. Because Ahab wants revenge. He wants to hunt them down and destroy them. This is it, Solace. This is where we learn how to strike back."

He sounded ridiculous to his own ears, but Solace and the

Myrmidons went quiet and still. He caught Heremon nodding slightly. *Not impressed? Not even surprised? Are Tothiat just really hard to shock, or...?*

"Most of all right now, though, I need to connect to Ahab and talk him into coming out, because he's hunting down there alone, and while the Machine's on, the shield's off. Nobody fight anyone until I'm out again."

There was a sudden clatter from above, as of someone slipping down a ladder too quickly.

"No promises," Solace said. "There are a pack of Voyenni out there, and they'll be in here soon enough, if they can navigate worth a damn."

"Why did you bring Voyenni?" Idris demanded.

"Believe me, we did our very best to bring as few of them as possible." Her Myrmidons were now spreading out, guns levelled upwards. Then there was a colossal retort that shook all the walls around them and seemed to go on forever, echoing into the cavernous depths.

Jaine swore. "I think that was something structural. Go get Ahab, Telemmier. I can't patch this place until he's out. If it's even possible."

Then he was in the chair, and in the Machine, and nothing else mattered. There was a second, perhaps, when the presence of Solace snagged at his conscience, but unspace beckoned, and in this seat he had a leverage over it that a spaceship never gave him. In the lion's den, but he had a whip.

Ahab, already sunk deep, called to him. "Come! We must understand!" In the heart of that cluster of organization and energy that they'd found and which had so baffled them both. Right then, Idris had no thought for the installation or its longevity, for Jaine's repairs, the *Vulture God*, any of it. He needed to know. He had to discover the truth behind the Architects and their masters. Though he'd tell himself it was to save the universe from them, in reality he just wanted to *know*.

He joined Ahab and the assemblage of activity and motion deep in unspace. Abruptly they were there: the Architects, their intelligences. They brushed against the pair of explorers, flinching away, and were already in motion, he realized. They were coming for Criccieth's Hell, to test themselves against the planet's fires. They would burn up their crystal soldiers in an attempt to excise the installation. Anything to prevent Idris and Ahab from making their discovery. He had moments of connection, like needles in his brain. They were terrified of him, in that moment. They were terrified of Ahab too. They, who could reshape planets.

Data shuttled back and forth, Idris to Ahab and back. The Naeromathi's long life, experience and driving purpose, Idris's Intermediary perspective that unpacked unspace like an opening flower.

Then he knew. And it wasn't what he'd thought. He felt leaden and bitter, even as Ahab exulted that the universe had finally given up its secrets.

31.

Solace

Metal shrilled and squealed somewhere above, and Solace winced. Light assault armour was all very well and covered a multitude of threats, but nothing she had would stave off the radiant life of this planet. Her Myrmidons stayed very still, and she was proud of them for it. Right now she could feel the local gravity tugging and shifting around her, and the air was full of distant thunder, coming closer. The local biosphere was savaging the outside of this place for the temerity of even existing.

She'd had the lowdown from the cyborg called Tokamak Jaine about why this was here. So the old Originators had run into something on Criccieth's Hell even they couldn't deal with. Which meant that this planet wasn't just a death-world *now*; it had been like that however many hundreds of millions of years ago too, and got no less death-y since.

"So what were they actually doing?" she asked, because right now talking lent her the illusion of having some control of the situation.

"Say what now?" Jaine asked.

"The Originators. I mean they were all over, and the universe and unspace are vast. Why here?"

"Just an engineer," Jaine told her with a shrug. "I don't do the big-picture stuff."

Then Shinandri's voice rose from the seat he was occupying, from the faceless visor of his helmet. "It isn't known, precisely. A mystery, as it were, but we can guess." She'd thought he was under, like Idris, but apparently his role was some sort of halfway house, monitoring what was going on without actually submerging himself in it. "From the data brought back, from the structure of this place, from everything, indeed, we know about both the Originators and how manipulation of unspace works."

Solace waited, but apparently that was supposed to be enough, so she kicked the overbuilt couch he was in, to Jaine's alarmed squawk. "Meaning what?"

"Sometimes it's all about the precise spatial relationship," Shinandri's voice floated to her, as though from far away. "Not the walls but the spaces in between. So they came here simply because they needed part of their overarching device *here*. Because being *here* was the point. The part of the plan that actually *does* things isn't the points, but the arrangement of the points. A plan as big as the universe. I hypothesized as much in my early academiotypes. They'll still have them on Deathknell, if you fancy some reading."

Solace suspected that kind of reading was above her pay grade. Any further questions she might have pressed were obliterated when something else colossal gave way far above. She couldn't see any rent in the metal sky directly, but there was an abrupt and hideously lurid glare up there, the outside leaking in.

"These plants, the nasty ones," she said. "They move about?"

"They grow," Jaine said flatly. She was absolutely motionless, staring up. And frightened, very obviously frightened. Given she'd lived with this horror for decades apparently, that fear communicated itself readily to Solace.

"Fast?"

"This is possibly the highest-energy ecology known to humanity," Jaine said. "They can grow as fast as you can run."

Then there was a much closer disturbance, a clattering of boots on ladders. Just in case she didn't have enough to worry about, the Voyenni were finally making their move.

"When we fought these clowns before," she said, "our shot just ended up magnetized to the walls or something."

"It does that sometimes. When the Machine's on. Plays hob with the electromagnetic fields," Jaine confirmed, still staring up.

"Only sometimes?"

"We're basically standing at the edge of a raw wound between unspace and the real. There's a lot of fluctuation we don't fully understand. Interference in the basic substructure of the matter universe," the cyborg offered, which was a lot of words to not really enlighten Solace any further.

One of her Myrmidons let fly with a burst of accelerator shot then suppressive fire up through the hatch above. Solace's eyes hurt as she saw not the shot itself, which was too fast to see, but a flare of bluish energy twisting the air along its path. The hatch rim ended up studded and pocked with spent shot. It clustered here and there unevenly, in something that her mind kept trying to make into a pattern. When she started seeing it as writing, she looked away. *This is a mad place. It will make us all crazy.*

Another shudder racked the structure around them, and she felt a lurch in her stomach as though the whole assembly of walls, platforms and Jaine's makeshift ladders had dropped five metres. Which of course it hadn't, but the gravitic fields were shifting, or possibly failing. Unless they had dropped, and this whole shitshow was about to just plummet into the bowels of Criccieth's Hell. Or else contract into a supergravitational mass the size of a fist and crush them all to death. So many ways to die on this planet. And the glare from above was brighter now, in all its eye-offending glory.

Then there was shouting.

It came from above, voices in Colvul with Magdan accents. For a moment she couldn't work out what they were saying. A challenge, surely, rough demands from the Uskaros' elite bully boys. Except it wasn't. Except things had got too much even for men who got whipped for a living and learned to like it.

"We're coming down!" they were yelling. "We surrender! You have a way to leave here?"

The soldier within her was urging her to just kill them. Gun them down, if the physics would even let her. Or keep them up there, closer to where the death was. But she'd been among civilians and Colonials a long time. Also, she'd been taught to think that the Parthenon were the right and the good. And rather than that meaning they got to do what they liked, and their actions would be whitewashed as right and good because of who they were, it meant they had to actually do right and good things. Active virtue, defending humanity and never, ever giving in to the temptation that Doctor Parsefer had strewn in their path when she'd cooked up her perfect vat-born warrior angels. *If these angels were ever to fall, we would be such a force for evil in the universe.* It was a terrible thing to look into the heart of your culture and know that you were intended for monstrosity and only an active devotion to the good of others would keep you from it, even when those others hated you.

"Discard your weapons and come down," she ordered. "Shinandri, tell me Idris is just about done, because otherwise I think this whole *place* is."

"I...think he is in communion with Ahab, that would be my very best guess," came the voice from the man's helm. "I think...they have made a discovery."

"This is not the time for discoveries!" Solace snapped at him.

"I...My very goodness..." Shinandri's voice was hushed. "They've *done it.*"

But up in the space above, her gaze threading the needle through a series of holes and portals, she saw a twisting tendril, advancing in a series of sharp-edged turns like a living lightning bolt. It shimmered in hues that were like screams on the retina. Then the Voyenni were rushing down, four of them and no guns in sight, cumbersome in their own armour. Things were getting crowded around the Machine couches now. There was no real room to hold them at gunpoint.

"You two, make yourselves useful," Solace said to Emmaneth and Heremon, who'd been maintaining a brooding silence until then. "Any of these clowns start anything, break all their arms."

Then Idris gasped and half sat up, flailing in the folds of his oversized suit. He bounced his helmet hard off one of the couch supports and half fell from the seat before Solace caught him. Across from him, Shinandri sat up gingerly.

"Idris." She tried to get his helmet off, then gave way to

Jaine. "He's clear, turn the Machine off." Around them, the grind and thunder of the angry planet was growing ever louder.

"It is already," Jaine said. "The moment he came back to himself I turned it off." She had the helmet off him now too and Idris's face looked pasty and agonized, sheened with sweat.

"It's not what we thought," he got out.

"I don't care," Solace told him. "Focus, Idris. We have to get out of here. Turn it off."

"It is off."

"How's Ahab?" Jaine asked.

"I don't know," Shinandri confessed. "I believe they're disconnected but I seem unable to communicate."

"Then why isn't the shield up?" Emmaneth asked, calm, quiet even. Of course, she'd come here to die, so her peace of mind wasn't a reliable litmus.

Jaine moved over to a console that was mostly a mess of exposed wiring and loose displays. "The field *is* up," she said flatly.

Another thunderous retort from above seemed to give the lie to that.

"Using the Machine damages this installation, and we've just crossed a threshold," Jaine explained. "There was damage to the Originator structure when we arrived. Cracks in the walls, where the roots got in. The field is actually holding most of the plants back right now, but the cracks are spreading faster and faster and..." She had a display turned towards them, pulling up complex figures into the air that nobody else could make sense of. "The corridor's...awry, intermittent."

"Corridor?" Solace echoed dumbly.

"The one leading into orbit. The safe approach you snuck in by, by the skin of your teeth," Jaine said. "It's like a corkscrew right now. A corkscrew that's not even there half the time. Unless I can fix it, there's no way off-planet."

Kris

Kris was leaning against the printer when the two of them piled in, Uskaro Senior and Junior, plus only a single Voyenni to guard them. She could hear something going wrong elsewhere on the ship, and her feet transmitted little shocks and thunders to her. She had a whole host of times from the last several years when she could have cursed out Olli furiously for over-reacting to some slight or other, but this wasn't one of them.

On the downside, the man they had with them, the particularly big and nasty-looking thug, was Beyon, last seen being whipped on Arc Pallator before having escaped that doomed world with his master.

"Gentlemen," she said sweetly, although the goon's reappearance in her life had thrown her a little. True, the whole whipping business had been aimed at Solace, but Kris had been given a front-row seat to it nonetheless.

The Morzarin Ravin Okosh Uskaro didn't appear his usual debonair self and nor did he look on her with much love. A flick of his fingers sent Beyon lumbering forwards with the clear intent of seizing her for nefarious purposes. "Human shield" was probably the best of those and Kris was fed up with auditioning for that role.

If she had been a sneakier son of a bitch, as per spacer standard, she'd probably just have let herself be dragged over to the two noblemen, so she could flip the tables on the old hostage routine and get her blade up to Ravin's throat. Beyon and Piter both had a gun and knife, but they probably couldn't draw them quickly enough to stop her. It would have been all very derring-do, and she could probably have pulled it off. Something inside her kicked at it, though: the Scintilla graduate, follower of rules, adherent of the law. Or at least some laws, whichever held jurisdiction, as appropriate.

So the knife came out early, wavering right before Beyon's nose and making a few deft circles as he tried to grab it. He then went for her, no patience and little enough finesse. She reckoned there was a whole school of unarmed combat they got taught, to make the most of their sheer size and strength. It did require him to actually get his hands on her, though, and her own training was all about remaining as hands-free as possible.

There was, she had to admit, an ugly little scuffle and a clash of styles. By the time they'd parted she was breathing heavily and Beyon's hands were short two fingers. The plastic knife Colvari had printed was insanely sharp. If she'd realized it was quite that keen she wouldn't have had it in her sleeve.

"Now," she told them, "let's have some alternative dispute resolution." She was in her duelling stance, making sure the knife was between her and Beyon. The big man looked incandescent, rage overwriting the pain. The blood had stopped almost immediately, suggesting that the favoured servants of the Uskaro clan got a little combat mod surgery. He was reassessing her, though. She'd gone, at least, from helpless civilian to credible threat.

"Mesdam Almier," Ravin snapped, "enough of this nonsense. There has been a considerable change in circumstances."

"A change in circumstances," Kris echoed. It was a good description of what Olli usually wreaked on the universe. "I'm sure. I'm afraid, Your Elegance, that I'm not particularly minded to cooperate with you anymore so I'll be walking out the door right about now."

Ravin's eyes flicked from her to the knife. She could see the calculations behind them: the possible leverage from holding onto her against the extra damage that might accrue. At last, he stepped back from the doorway with as much of his elegance as he could muster, tugging at his nephew's arm. Beyon was growling, low and insistent, and she couldn't quite make herself waltz blithely past within arm's reach of him. She made the best grace she could of a curving path around the room to the door.

And there, as she knew even with the words passing her lips, she pushed her luck.

"I will," she said, "be pressing charges. There will be recorded evidence of my kidnap on Deathknell, and you managed to burn your bridges there so they'll be only too glad to help. Your Elegances, I'll be seeing you in court."

Ravin, older and wiser, just rolled his eyes at the bravado, but she hadn't realized just how tightly wound Piter was. This, apparently, was one turn too many and he snapped.

When he went for her, she'd been so much into her own patter she wasn't ready for it. He actually managed to get a hand on her knife-arm, but not a grip, and her reflexes re-asserted themselves. A moment later she was three paces away and out of his reach. But back inside the room.

Ravin shouted at his nephew to leave her and control

himself, but Piter was evidently past the point of familial correction. "You said yourself it's all up," he snarled. "You as good as told me we're fucked now. That they know everything. If we're going down, it won't be so this jumped-up little clerk can laugh at us."

That meant literally nothing to Kris, except that apparently Olli tearing their ship up *wasn't* the change of circumstances they'd meant. She had so many questions, right then, but unfortunately Piter had his own knife out. Not his gun, even, but his knife, because he wanted to make this personal and that meant physical contact.

And Ravin was shouting, and now Beyon was moving in again, and this was a long way from a Scintilla duelling society bout. But what it *was* like, just a little, was one of the illegal honour matches the law school had simultaneously outlawed and covertly encouraged, where you could be arrested by the beadles any moment, and where people died. Where she'd ruined her career.

Beyon wasn't going to be stopped by the threat of a blade, nor a little pain. She went for him first, letting Piter chase her round the room. She didn't aim for his wounded hand, which would be so flooded with painkillers he wouldn't have felt it being amputated. She let her feet tap through the odd little jink she'd won several matches with and, rather than just threaten his throat, she slashed him across the face. Hard to slow down a man as inured to pain as all that, but the knife's razor edge did a lot of nasty work in that one pass. The blood was in his eyes and he was sucking in air through a new hole in his cheek. Ravin, still shouting, tried to get in the way so that Beyon's next blundering lunge actually ended up knocking his master down. The change in the big man was instant, from brute to cringing cur. He was out of the fight, at least for now, helping Ravin up, whimpering, apologizing, all with his face a mask of blood and carved flesh.

Piter came on past them, vaulting over the tangle of their limbs and almost landing a textbook impale right into her shoulder. A convulsive twist of her body turned it into a thin, cold line of pain, and for a moment she stopped, because that was a hit and she had to concede it. Her adherence to formalities almost got her killed as the next thrust went for her ribs. Her off-hand slapped it aside, though, even as she registered it. Then she got a shallow, bloody strike across Piter's forearm. One for one.

They resumed their distance. She could almost see the reach of his blade as a glinting circle in the air around him, and would have to enter this in order to bring him within the range of her own. She found she was smiling, because this moment was pure nostalgia, the best and the worst of it.

"Piter, I insist you stand down!" Ravin was shouting at him. "Beyon, restrain my idiot nephew!" The big man, his face half wiped of blood, vacillated wretchedly between the pair of them.

"We can call that a draw, Your Elegance," Kris invited, "or we can go for a deciding bout." She flourished her little plastic knife at him, a cavalier flip of the wrist she hadn't used in ages.

In retrospect, she reckoned it was that gesture that pushed him over. She'd marked him, and he didn't have the same pain-suppression as Beyon. For all his airs and the knife-scar he bore so proudly, he didn't like being hurt.

He brought the pistol awkwardly out with his left hand,

dragging it up towards her face. Possibly, it was only intended as a threat, a way of asserting dominance that didn't carry the risk of getting any more tears in his hide. If that had been his intent, it failed abysmally.

She did the only thing you could when someone brought a gun to a knife fight. She closed. He was caught up with pointing the gun at her, so she could bat aside his blade and push inside his guard. She was aiming to get her edge alongside his throat, to take control of the situation and put the gun out of play. He didn't cooperate, though, striking her across the head with the weapon's barrel, simultaneously trying an ungainly slash with his own knife. It would have cut up her arm but without doing serious harm.

She jerked forwards, and it was her final duel on Scintilla all over again. Because at the core of law-upholding, ever-so-civilized Keristina Soolin Almier was someone who really wanted to *win*. Not even survive, but win. In this case, winning involved driving her knife into Piter Tchever Uskaro's neck up to the hilt, and it was all she could do not to give him a second one for luck.

She jerked back as he fell, and then Beyon really was going for her. That might have progressed all manner of ways if Olli hadn't come violently in through the door that same moment, carving and crumpling her way through the metal in equal measure. This explosive introduction was enough to send Beyon scurrying back to protect Ravin. Kris descended on Piter instantly, stanching the blood, shouting for the love of God for someone to get her a medical kit. She'd been in this position before, but then everyone had been too terrified about being witness to a duel gone wrong to actually help.

It was Havaer bloody Mundy, late of Mordant House, who

actually got a compress applied and painkillers, and regenerative agents and all the rest. Piter was ashen by then, unconscious, and Kris still wasn't sure if he'd make it or not. Or, if he did, what sort of a scar he'd carry with him. Magda was sure to keep the Colonies' very best tissue replacement for its Boyarin, but she'd made a hell of a mess, and they were a long way from the Uskaros' home.

"These two going to be trouble?" Olli asked, indicating Ravin and the snarling Beyon. "They could have an accident. Maybe more than one."

"No, it's fine. You came for me. We'll go now," Kris said, feeling exhausted as all the adrenaline drained out of her. "Listen, though, what's going on? What's happening out there?"

"What?" Olli blinked at her.

"Kit was saying," Mundy grunted, still applying everything he could find in the Uskaros' medkit, "that we need to hurry and get out."

"Oh, right. Was a bit distracted fighting these clowns," Olli said.

"I was attempting to inform you," Ravin Uskaro said frostily, and somewhat disingenuously in Kris's opinion, as he hadn't been. "The circumstances out there have changed. The fighting between the *Intrepid* and your Partheni friends," quite the spitting tone over that, "has ended. There's been a new arrival."

32.

Idris

Idris saw Solace take a moment to digest the news about the disintegrating corridor. Then she said, "Erratic doesn't mean impossible," just like he knew she would. He also knew she was wrong this time. There was no way to climb out of Criccieth's gravity well, not now. The hideous ecology was having its last laugh at the rest of the universe.

Shinandri had his hoses detached, sitting sideways on his couch. "Is it possible we might prepare some sort of... beacon? To jettison what we've discovered into orbit, where it might be found, do you think? Because..." He met Idris's gaze. "We *have* found. At last, at this last moment, we have... understood what we were seeing, I suppose, is a—" and then another rending shriek from above stopped his flow of words. Everyone flinched, Partheni and Voyenni and Tothiat, the lot. No amount of toughness or tech was going to save them from what was coming.

The same went for any attempt at a beacon. "Doc," Jaine said, "the *Originators* couldn't build something to endure in this place without their gravity field bending the rads away. You reckon we can get a capsule up out of the atmosphere without it turning into free atoms?"

Then the voice came: *"No!"* Booming from every wall and failing strut, as though it was the planet speaking to them, the hungry ecosystem itself. "No! What we have found must not be buried!"

"Ahab," Emmaneth whispered. The Naeromathi's words were so distorted Idris hadn't recognized the speaker.

"You know what we have found! Idris! You *know!*" The mad-sounding series of exclamations that were all the translator could make of Ahab's thoughts. "The knowledge must survive!"

"Yes, I know what we've found." Idris resisted the urge to shout back. The angsty fit that might get his pitiful rage up wasn't on him right now, just a terrible sadness. "It's not what we thought."

"It is enough! The crusade continues!" Ahab boomed. "It must be preserved!"

"What?" Solace demanded suddenly. "What must be preserved? You stole Idris, brought him here to this hell, shoved him into your machine. Why? What's so important?" She practically rammed Mr. Punch up Shinandri's nose, leaving him spluttering around a lack of explanation. Saving them all was up to Idris, of course. It always seemed to come down to that.

"I thought we'd find the thing that enslaved the Architects," he said dully. "That was what I was looking for, in unspace. There was something, and we had to... It's like solving an equation. We had to interpret it, squint through the numbers until we worked out what we were looking at. And we did, in the end. It just wasn't what we thought."

"Idris," said Solace levelly, "I love you dearly and I am glad I found you alive but you have to learn to get to the *point.*"

"It's not their masters," he said heavily. "We found where Architects form, deep in unspace."

"Miraculous," Shinandri breathed.

"And this means...?" Solace prompted.

"We could theoretically find a way to assault them there. To destroy their breeding grounds, their nursery, or their probability field, whatever it is. To murder their children."

"Yes!" Ahab roared all around them. "Rightful revenge for all that was lost!" And Idris sympathized, he really did. He saw the same thought in Solace, too; in all of them. *Why not?* He would answer, *Because they're slaves and being forced to attack us*, but nobody would care.

"Maybe..." Jaine had her eyes closed to keep the maths in. "I could actually rig a signal, a big enough signal, to get the data out. Maybe. Somehow." He saw her lips move after the words stopped, arguing the practicalities with herself.

"No!" Ahab barked. "The engine must be preserved! We cannot surrender it. It is the point of our spear! Our weapon!"

"Boss," Jaine called into the groaning, creaking void. "This place ain't going to be here long, Machine and all. If you made your big damn discovery, then maybe I can...I don't even know if I can..."

"No!" again, that blind refusal in the face of the universe that had got Ahab this far. "Idris! You have lived within the engine's heart. You have seen what is here on this world. You understand the universe's sole truth! Nothing matters!" Ahab's voice vibrated the floor and walls. "That is the secret. Nothing matters!"

"Oh. Fuck," Emmaneth said quietly in the echo of that. "Nihilism. A philosophy I can get behind. Great."

"No," said Idris. He lay back down in the couch. "Jaine, I need to go in again."

"You go in and even the half-ass shield we've got is going to fail," she pointed out.

"You know it doesn't change anything but how fast the clock runs," he argued.

"Idris, wait, we can..." Solace's helmet looked up to the hatch above, the growing glare that seemed to eat at the edge of it. She wanted so badly to do what the Partheni always did, he knew. Grab him and battle through the worst Criccieth's Hell could throw at them, get on a ship, get off the world, save the day. But that light up there, *that* was the day. Nobody was saving them from that.

"*Nothing* matters," Shinandri echoed, but in a different tone, a speculative one. He understood. Unspace, the Originator walls, the Throughways, the universe, from the void between the stars to the whirling emptiness of atoms, it was all about the nothing and how you arranged it. Which meant that there were no walls at all, if you could just bend the pieces of nothing the right way. This was what a ship's gravitic drive did, every time it passed into or out of unspace. Even reality was subordinate to nothing. You could take a vessel and make it a dream, and then throw that dream across the universe and make it real again around another star.

The Machine was an eye into unspace, but it was such by virtue of being a gravitic engine, focusing its might upon the very boundary between real and unreal.

"This won't work," Idris declared, and then he was back in the focus of the Machine, staring into the wastes of unspace. Feeling the Presence down there, sluggishly registering his intrusion; feeling the far-off arrangement of energy and information, the place where the Architects were born, and the guilty weight that knowledge carried. Feeling the distortion of Criccieth's Hell's gravity well, that the Machine used to focus its immaterial eye. Finally there was the universe itself, in its precisely strung-out scatter of tiny distortions, to the nothing that were stars and planets ad infinitum, all set out to some plan or no plan or...

Some plan, he thought, helplessly losing traction against the funnel of nothing, with the Presence rising beneath him. Ahab is right: nothing matters. Shinandri is right: it's the precise arrangement of all the nothing, the spaces and not the things. There is a plan. And right now, I'm distorting that plan just by applying my mind to unspace. I am bringing ruin to something perfect.

He was about to do far worse, because Ahab understood. They'd got what they needed from the Eye of Criccieth's Hell. Now it was time to leave.

"This can't work," he said, because if it could then the Originators wouldn't have just left this jewel of their vanished crown encysted like a pearl in the killing radiation of Criccieth's Hell. *If I can do this, they could have done.* Except he could see the equations as clearly as if someone had engraved them onto his retinas with a razor blade. How you could manipulate the gravitic fields from *here*, but not if you were... *in unspace. The Originators were working from the other side of the boundary. All their ruins, all their works were just the tiniest intrusion into the real. Their civilization was never a real thing, and perhaps that's where they went, in the end. They ceased, and left only the Throughways and whatever litter they hadn't been able to reclaim.*

Impossible. Patently impossible. Nothing could live in

unspace. Except the Architects, of course. And the Thing That Lived In Unspace. Was it the Originators' inheritor or predator, or the adult form they'd pupated into, or . . . Perhaps there was a whole imaginary bestiary in the unreal and nobody had ever guessed.

But there wasn't time or space left for any more speculations. It was time to go.

He wanted to tell them to brace themselves, to warn everyone this wouldn't work, and that he was just about to accelerate the end of all of them. Or he might possibly murder half the planet, themselves included, through some spectacular release of energy. Or he'd accomplish nothing at all.

He wanted to say goodbye to Solace, who'd come for him despite everything. He didn't deserve the friends he had, and they certainty didn't deserve to get themselves killed on his account.

But none of that was possible, and the claws of Criccieth's Hell were tearing up the base even now, so he'd better do what he came here to do. Since Ahab had put the idea in his head, he was able to see how it could be done. Like, he thought, flicking a marble out of a basin. Tricky to stop it just rolling back down the gradient, in this case the planet's gravity. Also tricky because once the marble was in motion, its natural inclination would be to vanish down the drain. And this marble was also sitting on the very boundary of a vast energy discontinuity, the real versus the unreal. One issue regular marbles didn't have to deal with was a catastrophic reality dysfunction when you flicked them.

He'd seen it done before, though. The Essiel had managed it on Arc Pallator when they'd snatched their faithful from the jaws of death, ripping the entire temple from the ground to place it safely elsewhere. He'd observed the blueprint of it in the way the Originator city there had shouted back to the sky, twisting the boundary between real and unreal, even though it had been nothing but a dead ruin. And this installation here was *alive*.

He would have to trust that his subconscious could make the calculations. Sighting up on the marble that he was actually inside, he applied his mind. He dug his fingernails into the substance of the cosmos, the nothing of unspace, and twisted all the curves and gradients off every point of the compass.

Then the Presence was rising like the kraken, because he *really* had its attention now. He knew it of old, but never before had Idris actually managed to piss it off like this.

It was rising jaws agape, and although the thing he was moving was vast, as big as any ship he'd ever piloted, the whole would have fit within the circumference of those teeth with plenty of nothing to spare. Except, of course, it wasn't the teeth; it was the nothingness between them that would devour you.

Everyone else would feel the same, he knew. He hoped they'd be able to stand it. It would only be for a second and a half, though for him, balancing all the energy and mass of the universe on the head of a pin, it seemed to last for a hundred years.

They were then out of the Presence's reach and he was disconnecting from the Machine, emerging to find a terrible wailing of tortured air whistling away from them in every direction. The Machine, and a ragged chunk of the Originator installation, was now sitting in orbit above Criccieth's Hell.

He panicked for a moment, because he honestly hadn't thought beyond the exit part of the plan. Re-entry into hard vacuum and zero-G was way outside his contemplation. He jackknifed up in the couch and then Jaine killed power to the Machine, even over the screaming of the air.

This lessened. Not, as he might reasonably have feared, from running out of air, but because something of the facility's field snapped back into place the moment the Machine died. The atmosphere around them shuddered, shouldering back and forth through the spaces of the de-installed installation as flaws in the field began to erratically syphon it off. The gravity was back, but it too was unreliable, its strength fluctuating from half to three-quarters of Earth standard, by Idris's professional assessment. It was also complicated by the fact that the torn-out piece of facility was spinning. The outwards pull of the spin was at around seventy degrees to the actual gravitic plane the facility's engines were trying to instate.

"Some stability, Jaine, please." Doctor Shinandri was sitting on his own couch, clinging on for dear life. He had his helmet off but Jaine was forcing it back on.

"I have no control over this," she was saying. "We might lose atmosphere any moment. Just…suit up. Everyone that's got one, keep wearing it." Idris realized that she was the only one who hadn't. Not that his and the doctor's suits were intended for space, exactly, but they were better than nothing. The two Tothiat were definitely spacer-casual for protective gear, but then vacuum wouldn't kill them. Solace's people and the Voyenni had all come loaded for hard vacuum. Which left…

"Ahab," he got out. "Where's Ahab?"

"Not here," Jaine said shortly, still fiddling with Shinandri's suit. "Tried to raise him but comms are fritzed right now. The field is screwing with them, and half the tech I put in is still down on the surface. That," she added, "was something. I will be talking to you about what you just did, Menheer Telemmier. It was a thing. Right, Doc, you're good."

"We need to get out of here," Solace said. "Can you broadcast?"

"I can try," Jaine said. "What's your play?"

"Call our ship, get them over here. If they're even out there still. There was a war going on when we left." Idris could hear the strain in her voice.

"Let me..." Jaine was then over at another console, more of the tech she'd bolted to the tech Ahab had stapled to her original systems, which themselves were just parasites off the Originator originals. These were bleeding out into space right now for all he knew.

He felt a dreadful longing to get back on the couch and turn the Machine on, despite all the many reasons that would be a terrible idea. Unspace had always horrified him, an enemy he set himself against every time he did his job. But now he heard the Sirens calling from those unreal depths. *What truths you could learn!* The Machine had turned his entire perspective inside out. His hands were shaking just thinking about it. *They made me an addict to revelation.*

"I have...something?" Jaine said. For a moment there'd been a screen projected up from her console showing a scatter of ships. Apparently she'd scavenged some data from it because she went on, "The salvage ship was yours? She's still there. I'm signalling. Can't open a voice channel but I'm using spacer on-offs." Meaning that the most she could get out was a stream of signal/non-signal, little more than zeros and ones. Spacers had been getting themselves into dumbass deathtraps like this for generations since the Polyaspora, though. There were long-established codes.

Now Jaine watched her console hawkishly, and everyone, absolutely everyone, was utterly silent, waiting for her. "Received response," she said at last. "Coming for us." She looked up, eyes seeing not their immediate surroundings but the wider structure of what Idris had wrested from the ground. "Okay then, I have absolutely no idea what's intact between here and open space but I'm lighting a beacon at the edge of where my network reaches. We'll just have to hope that's the outside and it's somewhere your ship can reach. Doc, you're up to walking?"

"I would prefer it to eventually running out of air," he agreed, and she helped him off the couch, lurching in the weird gravity and the unquiet air.

"Give me the route," Solace ordered. Jaine flicked an eyebrow at that but nodded. "Just bear in mind what's between *here* and *there* may not match the maps anymore, after what your boy pulled."

"Do you have a suit?" Idris asked her.

She gave him a small smile. "Well I'm not exactly proofed for vacuum but," and rapped on her cybernetic torso, "I'll cope until I don't."

Before she'd let them set off, she tried calling Ahab again, more than once. But there was nothing.

"His Machine terminal should still be within this piece of installation you've left us with," she muttered. "Come *on*, boss." At last she gave up, because Solace was clearly just going to leave without her.

Moving through the wreck of the installation was a nightmare of three-dimensional navigation. Gravity was no longer their tame dog, and every open space became a battleground for changing weather, winds that scoured past them and tore people from their feet or tried to suck them away into the abyss. The air pressure was declining too. Not swiftly but enough that Idris could sense it. He had no idea whether they were even in a stable orbit, and the odds were that the whole salvaged chunk of installation would end up plummeting cataclysmically back into Criccieth's lethal radiationsphere. He wondered if any of it would survive to actually hit the ground.

I've saved nothing. I'm sorry, Ahab. Ahab, who he hadn't saved either.

They passed through a section of the wreck where the air was howling away into nowhere and the gravity followed a spiral across walls and ceiling, shifting as the chunk of facility rotated. Jaine faltered then, the thin atmosphere frosting her face and hands, and Idris and Shinandri had to help her. He saw her internal mechanisms working furiously. All those artificial organs in her torso putting in overtime to defrost her blood and keep her brain oxygenated, while her remaining skin went blue. Then Emmaneth shouldered him aside. There was a cold sheen across the Tothiat's face and her eyes were frozen open but she didn't seem to care. She just grabbed Jaine and leapt across the chamber, landing hard and badly—eye-twistingly on the wrong wall—but springing back up even as her knees reset themselves. Heremon hared right after her in case all this was some kind of escape attempt.

They all bundled into the next section and Shinandri got a hatch-cover shut that stopped the most urgent egress of air, but not all the other intermittent leaks that were yanking the atmosphere left and right. The two Tothiat were glowering at each other, on the brink of having it out, but then Emmaneth sneered and dismissed the other woman, pointedly turning her back. *What is Heremon going to do, after all? Punch her?*

"Will you two just—" Solace started, and then stopped. "I had comms, just for a moment."

"From who?" Jaine asked faintly. Colour was coming back to her face now they were back on the right side of freezing again.

"Sounded like Kittering."

"I'm not getting anything." They then clambered out through a Naeromathi-sized hatch into a big open level, and the gravity shifted sideways just as the wind started. Abruptly they were all sliding away down a suddenly sloping floor. Idris grappled Shinandri as the doctor lost his grip, and then he was in freefall himself until one of the Voyenni unexpectedly snagged the pair of them. They were only slowing their tumble, though, using magnetized boots and suits that turned a headlong fall into a weirdly stop-and-start descent, along an incline that couldn't make up its mind where *down* was supposed to be. In the middle of this, he heard a clear voice issuing from Solace's suit. Static lashed across it, but Kit's translator was clearly recognizable for all that.

"Docking has been accomplished!" the Hanni was saying.

Solace clamped down on the floor, which was becoming more flat than slope as the artificial gravity began to behave again. "Say again?"

"Hearing your voice is always welcome! The beacon is ours. Course to be maintained until we are reached."

Idris saw Solace take stock: everyone was still with them. The world was not quite as mad as it had been a moment ago, but teetering on the edge. *Down* was still darting about beneath them like an anxious fish under ice.

"Are you safe? What about the *Intrepid*?" Solace pressed. "Are we coming out into a firefight?"

"No, no, fighting discontinued," came Kit's distant, scratchy voice. "A change of circumstances occurred. There is a *Scythe*."

"Repeat," Solace asked blankly. "I thought you said there was a scythe?"

Idris actually registered the change in Heremon and Emmaneth but didn't have the context to understand it.

"Ship identified as the *Almighty Scythe of Morning*," Kit reported. "A stand-off is currently occurring."

"The Harvest is here? What do they...?" Solace's gaze twitched over to Emmaneth. "Surely not just for—"

Emmaneth hadn't cared that Heremon had come for her, right up until then. *You'll never hold me*, she'd said, and so the other Tothiat had just been a complication. But her lord and former master had come for her in person, and that changed a lot.

She had her gun still, and immediately emptied the magazine into Heremon, tearing the woman's torso open, enough fatal wounds for a dozen. A moment later she straight-armed the woman in her broken chest with enough force to fling her backwards. Idris saw the bones of Emmaneth's own arm shatter with the force. Then she was springing away and gravity chose that moment to skew, sending them all scattering down the rivet-studded iron jigsaw of the floor.

Emmaneth slammed into a bulkhead ahead of them. Idris saw half her body deform round it, but snap back into shape just as quickly. She cast one glance at them, as they scrabbled or tumbled towards her, and then set her fingers into the seams between plates.

"No!" Jaine was yelling, already ahead of her.

"Sorry!" Emmaneth shouted back, and then tore the wall open.

There must have been only half as much atmospheric pressure beyond the wall, because everyone took a violent left turn, ripped from their holds and sucked into the next section of the wreck. Emmaneth was bounding ahead, followed by Heremon—skin still knitting back together—giving chase.

The hand holding onto Idris's belt then suddenly yanked him into a close hold. He craned back to see the faceplate of one of the Voyenni. He could just make out the man's narrow, scarred face, see his lips move as he spoke into his own comms.

Then he was off, Idris bundled under his arm like a package. His fellows were with him, kicking out across the open space, heading away from the trail that the two Tothiat had taken and leaving the Partheni behind.

33.

Idris

Just once it would be good to be strong, he thought. Hereditary spacers with three generations of bad nutrition and close quarters tended towards the skinny, though, and Idris was a dwarfish scarecrow even for them. The Voyenni, on the other hand, were presumably recruited out of the very beefiest that long-settled Magda could offer, and then fattened up on red meat and steroids. Kick and struggle as much as he wanted, Idris was doing nothing more than putting the man slightly off his bounding course.

He heard the high singing notes of accelerators behind him and winced, even though his flinching would be coming solid moments *after* any shot might have found him. It hit something, though. There was an explosive moment just out of sight that sent a ragged skirt of blood lashing past his view, curling weirdly in the unreliable gravity. One of the other Voyenni running fatal interference, he guessed, or just getting in the way.

"You can't win this time," he shouted at his captor's armpit. The *this time* was wearily felt—how many chances had these goons missed to grab him? "I'm probably not even important anymore!" Events had, after all, moved on. But the Voyenni only had his last orders to go on, and they were here to get Idris.

"I am not," he insisted, "worth your life. Look, the ship coming to get us is my ship, with my friends on it. You could have just walked aboard and been repatriated. Now you're going to meet Olli and she will pull your goddamn head off."

"Shut up!" The man abruptly had him at arm's length, shaking him like a doll. "Failure is not an option!" He sounded as though he were close to tears. Idris caught sight of his face through his visor: pop-eyed, veins bulging, panicked beyond reason. A man who'd been big and strong all his life, who'd picked what he thought was the winning side, and that had always been enough. Now this, on the run through a dying chunk of labyrinth and alien tech, chased by an implacable enemy and with nowhere to go.

There was more shouting from behind—the Partheni hot on his trail.

"I'll kill you," the Voyenni said. "Rather than let them have you." He was fumbling in some pocket of his suit, even as he yanked Idris along like a toy balloon. The gravity was abruptly almost gone, and then a great howling rush of air had both of them in its teeth, bundling them end over end, off course and ramming into walls. Idris was clinging onto the man's arm now, letting the Voyenni blaze that particular trail and cushion the blows. The waves and fluctuations of the installation's fields were coming to him mind first, then body, his senses receiving briefings from the unspace boundary they rippled across. He saw the man's faceplate crack with one impact, and another tore open the pouch he was trying to open. A scatter of tools leapt out into the air and were immediately yanked sideways towards a metallic wall, along with both men. Every ferrous part of their suits had abruptly magnetized, dragging them there, along with the little toolkit and knife the man had surely been seeking.

The Voyenni tried to prise the blade loose but found it practically welded to the clunky Naeromathi ironwork. With a snarl he grabbed for Idris's throat, but Idris had been letting the shifting field whisper to him, *Now, now*. When he took the knife, it flew upwards to his hand like a pet bird.

The Voyenni made a gargling noise and Idris drove the blade into the man's elbow, between the plates of his suit. The puncture would have sealed instantly, except that Idris left the knife in there, jammed between armour and bones both. He then kicked off, anticipating the waxing gravity so that from a near-float he ended up on his feet. The Voyenni stared at him, apoplectic, lit by a weird light. Backing away.

That light: glaring across the man's visor, reflecting back from every shiny surface on his suit, colouring the very walls. A green light, a yellow and purple and orange light, all at once, jangling the eyes, screaming into the visual centres of the brain. Idris had seen that light before, but only with some serious layers of protection between him and the things that made it.

He turned around and saw, coming through the ceiling, a barbed, snaking tendril that glowed and seared and wept with that light. The flora of Criccieth's Hell hadn't been wholly left behind on the planet. Some of it had still been attached.

It twisted and writhed, lunging forwards in sudden starts, branching, weaving in the air. And it wasn't *moving*, he realized. It wasn't a serpent but a root, *growing* as fast as he could scrabble back from it. A severed but still-living thing flooding the air with its deadly radiation, mindlessly questing for whatever the hell it was that these monstrous plants desired.

The Voyenni had moved well back, climbing down the slope of the wall as though it was a steep hill. Idris was trying to do the same but the sight of the creeper was hypnotic. A primal part of him felt that if he turned away it would rush forwards, seize him, impale him. And it was getting closer. Much closer. All the alarms in his suit—or the few that Jaine had left functional—were screaming about the radiation exposure, and yet he couldn't let the thing out of his sight. Even as all the air about him shuddered and shunted off, another breach sucking it from the dying installation. Even as that angry, radiant tendril grew ever nearer to him.

Then Heremon was rushed into the room with a turbulent shift of atmosphere, sending him along the floor too in a direction that was momentarily both *down* and *up*. Emmaneth came right after her, landing on her enemy and delivering three blows that destroyed ribs and jaw as well as her own hands, with every injury seething back together a moment later.

Idris was shouting at them. He wasn't sure what he shouted, to be honest. Just raw emotions mostly. Just *Don't be so stupid this isn't the time* sort of noise. They were gone out of his sight a heartbeat later, and he could see nothing but that root and its poisonous light.

He thrust out a hand to ward it off and felt a fierce, fiery pain from the fingers of that hand, then down the arm to the elbow.

He would have run then, except the gravity was back,

pinning him to the floor. He had no strength left. He felt sick, and probably he was sick, just from being so near the thing.

Someone then took hold of him and just dragged him away by his nominally good arm, putting the shoulder well out of its socket. He screamed from the pain as he went skidding away across the floor, hitting every rivet and plate-edge as he did so. His suit became a ruin, and he felt the cold, thin air on his skin and in his lungs.

He ended up on his stomach, one arm shrieking agony at him from a shoulder that would click back into place readily enough. The other was terrifyingly numb, even though there was nothing much left of it past the charred stump of his elbow. The charred stump. He just stared at that for a second, trying to understand what he was seeing. Then he looked back and saw the end of it.

Emmaneth was the one who had hauled him away from the root. Her last service for the Criccieth's Hell research operation. Or possibly she had simply been getting him off that particular cross so she could take his place.

The root had pierced her through the abdomen, a sudden access of speed in its blind questing. Her body arched backwards, fingers clawing at the iron walls. For a moment it seemed that her monstrous metabolism could survive even this.

Then it was incinerating her. She just flaked away into ash below the ribs. Idris saw her eyes close and her face go slack, and he had no idea if this was what she had really wanted or not.

Heremon was screaming, though. Not rage, as he first thought: grief. Screaming at the death of a sister, getting as close as she dared, trying to steal from death's own table. She came back, her skin blistered and cracked, one eye gone, but she was clutching something to herself, shielding it from the terrible glare. The Tothir, he realized. The chitinous symbiote that had been part of what Emmaneth had become. He had no idea if it was still alive or not.

He lurched further away from the root, not wanting to see it work its way through the rest of Emmaneth's human remains. Not wanting to see what Heremon did next. Not wanting anything to do with any of it. Every movement was agony, but the field was still telling him how it was going to shift and change, so he tried to let the air and the gravity do the walking for him.

The Voyenni then kicked him hard in the stomach, and he went over, landing on the arm that was mostly gone now. He blacked out for a moment but then he was on his back, staring up at the man. The knife was still wedged between the plates of his elbow, but otherwise the Voyenni was in a better state than Idris. Which wasn't saying much.

For a moment they just stared at each other, and Idris wondered if there were some words he might say, if he could only find them, that would get through the pain and rage, and twenty years of abusive training, to bring the man round to the side of sanity. Then one big Voyenni boot was up in the air, ready to come down on any part of Idris that fell into its shadow.

But there was a larger shadow. A serpent that loomed over the Voyenni—not the glazing death-light of the Criccieth tendril, but a thing of dark scarred flesh and metal.

The Voyenni must have seen the movement reflected in Idris's battered visor because he hesitated, looking up, and in that moment the thing fell on him, thundering down like a fist. It struck and seized, a half-dozen tentacles and manipulator arms taking hold of the man. There were no jaws: if Ahab had ever possessed such a feature it was long gone behind its cybernetic additions. It didn't need them, though, shaking the Voyenni like a dog with a rat, and then throwing him at the tendril. Idris felt the shift of gravity coming in time to dig his heels into the floor. For a brief moment, that writhing root was the centre of their little universe and the Voyenni hurtled screaming towards it. He was destroyed utterly, nothing left that was visible to the eye.

Then Ahab grabbed Idris and hauled him away, and Heremon was hurrying after, cradling the curled-up lobster-thing which was all that was left of Emmaneth.

Solace and her Myrmidons found them soon after, Jaine and Shinandri still gamely following along. By then, the atmosphere was thin enough that Idris was having difficulty breathing and couldn't move under his own power, even after Heremon had unsympathetically reset his shoulder. They were within a last dash of the *Vulture God* by then, though, bundling one after another into its umbilical, with the steady gravity and atmosphere that came with it. Olli's expression when she saw just how many passengers she'd inherited was a picture. Her look at Ahab was one of sheer panic. The Naeromathi barely fit down the umbilical and could only just be crammed into the drone bay.

Then Solace was getting Idris to the *Vulture*'s rudimentary med bay to start what tissue repair was even possible.

*

In the end, they had to move Idris over to one of the Partheni ships because the *God*'s facilities were entirely inadequate. The medical officer there told him they'd need to flush his blood out entire and seed his bone marrow with regenerative nanos to even start repairing the radiation damage. The telltales around his heart said the organ had done its best just to stop dead during his encounter with the tendril, but the little knot of Trine's units there had gamely soldiered on and kept it beating for him. He hadn't even realized he had telltales.

He remembered thinking that he wanted to be strong, when the Voyenni had him. Looking back on what he'd survived in his life, he wondered if all those pieces came together into a kind of strength, despite himself.

And as for the Partheni...

Nobody seemed to know entirely what was going on. The actual crew of the ship he'd ended up on, the *Amina Mohamud*, wouldn't speak to him. They seemed to find having a Colonial aboard massively socially awkward, given that they were on a war footing. It took Solace's visit to start the enlightenment process, after she'd liaised with her superiors and been briefed herself.

The *Intrepid* was still sitting in orbit around Criccieth's Hell, as well as the flight of Partheni vessels and the original gunboat and escorts the Orichalk naval base had sent out. The two factions were all keeping a politic amount of the planet's curve between them. Most of the vessels were cut up and there had been deaths on both sides from the early fighting, but right now nobody was shooting.

The most obvious reason for this was the *Almighty Scythe of Morning*, the flagship of a Hegemonic gangster, which was somehow sitting unmolested here, in the heart of the Colonies. A vessel more than capable of holding off both little flotillas at once if it so chose. Not, Idris considered, more than capable of holding off everything currently docked at Orichalk, though. He'd have expected the naval base to be launching everything it had to clear the system of all foreign armed presence. Solace agreed, and yet they weren't doing that. The Partheni weren't just getting out with Idris either, which would seem to have been the sensible decision. Whatever was going on was doing so at a level above Solace's head. It was, she said, Aspirat business, and apparently unfit for anyone below Monitor Superior.

"They're going to put me under soon," Idris told her glumly. "I don't like it. Been happening a lot recently. I'm out of the habit of having slices of time I don't remember. Freaks me out."

"You need it. I've seen the full list of repairs your body requires. You don't want to be awake for that. And they can't even *get* you a prosthetic here. They're not able to restore enough nerve throughput to your arm. We'll have to get you to a specialist ward for that."

"I was hoping for a tissue graft, rather than a fake," grumbled Idris. That was probably complicated for the Partheni, who were used to working with a narrow range of genetic variance for the purposes of tissue rejection. "I guess I'll take what I can get right now. So...what next, basically?"

"We're still waiting for the *what*," was all Solace could say. "All the drives are hot and ready to go if it looks like this is going to turn into a shooting war again. Until then... high-ups are talking, and you get to have your blood replaced."

"Well I never liked it anyway. Mongrel spacer stuff. Maybe

they can give me better blood, make me heir to a kingdom or something," Idris said vaguely.

The others had come to see him, one at a time. Olli was on a high, having apparently trashed a very expensive yacht. Kris was as low as he'd ever seen her, having very nearly killed a very expensive Magdan nobleman. She'd killed before, he knew. Killing someone at knifepoint was exactly why she wasn't enjoying a lucrative legal career on some fancy core world somewhere. But she still had the shudders about it, and now it had almost happened again. Because it was something she was very good at, and because—Idris suspected—there was a part of her that came out of its cave and exulted in such things, and she hated that about herself. Kittering was fretting about the future, as he did—he was a planner by nature and right now they just didn't have the information to plan. Heremon and Agent Mundy hadn't put in an appearance and Idris wasn't particularly sorry for that. They had both ended up on the *Scythe*, apparently. The *Raptorid*, or what Olli had left of it, was docked with the *Intrepid* for the same reasons they'd brought Idris to the *Amina Mohamud*: Piter Uskaro had needed more work than his own med bay could handle.

Very shortly before they put him under, he received a call. It didn't come through the Partheni comms officer, nor did it apparently register on their system or leave a record of its coming and going. It was just a familiar voice issuing out of the speaker beside his bed, taking its moment when none of the crew were around.

"Idris? Do I find you well?"

Idris stared at the grey-blue of the ceiling. "Ash."

"None other." He pictured the alien, its inhuman form

crammed into a robe in the universe's least successful attempt at mimicry. Ash, speaking all languages, bearing ominous warnings, a Cassandra whom people had learned soon enough to heed.

"I'm alive. That's probably enough for now," he said to the air around him. In truth he was feeling exceptionally sick, even pumped full of drugs.

"And you were successful?" He had no idea if the emotion, as heard in Ash's voice, was something real or just a show the creature put on. Right now it sounded tremulously eager.

Idris himself only felt bitter, but he forced himself to confirm, "Yes. Ahab and I found it, and understood it."

"That's marvellous, Idris."

"Is it?"

"Idris, I have been looking for a way to strike against the Architects for a long time. Far longer even than Ahab. This is the first indication that such a thing is even possible."

"Except," Idris told it, "the Architects are not the problem. There's something out there that wants to kill us, or at least to wreck all our worlds, and it's not the Architects. They're innocent. They're under duress. I thought we'd find the masters, but instead we found...where Architects *come* from, Ash. We found their children."

"And will you put these 'children's' lives before every human and Hanni and Castigar, and all the other species in the universe, Idris?" Ash asked.

"No," Idris whispered. "But...Where *are* they, Ash?"

A silence on the channel.

"The Architects know where we are and what we've found. Why haven't they just turned up to twist us into pretzels? We're a threat now. One which they have the power to remove."

He continued, not leaving Ash time to speculate. "They're terrified of what we might do, too. I felt it down there. Yet they haven't come to slap us, because that's something they only do when their masters force them. I learned that before. I don't even know if they've told their masters what we're up to. Maybe they can't. Maybe that channel only goes one way."

He started to think that the link to Ash—wherever Ash even *was*—had died, but at last the voice came back to him. "We still have to stop them, Idris. Billions of lives are at stake. All the lives and thinking minds in the universe," and Idris broke in before he could stop himself.

"What are you, Ash?"

Another silence.

"Because you know what, you're right. All the thinking minds. Thought is the thing, isn't it. Thought distorts unspace. I'm living proof of that. When I was in the Machine, I could see all those thoughts, of all those sentient beings, pulling at the structure of everything just by virtue of existing. But you already knew that. Are you... Are *you* the last Originator?"

Ash laughed. It sounded exactly like a human laughing. "That would be satisfying, wouldn't it?" There was another long pause that Idris didn't feel able to break into. "Did Ahab live, by the way? Reports are contradictory."

"We got it out," Idris confirmed. "As well as Shinandri and Tokamak Jaine. Emmaneth died. Or most of her did."

"You actually transported a large piece of the Originator mechanism into orbit?"

"Let me guess, you can use that."

"Most certainly we can. You've really done very, very well, Idris."

Then the Partheni medics were coming in and Ash's voice was gone so abruptly he wondered if he'd just hallucinated the whole business. And then they put him under.

Havaer

Havaer Mundy didn't much care for Hegemonic interior ship design. But that was nothing compared to his feelings about The Unspeakable Aklu, the Razor and the Hook. The Essiel hovered in the centre of a star-shaped chamber there, lording it over the universe, with a half-dozen thugs in attendance. Heremon had already been repatriated to his side, though Havaer had no idea what had happened to the Tothir part of Emmaneth.

Also in attendance at this gathering of factions were a handful of men and women he recognized from Mordant House—not the flashy high-fliers but competent agents, people he'd worked with. People who had been on Chief Laery's shortlist for doing the dirty jobs and getting out with clean hands, like him.

Colvari was present too. *Delegate* Colvari, as the Hiver had apparently been promoted to, sitting off to one side, looking like nothing very much except for their antique legs. Not the same Colvari he'd hired after Hismin's Moon, really. The reinstantiation meant that they had the same memories and the same designation, but no continuation of self. In human terms, the Colvari he'd known had given up its life so that this more useful Colvari could come into being. The thought still vaguely depressed him.

And there was Ash. Havaer didn't trust Ash, despite the

alien's semi-benevolent history. Ash was, as far as he could tell, doing its best to pretend the whole business had been its plan all along. Havaer reckoned it was adapting to what was, though. It had something to do with whatever the hell had been on the planet, and was now in unstable orbit above it. Ash's retinue currently consisted of a cyborg, some kind of academic and a Naeromathi that looked like it had gone through a serial autopsy. And yet they'd apparently made some kind of grand discovery together, which was Ash's leverage for a seat at this table.

Finally, rounding out the conspiracy: Chief Laery. Standing right by Aklu as though that was a reasonable thing for anyone to accept.

She was wearing a Berlenhof-style suit bulked out by an exoskeleton to support her stick-insect frame. She'd just given an address—not just to the naval base at Orichalk and the little knot of Partheni, but to the whole of Hugh and the Parthenon, and possibly the entire Hegemony into the bargain.

"My name is Adela Laery," she'd said. Havaer had been wrong-footed a moment before remembering that yes, she did have a first name. "Formerly of the Intervention Board. Possibly still of, depending on how people feel like taking this, but frankly the distinction is of supreme indifference to me right now." She seemed simultaneously exhausted and strung tight as a wire, and Havaer wondered what cocktail of drugs she was on right then.

"I am speaking to you as the human element in a new alliance that has come together to deal with the threat the Architects pose to all life. The majority shareholder in this alliance is the Hiver Assembly in Aggregate, which has come to the conclusion that neither the Parthenon nor the Council of Human Interests is in a position to take the required steps. The Assembly is assisted by...certain elements of the Hegemony that are permitted to take such actions."

Because the Essiel did not *fight* the Architects, of course. They'd worked out their own détente hiding behind the fragments and ruins of the Originators. This strategy had stopped working, of course, when the Architects had begun taking their toys *back*. So much for the almighty Essiel Hegemony. Except, built into the byzantine and occult Hegemonic structure was their state-sanctioned devil. The maverick that could, by its very nature, do the things Essiel were forbidden to do, or perhaps were unable even to conceive of. Given Laery had deliberately delivered Havaer right into Heremon's lap on Matachin Below, he could only assume this particular partnership had been a fixture for a worryingly long time.

"Following recent developments," Laery explained, "we are now in possession of a means to strike against the Architects for the first time. We will be making overtures to both Hugh and Parthenon as to what assistance they can each provide, to develop this weapon. Until then, the Assembly in Aggregate is calling on both sides to at least suspend hostilities. Or in any event to tender what assistance we ask for while you go about killing one another."

After her speech, she'd beckoned Havaer over, looking profoundly pleased with herself, more than ready to start flexing the muscles her new allies were lending her. "First order of business," she'd told him. "Thanks to you, we happen to know that certain elements in Hugh have begun constructing a prototype ark fleet. Strikes me that's just the sort of ship frame we might have a use for, to house the new weapons we'll be developing. I feel some manner of confiscation is in order." He'd looked into her sere, gaunt face and wondered just how many scores Chief Laery was about to settle with the universe at large.

But that, apparently, was that. The Hiver Assembly in Aggregate, which had been a compliant partner to Hugh and the Parthenon through all the years since it had won its independence from human control, had decided to wake up and flex its muscles. Its factories and orbitals were spread throughout human-controlled space. A great many military and civilian leaders would right now be considering just how bad things might get if the Hivers weren't on their side any more.

Idris

When Idris woke up, he had new blood. It felt just like the old blood. They'd patched up about a million other problems too, but he was still without one arm from mid-bicep, which was, by half an upper arm, fewer arms than he'd had when he went under. Apparently what they'd left him with was everything that could be saved. Someone would be along to talk to him about replacements later, they told him, as if he'd lost a pair of shoes. At least the only pain was a faint background buzz that wasn't much different to everyday life.

He had visitors, they told him. He was expecting Solace and the crew, but instead he got a roomful of Partheni and one ebullient Hiver.

"Trine?"

"Just arrived, my old friend and adopted sibling," the archaeologist agreed cheerily. "They tell me you've been having adventures! You should stop that, it obviously fails to agree with you. I, on the other hand, have been summoned both for my inarguable expertise on the subject of Originator remains, and my new diplomatic authority. And you, my dear colleague and good old friend, have found me an *intact* Originator site!"

"Mostly intact," Idris agreed weakly, then one of the Partheni pointedly coughed for attention.

"Delegate, if you will?"

"If I will?" Trine turned their holographic face on the speaker. "Well I suppose I must."

"Menheer Telemmier, I am—"

"Monitor Superior Tact," Idris filled in for her. "Solace's boss."

"Even so," she agreed. "I am here to take you back to Partheni space, now the diplomatic niceties have been ironed out."

"You mean you've decided who owns me."

"Actually a great deal more than that," she said, not wrong-footed in the least. "It's not all about you, Menheer Telemmier. We are having something of a war, you may have heard."

"Solace told me." A beat. "The *Ceres*. How bad was it?" Remembering the ship he'd lived on for several months, the women he'd lived amongst. "The program...?"

Tact nodded, appreciating that he'd thought to ask. "There was considerable loss of life," she stated. "However, the bulk of our first class, the potential Intermediaries, were off-ship at the time, undergoing unspace exposure. We will rebuild. With your help." She couldn't quite shut that down without the slightest hint of a question mark at the end of it. They couldn't force him, after all.

"And the war?" he asked her.

"Is complicated. There has been a...declaration and an invitation of sorts. From a third party. We're still waiting to see what Hugh and our high command will say in response."

*

Idris got to hear Laery's declaration later, when they finally repatriated him to the *Vulture God*. He was there under Solace's watch, and the *God* was right in the middle of the Partheni expeditionary force, but it was still a gesture of trust, Tact trying to put him at his ease.

He watched, hearing the withered old Mordant House woman tell the universe about the new alliance, how things were going to be.

"This," Olli told him, "is some fucked-up mess we're all in. Hugh must be crapping themselves about the new players in town. *And* your lot must be too." Poking Solace's ankle with one leg of her walking frame.

Ash will be there in the centre of it all, Idris thought. *Pursuing his own ancient mission. Of which Ahab's crusade is maybe just a part.*

"That's a lot to take in," he admitted.

"Truly the dawn of a new golden age," Trine declared happily, to nobody's particular agreement.

"Yeah, well," Olli decided. "This new alliance can just get on with things, the lot of them, right?"

"It won't be that simple," Solace said quietly, and apparently this was news to everyone else as well as Idris. "They need us to go there, too. To their new base. The Partheni Int program is relocating there for starters."

"Why?" he demanded.

"Because it's neutral ground, and safe, and because they'll need Partheni pilots. For the ships they're building, or converting from these arks. If Tact and Laery and the others have us all working together right now, we need to make the most of it before something goes wrong. And their alliance will really need you, to work with those pilots. To help as many of them survive becoming Intermediaries as possible." It was unfair, for her to put that on him, to hit him right where he was most vulnerable. But it was true, as well.

He didn't want to take the war to the Architects. He didn't want to be any part of what might be genocide. But neither the universe nor the war was done with him yet.

THE UNIVERSE OF THE ARCHITECTS: REFERENCE

Glossary

Architects—moon-sized entities that can reshape populated planets and ships

Aspirat—Partheni intelligence services

The Betrayed—the violent extremist wing of the Nativists

Broken Harvest Society—a Hegemonic criminal cartel

Colonies—The surviving human worlds following the fall of Earth.

Council of Human Interests ("Hugh")—the governing body of the Colonies

Hegemony—a coalition of species ruled by the alien Essiel

Hegemonic cult—humans who serve and worship the Essiel

Intermediaries—surgically modified navigators who can pilot ships off the Throughways, developed as weapons against the Architects during the war

Intermediary Program—Colonial wartime body responsible for creating the Intermediaries

Intervention Board ("Mordant House")—Colonial policing and intelligence service

Kybernet—an AI system responsible for overseeing a planet or orbital

Liaison Board—current Colonial body responsible for

creating Intermediaries en masse for commercial purposes

Nativists—a political movement that believes in "pure-born" humans and "humanity first"

Orbital—an orbiting habitat

Parthenon—a breakaway human faction composed of parthenogenetically grown women

Throughways—paths constructed within unspace by unknown hands, joining habitable planets. Without a special navigator, ships can only travel along existing Throughways

Unspace—a tenuous layer beneath real space, which can be used for fast travel across the universe

Voyenni—the house guard of a Magdan noble

Characters
Crew of the *Vulture God*

Rollo Rostand—Captain, deceased

Idris Telemmier—Intermediary navigator

Keristina "Kris" Soolin Almier—lawyer

Olian "Olli" Timo—drone specialist

Kittering "Kit"—Hannilambra factor

Musoku "Barney" Barnier—engineer, deceased

Medvig—Hiver search and catalogue specialist, deceased

Myrmidon Executor Solace—Partheni soldier and agent

*

Other key characters

Ahab—Naeromathi visionary and engineer
The Unspeakable Aklu, the Razor and the Hook—Essiel
  gangster
Beyon—Voyenni in the service of the Uskaro family
Colvari—Hiver data analyst
Drayfus—retired pirate
Emmaneth (Emma Ostri)—rogue Tothiat
Cognosciente Superior Felicity—Partheni scientist
Professor Granduja—academic on Deathknell
Cognosciente Grave—Partheni technician
Heremon—Tothiat in Aklu's employ
Ismia—Hegemonic cult liaison
Tokamak Jaine—engineer
Exemplar Keen—Partheni captain of the *Grendel's Mother*
Kenyon—Intervention Board agent, Havaer's second
Chief Laery—Havaer's superior on the Intervention Board
Lombard—Intervention Board officer
Karl Mannec—Colonial diplomat
Havaer Mundy—Intervention Board agent
Reams—Intervention Board agent
Doctor Sang Sian Parsefer—founder of the Parthenon
Doctor Haleon Shinandri—maverick scientist
The Radiant Sorteel, the Provident and the Prescient—
  divine Essiel
Professor Tiber Storquel—Colonial expert on Originator
  technology
Monitor Superior Tact—Solace's superior in the Aspirat
Xavienne "Saint Xavienne" Torino—the first Intermediary,
  deceased

Delegate Trine—Hiver archaeologist
Demi Ulo—Intermediary, first class
Boyarin Piter Tchever Uskaro—nobleman from Magda
Morzarin Ravin Okosh Uskaro—nobleman from Magda, Piter's uncle.

Worlds

Amraji—world destroyed by the Architects
Arc Pallator—Hegemonic world
Berlenhof—administrative and cultural heart of the Colonies
Criccieth's Hell—death-world
Earth—world destroyed by the Architects
Far Lux—where Intermediaries ended the war
Forthbridge Port—where Saint Xavienne first managed to contact an Architect
Hismin's Moon—Hanni mining colony
Huei-Cavor—prosperous world which passed from the Colonies to the Hegemony
Ittring—Hanni residence world
Jericho—wild planet rich in Originator ruins
Kodo—Colonial mining world
Matachin—Colonial industrial system
Nillitik—Hanni–human world destroyed by the Architects
Orichalk—Colonial world, site of a naval base
Roshu—a mining world and Throughway hub
Scintilla—planet noted for its legal schools and duelling code
Tarekuma—a lawless, hostile planet.

Species

Ash—the Harbinger, a singular alien that brought warning of the Architects to Earth

Athamir—fungal-looking species subject to the Essiel

Castigar—alien species with several castes and shapes, naturally wormlike

Essiel—the "divine" masters of the Hegemony

Hannilambra ("Hanni")—crab-shaped aliens, enthusiastic merchants

Hivers—composite cyborg insect intelligences, originally created by humans but now independent

Naeromathi ("Locusts")—nomadic aliens that deconstruct worlds to create more of their "Locust Arks"

Ogdru—a species from the Hegemony that produces void-capable navigators

Originators—a hypothetical elder race responsible for the Throughways and certain enigmatic ruins

Tothiat—a hybrid of the symbiotic Tothir and another species, often human. Phenomenally resilient

Tymeree—diminutive species subject to the Essiel

Ships

Almighty Scythe of Morning—flagship belonging to the Broken Harvest cartel

Beagle—Colonial science vessel

Byron—Colonial warship

Ceres—Partheni garden ship

Grendel's Mother—Partheni warship

Griper—Intervention Board launch

Hale—Partheni light carrier

Heaven's Sword—Partheni warship, both the original that was destroyed at Berlenhof and its replacement currently in service

Intrepid—Colonial warship

Nereid—Partheni shuttle

Raptorid—private yacht of Boyarin Piter Uskaro

Sturgeon—Partheni shuttle

Vulture God—salvage vessel

TIMELINE

107 Before: Probes sent by Earth to neighbouring star systems attract the attention of an alien ship. Humanity's first alien contact follows shortly afterwards. Once the initial revulsion over the wormlike Castigar fades, humans begin to learn about unspace, Throughways and the wider universe. The Castigar themselves have only been travelling between stars for under a century and have a practice of making small colonies on many planets, but not engaging in large-scale colonization. Castigar ships reach deals to ferry Earth colonists to habitable worlds they had discovered. They also give humans some details about the Naeromathi and the Hegemony.

91 Before: Humans establish their first interstellar colony on Second Dawn, a planet with a dense ecosystem of plant/fungal-like life. Second Dawn is pleasantly balmy for the Castigar but proves difficult for humans.

90 Before: Humans establish a colony on Berlenhof, a warm world with 90% ocean coverage. This thrives and is patronized by a number of powerful companies and rich families.

88 Before: A colony is established on Lief, an ice world in a system with valuable minerals in several asteroid belts. A colony is also established on Amber, a hot world with a crystalline ecosystem where humans live in cooled domes.

75 Before: Several minor colonies are established in other systems with Castigar help, mostly for industrial purposes. Reliance on the Castigar for all shipping is becoming problematic to expanding humanity, and to the Castigar. Castigar scientists work with humans to help them build their own gravitic drives.

72 Before: The first human gravitic drive spaceship, the *Newton's Bullet*, opens the doors to a greater era of human colonization.

61 Before: On the forested world of Lycos, humans discover their first Originator ruins.

45 Before: A Naeromathi Ark arrives in the colonized Cordonier system and begins dismantling some of the inhabited world's moons. Contact goes poorly and degenerates into fighting. There is never a formal Naeromathi–human war, as there is not really a Naeromathi state to declare war on. However, other Ark ships are seen across the Throughway network, and there are several clashes with losses on both sides.

25 Before: Contact is made with the Essiel Hegemony as a result of human travel and expansion. Initial contact is not hostile but humans find it baffling as they and the Essiel fail to understand one another. Human diplomats recognize that the

Essiel appear to be offering humans some kind of master–subject relationship. However, they are confused that it does not appear to be accompanied by threats. In retrospect, warnings about the Architects were present, but not grasped. Over the next decades human emissaries understand that the Hegemony appears to value Originator ruins, though not displaced Originator relics. Several worlds with Originator sites are effectively sold to the Hegemony as a result.

22 Before: As a response to conditions on Earth, and what she sees as deep flaws in human nature, Doctor Sang Sian Parsefer and her allies found the Parthenon. They genetically engineer what they consider to be an ideal version of humanity. The Parthenon is founded as a military force and uses parthenogenetic vat birth as a means of creating human beings artificially. This happens more swiftly than natural means would allow. The Parthenon pushes the limits of human science and is viewed as a threat by the rest of humanity.

5 Before: A Castigar ship brings the alien Ash to Earth, warning of the arrival of the Architects. Few take him seriously; the Castigar themselves have not encountered the Architects. But some nations and groups do make limited preparations.

0: An Architect larger than Earth's moon exits unspace close to Earth. It reworks the planet into the bizarre, coiling structure now familiar to all, causing appalling loss of life and tearing the heart out of the human race. Every space-worthy ship evacuates as many people as it can carry, but billions are left behind to die. The ships flee to various colony worlds. Some reach them, others founder, insufficiently prepared for the voyage. The Polyaspora begins, as does the First Architect War.

15 After: The largest solar system colony on Titan is deconstructed by the Architects around 7AE. Over the next few years, several extrasolar colonies are also reworked. Every human colony is on high alert, with evacuation measures in place as standard. Many colonies become short on food and supplies. Attempts to fight the Architects fail to even attract their notice.

21 After: The small religious colony on Charm Prime establishes communication with Hegemony envoys and becomes the first human Hegemonic cult cell. In return, the Hegemony establishes a shrine, and their human cult declares that the Hegemony can ward off Architects. The majority of other colonies do not believe this, and some claim the Hegemony controls or can even summon Architects to scare humanity into accepting alien overlords. There is little human take-up of Hegemonic rule for the next few decades.

28 After: Experiments in autonomous distributed intelligence, originally intended as a resource-stripping tool, are turned to the war effort. And so the first Hive entity is developed and added to humanity's arsenal.

43 After: In the midst of war, the first Hannilambra–human contact occurs—with Hanni venture-ships narrowly escaping a hostile response when they turn up at Clerk's World. The Hanni will subsequently create a sporadic lifeline of goods, at cost, to beleaguered human colonies. They will also transport humans from colonies under threat.

48 After: Architects at Lycos leave without touching the colony. From this and other clues it becomes clear that the Architects do indeed have some relationship with Originator sites and their relics. The shrine at Charm Prime is found to contain Originator relics and there is a doomed attempt to use these to repel Architects from other colonies by simply transporting them off-world. After the destruction of Karis Commune, whose inhabitants relied on relics taken from Charm Prime, the Hegemony manages to communicate dire news: only they can transport relics in a manner that retains their anti-Architect properties. Between now and the end of the war, a number of human colonies will accept Hegemonic rule in return for such protection.

51 After: The Architects come to Amraji, a large human–Castigar colony swollen with refugees. There is a considerable human military force in place already, owing to the arrival and depredations of a Naeromathi Ark. Parthenon, Hive and regular human forces attack the Architect to buy the evacuation more time and the Naeromathi join the battle on humanity's side. Combined efforts allow over half the colony's population to escape off-planet. However, this initiative also results in the majority of the defenders being destroyed, including the Ark. The "Amraji Peace" is no more a formal human–Naeromathi détente than the hostilities were a war. But from here onwards, fighting between humans and Naeromathi will be minimal.

During these years, at the height of the First Architect War, humanity is living hand to mouth under the constant shadow of annihilation. Everyone lives with an emergency bag and a knowledge of where to go if the worst happens. The entire species suffers from a multigenerational traumatic shock.

68 After: A refugee transport, the *Mylender*, arrives at Forthbridge Port at the same time as an Architect. Aboard is Xavienne Torino, aged 15, who claims that she can hear the Architect's thoughts. Through a process that is entirely mysterious at the time, Xavienne is able to demand that the Architect leaves the system. To everyone's astonishment, it does.

76 After: Human scientists work with Xavienne Torino to isolate the precise genetic and neurological fluke that allowed her to interact with the Architects by way of unspace. By 76AE, the first generation of artificial Intermediaries has been developed. Of the suitable volunteers, fewer than ten per cent survive the process and come out sane. Idris, one of the first generation, is 20 years old when he completes the Program.

78 After: Battle of Berlenhof. The wealthiest and most populous human world detects the approach of an Architect—and military forces race to intervene. The full force of the Parthenon navy, several Hive lattices, human regular forces and alien allies fight to preserve the world. The defenders pay a colossal cost but top-of-the-line Parthenon weapons are able to damage the Architect. Early use of Intermediaries also appears to be effective. However, of the eight Ints deployed, three are killed and another two go insane trying to contact the Architects. Yet Berlenhof is saved.

In the next six years, the Architects destroy two more human colonies. In each case, a spirited defence only buys time for a more thorough evacuation.

80 After: The Intermediary Program reaches its greatest strength with thirty combat Intermediaries. Their training builds on the lessons learned at Berlenhof. They begin meeting the Architects when they manifest, making contact, trying to get the creatures to notice them. Their attempts prove more and more successful.

84 After: Intermediary successes culminate with Idris and two other Ints contacting an Architect at Far Lux. They report that the enemy was momentarily aware of them this time. After this event, there are no further Architect sightings.

As people realize that the war has finally finished, three generations after it started, human society and economy are in a poor way. People are desperate, colonies are under-resourced and overpopulated. There is no real political unity and friction develops between needy colonies and alien neighbours. Growing discontent seems likely to fragment the Polyasporic human presence into dozens of feuding states.

88 After: The Council of Human Interests or "Hugh" is formed. This happens when the various human colonies come together to prevent internecine war and to regulate their affairs. The initial line-up does not include many smaller colonies. It also excludes expatriate communities within alien colonies, who will be given a voice at a later stage. However, it does include both the Parthenon and human colonies that have sworn fealty to the Hegemony.

96 After: The Hivers, the cyborg intelligence developed during the war, remain under human control but elements of this distributed intelligence find ways to demand independence and self-determination. There are several brutal human crackdowns on Hive cells that refuse to perform their functions. The Hive cites its service during the war as a reason to grant it independence.

103 After: Human worlds sworn to the Hegemony make vocal attempts at proselytizing, including some terrorist activity. Following this, Hugh votes to exclude human colonies that have sworn allegiance to the Hegemony from its ranks. There are fears that a war with the Essiel will result, but this never manifests. The Hegemony's stated policy, as translated by its human mouthpieces, remains that the Hegemony is ready to accept the fealty of any who wish to join it.

105 After: The political struggle over the future of the Hivers comes to a head, as the Parthenon faction demands it be released from human control. The decision to allow this, forced through by Parthenon military superiority, is contentious. The Hivers are released from service and promptly evacuate to worlds outside human control and unsuitable for human colonization. The Hive's initial contacts with its former masters are almost entirely through the Parthenon. Over time Hive elements will re-enter human space and commerce to offer their services and skills.

107 After: More than twenty years after the war, the first stirrings of the Nativist movement are felt. This manifests as increased hostility towards alien powers, especially the Hegemony. It also shows in antagonistic behaviour towards human elements seen as deviating from a "traditional" human lifestyle, especially the Parthenon. Hugh has only been in existence for nineteen years at this point, and many human colonies are still in a very bad shape. Many traditionally born humans believe that the Parthenon intends to impose its "unnatural" way of life on all of humanity at gunpoint. Others fear that the Hive will take revenge for their previous servitude. Another popular Nativist belief is that Hegemonic cultists—both overt and hidden— are a fifth column on many worlds, aiming to manipulate governments into submitting to alien overlords. There are riots, demonstrations, coups and popular movements.

109 After: The Betrayed movement starts to gain traction. They spread the story that the Architects could have been fully defeated save that certain parties struck a deal to limit human expansion and power for their own benefit. They include amongst these "betrayers" the Intermediaries, Parthenon agents and aliens. The Betrayed fan the flames of anti-Parthenon and anti-Hegemony feeling and enact several terrorist attacks against Parthenon citizens.

110 After: The Parthenon officially secedes from Hugh, declaring its fleet and colonies a state outside traditional human control. War is feared but does not materialize, and diplomatic relations are maintained. As a result, relations become perhaps less fraught than in the last few years of the Parthenon's Hugh membership.

Over the next decade, human colonial life slowly improves, but political differences become ever more divisive. Hugh's ability to influence the recovering colonies decreases, as more extreme and populist factions take over. The larger and more powerful colonies form a relatively self-interested core. On the fringes of human space, there is a rich melting pot of humans and aliens prospecting, salvaging, colonizing and exploring.

123 After: The Architects return, destroying Far Lux and then arriving at Berlenhof. In the second battle of Berlenhof, Idris Telemmier reaches a communion with the attaching Architect, sending it away. Immediately after, Telemmier defects to the Parthenon, to general condemnation across the Colonies.

124 After: Present day

ACKNOWLEDGEMENTS

With thanks as ever to my agent, Simon, the architect (in a good way) of so many things.

Thanks to Wayne Stevens for inspiring the last breath of the Athamir.

The lyric *"We're all acquainted with the tragedy of being you"* is from Jonathan Coulton's "Someone Is Crazy," used here with permission.